Out of the night...

"A kiss in payment, señorita," he said. "It will be a pleasure to tame such a wild one."

She tried to fight again, but could not. She called upon the saints to aid her. And Captain Ramôn laughed more and bent his head, and his lips came close to hers. But he never claimed the kiss. From a corner of the room there came a voice that was at once deep and stern.

"One moment, Señor!" it said.

Captain Ramôn released the girl and whirled on one heel. He blinked his eyes to pierce the gloom of the corner; he heard Señorita Lolita give a glad cry.

Then Captain Ramôn, disregarding the presence of the lady, cursed, once and loudly, for Señor Zorro stood before him.

"Outlaw I may be, but I respect women," the Curse of Capistrano said. "I heard a lady's scream, which is warrant enough for caballero to enter any place, señor. It appears to me that you have broken all the conventions."

"Perhaps the lady has broken them also."

"Señor!" roared the highwayman. "Another thought like that and I cut you down where you stand, though you are a wounded man! How shall I punish you?"

*Under one cover—***The Mark of Zorro** *and two additional adventures by Johnston McCulley, featuring the legendary fighting hidalgo!*

Zorro

THE COMPLETE PULP ADVENTURES™ VOL. 1

Johnston McCulley

Featuring
The Mark of Zorro
Illustrated by Ed Coutts

BOLD VENTURE

Rich Harvey
Editor & Designer

Ed Coutts, Illustrations
*Pages 38-39, 65, 125,
160, 240-241, 261*

Zorro ® & © Zorro Productions, Inc. All Rights Reserved.
Published under license from Zorro Productions, Inc.

Pulp Adventures TM & © 2016 Bold Venture Press, All Rights Reserved.

"The Curse of Capistrano" by Johnston McClley originally appeared in *The All-Story Weekly*, August 9, August 16, August 23, August 30, and September 6, 1919. Copyright ©1919 Johnston McCulley. Copyright © renewed 1947 and assigned to Zorro Productions, Inc. All Rights Reserved.

"Zorro Saves a Friend" by Johnston McCulley originally appeared in Argosy, November 12, 1932. Copyright ©1932 Johnston McCulley. Copyright renewed ©1960 and assigned to Zorro Productions, Inc. All Rights Reserved.

"Zorro Hunts a Jackal" originally appeared in Argosy, April 22, 1933. Copyright ©1933 Johnston McCulley. Copyright renewed ©1961 and assigned to Zorro Productions, Inc. All Rights Reserved.

"Zorro's California" by Sandra Curtis ©1997 Zorro Productions, Inc. All Rights Reserved.

"From Pulp Page to Silver Screen" ©2010 Ed Hulse. All Rights Reserved.

ISBN-13: 978-1530392445
Retail cover price $19.95

All rights reserved. No part of this book may be reproduced or transmitted in any form or by any means without express permission of the publisher and author.

All persons, places and events in this book are fictitious, and any resemblance to any actual persons, places or events is purely coincidental.

Printed and bound in the United States.
10 9 8 7 6 5 4 3 2 1

Published by Bold Venture Press
www.boldventurepress.com

Contents

Zorro's California
by Sandra R. Curtis 7

The Mark of Zorro 21
Zorro Saves a Friend 263
Zorro Hunts a Jackal 301

Pulp Page to Silver Screen
by *Ed Hulse* 333

Zorro's California

by Sandra R. Curtis

SEÑOR Zorro was first introduced in *The Curse of Capistrano* on August 9, 1919, in the pulp magazine *All-Story Weekly* by writer Johnston McCulley. The story ran as a series in five parts through September 6, 1919. Zorro, the fox, defended the oppressed against injustice in the pueblo of *Reyna de Los Angeles.* The fox's popularity both in print and subsequent film (1920) prompted Grosset & Dunlap to republish the tale in a hardcover edition (1924) retitled *The Mark of Zorro.*

Ninety-five years have passed since Zorro initially appeared. As social values have evolved, so too has the character. The Zorro familiar to those who knew Guy Williams in the role in the Walt Disney television series of 1957-1959 would find McCulley's character more violent and romantic. Williams' handsome fox with the beaming smile never carved a Z in the flesh of his adversaries, as did McCulley's original fox. Disney's Zorro did, however, repeatedly embarrass the bumbling Sergeant Garcia by carving a Z in his clothing. The sadistic, gruff and bombastic Sergeant Gonzales whom early readers met in McCulley's story also evolved with the times, having been transformed into the lovable Sergeant Garcia.

In his cloak and mask, Zorro masqueraded behind an improbable dual identity as the languid Don Diego Vega, son of wealthy widower Alejandro Vega. No one suspected that the gentle Diego—who absolutely abhorred violence—could be the heroic masked rider. Zorro was known to the soldiers up and down El Camino Real, the highway connecting California's missions, as the "terror of the highway." To the people, he was a hero who defended them against injustice. Diego, a man who preferred talk of poetry to the ardors of the duel, was the perfect foil for his alter ego, the fox. Zorro's devil-may-care attitude, his superior skill with a sword, and his dedication to justice captured the imagination of the public. The noble fox, at once romantic, passionate, and righteous became Johnston McCulley's most endearing creation.

McCulley enmeshed his swashbuckling hero in the era of Spanish California—a romanticized time of peaceful life on sprawling cattle ranchos—when gentle padres civilized the Native Americans working at the missions and serenading caballeros romanced dark-eyed senoritas. Zorro has attracted millions of fans across generations, even inspiring other writers to create their own dual-identity heroes, notably Bob Kane's Batman. The fox's most influential fan, however, was silent film star Douglas Fairbanks, Sr.

While on his honeymoon with Mary Pickford, America's film sweetheart in the early days of cinema, Fairbanks read McCulley's *The Curse of Capistrano* in serial form. He was looking for a new character who could expand his career, especially one who would attract female matinee audiences. The actor was known for his on-screen energy and daring physical prowess. Zorro fit the bill, for as the dual-identity fox, Fairbanks could combine action as Zorro with comedy as Diego. The combination led to a whole new film genre: the adventure comedy.

Fairbanks gave his film the title *The Mark of Zorro*, a phrase taken from the climax of McCulley's *The Curse of Capistrano*. Zorro had defeated Captain Ramón in a duel and marked his forehead with a Z:

> "Like the tongue of a serpent, Señor Zorro's blade shot in. Thrice it darted forward, and upon the fair brow of Ramon just between the eyes there flamed suddenly a red bloody letter Z. 'The mark of Zorro!' the highwayman cried. 'You wear it forever now, Commandante.'

The Mark of Zorro debuted on November 28, 1920 at the Capitol Theater in New York City, playing to record crowds. It was an immediate hit as Zorro confounded the soldiers, wielding his sword with audacious flair, and ardently wooed the lovely señorita, Lolita Pulido. Audiences were captivated by Diego as well, with his wistful, languid demeanor and his magic tricks. Women flocked to matinees to see this debonair, poetic, heroic lover. Zorro fulfilled his mission, setting Fairbanks' career on a new course and securing the actor's place as a media legend.

Zorro's success on film embellished his image on the printed page. When *The Further Adventures of Zorro* appeared as a six-part series, beginning on May 6, 1922, in *Argosy's All Story Weekly*, McCulley had added magic tricks to Diego's repertoire, as Fairbanks had done.

FROM his humble beginning as a newspaperman from Ottawa, Illinois, McCulley's success with Zorro propelled him into an extensive career as playwright, screenwriter, novelist, and prolific author. His stories ranged from crime thrillers to Westerns. Still, it was the fox who remained intimately identified with the author until McCulley's death forty years after Zorro's introduction. Over his career, McCulley published a total of sixty-five Zorro stories for the pulps, several in serial format. His last one, "The Mask of Zorro," appeared in 1959 in *Short Stories for Men*. The same title was given to the 1998 Zorro film produced by TriStar Pictures and Steven Spielberg's Amblin Entertainment, starring Anthony Hopkins and Antonio Banderas.

Zorro has become an enduring early California legend, but historians have questioned the historical accuracy of his adventures. An interesting debate occurred in California history journals in the mid 1980s, prompting a deeper understanding of the legend by examining the origins of its embedded prejudices and the basis of its romantic appeal. The issues raised in the journal articles offer an historical frame within which to set this current reissue of *The Mark of Zorro*.

Johnston McCulley placed his original Zorro story in the "day of the decadence of the missions." This description corresponds to the period between 1822 and 1848, when California was under Mexican rule. The province had begun as a Spanish colony in 1769 with the founding at San Diego of the first in a chain of twenty-one missions. When Mexico gained independence from Spain in 1822, California became part of the Mexican Republic.

While claiming to be set in Spanish California, McCulley's Zorro stories actually combine elements from both the Spanish and the Mexican periods. The former period, 1769-1821, is known as "the days of the missions." The latter period, 1822-1848, is known as "the days of the ranchos." The missions dominated California's economy from 1769 until secularization began in 1834. Afterward, the ranchos became dominant. In McCulley's world, the two coexist, equally powerful and important.

The author also invented a *presidio* in Los Angeles. Though there were four *presidios* built in California during the Spanish period, none ever existed in Los Angeles. The town was created in 1781 as one of three civilian *pueblos* in the province. Historian Abraham Hoffman viewed the greatest shortcoming of the Zorro legend as:

"...its existence in a historical vacuum, one that neglected entirely the dramatic events in which California was involved that would profoundly affect California's future—Mexican independence from Spain, contact with Yankees through the hide and tallow trade, the arrival of American fur trappers, secularization of the missions, the Russians at Fort Ross, Sutter's personal empire, the events leading to the Mexican—American War, and the acquisition of California by the United States. McCulley mentioned not one of these; his story might as well have taken place on Mars." [1]

While McCulley's original title may have been poetic, it didn't quite fit his story. The only Capistrano near the Los Angeles *pueblo* was the mission at San Juan Capistrano, sixty miles south of Los Angeles along the coast. The author created a *pueblo* to suit his story, augmenting it with some historical elements, but by no means depicting the actual site.

The tavern in which both McCulley's opening chapters are set and his story's climax occurs did not exist, nor were there fancy homes like Diego's gracing the plaza. There were only single-story adobes with flat, tar-covered roofs. The pueblo was not ruled by the commandante of the *presidio* either, but by the *alcalde*, or mayor, with his *ayuntamiento*, the town council, and six *regidores*, or councilmen.

Though California's rancho period followed the mission period, there was some overlap. The King of Spain authorized land grants to private persons prior to the secularization of mission lands, when most of the ranchos were created. McCulley incorporated this knowledge into *Zorro Races with Death* (1947). Don Alejandro Vega protested the new commandante at his rancho, claiming, "I hold this property under a grant from the King of Spain himself ..."

Five private ranchos were granted near Los Angeles by the

---
[1] Hoffman, A., "Zorro: Generic Swashbuckler," *The Californians*, Sept./Oct., 1985.

king himself during the Spanish period.[2] The largest, which covered over 300,000 acres,[3] was given to Manuel Nietos in 1784. His grant extended from the Santa Ana River to the San Gabriel River and from the ocean to the mountains. The Nietos land grant may have been McCulley's model for the Vega rancho.

Historians have referred to the years between 1782 and 1810 as California's "romantic period." McCulley drew on this period to evoke images of early California, where life was:

> "...one continuous round of hospitality and social amenities, tempered with vigorous outdoor sport. There were no hotels in California. Every door was open, and food, lodging, a fresh horse, and money even, were free to the guest, whether friend or stranger. No white man had to concern himself greatly with work, and even school books were a thing apart. Music, games, dancing, and sprightly conversation—these were the occupations of the time—these constituted education. Also, men and women were much in the open, all were expert horsemen, could throw a lasso and shoot unerringly, even the women, accomplishments which fitted their type of life and made hunting a general pastime. When foreign ships came, there were balls and the gayest of festivals, nor were these visits the only occasion for that type of entertainment." [4]

McCulley described Lolita as an excellent horsewoman, as tradition indicated. In a climatic scene near the end of *The Curse of Capistrano*, Zorro believed he was being pursued by soldiers. He ...

> "glanced back over his shoulder and gasped his surprise. For it was Señorita Lolita Pulido who rode that horse and was pursued by the half-dozen troopers and

---
2 Knill, H., *Early Los Angeles*. Bellerophon Books, Santa Barbara, California, 1984.
3 Sanchez, N., *Spanish Arcadia*. Powell Publishing Co., Los Angeles, 1929.
4 Chapman, C.E., *A History of California, the Spanish Period*. The MacMillan Co., New York. 1921.

The legend begins — Zorro, *The Curse of Capistrano*, makes his world debut in the pages of *All-Story Weekly*. A year later, 1920, it became a film starring matinee idol Douglas Fairbanks, Jr.   Cover painting by P. J. Monahan.

he had thought her safe at the *hacienda* of Fray Felipe. Her long black hair was down and streaming out behind her. Her tiny heels were holding the reins low down, and Señor Zorro, even in that instant, marveled at her skill with a mount."

A distinct aristocracy existed in Spanish California, where social class was based on rank, bloodlines, and parentage. The patriarch of the family ruled with autocratic authority, to the extent that he even determined when young men under his charge could begin shaving. This social hierarchy and elitism found its way into McCulley's Zorro stories. Diego courted Lolita at his father's insistence, a filial obligation with historic underpinnings. McCulley's characters were also preoccupied with bloodlines. Diego was "a fair youth of excellent blood." The friendship between Diego and Sergeant Gonzales was described as "peculiar," given their differences in breeding and birth, for Diego came from a "family of blood." When Diego visited the Pulidos to pursue Lolita in marriage, he told Don Carlos, Lolita's father:

> " '…you are of excellent blood, Señor, of the best blood in the land. Everybody knows it, Señor. And a Vega, naturally, when he takes a mate, must seek out a woman of excellent blood.' "

The strict social hierarchy and paternal authority extended to rancho operations. They were organized as feudal estates had been in Europe during the Middle Age in, each run by its overlord, or majordomo, with a large contingent of laborers and underlings.

The year 1810 was pivotal in California's Spanish colonial history. The independence movement had begun In South America and spread north through Central America to Mexico. The Spanish ships that had been coming to California from San Blas, Mexico, bringing goods and salaries for the soldiers, ceased. Spain had forbidden her colony in California to trade with the ships of other countries, but once the Spanish ships stopped arriving, trade opened along the Pacific coast. Hides and tallow became valuable trade items for the English colonies on the Atlantic coast.

Centered at the missions, the hide and tallow trade became the principal means of economic survival for California. Extensive work was required to prepare the hides for trade, from scraping to drying, as well as rendering the fat into tallow for candles. The work was done by the mission Indians, under the supervision of the padres. Hide swindles take center stage in several of McCulley's Zorro stories, including *The Curse of Capistrano*, in which buyers accuse sellers of trading improperly cured hides.

Though Mexican independence was declared on February 24, 1821, news did not reach isolated California until January of 1822. California was the last of Spain's northernmost provinces to swear loyalty to the new Mexican Republic. A volatile period in California history was ushered in under Mexican rule. The *Californios* had not supported the independence movement against Spain, and they chafed under the new rule of theft Mexican governors.

Rivalries between tine north and the south of the state commenced, with the southerners in favor of greater independence, the northerners seeking stronger ties to Mexico. San Francisco and Monterey fought with Los Angeles and San Diego over which would be the province's seat of government. Greed and petty rivalries characterize the period. McCulley could easily have drawn on the unscrupulous leaders of the time as models for the evil commandantes against whom Zorro matched wits.

Secularization of the mission lands took place during California's years under Mexican rule. The Spanish government originally intended that the mission lands would be turned into civilian towns ten years after their founding. In the interim period, Native Americans would be converted to

Christianity and trained to work. The lands would subsequently be turned over to the Indians to be managed as part of the Spanish empire. However, sixty-five years passed before the California missions were secularized.

California's Governor Echeandia implemented a three-year plan for secularization, beginning in 1834. Half of the mission properties were distributed among the Indians and the rest put in charge of secular administrators. A few of the latter were honest, but others enriched themselves and their friends. Non-Indian mission lands were distributed as political spoils. The Indians did not understand the concept of private property. They had not been prepared for independent living. As neophytes at the missions, they were essentially slaves. Without the discipline of the mission system, the inevitable consequence was that they were unable to hold onto their lands.

The padres were unhappy about losing their empire. McCulley alludes to the friars' discontent with the secularization plan in *The Curse of Capistrano*. Fray Felipe complains to Diego after receiving an unjust lashing:

> "'It is but another instance of injustice. For twenty years we of the missions have been subjected to it, and it grows. The sainted Junipero Serra invaded this land when other men feared, and at San Diego de Alcala he built the first mission of what became a chain, thus giving an empire to the world. Our mistake was that we prospered. We did the work, and others reap the advantages.... They began taking our mission lands from us, lands we had cultivated, which had formed a wilderness and which my brothers had turned into gardens and orchards. They robbed us of worldly goods. And not content with that, they now are persecuting us. The mission empire is doomed, *caballero*. The time is not far distant when mission roofs will fall in and the walls crumble away.'"

From the historical record, we understand that the padre was not referring to the Indians as those reaping the advantages, but to the *Californio* soldiers and settlers who coveted the valuable mission property.

The rank-and-file soldiers were eager to acquire the rich mission lands. Having gone without pay since 1810, they expected their delayed compensation in terms of the choice mission properties. Even though it was unlawful for Indians to sell their property, the soldiers were eager buyers, often acquiring Indian land grants by trickery.

California was ceded to the United States for $15 million in 1848 as part of the Treaty of Guadalupe Hildalgo. The *Californios* became an alien culture in their own land. Forced to adapt to a new way of life, they had to defend not only their culture, but their property. The inexact boundaries used to define their ranchos—a boulder here, a stream there, but no definitive deeds—left the *Californios* vulnerable in American courts of law. Vast acres of prime real estate ended in the hands of greedy Yankees, reminiscent of the earlier land grab from the Indians.

A further insult was dealt in 1850, when California became a state. A Foreign Miner's Tax was passed, penalizing gold miners who were not natural-born U.S. citizens. The tax struck the *Californios* with particular severity because not only did they not consider themselves foreigners, they had taught the forty-niners gold-panning and sluicing techniques.

The rejection of *Californio* customs and values resulted in a major clash between the Anglo and Hispanic cultures. The *Californios* who resisted the invading Yankee immigrants became outlaws.[5] These *bandidos* may have been McCulley's model for Zorro. The American judicial system of the 1840s and 1850s considered Tiburcio Vasquez an outlaw, but his people idealized him as a hero for refusing to submit to the Anglo conquest.

---

5   Burciago, J.A., "Tiburcio Vasques: A Chicano Perspective," *The Californians*, May/June, 1985.

California's greatest legendary badman, Joaquin Murrieta, reportedly terrorized Calaveras County for three years in the early 1850s. Governor Bigler hired Captain Harry S. Love to track down this *bandido*. With a contingent of twenty men, Love's California Rangers pursued Murrieta for three months. In a major gunfight at Panoche Pass, Love's men killed two bandits whom they claimed were Joaquin and his lieutenant, Three-fingered Jack. The Rangers cut off the head of one and the hand of the other and bottled the trophies in whiskey. These grisly relics became popular attractions in San Francisco.

Murrieta's capture, however—even his actual existence—continues to be disputed. Whether the legend was true or not, it definitely altered the image of the *Californio*. Prior to 1854, the *Californio* evoked romantic idylls of peaceful ranchos, but after the spread of the Murrieta legend, that image turned to one of terror. Murrieta's romantic prowess and aristocratic background, along with his concern for justice, may well have fueled McCulley's imagination in creating Zorro.

Other well-known bandidos—Jack Powers, for instance—may have influenced McCulley's character development, too. Powers' shrewdness and his exceptional riding ability helped him to appear ubiquitous, never putting him at the scene of violence.[6] Just as it is difficult to pinpoint the historical period for Zorro, neither can a single historical figure be identified on whom Zorro was based.

McCulley wove elements of the Spanish-Mexican Period of early California into his Zorro stories, setting them in a novelistic genre. He fabricated a *presidio* in Los Angeles and merged aspects of two historical periods, but that mattered little to his readers. The author played fast and loose with his facts to create a colorful, intriguing legend. As Zorro used his sword to toy with his adversaries, McCulley used his pen to weave Señor Zorro's adventurous tales into the pursuit of justice.

---

6 Forsythe, H., "Santa Barbara's Blue-Blood Bandit," *The California Highway Patrolman*, 1968.

McCulley avoided making his writing an instrument of social criticism. He never confronted the repressive, paternalistic role of the church toward the Indians, nor did he challenge the view of "good blood" as voiced by some of his characters. Though such attitudes were authentic at the time and in the place, McCulley let his tales of good versus evil speak for themselves.

Despite his shortcomings as a writer, McCulley created a folk hero so familiar to so many that he can be recognized by a mere sign: "All you have to do is go *shhh, shhh, shhh*, and you've got Zorro," observed historian Hoffman as he inscribed the air with three rapid strokes.[7]

The original Señor Zorro rides again in this reissue of Johnston McCulley's *The Mark of Zorro*. We hope you enjoy your return (or your introduction) to the romance of early California as the wily fox defends the oppressed. Not even the realities of history can diminish Zorro's noble pursuit of justice. His quest claims, as ever, our admiration.

Sandra.R. Curtis
Berkeley, California
May, 1997

---

[7] Hoffman, A. Interview, "The History of Zorro," Arts and Entertainment *Biography* series, aired June 26, 1996.

Oppression—by its very nature—creates the power that crushes it. A champion arises—a champion of the oppressed—whether it be a Cromwell or someone unrecorded, he will be there. He is born.

In California, nearly two hundred years ago, with its warmth, its romance, its peaceful beauties, this dread disease, oppression, had crept in.

Then—out of the mystery of the unknown—appeared a masked rider who rode up and down the great highway—punishing and protecting—and leaving upon the vicious oppressor ...

The Mark of Zorro

®

Chapter 1
Pedro, the Boaster

AGAIN the sheet of rain beat against the roof of red Spanish tile, and the wind shrieked like a soul in torment, and smoke puffed from the big fireplace as the sparks were showered over the hard dirt floor.

"'Tis a night for evil deeds!" declared Sergeant Pedro Gonzales, stretching his great feet in their loose boots toward the roaring fire and grasping the hilt of his sword in one hand and a mug filled with thin wine in the other. "Devils howl in the wind, and demons are in the raindrops! Tis an evil night, indeed—eh, señor?"

"It is!" The fat landlord agreed hastily; and he made haste, also, to fill the wine mug again, for Sergeant Pedro Gonzales had a temper that was terrible when aroused, as it always was when wine was not forthcoming.

"An evil night," the big sergeant repeated, and drained the mug without stopping to draw breath, a feat that had attracted considerable attention in its time and had gained the sergeant a certain amount of notoriety up and down El Camino Real, as they called the highway that connected the missions in one long chain.

Gonzales sprawled closer to the fire and cared not that

other men thus were robbed of some of its warmth. Sergeant Pedro Gonzales often had expressed his belief that a man should look out for his own comfort before considering others; and being of great size and strength, and having much skill with the blade, he found few who had the courage to declare that they believed otherwise.

Outside the wind shrieked, and the rain dashed against the ground in a solid sheet. It was a typical February storm for southern California. At the missions the frailes had cared for the stock and had closed the buildings for the night. At every great hacienda big fires were burning in the houses. The timid natives kept to their little adobe huts, glad for shelter.

And here in the little pueblo of Reina de Los Angeles, where, in years to come, a great city would grow, the tavern on one side of the plaza housed for the time being men who would sprawl before the fire until the dawn rather than face the beating rain.

Sergeant Pedro Gonzales, by virtue of his rank and size, hogged the fireplace, and a corporal and three soldiers from the presidio sat at table a little in rear of him, drinking their thin wine and playing at cards. An Indian servant crouched on his heels in one corner, no neophyte who had accepted the religion of the frailes, but a gentile and renegade.

For this was in the day of the decadence of the missions, and there was little peace between the robed Franciscans who followed in the footsteps of the sainted Junipero Serra, who had founded the first mission at San Diego de Alcala, and thus made possible an empire, and those who followed the politicians and had high places in the army. The men who drank wine in the tavern at Reina de Los Angeles had no wish for a spying neophyte about them.

Just now conversation had died out, a fact that annoyed the fat landlord and caused him some fear; for Sergeant Pedro Gonzales in an argument was Sergeant Gonzales at peace; and unless he could talk the big soldier might feel moved to action and start a brawl.

Twice before Gonzales had done so, to the great damage of furniture and men's faces; and the landlord had appealed to the comandante of the presidio, Captain Ramôn, only to be informed that the captain had an abundance of troubles of his own, and that running an inn was not one of them.

So the landlord regarded Gonzales warily and edged closer to the long table and spoke in an attempt to start a general conversation and so avert trouble.

"They are saying in the pueblo," he announced, "that this Señor Zorro is abroad again."

His words had an effect that was both unexpected and terrible to witness. Sergeant Pedro Gonzales hurled his half-filled wine mug to the hard dirt floor, straightened suddenly on the bench, and crashed a ponderous fist down upon the table, causing wine mugs and cards and coins to scatter in all directions.

The corporal and the three soldiers retreated a few feet in sudden fright, and the red face of the landlord blanched; the native sitting in the corner started to creep toward the door, having determined that he preferred the storm outside to the big sergeant's anger.

"Señor Zorro, eh?" Gonzales cried in a terrible voice. "Is it my fate always to hear that name? Señor Zorro, eh? Mr. Fox, in other words! He imagines, I take it, that he is as cunning as one. By the saints, he raises as much stench!"

Gonzales gulped, turned to face them squarely, and continued his tirade.

"He runs up and down the length of El Camino Real like a goat of the high hills! He wears a mask, and he flashes a pretty blade, they tell me. He uses the point of it to carve his hated letter Z on the cheek of his foe! Ha! The mark of Zorro they are calling it! A pretty blade he has, in truth! But I cannot swear as to the blade—I never have seen it. He will not do me the honor of letting me see it! Señor Zorro's depredations never occur in the vicinity of Sergeant Pedro Gonzales! Perhaps this Señor Zorro can tell us the reason for that? Ha!"

He glared at the men before him, threw up his upper lip, and let the ends of his great black mustache bristle.

"They are calling him the Curse of Capistrano now," the fat landlord observed, stooping to pick up the wine mug and cards and hoping to filch a coin in the process.

"Curse of the entire highway and the whole mission chain!" Sergeant Gonzales roared. "A cutthroat, he is! A thief! Ha! A common fellow presuming to get him a reputation for bravery because he robs a hacienda or so and frightens a few women and natives! Señor Zorro, eh? Here is one fox it gives me pleasure to hunt! Curse of Capistrano, eh? I know I have led an evil life, but I only ask of the saints one thing now—that they forgive me my sins long enough to grant me the boon of standing face to face with this pretty highwayman!"

"There is a reward—" the landlord began.

"You snatch the very words from my lips!" Sergeant Gonzales protested. "There is a pretty reward for the fellow's capture, offered by his excellency the governor. And what good fortune has come to my blade? I am away on duty at San Juan Capistrano, and the fellow makes his play at Santa Barbara. I am at Reina de Los Angeles, and he takes a fat purse at San Luis Reydine at San Gabriel, let us say, and he robs at San Diego de Alcala! A pest, he is! Once I met him—"

Sergeant Gonzales choked on his wrath and reached for the wine mug, which the landlord had filled again and placed at his elbow. He gulped down the contents.

"Well, he never has visited us here," the landlord said with a sigh of thanksgiving.

"Good reason, fat one! Ample reason! We have a presidio here and a few soldiers. He rides far from any presidio, does this pretty Señor Zorro! He is like a fleeting sunbeam, I grant him that—and with about as much real courage!"

Sergeant Gonzales relaxed on the bench again, and the

landlord gave him a glance that was full of relief, and began to hope that there would be no breakage of mugs and furniture and men's faces this rainy night.

"Yet this Señor Zorro must rest at time—he must eat and sleep," the landlord said. "It is certain that he must have some place for hiding and recuperation. Some fine day the soldiers will trail him to his den."

"Ha!" Gonzales replied. "Of course the man has to eat and sleep. And what is it that he claims now? He says that he is no real thief, by the saints! He is but punishing those who mistreat the men of the missions, he says. Friend of the oppressed, eh? He left a placard at Santa Barbara recently stating as much, did he not? Ha! And what may be the reply to that? The frailes of the missions are shielding him, hiding him, giving him his meat and drink! Shake down a robed fray and you'll find some trace of this pretty highwayman's whereabouts, else I am a lazy civilian!"

"I have no doubt that you speak the truth," the landlord replied. "I put it not past the frailes to do such a thing. But may this Señor Zorro never visit us here!"

"And why not, fat one?" Sergeant Gonzales cried in a voice of thunder. "Am I not here? Have I not a blade at my side? Are you an owl, and is this daylight that you cannot see as far as the end of your puny, crooked nose? By the saints—"

"I mean," said the landlord quickly and with some alarm, "that I have no wish to be robbed."

"To be—robbed of what, fat one? Of a jug of weak wine and a meal? Have you riches, fool? Ha! Let the fellow come! Let this bold and cunning Señor Zorro but enter that door and step before us! Let him make a bow, as they say he does, and let his eyes twinkle through his mask! Let me but face the fellow for an instant—and I claim the generous reward offered by his excellency!"

"He perhaps is afraid to venture so near the presidio," the landlord said.

"More wine!" Gonzales howled. "More wine, fat one, and place it to my account! When I have earned the reward, you shall be paid in full. I promise it on my word as a soldier! Ha! Were this brave and cunning Señor Zorro, this Curse of Capistrano, but to make entrance at that door now—"

The door suddenly was opened.

Chapter 2
On the Heels of the Storm

IN CAME a gust of wind and rain and a man with it, and the candles flickered and one was extinguished. This sudden entrance in the midst of the sergeant's boast startled them all; and Gonzales drew his blade halfway from its scabbard as his words died in his throat. The native was quick to close the door again to keep out the wind.

The newcomer turned and faced them; the landlord gave another sigh of relief. It was not Señor Zorro, of course. It was Don Diego Vega, a fair youth of excellent blood and twenty-four years, noted the length of El Camino Real for his small interest in the really important things of life.

"Ha!" Gonzales cried, and slammed his blade home.

"Is it that I startled you somewhat, señores?" Don Diego asked politely and in a thin voice, glancing around the big room and nodding to the men before him.

"If you did, señor, it was because you entered on the heels of the storm," the sergeant retorted. "'Twould not be your own energy that would startle any man!"

"H-m!" grunted Don Diego, throwing aside his sombrero and flinging off his soaked serape. "Your remarks border on the perilous, my raucous friend."

"Can it be that you intend to take me to task?"

"It is true," continued Don Diego, "That I do not have a reputation for riding like a fool at risk of my neck, fighting like an idiot with every newcomer, and playing the guitar under every woman's window like a simpleton. Yet I do not care to have these things you deem my shortcomings flaunted in my face!"

"Ha!" Gonzales cried, half in anger.

"We have an agreement, Sergeant Gonzales, that we can be friends, and I can forget the wide difference in birth and breeding that yawns between us only as long as you curb your tongue and stand my comrade. Your boasts amuse me, and I buy for you the wine that you crave—it is a pretty arrangement. But ridicule me again, señor, either in public or private, and the agreement is at an end. I may mention that I have some small influence—"

"Your pardon, *caballero* and my very good friend!" the alarmed Sergeant Gonzales cried now. "You are storming worse than the tempest outside, and merely because my tongue happened to slip. Hereafter, if any man ask, you are nimble of wit and quick with a blade, always ready to fight or to make love. You are a man of action, caballero! Ha! Does any dare doubt it?"

He glared around the room, half drawing his blade again, and then he slammed the sword home and threw back his head and roared with laughter, and then clapped Don Diego between the shoulders; and the fat landlord hurried with more wine, knowing well that Don Diego Vega would stand the score.

For this peculiar friendship between Don Diego and Sergeant Gonzales was the talk of El Camino Real. Don Diego came from a family of blood that ruled over thousands of broad acres, countless herds of horses and cattle, great fields of grain. Don Diego, in his own right, had a hacienda that was like a small empire, and a house in the pueblo also, and was destined to inherit form his father more than thrice what he had now.

But Don Diego was unlike the other full-blooded youths of the times. It appeared that he disliked action. He seldom wore his blade, except as a matter of style and apparel. He was damnably polite to all women and paid court to none.

He sat in the sun and listened to the wild tales of other men—and now and then he smiled. He was the opposite of Sergeant Pedro Gonzales in all things, and yet they were together frequently. It was as Don Diego had said—he enjoyed the sergeant's boasts, and the sergeant enjoyed the free wine. What more could either ask in the way of a fair arrangement?

Now Don Diego went to stand before the fire and dry himself, holding a mug of red wine in one hand. He was only medium in size, yet he possessed health and good looks, and it was the despair of proud dueñas that he would not glance a second time at the pretty señoritas they protected, and for whom they sought desirable husbands.

Gonzales, afraid that he had angered his friend and that the free wine would be at an end, now strove to make peace.

"Caballero, we have been speaking of this notorious Señor Zorro," he said. "We have been regarding in conversation this fine Curse of Capistrano, as some nimble-witted fool has seen, fit to term the pest of the highway."

"What about him?" Don Diego asked, putting down his wine mug and hiding a yawn behind his hand. Those who knew Don Diego best declared he yawned ten score times a day.

"I have been remarking, caballero," said the sergeant, "that this fine Señor Zorro never appears in my vicinity, and that I am hoping the good saints will grant me the chance of facing him some fine day, that I may claim the reward offered by the governor. Señor Zorro, eh? Ha!"

"Let us not speak of him," Don Diego begged, turning from the fireplace and throwing out one hand as if in protest. "Shall it be that I never hear of anything except deeds of bloodshed and violence? Would it be possible in these turbulent times for a man to listen to words of wisdom regarding music or the poets?"

"Meal mush and goat's milk!" snorted Sergeant Gonzales in huge disgust. "If this Señor Zorro wishes to risk his neck, let him. It is his own neck, by the saints! A cutthroat! A thief! Ha!"

"I have been hearing considerable concerning his work," Don Diego went on to say. "The fellow, no doubt, is sincere in his purpose. He has robbed none except officials who have stolen from the missions and the poor, and punished none except brutes who mistreat natives. He has slain no man, I understand. Let him have his little day in the public eye, my sergeant."

"I would rather have the reward!"

"Earn it," Don Diego said. "Capture the man!"

"Ha! Dead or alive, the governor's proclamation says. I myself have read it."

"Then stand you up to him and run him through, if such a thing pleases you," Don Diego retorted. "And tell me all about it afterward—but spare me now."

"It will be a pretty story!" Gonzales cried. "And you shall have it entire, caballero, word by word! How I played with him, how I laughed at him as we fought, how I pressed him back after a time and ran him through—"

"Afterward—but not now!" Don Diego cried, exasperated. "Landlord, more wine! The only manner in which to stop this raucous boaster is to make his wide throat so slick with wine that the words cannot climb out of it!"

The landlord quickly filled the mugs. Don Diego sipped at his wine slowly, as a gentleman should, while Sergeant Gonzales took his in two great gulps. And then the scion of the house of Vega stepped across to the bench and reached for his sombrero and his serape.

"What?" the sergeant cried. "You are going to leave us at such an early hour, caballero? You are going to face the fury of that beating storm?"

"At least I am brave enough for that," Don Diego replied, smiling. "I but ran over from my house for a pot of honey. The fools feared the rain too much to fetch me some this day from the hacienda. Get me one, landlord."

"I shall escort you safely home through the rain!" Sergeant Gonzales cried, for he knew full well that Don Diego had excellent wine of age there.

"You shall remain here before the roaring fire," Don Diego told him firmly. "I do not need an escort of soldiers from the presidio to cross the plaza. I am going over accounts with my secretary, and possibly may return to the tavern after we have finished. I wanted the pot of honey that we might eat as we worked."

"Ha! And why did you not send that secretary of yours for the honey, caballero? Why be wealthy and have servants, if a man cannot send them on errands on such a stormy night?"

"He is an old man and feeble," Don Diego explained. "He also is secretary to my aged father. The storm would kill him. Landlord, serve all here with wine and put it to my account. I may return when my books have been straightened."

Don Diego Vega picked up the pot of honey, wrapped his serape around his head, opened the door, and plunged into the storm and darkness.

"There goes a man!" Gonzales cried, flourishing his arms. "He is my friend, that caballero, and I would have all men know it! He seldom wears a blade, and I doubt whether he can use one—but he is my friend! The flashing dark eyes of lovely *señoritas* do not disturb him, yet I swear he is a pattern of a man!

"Music and the poets, eh? Ha! Has he not the right, if such is his pleasure? Is he not Don Diego Vega? Has he not blue blood and broad acres and great storehouses filled with goods? Is he not liberal? He may stand on his head or wear petticoats, if it please him—yet I swear he is a pattern of a man!"

The soldiers echoed his sentiments since they were drinking Don Diego's wine and did not have the courage to combat the sergeant's statements anyway. The fat landlord served them with another round since Don Diego would pay. For it was beneath a Vega to look at his score in a public tavern, and the fat landlord many times had taken advantage of this fact.

"He cannot endure the thought of violence or bloodshed," Sergeant Gonzales continued. "He is as gentle as a breeze of spring. Yet he has a firm wrist and a deep eye. It merely is the caballero's manner of seeing life. Did I but have his youth and good looks and riches—Ha! There would be a stream of broken hearts from San Diego de Alcala to San Francisco de Asis!"

"And broken heads!" the corporal offered.

"Ha! And broken heads, comrade! I would rule the country! No youngster should stand long in my way. Out with blade and at them! Cross Pedro Gonzales, eh? Ha! Through the shoulder—neatly! Ha! Through a lung!"

Gonzales was upon his feet now, and his blade had leaped from its scabbard. He swept it back and forth through the air, thrust, parried, lunged, advanced, and retreated, shouted his oaths, and roared his laughter as he fought with shadows.

"That is the manner of it!" he screeched at the fireplace. "What have we here? Two of you against one? So much the better, señores! We love brave odds! Ha! Have at you, dog! Die, hound! One side, poltroon!"

He reeled against the wall, gasping, his breath almost gone, the point of his blade resting on the floor, his great face purple with the exertion and the wine he had consumed, while the corporal and the soldiers and the fat landlord laughed long and loudly at this bloodless battle from which Sergeant Pedro Gonzales had emerged the unquestioned victor.

"Were—were this fine Señor Zorro only before me here and now!" the sergeant gasped.

And again the door was opened suddenly, and a man entered the inn on a gust of the storm.

Chapter 3
Señor Zorro Pays a Visit

THE native hurried forward to fasten the door against the force of the wind, and then retreated to his corner again. The newcomer had his back toward those in the long room. They could see that his sombrero was pulled far down on his head, as if to prevent the wind from whisking it away, and that his body was enveloped in a long cloak that was wringing wet.

With his back still toward them, he opened the cloak and shook the raindrops from it and then folded it across his breast again as the fat landlord hurried forward, rubbing his hands together in expectation, for he deemed that here was some caballero off the highway who would pay good coin for food and bed and care for his horse.

When the landlord was within a few feet of him and the door the stranger whirled around. The landlord gave a little cry of fear and retreated with speed. The corporal gurgled deep down in his throat; the soldiers gasped; Sergeant Pedro Gonzales allowed his lower jaw to drop and let his eyes bulge.

For the man who stood straight before them had a black mask over his face that effectually concealed his features, and through the two slits in it his eyes glittered ominously.

"Ha! What have we here?" Gonzales gasped finally, some presence of mind returning to him.

The man before them bowed.

"Señor Zorro, at your service," he said.

"By the saints! Señor Zorro, eh?" Gonzales cried.

"Do you doubt it, señor?"

"If you are indeed Señor Zorro, then have you lost your wits!" the sergeant declared.

"What is the meaning of that speech?"

"You are here, are you not? You have entered the inn, have you not? By all the saints, you have walked into a trap, my pretty highwayman!"

"Will the señor please explain?" Señor Zorro asked. His voice was deep and held a peculiar ring.

"Are you blind? Are you without sense?" Gonzales demanded. "Am I not here?"

"And what has that to do with it?"

"Am I not a soldier?"

"At least you wear a soldier's garb, señor."

"By the saints, and cannot you see the good corporal and three of our comrades? Have you come to surrender your wicked sword, señor? Are you finished playing at rogue?"

Señor Zorro laughed, not unpleasantly, but he did not take his eyes from Gonzales.

"Most certainly I have not come to surrender," he said. "I am on business, señor."

"Business?" Gonzales queried.

"Four days ago, Señor, you brutally beat a native who had won your dislike. The affair happened on the road between here and the mission at San Gabriel."

"He was a surly dog and got in my way! And how does it concern you, my pretty highwayman?"

"I am the friend of the oppressed, Señor, and I have come to punish you."

"Come to—to punish me, fool? You punish me? I shall die

of laughter before I can run you through! You are as good as dead, Señor Zorro! His excellency has offered a pretty price for your carcass! If you are a religious man, say your prayers! I would not have it said that I slew a man without giving him time to repent his crimes. I give you the space of a hundred heartbeats."

"You are generous, Señor, but there is no need for me to say my prayers."

"Then must I do my duty," said Gonzales, and lifted the point of his blade. "Corporal, you will remain by the table, and the men also. This fellow and the reward he means are mine!"

He blew out the ends of his mustache and advanced carefully, not making the mistake of underestimating his antagonist, for there had been certain tales of the man's skill with a blade. And when he was within the proper distance he recoiled suddenly, as if a snake had warned of a strike.

For Señor Zorro had allowed one hand to come from beneath his cloak, and the hand held a pistol, most damnable of weapons to Sergeant Gonzales.

"Back, Señor!" Señor Zorro warned.

"Ha! So that is the way of it!" Gonzales cried. "You carry that devil's weapon and threaten men with it! Such things are for use only at a long distance and against inferior foes. Gentlemen prefer the trusty blade."

"Back, Señor! There is death in this you call the devil's weapon. I shall not warn again."

"Somebody told me you were a brave man," Gonzales taunted, retreating a few feet. "It has been whispered that you would meet any man foot to foot and cross blades with him. I have believed it of you. And now I find you resorting to a weapon fit for nothing except to use against red natives. Can it be, señor, that you lack the courage I have heard you possess?"

Señor Zorro laughed again.

The Mark of Zorro

"*Señor Zorro, at your service,*" he said.

"As to that you shall see presently," he said. "The use of this pistol is necessary at the present time. I find myself pitted against large odds in this tavern, señor. I shall cross blades with you gladly when I have made such a proceeding safe."

"I wait anxiously," Gonzales sneered.

"The corporal and soldiers will retreat to that far corner," Señor Zorro directed. "Landlord, you will accompany them. The native will go there also. Quickly, señores. Thank you. I do not wish to have any of you disturbing me while I am punishing this sergeant here."

"Ha!" Gonzales screeched in fury. "We shall soon see as to the punishing, my pretty fox!"

"I shall hold the pistol in my left hand," Señor Zorro continued. "I shall engage this sergeant with my right, in the proper manner, and as I fight I shall keep an eye on the corner. The first move from any of you, señores, means that I fire. I am expert with this you have termed the devil's weapon, and if I fire some men shall cease to exist on this earth of ours. It is understood?"

The corporal and soldiers and landlord did not take the trouble to answer. Señor Zorro looked Gonzales straight in the eyes again, and a chuckle came from behind his mask.

"Sergeant, you will turn your back until I can draw my blade," he directed. "I give you my word as a caballero that I shall not make a foul attack."

"As a caballero?" Gonzales sneered.

"I said it, señor!" Zorro replied, his voice ringing a threat. Gonzales shrugged his shoulders and turned his back. In an instant he heard the voice of the highwayman again.

"On guard, señor!"

Chapter 4
Swords Clash — and Pedro Explains

GONZALES whirled at the word, and his blade came up. He saw that Señor Zorro had drawn his sword, and that he was holding the pistol in his left hand high above his head. Moreover, Señor Zorro was chuckling still, and the sergeant became infuriated. The blades clashed.

Sergeant Gonzales had been accustomed to battling with men who gave ground when they pleased and took it when they could, who went this way and that seeking an advantage, now advancing, now retreating, now swinging to left or right as their skill directed them.

But here he faced a man who fought in quite a different way. For Señor Zorro, it appeared, was as if rooted to one spot and unable to turn his face in any other direction. He did not give an inch, nor did he advance, nor step to either side.

Gonzales attacked furiously, as was his custom, and he found the point of his blade neatly parried. He used more caution then and tried what tricks he knew, but they seemed to avail him nothing. He attempted to pass around the man before him, and the other's blade drove him back. He tried a retreat, hoping to draw the other out, but Señor Zorro stood his ground and forced Gonzales to attack again. As for the highwayman, he did naught except put up a defense.

Anger got the better of Gonzales then, for he knew the corporal was jealous of him and that the tale of this fight would be told to all the pueblo tomorrow, and so travel up and down the length of El Camino Real.

He attacked furiously, hoping to drive Señor Zorro off his feet and make an end of it But he found that his attack ended as if against a stone wall, his blade was turned aside, his breast crashed against that of his antagonist, and Señor Zorro merely threw out his chest and hurled him back half a dozen steps.

"Fight, señor!" Señor Zorro said.

"Fight yourself, cutthroat and thief!" the exasperated sergeant cried. "Don't stand like a piece of the hills, fool! Is it against your religion to take a step?"

"You cannot taunt me into doing it," the highwayman replied, chuckling again.

Sergeant Gonzales realized then that he had been angry, and he knew an angry man cannot fight with the blade as well as a man who controls his temper. So he became deadly cold now, and his eyes narrowed, and all boasting was gone from him.

He attacked again, but now he was alert, seeking an unguarded spot through which he could thrust without courting disaster himself. He fenced as he never had fenced in his life before. He cursed himself for having allowed wine and food to rob him of his wind. From the front, from either side, he attacked, only to be turned back again, all his tricks solved almost before he tried them.

He had been watching his antagonist's eyes, of course, and now he saw a change. They had seemed to be laughing through the mask, and now they had narrowed and seemed to send forth flakes of fire.

"We have had enough of playing," Señor Zorro said. "It is time for the punishment!"

And suddenly he began to press the fighting, taking step

after step, slowly and methodically going forward and forcing Gonzales backward. The tip of his blade seemed to be a serpent's head with a thousand tongues. Gonzales felt himself at the other's mercy, but he gritted his teeth and tried to control himself and fought on.

Now he was with his back against the wall, but in such a position that Señor Zorro could give him battle and watch the men in the corner at the same time. He knew the highwayman was playing with him. He was ready to swallow his pride and call upon the corporal and soldiers to rush in and give him aid.

And then there came a sudden battering at the door, which the native had bolted. The heart of Gonzales gave a great leap. Somebody was there, wishing to enter. Whoever it was would think it peculiar that the door was not thrown open instantly by the fat landlord or his servant. Perhaps help was at hand.

"We are interrupted, señor," the highwayman said. "I regret it, for I will not have the time to give you the punishment you deserve, and will have to arrange to visit you another time. You scarcely are worth a double visit."

The pounding at the door was louder now. Gonzales raised his voice:

"Ha! We have Señor Zorro here!"

"Poltroon!" the highwayman cried.

His blade seemed to take on new life. It darted in and out with a speed that was bewildering. It caught a thousand beams of light from the flickering candles and hurled them back.

And suddenly it darted in and hooked itself properly, and Sergeant Gonzales felt his sword torn from his grasp and saw it go flying through the air.

"So!" Señor Zorro cried.

Gonzales awaited the stroke. A sob came into his throat that this must be the end instead of on a field of battle where a soldier wishes it. But no steel entered his breast to bring forth his life's blood.

Instead, Señor Zorro swung his left hand down, passed the hilt of his blade to it and grasped it beside the pistol's butt, and with his right he slapped Pedro Gonzales once across the cheek.

"That for a man who mistreats helpless natives!" he cried.

Gonzales roared in rage and shame. Somebody was trying to smash the door in now. But Señor Zorro appeared to give it little thought. He sprang back, and sent his blade into its scabbard like a flash. He swept the pistol before him and thus threatened all in the long room. He darted to a window, sprang upon a bench.

"Until a later time, señor!" he cried.

And then he went through the window as a mountain goat jumps from a cliff, taking its covering with him. In rushed the wind and rain, and the candles went out.

"After him!" Gonzales screeched, springing across the room and grasping his blade again. "Unbar the door! Out and after him! Remember, there is a generous reward—"

The corporal reached the door first, and threw it open. In stumbled two men of the pueblo, eager for wine and an explanation of the fastened door. Sergeant Gonzales and his comrades drove over them, left them sprawling, and dashed into the storm.

But there was little use in it. It was so dark a man could not see a distance of a horse's length. The beating rain was enough to obliterate tracks almost instantly. Señor Zorro was gone—and no man could tell in what direction.

There was a tumult, of course, in which the men of the pueblo joined. Sergeant Gonzales and the soldiers returned to the inn to find it full of men they knew. And Sergeant Gonzales knew, also, that his reputation was now at stake.

"Nobody but a highwayman, nobody but a cutthroat and thief would have done it!" he cried aloud.

"How is that, brave one?" cried a man in the throng near the doorway.

"This pretty Señor Zorro knew, of course! Some days ago I broke the thumb of my sword hand while fencing at San Juan Capistrano. No doubt the word was passed to this Señor Zorro. And he visits me at such a time that he may afterward say he had vanquished me."

The corporal and soldiers and landlord stared at him, but none was brave enough to say a word.

"Those who were here can tell you, señores," Gonzales went on. "This Señor Zorro came in at the door and immediately drew a pistol—devil's weapon—from beneath his cloak. He presents it at us, and forces all except me to retire to that corner. I refused to retire.

"'Then you shall fight me,' says this pretty highwayman, and I draw my blade, thinking to make an end of the pest. And what does he tell me then? 'We shall fight,' he says, 'and I will outpoint you, so that I may boast of it afterward, in my left hand I hold the pistol. If your attack is not to my liking, I shall fire, and afterward run you through, and so make an end of a certain sergeant.'"

The corporal gasped, and the fat landlord was almost ready to speak, but thought better of it when Sergeant Gonzales glared at him.

"Could anything be more devilish?" Gonzales asked. "I was to fight, and yet I would get a devil's chunk of lead in my carcass if I pressed the attack. Was there ever such a farce? It shows the stuff of which this pretty highwayman is made. Some day I shall meet him when he holds no pistol—and then—"

"But how did he get away?" someone in the crowd asked.

"He heard those at the door. He threatened me with the devil's pistol and forced me to toss my blade in yonder far corner. He threatened us all, ran to the window, and sprang through. And how could we find him in the darkness or track him through the sheets of rain? But I am determined now! In the morning I go to my Captain Ramón and ask permission to be absolved from all other duty, that I may take some comrades and run down this pretty Señor Zorro. Ha! We shall go fox hunting!"

The excited crowd about the door suddenly parted, and Don Diego Vega hurried into the tavern.

"What is this I hear?" he asked. "They are saying that Señor Zorro has paid a visit here."

"'Tis a true word, caballero!" Gonzales answered. "And we were speaking of the cutthroat here this evening. Had you remained instead of going home to work with your secretary, you should have seen the entire affair."

"Were you not here? Can you not tell me?" Don Diego asked. "But I pray you make not the tale too bloody. I cannot see why men must be violent. Where is the highwayman's dead body?"

Gonzales choked; the fat landlord turned away to hide his smile; the corporal and soldiers began picking up wine mugs to keep busy at this dangerous moment.

"He—that is, there is no body," Gonzales managed to say.

"Have done with your modesty, sergeant!" Don Diego cried. "Am I not your friend? Did you not promise to tell me the story if you met this cutthroat? I know you would spare my feelings, knowing that I do not love violence, yet I am eager for the facts because you, my friend, have been engaged with this fellow. How much was the reward?"

"By the saints!" Gonzales swore.

"Come, sergeant! Out with the tale! Landlord, give all of us wine, that we may celebrate this affair! Your tale, sergeant! Shall you leave the army, now that you have earned the reward, and purchase a hacienda and take a wife?"

Sergeant Gonzales choked again and reached gropingly for a wine mug.

"You promised me," Don Diego continued, "that you would tell me the whole thing, word by word. Did he not say as much, landlord? You declared that you would relate how you played with him; how you laughed at him while you fought; how you pressed him back after a time and then ran him through—"

"By the saints!" Sergeant Gonzales roared, the words coming from between his lips like peals of thunder. "It is beyond the endurance of any man! You—Don Diego—my friend—"

"Your modesty ill becomes you at such a time," Don Diego said. "You promised the tale, and I would have it. What does this Señor Zorro look like? Have you peered at the dead face beneath the mask? It is, perhaps, some man that we all know? Cannot some one of you tell me the facts? You stand here like so many speechless images of men—"

"Wine—or I choke!" Gonzales howled. "Don Diego, you are my good friend, and I will cross swords with any man who belittles you! But do not try me too far this night—"

"I fail to understand," Don Diego said. "I have but asked you to tell me the story of the fight—how you mocked him as you battled; how you pressed him back at will, and presently ended it by running him through—"

"Enough! Am I to be taunted?" the big sergeant cried. He gulped down the wine and hurled the mug far from him.

"Is it possible that you did not win the battle?" Don Diego asked. "But surely this pretty highwayman could not stand up before you, my sergeant. How was the outcome?"

"He had a pistol—"

"Why did you not take it away from him, then, and crowd it down his throat? But perhaps that is what you did. Here is more wine, my sergeant. Drink!"

But Sergeant Gonzales was thrusting his way through the throng at the door.

"I must not forget my duty!" he said. "I must hurry to the presidio and report this occurrence to the comandante!"

"But, sergeant—"

"And as to this Señor Zorro, he will be meat for my blade before I am done!" Gonzales promised.

And then, cursing horribly, he rushed away through the rain, the first time in his life he ever had allowed duty to interfere with his pleasure and had run from good wine.

Don Diego Vega smiled as he turned toward the fireplace.

Chapter 5
A Ride in the Morning

THE following morning found the storm at an end, and there was not a single cloud to mar the perfect blue of the sky, and the sun was bright, and palm fronds glistened in it, and the air was bracing as it blew down the valleys from the sea.

At midmorning, Don Diego Vega came from his house in the pueblo, drawing on his sheepskin riding-mittens, and stood for a moment before it, glancing across the plaza at the little tavern. From the rear of the house an Indian servant led a horse.

Though Don Diego did not go galloping across the hills and up and down El Camino Real like an idiot, yet he owned a fairish bit of horseflesh. The animal had spirit and speed and endurance, and many a young blood would have purchased him, except that Don Diego had no use for more money and wanted to retain the beast.

The saddle was heavy and showed more silver than leather on its surface. The bridle was heavily chased with silver, too, and from its sides dangled leather globes studded with semi-precious stones that now glittered in the bright sunshine as if to advertise Don Diego's wealth and prestige to all the world.

Don Diego mounted, while half a score of men loitering around the plaza watched and made efforts to hide their grins. It was quite the thing in those days for a youngster to spring from the ground into his saddle, gather up the reins, rake the beast's flanks with his great spurs, and disappear in a cloud of dust all in one motion.

But Don Diego mounted a horse as he did everything else—without haste or spirit. The native held a stirrup, and Don Diego inserted the toe of his boot. Then he gathered the reins in one hand, and pulled himself into the saddle as if it had been quite a task.

Having done that much, the native held the other stirrup and guided Don Diego's other boot into it, and then he backed away, and Don Diego clucked to the magnificent beast and started it, at a walk, along the edge of the plaza toward the trail that ran to the north.

Having reached the trail, Don Diego allowed the animal to trot, and after having covered a mile in this fashion, he urged the beast into a slow gallop, and so rode along the highway.

Men were busy in the fields and orchards, and natives were tending the herds. Now and then Don Diego passed a lumbering carreta, and saluted whoever happened to be in it Once a young man he knew passed him at a gallop, going toward the pueblo, and Don Diego stopped his own horse to brush the dust from his garments after the man had gone his way.

Those same garments were more gorgeous than usual this bright morning. A glance at them was enough to establish the wealth and position of the wearer. Don Diego had dressed with much care, admonishing his servants because his newest serape was not pressed properly, and spending a great deal of time over the polishing of his boots.

He traveled for a distance of four miles and then turned from the highroad and started up a narrow, dusty trail that led to a group of buildings against the side of a hill in the distance. Don Diego Vega was about to pay a visit to the hacienda of Don Carlos Pulido.

This same Don Carlos had experienced numerous vicissitudes during the last few years. Once he had been second to none except Don Diego's father in position, wealth, and breeding. But he had made the mistake of getting on the wrong side of the fence politically, and he found himself stripped of a part of his broad acres, and tax-gatherers bothering him in the name of the governor, until there remained but a remnant of his former fortune, but all his inherited dignity of birth.

On this morning Don Carlos was sitting on the veranda of the hacienda meditating on the times, which were not at all to his liking. His wife, Doña Catalina, the sweetheart of his youth and age, was inside directing her servants. His only child, the Señorita Lolita, likewise was inside, plucking at the strings of a guitar and dreaming as a girl of eighteen dreams.

Don Carlos raised his silvered head and peered down the long, twisting trail, and saw in the distance a small cloud of dust. The dust cloud told him that a single horseman was approaching, and Don Carlos feared another gatherer of taxes.

He shaded his eyes with a hand and watched the approaching horseman carefully. He noted the leisurely manner in which he rode his mount, and suddenly hope sang in his breast, for he saw the sun flashing from the silver on saddle and bridle, and he knew that men of the army did not have such rich harness to use while on duty.

The rider had made the last turning now and was in plain sight from the veranda of the house, and Don Carlos rubbed his eyes and looked again to verify the suspicion he had. Even at that distance the aged don could establish the identity of the horseman.

" 'Tis Don Diego Vega," he breathed. "May the saints grant that here is a turn in my fortunes for the better at last."

Don Diego, he knew, might only be stopping to pay a friendly visit, and yet that would be something, for when it was known abroad that the Vega family was on excellent terms with the Pulido establishment, even the politicians would stop to think twice before harassing Don Carlos further, for the Vegas were a power in the land.

So Don Carlos slapped his hands together, and a native hurried out from the house, and Don Carlos bade him draw the shades so that the sun would be kept from a corner of the veranda, and place a table and some chairs, and hurry with small cakes and wine.

He sent word into the house to the women, too, that Don Diego Vega was approaching. Doña Catalina felt her heart beginning to sing, and she herself began to hum a little song, and Señorita Lolita ran to a window to look out at the trail.

When Don Diego stopped before the steps that led to the veranda, there was a native waiting to care for his horse, and Don Carlos himself walked halfway down the steps and stood waiting, his hand held out in welcome.

"I am glad to see you a visitor at my poor hacienda, Don Diego," he said, as the young man approached, drawing off his mittens.

"It is a long and dusty road," Don Diego said. "It wearies me, too, to ride a horse the distance."

Don Carlos almost forgot himself and smiled at that, for surely riding a horse a distance of four miles was not enough to tire a young man of blood. But he remembered Don Diego's lifelessness and did not smile, lest the smile cause anger.

He led the way to the shady nook on the veranda, and offered Don Diego wine and cakes, and waited for his guest to speak. As became the times, the women remained inside the house, not ready to show themselves unless the visitor asked for them, or their lord and master called.

"How are things in the pueblo of Reina de Los Angeles?" Don Carlos asked. "It has been a space of several score days since I visited there."

"Everything is the same," said Don Diego, "except that this

Señor Zorro invaded the tavern last evening and had a duel with the big Sergeant Gonzales."

"Ha! Señor Zorro, eh? And what was the outcome of the fighting?"

"Though the sergeant has a crooked tongue while speaking of it," said Don Diego, "it has come to me through a corporal who was present that this Señor Zorro played with the sergeant and finally disarmed him and sprang through a window to make his escape in the rain. They could not find his tracks."

"A clever rogue," Don Carlos said. "At least, I have nothing to fear from him. It is generally known up and down El Camino Real, I suppose, that I have been stripped of almost everything the governor's men could carry away. I look for them to take the hacienda next."

"Um! Such a thing should be stopped!" Don Diego said, with more than his usual amount of spirit.

The eyes of Don Carlos brightened. If Don Diego Vega could be made to feel some sympathy, if one of the illustrious Vega family would but whisper a word in the governor's ear, the persecution would cease instantly, for the commands of a Vega were made to be obeyed by all men of whatever rank.

CHAPTER 6
Diego Seeks a Bride

D ON DIEGO sipped his wine slowly and looked out across the mesa, and Don Carlos looked at him in puzzled fashion, realizing that something was coming, and scarcely knowing what to expect.

"I did not ride through the damnable sun and dust to talk with you concerning this Señor Zorro, or any other bandit," Don Diego explained after a time.

"Whatever your errand, I am glad to welcome one of your family, caballero," Don Carlos said.

"I had a long talk with my father yesterday morning," Don Diego went on. "He informed me that I am approaching the age of twenty-five, and he is of a mind that I am not accepting my duties and responsibilities in the proper fashion."

"But surely—"

"Oh, doubtless he knows. My father is a wise man."

"And no man can dispute that, Don Diego!"

"He urged upon me that I awaken and do as I should. I have been dreaming, it appears. A man of my wealth and station—you will pardon me if I speak of it—must do certain things."

"It is the purse of position, señor."

"When my father dies I come into his fortune, naturally,

being the only child. That part of it is all right. But what will happen when I die? That is what my father asks."

"I understand."

"A young man of my age, he told me, should have a wife, a mistress of his household, and should—er—have offspring to inherit and preserve an illustrious name."

"Nothing could be truer than that," said Don Carlos.

"So I have decided to get me a wife."

"Ha! It is something every man should do, Don Diego. Well do I remember when I courted Doña Catalina. We were mad to get into each other's arms, but her father kept her from me for a time. I was only seventeen, though, so perhaps he did right. But you are nearly twenty-five. Get you a bride, by all means."

"And so I have come to see you about it," Don Diego said.

"To see me about it?" gasped Don Carlos, with something of fear and a great deal of hope in his breast.

"It will be rather a bore, I expect. Love and marriage, and all that sort of thing, is rather a necessary nuisance in its way. The idea of a man of sense running about a woman, playing a guitar for her, making up to her like a loon when everyone knows his intention! And then the ceremony! Being a man of wealth and station, I suppose the wedding must be an elaborate one, and the natives will have to be feasted, and all that, simply because a man is taking a bride to be mistress of his household."

"Most young men," Don Carlos observed, "delight to win a woman and are proud if they have a great and fashionable wedding."

"No doubt. But it is an awful nuisance. However, I will go through with it, señor. It is my father's wish, you see. You—if you will pardon me again—have fallen upon evil days. That is the result of politics, of course. But you are of excellent blood, señor, of the best blood in the land."

"I thank you for remembering that truth," said Don Carlos,

rising long enough to put one hand over his heart and bow.

"Everybody knows it, señor. And a Vega, naturally, when he takes a mate, must seek out a woman of excellent blood."

"To be sure!" Don Carlos exclaimed.

"You have an only daughter, the Señorita Lolita."

"Ah! Yes, indeed, señor. Lolita is eighteen now, and a beautiful and accomplished girl, if her father is the man to say it."

"I have observed her at the mission and at the pueblo," Don Diego said. "She is, indeed, beautiful, and I have heard that she is accomplished. Of her birth and breeding there can be no doubt. I think she would be a fit woman to preside over my household."

"Señor?"

"That is the object of my visit today, señor."

"You—you are asking my permission to pay addresses to my fair daughter?"

"I am, señor."

Don Carlos's face beamed, and again he sprang from his chair, this time to bend forward and grasp Don Diego by the, hand.

"She is a fair flower," the father said. "I would see her wed, and I have been to some anxiety about it, for I did not wish her to marry into a family that did not rank with mine. But there can be no question where a Vega is concerned. You have my permission, señor."

Don Carlos was delighted. An alliance between his daughter and Don Diego Vega! His fortunes were retrieved the moment that was consummated. He would be important and powerful again!

He called a native and sent for his wife, and within a few minutes the Doña Catalina appeared on the veranda to greet the visitor, her face beaming, for she had been listening.

"Don Diego has done us the honor to request permission to pay his respects to our daughter," Don Carlos explained.

"You have given consent?" Doña Catalina asked; for it

would not do, of course, to jump for the man.

"I have given my consent," Don Carlos replied.

Doña Catalina held out her hand, and Don Diego gave it a languid grasp and then released it.

"Such an alliance would be a proud one," Doña Catalina said. "I hope that you may win her heart, señor."

"As to that," said Don Diego, "I trust there will be no undue nonsense. Either the lady wants me and will have me, or she will not. Will I change her mind if I play a guitar beneath her window, or hold her hand when I may, or put my hand over my heart and sigh? I want her for wife, else I would not have ridden here to ask her father for her."

"I—I—of course," said Don Carlos.

"Ah, señor, but a maid delights to be won," said the Doña Catalina. "It is her privilege, señor. The hours of courtship are held in memory during her lifetime. She remembers the pretty things her lover said, and the first kiss, when they stood beside the stream and looked into each other's eyes, and when he showed sudden fear for her while they were riding and her horse bolted—those things, señor.

"It is like a little game, and it has been played since the beginning of time. Foolish, señor? Perhaps when a person looks at it with cold reason. But delightful, nevertheless."

"I don't know anything about it," Don Diego protested. "I never ran around making love to women."

"The woman you marry will not be sorry because of that, señor."

"You think it is necessary for me to do these things?"

"Oh," said Don Carlos, afraid of losing an influential son-in-law, "a little bit would not hurt. A maid likes to be wooed, of course, even though she has made up her mind."

"I have a servant who is a wonder at the guitar," Don Diego said. "Tonight I shall order him to come out and play beneath the señorita's window."

"And not come yourself?" Doña Catalina gasped.

"Ride out here again tonight, when the chill wind blows in from the sea?" gasped Don Diego. "It would kill me. And the native plays the guitar better than I."

"I never heard of such a thing!" Doña Catalina gasped, her sense of the fitness of things outraged.

"Let Don Diego do as he wills," Don Carlos urged.

"I had thought," said Don Diego, "that you would arrange everything and then let me know. I would have my house put in order, of course, and get me more servants. Perhaps I should purchase a coach and drive with my bride as far as Santa Barbara and visit a friend there. Is it not possible for you to attend to everything else? Just merely send me word when the wedding is to be."

Don Carlos Pulido was nettled a little himself now.

"Caballero," he said, "when I courted Doña Catalina she kept me on needles and pins. One day she would frown, and the next day smile. It added a spice to the affair. I would not have had it different. You will regret it, señor, if you do not do your own courting. Would you like to see the señorita now?"

"I suppose I must," Don Diego said.

Doña Catalina threw up her head and went into the house to fetch the girl; and soon she came, a dainty little thing with black eyes that snapped, and black hair that was wound around her head in a great coil, and dainty little feet that peeped from beneath skirts of bright hue.

"I am happy to see you again, Don Diego," she said.

He bowed over her hand and assisted her to one of the chairs.

"You are as beautiful as you were when I saw you last," he said.

"Always tell a señorita that she is more beautiful than when you saw her last," groaned Don Carlos. "Ah, that I were young again and could make love anew!"

He excused himself and entered the house, and Doña Catalina moved to the other end of the veranda, so that the pair could talk without letting her hear the words, but from where she could watch, as a good dueña always must.

"Señorita," Don Diego said, "I have asked your father this morning for permission to seek you in marriage."

"Oh, señor!" the girl gasped.

"Do you think I would make a proper husband?"

"Why, I—that is—"

"Just say the word, señorita, and I shall tell my father, and your family will make arrangements for the ceremony. They can send word in to me by some native. It fatigues me to ride abroad when it is not at all necessary."

Now the pretty eyes of the Señorita Lolita began flashing warning signals, but Don Diego, it was evident, did not see them, and so he rushed forward to his destruction.

"Shall you agree to becoming my wife, señorita?" he asked, bending slightly toward her.

Señorita Lolita's face burned red, and she sprang from her chair, her tiny fists clenched at her side.

"Don Diego Vega," she replied, "you are of a noble family and have much wealth and will inherit more. But you are lifeless, señor! Is this your idea of courtship and romance? Can you not take the trouble to ride four miles on a smooth road to see the maid you would wed? What sort of blood is in your veins, señor?"

Doña Catalina heard that, and now she rushed across the veranda toward them, making signals to her daughter, which Señorita Lolita refused to see.

"The man who weds me must woo me and win my love," the girl went on. "He must touch my heart. Think you that I am some bronze native wench to give myself to the first man who asks? The man who becomes my husband must be a man with life enough in him to want me. Send your servant to play a guitar beneath my window? Oh, I heard, Señor! Send him, Señor, and I'll throw boiling water upon him and bleach his red skin! Buenos dias, señor!"

She threw up her head proudly, lifted her silken skirts aside, and so passed him to enter the house, disregarding her mother also. Doña Catalina moaned once for her lost hopes. Don Diego Vega looked after the disappearing señorita and scratched at his head thoughtfully and glanced toward his horse.

"I—I believe she is displeased with me," he said in his timid voice.

Chapter 7

A Different Sort of Man

Don Carlos lost no time in hurrying out to the veranda again—since he had been listening and so knew what had happened—and endeavoring to placate the embarrassed Don Diego Vega. Though there was consternation in his heart, he contrived to chuckle and make light of the occurrence.

"Women are fitful and filled with fancies, señor," he said. "At times they will rail at those whom they in reality adore. There is no telling the workings of a woman's mind—she cannot explain it with satisfaction herself."

"But I—I scarcely understand," Don Diego gasped. "I used my words with care. Surely I said nothing to insult or anger the señorita."

"She would be wooed, I take it, in the regular fashion. Do not despair, Señor. Both her mother and myself have agreed that you are a proper man for her husband. It is customary that a maid fight off a man to a certain extent, and then surrender. It appears to make the surrender the sweeter. Perhaps the next time you visit us she will be more agreeable. I feel quite sure of it."

So Don Diego shook hands with Don Carlos Pulido and

mounted his horse and rode slowly down the trail; and Don Carlos turned about and entered his house again and faced his wife and daughter, standing before the latter with his hands on his hips and regarding her with something akin to sorrow.

"He is the greatest catch in all the country!" Doña Catalina was wailing; and she dabbed at her eyes with a delicate square of filmy lace.

"He has wealth and position and could mend my broken fortunes if he were but my son-in-law," Don Carlos declared, not taking his eyes from his daughter's face.

"He has a magnificent house and a hacienda besides, and the best horses near Reina de Los Angeles, and he is sole heir to his wealthy father," Doña Catalina said.

"One whisper from his lips into the ear of his excellency, the governor, and a man is made—or unmade," added Don Carlos.

"He is handsome—"

"I grant you that!" exclaimed the Señorita Lolita, lifting her pretty head and glaring at them bravely. "That is what angers me! What a lover the man could be, if he would! Is it anything to make a girl proud to have it said that the man she married never looked at another woman, and so did not select her after dancing and talking and playing at love with others?"

"He preferred you to all others, else he would not have ridden out today," Don Carlos said.

"Certainly it must have fatigued him!" the girl said. "Why does he let himself be made the laughingstock of the country? He is handsome and rich and talented. He has health, and could lead all the other young men. Yet he has scarcely enough energy to dress himself, I doubt not."

"This is all beyond me," the Doña Catalina wailed. "When I was a girl, there was nothing like this. An honorable man comes seeking you as wife—"

"Were he less honorable and more of a man, I might look at him a second time," said the señorita.

"You must look at him more than a second time," put in Don Carlos, with some authority in his manner. "You cannot throw away such a fine chance. Think on it, my daughter. Be in a more amiable mood when Don Diego calls again."

Then he hurried to the patio on pretense that he wished to speak to a servant, but in reality to get away from the scene. Don Carlos had proved himself to be a courageous man in his youth, and now he was a wise man, also, and hence he knew better than to participate in an argument between women.

Soon the siesta hour was at hand, and the Señorita Lolita went into the patio and settled herself on a little bench near the fountain. Her father was dozing on the veranda, and her mother in her room, and the servants were scattered over the place, sleeping also. But Señorita Lolita could not sleep, for her mind was busy.

She knew her father's circumstances, of course, for it had been some time since he could hide them, and she wanted, naturally, to see him in excellent fortune again. She knew, too, that did she wed with Don Diego Vega, her father was made whole. For a Vega would not let the relatives of his wife be in any but the best of circumstances.

She called up before her a vision of Don Diego's handsome face, and wondered what it would be like if lighted with love and passion. 'Twere a pity the man was so lifeless, she told herself. But to wed a man who suggested sending a native servant to serenade her in his own place!

The splashing of the water in the fountain lulled her to sleep, and she curled up in one end of the bench, her cheek pillowed on one tiny hand, her black hair cascading to the ground.

And suddenly she was awakened by a touch on her arm, and sat up quickly, and then would have screamed except that a hand was crushed against her lips to prevent her.

Before her stood a man whose body was enveloped in a long cloak, and whose face was covered with a black mask so that she could see nothing of his features except his glittering eyes. She had heard Señor Zorro, the highwayman, described, and she guessed that this was he, and her heart almost ceased to beat, she was so afraid.

"Silence, and no harm comes to you, señorita," the man whispered hoarsely.

"You—you are—" she questioned on her breath.

He stepped back, removed his sombrero, and bowed low before her.

"You have guessed it, my charming señorita," he said. "I am known as Señor Zorro, the Curse of Capistrano."

"And—you are here—"

"I mean you no harm, no harm to any of this hacienda, señorita. I punish those who are unjust, and your father is not that. I admire him greatly. Rather would I punish those who do him evil than to touch him."

"I—I thank you, Señor."

"I am weary, and the hacienda is an excellent place to rest," he said. "I knew it to be the siesta hour, also, and thought everyone would be asleep. It were a shame to awaken you, señorita, but I felt that I must speak. Your beauty would hinge a man's tongue in its middle so that both ends might be free to sing your praises."

Señorita Lolita had the grace to blush.

"I would that my beauty affected other men so," she said.

"And does it not? Is it that the Señorita Lolita lacks suitors? But that cannot be possible!"

"It is, nevertheless, Señor. There are few bold enough to seek to ally themselves with the family of Pulido, since it is out of favor with the powers. There is one—suitor," she went on. "But he does not seem to put much life into his wooing."

"Ha! A laggard at love—and in your presence? What ails the man? Is he ill?"

"He is so wealthy that I suppose he thinks he has but to request it and a maiden will agree to wed him."

"What an imbecile! 'Tis the wooing gives the spice to romance."

"But you, Señor! Somebody may come and see you here! You may be captured!"

"And do you not wish to see a highwayman captured? Perhaps it would mend your father's fortune were he to capture me. The governor is much vexed, I understand, concerning my operations."

"You—you had best go," she said.

"There speaks mercy in your heart. You know that capture would mean my death. Yet must I risk it, and tarry a while."

He seated himself upon the bench, and Señorita Lolita moved away as far as she could, and then started to rise.

But Señor Zorro had been anticipating that. He grasped one of her hands and, before she guessed his intention, had bent forward, raised the bottom of his mask, and pressed his lips to its pink, moist palm.

"Señor!" she cried, and jerked her hand away.

"It were bold, yet a man must express his feelings," he said. "I have not offended beyond forgiveness, I hope."

"Go, señor, else I make an outcry!"

"And get me executed?"

"You are but a thief of the highroad!"

"Yet I love life as any other man."

"I shall call out, señor! There is a reward offered for your capture."

"Such pretty hands would not handle blood money."

"Go!"

"Ah, señorita, you are cruel. A sight of you sends the blood pounding through a man's veins. A man would fight a horde at the bidding of your sweet lips."

"Señor!"

"A man would die in your defense, señorita. Such grace, such fresh beauty."

"For the last time, señor! I shall make an outcry—and your

fate be on your own head!"

"Your hand again—and I go."

"It may not be!"

"Then here I sit until they come and take me. No doubt I shall not have to wait long. That big Sergeant Gonzales is on the trail, I understand, and may have discovered track of me. He will have soldiers with him—"

"Señor, for the love of the saints—"

"Your hand."

She turned her back and gave it, and once more he pressed his lips to the palm. And then she felt herself being turned slowly, and her eyes looked deep into his. A thrill seemed to run through her. She realized that he retained her hand, and she pulled it away. And then she turned and ran quickly across the patio and into the house.

With her heart pounding at her ribs, she stood behind the curtains at a window and watched. Señor Zorro walked slowly to the fountain and stooped to drink. Then he put his sombrero on, looked once at the house, and stalked away. She heard the galloping hoofs of a horse die in the distance.

"A thief—yet a man!" she breathed. "If Don Diego had only half as much dash and courage!"

Chapter 8
Don Carlos Plays a Game

SHE turned away from the window, thankful that none of the household had seen Señor Zorro or knew of his visit. The remainder of the day she spent on the veranda, half the time working on some lace she was making, and the other half gazing down the dusty trail that ran toward the highway.

And then came evening, and down by the natives' adobe huts big fires were lighted, and the natives gathered around them to cook and eat and speak of the events of the day. Inside the house the evening meal had been prepared, and the family was about to sit at table when someone knocked upon the door. An Indian ran to open it, and Señor Zorro strode into the room. His sombrero came off, he bowed, and then he raised his head and looked at the speechless Doña Catalina and the half-terrified Don Carlos.

"I trust you will pardon this intrusion," he said. "I am the man known as Señor Zorro. But do not be frightened, for I have not come to rob."

Don Carlos got slowly upon his feet, while Señorita Lolita gasped at this display of the man's courage, and feared he would mention the visit of the afternoon, of which she had refrained from telling her mother.

"Scoundrel!" Don Carlos roared. "You dare to enter an honest house?"

"I am no enemy of yours, Don Carlos," Señor Zorro replied. "In fact, I have done some things that should appeal to a man who has been persecuted."

That was true, Don Carlos knew, but he was too wise to admit it and so speak treason. Heaven knew he was enough in the bad graces of the governor now without offending him more by treating with courtesy this man for whose carcass the governor had offered a reward.

"What do you wish here?" he asked.

"I crave your hospitality, Señor. In other words, I would eat and drink. I am a caballero, hence make my claim in justice."

"Whatever good blood once flowed in your veins has been fouled by your actions," Don Carlos said. "A thief and highwayman has no claim upon the hospitality of this hacienda."

"I take it that you fear to feed me, since the governor may hear of it," Señor Zorro answered. "You may say that you were forced to do it. And that will be the truth."

Now one hand came from beneath the cloak, and it held a pistol. Doña Catalina shrieked and fainted, and Señorita Lolita cowered in her chair.

"Doubly a scoundrel, since you frighten women!" Don Carlos exclaimed angrily. "Since it is death to refuse, you may have meat and drink. But I ask you to be caballero enough to allow me to remove my wife to another room and call a native woman to care for her."

"By all means," Señor Zorro said. "But the señorita remains here as hostage for your good conduct and return."

Don Carlos glanced at the man, and then at the girl, and saw that the latter was not afraid. He picked his wife up in his arms and bore her through the doorway, roaring for servants to come.

Señor Zorro walked around the end of the table, bowed to

Lolita again, and sat down in a chair beside her.

"This is foolhardiness, no doubt, but I had to see your beaming face again," he said.

"Señor!"

"The sight of you this afternoon started a conflagration in my heart, señorita. The touch of your hand was new life to me."

Lolita turned away, her face flaming, and Señor Zorro moved his chair nearer and reached for her hand, but she eluded him.

"The longing to hear the music of your voice, señorita, may lure me here often," he said.

"Señor! You must never come again! I was lenient with you this afternoon, but I can not be again. The next time I shall shriek, and you will be taken."

"You could not be so cruel," he said.

"Your fate would be upon your own head, señor."

Then Don Carlos came back into the room, and Señor Zorro arose and bowed once more.

"I trust your wife has recovered from her swoon," he said. "I regret that the sight of my poor pistol frightened her."

"She has recovered," Don Carlos said. "I believe you said that you wished meat and drink. Now that I come to think of it, señor, you have indeed done some things that I have admired, and I am happy to grant you hospitality for a time. A servant shall furnish you food immediately."

Don Carlos walked to the door, called a native, and gave his orders. Don Carlos was well pleased with himself. Carrying his wife into the next room had given him his chance. For servants had answered his call, and among them had been one he trusted. And he had ordered the man to take the swiftest horse and ride like the wind the four miles to the pueblo, and there to spread the alarm that Señor Zorro was at the Pulido hacienda.

His object now was to delay this Señor Zorro as much as

possible. For he knew the soldiers would come and the highwayman be killed or captured, and surely the governor would admit that Don Carlos was entitled to some consideration for what he had done.

"You must have had some stirring adventures, señor," Don Carlos said as he returned to the table.

"A few," the highwayman admitted.

"There was that affair at Santa Barbara, for instance. I never did hear the straight of that."

"I dislike to speak of my own work, señor."

"Please," the Señorita Lolita begged; and so Señor Zorro overcame his scruples for the time being.

"It really was nothing," he said. "I arrived in the vicinity of Santa Barbara at sunset. There is a fellow there who runs a store, and he had been beating natives and stealing from the frailes. He would demand that the frailes sell him goods from the mission, and then complain that the weight was short, and the governor's men would make the frailes deliver more. So I resolved to punish the man."

"Pray continue, señor," said Don Carlos, bending forward as if deeply interested.

"I dismounted at the door of his building and walked inside. He had candles burning, and there were half a dozen fellows trading with him. I covered them with my pistol and drove them into a corner and ordered this storekeeper before me. I frightened him thoroughly, and forced him to disgorge the money he had in a secret hiding-place. And then I lashed him with a whip taken from his own wall, and told him why I had done it."

"Excellent!" Don Carlos cried.

"Then I sprang on my horse and dashed away. At a native's hut I made a placard, saying that I was a friend of the oppressed. Feeling particularly bold that evening, I galloped up to the door of the presidio, brushed aside the sentry—who took me for a courier—and pinned the placard to the door of the presidio with my knife. Just then the soldiers came rushing out. I fired over their heads, and while they were bewildered I rode away toward the hills."

"And escaped!" Don Carlos exclaimed.

"I am here!—that is your answer."

"And why is the governor so particularly bitter against you, Señor?" Don Carlos asked. "There are other highwaymen to whom he gives not a thought."

"Ha! I had a personal clash with his excellency. He was driving from San Francisco de Asis to Santa Barbara on official business, with an escort of soldiers about him. They stopped at a brook to refresh themselves, and the soldiers scattered while the governor spoke with his friends. I was hiding in the forest and suddenly dashed out and at them.

"Instantly I was at the open door of the coach. I presented my pistol at his head and ordered him to hand over his fat purse—which he did. Then I spurred through his soldiers, upsetting several as I did so—"

"And escaped!" Don Carlos cried.

"I am here," assented Señor Zorro.

The servant brought a tray of food and placed it before the highwayman, retreating as soon as possible, his eyes big with fear and his hands trembling, for many weird tales had been told of this same Señor Zorro and his brutality, none of which was true.

"I am sure that you will pardon me," Señor Zorro said, "when I ask you to sit at the far end of the room. As I take each bite, I must raise the bottom of my mask, for I have no wish to become known. I put the pistol before me on the table, so, to discourage treachery. And now, Don Carlos Pulido, I shall do justice to the meal you have so kindly furnished."

Don Carlos and his daughter sat where they had been directed, and the bandit ate with evident relish. Now and then he stopped to talk to them, and once he had Don Carlos send out for more wine, declaring it to be the best he had tasted for a year.

Don Carlos was only too glad to oblige him. He was playing to gain time. He knew the horse the native rode, and judged that he had reached the presidio at Reina de Los Angeles before this, and that the soldiers were on their way. If he could hold this Señor Zorro until they arrived!

"I am having some food prepared for you to carry with you, señor," he said. "You will pardon me while I get it? My daughter will entertain you."

Señor Zorro bowed, and Don Carlos hurried from the room. But Don Carlos had made a mistake in his eagerness. It was an unusual thing for a girl to be left alone in the company of a man in such fashion, especially with a man known to be an outlaw. Señor Zorro guessed at once that he was being delayed purposely. For, again, it was an unusual thing for a man like Don Carlos to go for the package of food himself when there were servants that could be called by a mere clapping of the hands. Don Carlos, in fact, had gone into the other room to listen at a window for sounds of galloping horses.

"Señor!" Lolita whispered across the room.

"What is it, señorita?"

"You must go—at once. I am afraid that my father has sent for the soldiers."

"And you are kind enough to warn me?"

"Do I wish to see you taken here? Do I wish to see fighting and bloodshed?" she asked.

"That is the only reason, señorita?"

"Will you not go, señor?"

"I am loath to rush away from such a charming presence, señorita. May I come again at the next siesta hour?"

"By the saints—no! This must end, Señor Zorro. Go your way—and take care. You have done some things that I admire, hence I would not see you captured. Go north as far as San Francisco de Asis and turn honest, señor. It is the better way."

"Little priest," he said.

"Shall you go, señor?"

"But your father has gone to fetch food for me. And could I depart without thanking him for this meal?"

Don Carlos came back into the room then, and Señor Zorro knew by the expression on his face that the soldiers were coming up the trail. The don put a package on the table.

"Some food to carry with you, señor," he said. "And we would relish more of your reminiscences before you start on your perilous journey."

"I have spoken too much of myself already, señor, and it ill becomes a caballero to do that. It were better that I thank you and leave you now."

"At least, señor, drink another mug of wine."

"I fear," said Señor Zorro, "that the soldiers are much too close, Don Carlos."

The face of the don went white at that, for the highwayman was picking up his pistol, and Don Carlos feared he was about to pay the price for his treacherous hospitality. But Señor Zorro made no move to fire.

"I forgive you this breach of hospitality, Don Carlos, because I am an outlaw and there has been a price put upon my head," he said. "And, also, I hold you no ill will because of it. Buenos noches, señorita! Señor, adios!"

Then a terrified servant who knew little concerning the events of the evening rushed in at the door.

"Master! The soldiers are here!" he cried. "They are surrounding the house!"

Chapter 9
The Clash of Blades

ON THE table, near its middle, was an imposing candelero in which half a score of candles burned brightly. Señor Zorro sprang toward it now, and with one sweep of his hand dashed it to the floor, extinguishing all the candles in an instant and plunging the room into darkness.

He evaded the wild rush of Don Carlos, springing across the room so lightly that his soft boots made not the slightest noise to give news of his whereabouts. For an instant the Señorita Lolita felt a man's arm around her waist, gently squeezing it, felt a man's breath on her cheek, and heard a man's whisper in her ear:

"Until later, señorita."

Don Carlos was bellowing like a bull to direct the soldiers to the scene; and already some of them were pounding at the front door. Señor Zorro rushed from the room and into the one adjoining, which happened to be the kitchen. The native servants fled before him as if he had been a ghost, and he quickly extinguished all the candles that burned there.

Then he ran to the door that opened into the patio and raised his voice and gave a call that was half moan and half shriek, a peculiar call, the like of which none at the Pulido hacienda had heard before.

As the soldiers rushed in at the front door, and as Don Carlos called for a brand with which to light the candles again, the sound of galloping hoofs was heard from the rear of the patio. Some powerful horse was getting under way there, the soldiers guessed immediately.

The sound of hoofs died away in the distance, but the soldiers had noted the direction in which the horse was traveling.

"The fiend escapes!" Sergeant Gonzales shrieked, he being in charge of the squad. "To horse and after him! I give the man who overtakes him one third of all the reward!"

The big sergeant rushed from the house, the men at his heels, and they tumbled into their saddles and rode furiously through the darkness, following the sound of the beating hoofs.

"Lights! Lights!" Don Carlos was shrieking inside the house.

A servant came with a brand, and the candles were lighted again. Don Carlos stood in the middle of the room, shaking his fists in impotent rage. Señorita Lolita crouched in a corner, her eyes wide with fear. Doña Catalina, fully recovered now from her fainting-spell, came from her own room to ascertain the cause of the commotion.

"The rascal got away!" Don Carlos said. "It is to be hoped that the soldiers capture him."

"At least he is clever and brave," Señorita Lolita said.

"I grant him that, but he is a highwayman and a thief!" Don Carlos roared. "Why should he torment me by visiting my house?"

Señorita Lolita thought she knew, but she would be the last one to explain to her parents. There was a faint blush on her face yet because of the arm that had squeezed her and the words that had been whispered in her ear.

Don Carlos threw the front door open wide and stood in it, listening. To his ears came the sound of galloping hoofs once more.

"My sword!" he cried to a servant. "Someone comes—it may be the rascal returning! It is but one rider, by the saints!"

The galloping stopped; a man made his way across the veranda and hurried through the door into the room.

"Thank the good saints!" Don Carlos gasped.

It was not the highwayman returned; it was Captain Ramón, comandante of the presidio at Reina de Los Angeles.

"Where are my men?" the captain cried.

"Gone, señor! Gone after that pig of a highwayman!" Don Carlos informed him.

"He escaped?"

"He did, with your men surrounding the house. He dashed the candles to the floor, ran through the kitchen—"

"The men took after him?"

"They are upon his heels, señor."

"Ha! It is to be hoped that they catch this pretty bird. He is a thorn in the side of the soldiery. We do not catch him, and because we do not the governor sends sarcastic letters by his courier. This Señor Zorro is a clever gentleman, but he will be captured yet!"

And then Captain Ramón walked farther into the room and perceived the ladies and swept off his cap and bowed before them.

"You must pardon my bold entrance," he said. "When an officer is on duty—"

"The pardon is granted freely," said Doña Catalina. "You have met my daughter?"

"I have not had the honor."

The Doña presented them, and Lolita retreated to her corner again and observed the soldier. He was not ill to look at —tall and straight and in a brilliant uniform, and with sword dangling at his side. As for the captain, he never had set eyes upon Señorita Lolita before, for he had been at the post at Reina de Los Angeles but a month, having been transferred there from Santa Barbara.

But now that he had looked at her once he looked a second time and a third. There was a sudden light in his eyes that pleased Doña Catalina. If Lolita could not look with favor upon Don Diego Vega, perhaps she would look with favor upon this Captain Ramón, and to have her wedded to an officer would mean that the Pulido family would have some protection.

"I could not find my men now in the darkness," the captain said, "and so, if it is not presuming too much, I shall remain here and await their return."

"By all means," Don Carlos said. "Be seated, señor, and I'll have a servant fetch wine."

"This Señor Zorro has about had his run," the captain said, after the wine had been tasted and found excellent. "Now and then a man of his sort pops up and endures for a little day, but he never lasts long. In the end he meets the fate."

"That is true," said Don Carlos. "The fellow was boasting to us tonight of his accomplishments."

"I was comandante at Santa Barbara when he made his famous visit there," the captain explained. "I was visiting at one of the houses at the time else there might have been a different story. And tonight, when the alarm came, I was not at the presidio, but at the residence of a friend. That is why I did not ride out with the soldiers. As soon as I was notified I came. It appears that this Señor Zorro has some knowledge of my whereabouts and is careful that I am not in a position to clash with him. I hope one day to do so."

"You think you could conquer him, señor?" Doña Catalina asked.

"Undoubtedly! I understand he really is an ordinary hand with a blade. He made a fool of my sergeant, but that is a different proposition—and I believe he held a pistol in one hand while he fenced, too. I should make short work of the fellow."

There was a closet in one corner of the room, and now its door was opened a crack.

"The fellow should die the death," Captain Ramón went on to say. "He is brutal in his dealings with men. He kills wantonly, I have heard. They say he caused a reign of terror in the north, in the vicinity of San Francisco de Asis. He slew men regardless, insulted women—"

The closet door was hurled open—and Señor Zorro stepped into the room.

"I shall take you to task for that statement, señor, since it is a falsehood!" the highwayman cried.

Don Carlos whirled around and gasped his surprise. Doña Catalina felt suddenly weak in the knees and collapsed on a chair. Señorita Lolita felt some pride in the man's statement, and a great deal of fear for him.

"I—I thought you had escaped," Don Carlos gasped.

"Ha! It was but a trick. My horse escaped—but I did not."

"Then there shall be no escape for you now!" Captain Ramón cried, drawing his blade.

"Back, señor!" Zorro cried, exhibiting a pistol suddenly. "I shall fight you gladly, but the fight must be fair. Don Carlos, gather your wife and daughter beneath your arms and retire to the corner while I cross blades with this teller of falsehoods. I do not intend to have a warning given out that I still am here!"

"I thought—you escaped!" Don Carlos gasped again, seemingly unable to think of anything else, and doing as Señor Zorro commanded.

"A trick!" the highwayman repeated, laughing. "It is a noble horse I have. Perhaps you heard a peculiar cry from my lips? My beast is trained to act at that cry. He gallops away wildly, making considerable noise, and the soldiers follow him. And when he has gone some distance he turns aside and stops, and after the pursuit has passed he returns to await my bidding. No doubt he is behind the patio now. I shall punish this captain and then mount and ride away."

"With a pistol in your hand!" Ramón cried.

"I put the pistol upon the table—so. There it remains if Don Carlos stays in the corner with the ladies. Now, captain!"

Señor Zorro extended his blade, and with a glad cry Captain Ramón crossed it with his own. Captain Ramón had some reputation as a master of fence, and Señor Zorro evidently knew it, for he was cautious at first, leaving no opening, on defense rather than attack.

The captain pressed him back, his blade flashing like streaks of lightning in a troubled sky. Now Señor Zorro was almost against the wall near the kitchen door, and in the captain's eyes the light of triumph already was beginning to burn. He fenced rapidly, giving the highwayman no rest, standing his ground and keeping his antagonist against the wall.

And then Señor Zorro chuckled. For now he had solved the other's manner of combat, and knew that all would be well. The captain gave ground a little as the defense turned into an attack that puzzled him. Señor Zorro began laughing lightly.

"'Twere a shame to kill you," he said. "You are an excellent officer, I have heard, and the army needs a few such. But you have spoken falsehood regarding me, and so must pay a price. Presently I shall run you through, but in such manner that your life will not emerge when I withdraw my blade."

"Boaster!" the captain snarled.

"As to that we shall see presently. Ha! I almost had you there, my captain. You are more clever than your big sergeant, but not half clever enough. Where do you prefer to be touched—the left side or the right?"

"If you are so certain run me through the right shoulder," the captain said.

"Guard it well, my captain, for I shall do as you say. Ha!"

The captain circled, trying to get the light of the candles in the highwayman's eyes, but Señor Zorro was too clever for that. He caused the captain to circle back, forced him to retreat, fought him to a corner.

"Now, my captain!" he cried.

And so he ran him through the right shoulder, as the captain had said, and twisted the blade a bit as he brought it out. He had struck a little low, and Captain Ramôn dropped to the floor, a sudden weakness upon him.

Señor Zorro stepped back and sheathed his blade.

"I ask the pardon of the ladies for this scene," he said. "And I assure you that this time I am, indeed, going away. You will find that the captain is not badly injured, Don Carlos. He may return to his presidio within the day."

He removed his sombrero and bowed low before them, while Don Carlos sputtered and failed to think of anything to say that would be mean and cutting enough. His eyes, for a moment, met those of the Señorita Lolita, and he was glad to find that in hers there was no repugnance.

"Buenos noches," he said and laughed again.

And then he dashed through the kitchen and into the patio, and found the horse awaiting him there as he had said it would be, and was quick to mount and ride away.

Chapter 10
A Hint of Jealousy

WITHIN the space of half an hour Captain Ramôn's wounded shoulder had been cleansed of blood and bandaged, and the captain was sitting at one end of the table, sipping wine and looking very white in the face and tired.

Doña Catalina and Señorita Lolita had shown much sympathy, though the latter could scarcely refrain from smiling when she remembered the captain's boast regarding what he purposed doing to the highwayman, and compared it to what had happened. Don Carlos was outdoing himself to make the captain feel at home since it was well to seek influence with the army, and already had urged upon the officer that he remain at the hacienda a few days until his wound had healed.

Having looked into the eyes of the Señorita Lolita, the captain had answered that he would be glad to remain at least for a day and, despite his wound, was attempting polite and witty conversation, yet failing miserably.

Once more there could be heard the drumming of a horse's hoofs, and Don Carlos sent a servant to the door to open it so that the light would shine out, for they supposed that it was one of the soldiers returning.

The horseman came nearer and presently stopped before the house, and the servant hurried out to care for the beast.

There passed a moment during which those inside the house heard nothing at all, and then there were steps on the veranda, and Don Diego Vega hurried through the door.

"Ha!" he cried, as if in relief. "I am rejoiced that you all are alive and well!"

"Don Diego!" the master of the house exclaimed. "You have ridden out from the pueblo a second time in one day?"

"No doubt I shall be ill because of it," Don Diego said. "Already I am feeling stiff, and my back aches. Yet I felt that I must come. There was an alarm in the pueblo, and it was noised abroad that this Señor Zorro, the highwayman, had paid a visit to the hacienda. I saw the soldiers ride furiously in this direction, and fear came into my heart. You understand, Don Carlos, I feel—sure."

"I understand, caballero," Don Carlos replied, beaming upon him and glancing once at Señorita Lolita.

"I—er—felt it my duty to make the journey. And now I find that it has been made for nought—you all are alive and well. How does it happen?"

Lolita sniffed, but Don Carlos was quick to make reply.

"The fellow was here, but he made his escape after running Captain Ramón through the shoulder."

"Ha!" Don Diego said, collapsing into a chair. "So you have felt his steel, eh, captain? That should feed your desire for vengeance. Your soldiers are after the rogue?"

"They are," the captain replied shortly, for he did not like to have it said that he had been defeated in combat. "And they will continue to be after him until he is captured. I have a big sergeant, Gonzales—I think he is a friend of yours, Don Diego—who is eager to make the arrest and earn the governor's reward. I shall instruct him, when he returns, to take his squad and pursue this highwayman until he has been dealt with properly."

"Let me express the hope that the soldiers will be successful, Señor. The rogue has annoyed Don Carlos and the ladies—and Don Carlos is my friend. I would have all men know it."

Don Carlos beamed, and Doña Catalina smiled bewitchingly, but the Señorita Lolita fought to keep her pretty upper lip from curling with scorn.

"A mug of your refreshing wine, Don Carlos," Don Diego Vega continued. "I am fatigued. Twice today have I ridden here from Reina de Los Angeles, and it is about all a man can endure."

" 'Tis not much of a journey—four miles," said the captain.

"Possibly not for a rough soldier," Don Diego replied, "but it is for a caballero."

"May not a soldier be a caballero?" Ramón asked, nettled somewhat at the other's words.

"It has happened before now, but we come across it rarely," Don Diego said. He glanced at Lolita as he spoke, intending that she should take notice of his words, for he had seen the manner in which the captain glanced at her, and jealousy was beginning to burn in his heart.

"Do you mean to insinuate, señor, that I am not of good blood?" Captain Ramón asked.

"I cannot reply as to that, señor, having seen none of it. No doubt this Señor Zorro could tell me. He saw the color of it, I understand."

"By the saints!" Captain Ramón cried. "You would taunt me?"

"Never be taunted by the truth," Don Diego observed. "He ran you through the shoulder, eh? Tis a mere-scratch, I doubt not. Should you not be at the presidio instructing your soldiers?"

"I await their return here," the captain replied. "Also, it is a fatiguing journey from here to the presidio, according to your own ideas, señor."

"But a soldier is inured to hardship, señor."

"True, there are many pests he must encounter," the captain said, glancing at Don Diego with meaning.

"You term me a pest, señor?"

"Did I say as much?"

This was perilous ground, and Don Carlos had no mind to let an officer of the army and Don Diego Vega have trouble in his hacienda, for fear he would get into greater difficulties.

"More wine, señores!" he exclaimed in a loud voice, and stepping between their chairs in utter disregard of proper breeding. "Drink, my captain, for your wound has made you weak. And you, Don Diego, after your wild ride—"

"I doubt its wildness," Captain Ramôn observed.

Don Diego accepted the proffered wine mug and turned his back upon the captain. He glanced across at Señorita Lolita and smiled. He got up deliberately and picked up his chair and carried it across the room to set it down beside her.

"And did the rogue frighten you, señorita?" he asked.

"Suppose he did, señor? Would you avenge the matter? Would you put blade at your side and ride abroad until you found him, and then punish him as he deserves?"

"By the saints, were it necessary, I might do as much. But I am able to employ a raft of strong fellows who would like nothing better than to run down the rogue. Why should I risk my own neck?"

"Oh!" she exclaimed, exasperated.

"Let us not talk further of this bloodthirsty Señor Zorro," he begged. "There are other things fit for conversation. Have you been thinking, señorita, on the object of my visit earlier in the day?"

Señorita Lolita thought of it now. She remembered again what the marriage would mean to her parents and their fortunes, and she recalled the highwayman, too, and remembered his dash and spirit, and wished that Don Diego could be such a man. And she could not say the word that would make her the betrothed of Don Diego Vega.

"I—I have scarcely had time to think of it, caballero," she replied.

"I trust you will make up your mind soon," he said.

"You are so eager?"

"My father was at me again this afternoon. He insists that I should take a wife as soon as possible. It is rather a nuisance, of course, but a man must please his father."

Lolita bit her lips because of her quick anger. Was ever girl so courted before? she wondered.

"I shall make up my mind as soon as possible, Señor," she said finally.

"Does this Captain Ramôn remain long at the hacienda?"

A little hope came into Lolita's breast. Could it be possible that Don Diego Vega was jealous? If that were true, possibly there might be stuff in the man after all. Perhaps he would awaken, and love and passion come to him, and he would be as other young men.

"My father has asked him to remain until he is able to travel to the presidio," she replied.

"He is able to travel now. A mere scratch."

"You will not return tonight?" she asked.

"It probably will make me ill, but I must return. There are certain things that must engage my interest early in the morning. Business is such a nuisance."

"Perhaps my father will offer to send you in the carriage."

"Ha! It were kindness if he does. A man may doze a bit in a carriage."

"But, if this highwayman should stop you?"

"I need not fear, Señorita. Have I not wealth? Could I not purchase my release?"

"You would pay ransom rather than fight him, Señor?"

"I have lots of money, but only one life, señorita. Would I be a wise man to risk having my blood let out?"

"It would be the manly part, would it not?" she asked.

"Any male can be manly at times, but it takes a clever man

to be sagacious," he said.

Don Diego laughed lightly, as if it cost him an effort, and bent forward to speak in lower tones.

On the other side of the room, Don Carlos was doing his best to make Captain Ramôn comfortable, and was glad that he and Don Diego remained apart for the time being.

"Don Carlos," the captain said, "I come from a good family, and the governor is friendly toward me, as no doubt you have heard. I am but twenty-three years of age, else I would hold a higher office. But my future is assured."

"I am rejoiced to learn it, señor."

"I never set eyes upon your daughter until this evening, but she has captivated me, señor. Never have I seen such grace and beauty, such flashing eyes! I ask your permission, señor, to pay my addresses to the señorita."

Chapter 11
Three Suitors

HERE was a fix. Don Carlos had no wish to anger Don Diego Vega or a man who stood high in the governor's regard. And how was he to evade it? If Lolita could not force her heart to accept Don Diego, perhaps she could learn to love Captain Ramón. After Don Diego, he was the best potential son-in-law in the vicinity.

"Your answer, señor?" the captain was asking.

"I trust you will not misunderstand me, señor," Don Carlos said, in lower tones. "I must make a simple explanation."

"Proceed, señor."

"But this morning Don Diego Vega asked me the same question."

"Ha!"

"You know his blood and his family, señor. Could I refuse him? Of rights I could not. But I may tell you this—the señorita weds no man unless it is her wish. So Don Diego has my permission to pay his addresses, but if he fails to touch her heart—"

"Then I may try?" the captain asked.

"You have my permission, señor. Of course, Don Diego has great wealth, but you have a dashing way with you, and Don Diego—that is—he is rather—"

"I understand perfectly, señor," the captain said, laughing. "He is not exactly a brave and dashing caballero. Unless your daughter prefers wealth to a genuine man—"

"My daughter will follow the dictates of her heart, señor!" Don Carlos said proudly.

"Then the affair is between Don Diego Vega and myself?"

"So long as you use discretion, señor. I would have nothing happen that would cause enmity between the Vega family and mine."

"Your interests shall be protected, Don Carlos," Captain Ramón declared.

As Don Diego talked, the Señorita Lolita observed her father and Captain Ramón, and guessed what was being said. It pleased her, of course, that a dashing officer should enter the lists for her hand, and yet she had felt no thrill when first she looked into his eyes.

Señor Zorro, now, had thrilled her to the tips of her tiny toes, and merely because he had talked to her, and touched the palm of her hand with his lips. If Don Diego Vega were only more like the highwayman! If some man appeared who combined Vega's wealth with the rogue's spirit and dash and courage!

There was a sudden tumult outside, and into the room strode the soldiers, Sergeant Gonzales at their head. They saluted their captain, and the big sergeant looked with wonder at his wounded shoulder.

"The rogue escaped us," Gonzales reported. "We followed him for a distance of three miles or so as he made his way into the hills, where we came upon him."

"Well?" Ramón questioned.

"He has allies."

"What is this?"

"Fully ten men were waiting for him there, my captain. They set upon us before we were aware of their presence. We fought them well, and three of them we wounded, but they made their escape and took their comrades with them. We had not been expecting a band, of course, and so rode into their ambush."

"Then we have to contend with a band of them!" Captain Ramón said. "Sergeant, you will select a score of men in the morning, and have command over them. You will take the trail of this Señor Zorro, and you will not stop until he is either captured or slain. I will add a quarter's wages to the reward of his excellency, the governor, if you are successful."

"Ha! It is what I have wished!" Sergeant Gonzales cried. "Now we shall run this coyote to earth in short order! I shall show you the color of his blood—"

"'Twould be no more than right, since he has seen the color of the captain's," Don Diego put in.

"What is this, Don Diego, my friend? Captain, you have crossed blades with the rogue?"

"I have," the captain assented. "You but followed a tricky horse, my sergeant. The fellow was here, in a closet, and came out after I had entered. So it must have been some other man you met with his companions up in the hills. This Señor Zorro treated me much as he treated you in the tavern—had a pistol handy in case I should prove too expert with the blade."

Captain and sergeant looked at each other squarely, each wondering how much the other had been lying; while Don Diego chuckled faintly and tried to press the Señorita Lolita's hand and failed.

"This thing can be settled only in blood!" Gonzales declared. "I shall pursue the rascal until he is run to earth. I have permission to select my men?"

"You may take any at the presidio," the captain said.

"Sergeant Gonzales, I should like to go with you," Don Diego said suddenly.

"By the saints! It would kill you, caballero. Day and night in the saddle, uphill and downhill, through dust and heat, and with a chance at fighting."

"Well, perhaps it were best for me to remain in the pueblo," Don Diego admitted. "But he has annoyed this family, of which I am a true friend. At least you will keep me informed? You will tell me how he escapes if he dodges you? I at least may know that you are on his trail, and where you are riding, so I may be with you in spirit?"

"Certainly, caballero—certainly," Sergeant Gonzales replied. "I shall give you the chance of looking upon the rogue's dead face. I swear it!"

"'Tis a terrible oath, my sergeant. Suppose it should come to pass—"

"I mean if I slay the rascal, caballero. My captain, do you return this night to the presidio?"

"Yes," Ramón replied. "Despite my wound, I can ride a horse."

He glanced toward Don Diego as he spoke, and there was almost a sneer upon his lips.

"What magnificent grit!" Don Diego said. "I, too, shall return to Reina de Los Angeles, if Don Carlos will be as good as to have his carriage around. I can tie my horse to the rear of it. To ride horseback the distance again this day would be the death of me."

Gonzales laughed and led the way from the house. Captain Ramón paid his respects to the ladies, glowered at Don Diego, and followed. The caballero faced Señorita Lolita again as her parents escorted the captain to the door.

"You will think of the matter?" he asked. "My father will be at me again within a few days, and I shall escape censure if I am able to tell him that it is all settled. If you decide to wed me, have your father send me word by a servant. Then I shall put my house in order against the wedding day."

"I shall think of it," the girl said.

"We could be married at the mission of San Gabriel, only we should have to make the confounded journey there. Fray Felipe, of the mission, has been my friend from the days of my boyhood, and I would have him say the words, unless you 'prefer otherwise. He could come to Reina de Los Angeles and read the ceremony in the little church on the plaza there."

"I shall think of it," the girl said again.

"Perhaps I may come out again to see you within a few days, if I survive this night. Buenos noches, señorita. I suppose I should—er—kiss your hand?"

"You need not take the trouble," Señorita Lolita replied, "It might fatigue you."

"Ah—thank you. You are thoughtful, I see. I am fortunate if I get me a thoughtful wife."

Don Diego sauntered to the door. Señorita Lolita rushed into her own room and beat at her breasts with her hands, and tore at her hair a bit, too angry, too enraged to weep. Kiss her hand, indeed! Señor Zorro had not suggested it—he had done it. Señor Zorro had dared death to visit her. Señor Zorro had laughed as he fought, and then had escaped by a trick! Ah, if Don Diego Vega were half the man this highwayman appeared!

She heard the soldiers gallop away, and after a little time she heard Don Diego Vega depart in her father's carriage. And then she went out into the great room again to her parents.

"My father, it is impossible that I wed with Don Diego Vega," she said.

"What has caused your decision, my daughter?"

"I scarcely can tell, except that he is not the sort of man I wish for my husband. He is lifeless; existence with him would be a continual torment."

"Captain Ramón also has asked permission to pay you his addresses," Doña Catalina said.

"And he is almost as bad. I do not like the look in his eyes," the girl replied.

"You are too particular," Don Carlos told her. "If the persecution continues another year we shall be beggars. Here is the best catch in the country seeking you, and you would refuse him. And you do not like a high army officer because you do not fancy the look in his eyes.

"Think on it, girl! An alliance with Don Diego Vega is much to be desired. Perhaps when you know him better, you will like him more. And the man may awaken. I thought I saw a flash of it this night, deemed him jealous because of the presence of the captain here. If you can arouse his jealousy—"

Señorita Lolita burst into tears, but soon the tempest of weeping passed, and she dried her eyes.

"I—I shall do my best to like him," she said. "But I cannot bring myself to say, yet, that I will be his wife."

She hurried into her room again, and called for the native woman who attended her. Soon the house was in darkness, and the grounds about it, save for the fires down by the adobe huts, where the natives told one another grim tales of the night's events, each trying to make his falsehood the greatest. A gentle snore came from the apartment of Don Carlos Pulido and his wife.

But the Señorita Lolita did not slumber. She had her head propped on one hand, and she was looking through a window at the fires in the distance, and her mind was full of thoughts of Señor Zorro.

She remembered the grace of his bow, the music of his deep voice, the touch of his lips upon her palm.

"I would he were not a rogue." She sighed. "How a woman could love such a man!"

Chapter 12
A Visit

SHORTLY after daybreak the following morning there was considerable tumult in the plaza at Reina de Los Angeles. Sergeant Pedro Gonzales was there with a score of troopers, almost all that were stationed at the local presidio, and they were preparing for the chase of Señor Zorro.

The big sergeant's voice roared out above the din as men adjusted saddles and looked to bridles and inspected then-water bottles and small supplies of provisions. For Sergeant Gonzales had ordered that his force travel light, and live off the country as much as possible. He had taken the commands of his captain seriously—he was going after Señor Zorro and did not propose to return until he had him—or had died in an effort to effect a capture.

"I shall nail the fellow's pelt to the presidio door, my friend," he told the fat landlord. "Then I shall collect the governors reward and pay the score I owe you."

"I pray the saints it may be true," the landlord said.

"What, fool? That I pay you? Do you fear to lose a few small coins?"

"I meant that I pray you may be successful in capturing the man," the landlord said, telling the falsehood glibly.

Captain Ramôn was not up to see the start, having a small fever because of his wound, but the people of the pueblo crowded around Sergeant Gonzales and his men, asking a multitude of questions, and the sergeant found himself the center of interest.

"This Curse of Capistrano soon shall cease to exist!" he boasted loudly. "Pedro Gonzales is on his trail. Ha! When I stand face to face with the fellow—"

The front door of Don Diego Vega's house opened at that juncture, and Don Diego himself appeared, at which the townsmen wondered a bit, since it was so early in the morning. Sergeant Gonzales dropped a bundle he was handling, put his hands upon his hips, and looked at his friend with sudden interest.

"You have not been to bed," he charged.

"But I have!" Don Diego declared.

"And are up again so soon? Here is some devilish mystery that needs an explanation."

"You made noise enough to awaken the dead," Don Diego said.

"It could not be helped, caballero, since we are acting under orders."

"Were it not possible to make your preparations at the presidio instead of here in the plaza, or did you think not enough persons would see your importance there?"

"Now, by the—"

"Do not say it!" Don Diego commanded. "As a matter of fact, I am up early because I must make a confounded trip to my hacienda, a journey of some ten miles, to inspect the flocks and herds. Never become a wealthy man, Sergeant Gonzales, for wealth asks too much of a man."

"Something tells me that never shall I suffer on that account," said the sergeant, laughing. "Yon go with escort, my friend?"

"A couple of natives, that is all."

"If you should meet up with this Señor Zorro, he probably would hold you for a pretty ransom."

"Is he supposed to be between this place and my hacienda?" Don Diego asked.

"A native arrived a short time ago with word that he had been seen on the road running to Pala and San Luis Rey. We ride in that direction. And since your hacienda is the other way, no doubt you will not meet the rascal now."

"I feel somewhat relieved to hear you say it. So you ride toward Pala, my sergeant?"

"We do. We shall try to pick up his trail as soon as possible, and once we have it we shall run this fox down. Meanwhile, we also shall attempt to find his den. We start at once."

"I shall await news eagerly," Don Diego said. "Good fortune go with you!"

Gonzales and his men mounted, and the sergeant shouted an order, and they galloped across the plaza, raising great clouds of dust, and took the highway toward Pala and San Luis Rey.

Don Diego looked after them until nothing could be seen but a tiny dust cloud in the distance, then called for his own horse. He, too, mounted and rode away toward San Gabriel, and two native servants rode mules and followed a short distance behind.

But before he departed, Don Diego wrote a message and sent it by native courier to the Pulido hacienda. It was addressed to Don Carlos, and read:

> The soldiers are starting this morning to pursue this Señor Zorro, and it has been reported that the highwayman has a band of rogues under his command and may offer battle. There is no telling, my friend, what may happen. I dislike having one in whom I am interested subjected to danger, meaning your daughter particularly, but also the Doña Catalina and yourself. Moreover, this bandit saw your daughter last evening, and certainly

must have appreciated her beauty, and he may seek to see her again.

I beg of you to come at once to my house in Reina de Los Angeles, and make it as your home until matters are settled. I am leaving this morning for my hacienda, but have left orders with my servants that you are to give what commands you will. I shall hope to see you when I return, which will be in two or three days.

Diego.

Don Carlos read that epistle aloud to his wife and daughter, and then looked up to see how they took it. He scoffed at the danger himself, being an old war horse, but did not wish to put his womenfolk in jeopardy.

"What think you?" he asked.

"It has been some time since we have visited the pueblo," Doña Catalina said. "I have some friends left among the ladies there. I think it will be an excellent thing to do."

"It certainly will not injure our fortunes to have it become known we are house guests of Don Diego Vega," Don Carlos said. "What does our daughter think?"

It was a concession to ask her, and Lolita realized that she was granted this unusual favor because of Don Diego's wooing. She hesitated some time before answering.

"I believe it will be all right," she said. "I should like to visit the pueblo, for we see scarcely anybody here at the hacienda. But people may talk concerning Don Diego and myself."

"Nonsense!" Don Carlos exploded. "Could there be anything more natural than that we should visit the Vegas, since our blood is almost as good as theirs and better than that of others?"

"But it is Don Diego's house, and not that of his father. Still—he will not be there for two or three days, he says, and we can return when he comes."

"Then it is settled," Don Carlos declared. "I shall see my superintendent and give him instructions."

He hurried into the patio and rang the big bell for the superintendent, being well pleased. For when the Señorita Lolita saw the rich furnishings in the house of Don Diego Vega, she might the more readily accept Don Diego as a husband, he thought. When she saw the silks and satins, the elegant tapestries, the furniture inlaid with gold and studded with precious stones, when she realized that she could be mistress of this and much more besides—Don Carlos flattered himself that he knew the feminine heart.

Soon after the siesta hour, a carreta was brought before the door, drawn by mules and driven by a native. Doña Catalina and Lolita got into it, and Don Carlos bestrode his best horse and rode at its side. And so they went down the trail to the highway, and down the highway toward Reina de Los Angeles.

They passed folk who marveled to see the Pulido family thus going abroad, for it was well known that they had met with ill fortune and scarcely went anywhere now. It was even whispered that the ladies did not keep up with the fashions, and that the servants were poorly fed, but remained at the hacienda because their master was so kind.

But Doña Catalina and her daughter held their heads proudly, as did Don Carlos, and they greeted the people they knew, and so continued along the highway.

Presently they made a turning and could see the pueblo in the distance—the plaza and the church with its high cross on one side of it and the inn and storehouses and a few residences of the more pretentious sort, like Don Diego's, and the scattered huts of natives and poor folk.

The carreta stopped before Don Diego's door, and servants rushed out to make the guests welcome, spreading a carpet from the carreta to the doorway, that the ladies would not have to step in the dust. Don Carlos led the way into the house, after ordering that the horse and mules be cared for and the carreta put away, and there they rested for a time, and the servants brought out wine and food.

They went through the rich house then, and even the eyes of Doña Catalina, who had seen many rich houses, widened at what she saw here in Don Diego's home.

"To think that our daughter can be mistress of all this when she speaks the word!" she gasped.

Señorita Lolita said nothing, but she began thinking that perhaps it would not be so bad after all to become the wife of Don Diego. She was fighting a mental battle, was Señorita Lolita. On the one side was wealth and position, and the safety and good fortune of her parents—and a lifeless man for husband; and on the other side was the romance and ideal love she craved. Until the last hope was gone she could not give the latter up.

Don Carlos left the house and crossed the plaza to the inn, where he met several gentlemen of age, and renewed acquaintance with them, albeit he noticed that none was enthusiastic in his greeting. They feared, he supposed, to appear openly friendly to him, since he was in the bad graces of the governor.

"You are in the pueblo on business?" one asked.

"Not so, Señor," Don Carlos replied, and gladly, since here was a chance to set himself right in part. "This Señor Zorro is abroad, and the soldiers after him."

"We are aware of that."

"There may be a battle, or a series of raids, since it is whispered that now Señor Zorro has a band of cutthroats with him, and my hacienda is off by itself and would be at the mercy of the thief."

"Ah! And so you bring your family to the pueblo until the matter is at an end?"

"I had not thought of doing so, but this morning Don Diego Vega sent out to me a request that I bring my family here and make use of his house for the time being. Don Diego has gone to his hacienda, but will return within a short time."

The eyes of those who heard opened a bit at that, but Don

Carlos pretended not to notice, and went on sipping his wine.

"Don Diego was out to visit me yesterday morning," he continued. "We renewed old times. And my hacienda had a visit from this Señor Zorro last night, as doubtless you have heard, and Don Diego, learning of it, galloped out again, fearing we had met with disaster."

"Twice in one day!" gasped one of those who heard.

"I have said it, Señor."

"You—that is—your daughter is very beautiful, is she not, Don Carlos Pulido? And seventeen, is she not—about?"

"Eighteen, Señor. She is called beautiful, I believe," Don Carlos admitted.

Those around him glanced at one another. They had the solution now. Don Diego Vega was seeking to wed Señorita Lolita Pulido. That meant that Pulido's fortunes would soon be at the flood again, and that he might feel called upon to remember his friends and look askance at those who had not stood by him.

So now, they crowded forward, alert to do him honor, and asked concerning crops and the increase of his herds and flocks, and whether the bees were doing as well as usual, and did he think the olives were excellent this year.

Don Carlos appeared to take it all as a matter of course. He accepted the wine they bought, and purchased himself, and the fat landlord darted about doing their bidding and trying to compute the day's profits in his head, which was a hopeless task for him.

When Don Carlos left the inn at dusk, several of them followed him to the door, and two of the more influential walked with him across the plaza to the door of Don Diego's house. One of these begged that Don Carlos and his wife visit his house that evening for music and talk, and Don Carlos graciously accepted the invitation.

Doña Catalina had been watching from a window, and her face was beaming when she met her husband at the door.

"Everything goes well," he said. "They have met me with open arms. And I have accepted an invitation to visit tonight."

"But Lolita?" Doña Catalina protested.

"She must remain here, of course. Will it not be all right? There are half a hundred servants about. And I have accepted the invitation, my dear."

Such a chance to win favor again could not be disregarded, of course, and so Lolita was made acquainted with the arrangement. She was to remain in the great living-room, reading a volume of verse she had found there, and if she grew sleepy she was to retire to a certain chamber. The servants would guard her, and the despensero would look after her wishes personally.

Don Carlos and his wife went to make their evening visit, being lighted across the plaza by half a dozen natives who held torches in their hands, for the night was without a moon, and rain was threatening again.

Señorita Lolita curled up on a couch, the volume of verse in her lap, and began to read. Each verse treated of love, romance, passion. She marveled that Don Diego would read such, being so lifeless himself, but the volume showed that it had been much handled. She sprang from the couch to look at other books on a bench not far away. And her amazement increased.

Volume after volume of poets who sang of love; volumes that had to do with horsemanship; books that had been written at the dictation of masters of fence; tales of great generals and warriors were there.

Surely these volumes were not for a man of Don Diego's blood, she told herself. And then she thought that perhaps he reveled in them, though not in the manner of life they preached. Don Diego was something of a puzzle, she told herself for the hundredth time; and she went back and began reading the poetry again.

Then Captain Ramón hammered at the front door.

CHAPTER 13
Love Comes Swiftly

THE despensero hurried to open it.

"I regret that Don Diego is not at home, señor," he said. "He has gone to his hacienda."

"I know as much. Don Carlos and wife and daughter are here, are they not?"

"Don Carlos and his wife are out on a visit this evening, señor."

"The Señorita—"

"Is here, of course."

"In that case, I shall pay my respects to the Señorita," Captain Ramôn said.

"Señor! Pardon me, but the little lady is alone."

"Am I not a proper man?" the captain demanded.

"It—it is scarcely right for her to receive the visit of a gentleman when her duenna is not present."

"Who are you to speak to me of the proprieties?" Captain Ramôn demanded. "Out of my way, scum! Cross me and you shall be punished. I know things concerning you."

The face of the despensero went white at that, for the captain spoke the truth and, at a word, could cause him considerable trouble and mayhap a term in cárcel. Yet he knew what was right.

"But, señor—" he protested.

Captain Ramón thrust him aside with his left arm and stalked into the big living-room. Lolita sprang up in alarm when she saw him standing before her.

"Ah, Señorita, I trust that I did not startle you," he said. "I regret that your parents are absent, yet I must have a few words with you. This servant would deny me entrance, but I imagine you have nought to fear from a man with one wounded arm."

"It—it is scarcely proper, is it, señor?" the girl asked, a bit frightened.

"I feel sure no harm can come of it," he said.

He went across the room and sat down on one end of the couch and admired her beauty frankly. The despensero hovered near.

"Go to your kitchen, fellow!" Captain Ramón commanded.

"No; allow him to remain," Lolita begged. "My father commanded it, and he courts trouble if he leaves."

"And if he remains. Go, fellow!"

The servant went.

Captain Ramón turned toward the girl again, and smiled upon her. He flattered himself that he knew women—they loved to see a man show mastery over other men.

"More beautiful than ever, señorita," he said in a purring voice. "I really am glad to find you thus alone, for there is something I would say to you."

"What can that be, señor?"

"Last night at your father's hacienda I asked his permission to pay my addresses to you. Your beauty has inflamed my heart, señorita, and I would have you for my wife. Your father consented, except that he said Don Diego Vega also had received permission. So it appears that it lies between Don Diego and myself."

"Should you speak of it, señor?" she asked.

"Certainly Don Diego Vega is not the man for you," he went on. "Has he courage, spirit? Is he not a laughingstock because of his weakness?"

"You speak ill of him in his own house?" the señorita asked, her eyes flashing.

"I speak the truth, señorita. I would have your favor. Can you not look upon me with kindness? Can you not give me hope that I may win your heart and hand?"

"Captain Ramón, all this is unworthy," she said. "It is not the proper manner, and you know it. I beg you to leave me now."

"I await your answer, señorita."

Her outraged pride rose up at that. Why could she not be wooed as other, Señoritas, in the proper fashion? Why was this man so bold in his words? Why did he disregard the conventions?

"You must leave me," she said firmly. "This is all wrong, and you are aware of it. Would you make my name a byword, Captain Ramón? Suppose somebody was to come and find us like this—alone?"

"Nobody will come, señorita. Can you not give me an answer?"

"No!" she cried, starting to get to her feet. "It is not right that you should ask it. My father, I assure you, shall hear of this visit!"

"Your father," he sneered. "A man who has the ill will of the governor. A man who is being plucked because he possessed no political sense. I fear not your father. He should be proud of the fact that Captain Ramón looks at his daughter."

"Señor!"

"Do not run away," he said, clutching her hand. "I have done you the honor to ask you to be my wife—"

"Done me the honor!" she cried angrily, and almost in tears. "It is the man who is done the honor when a woman accepts him."

"I like you when you rage," he observed. "Sit down again

—beside me here. And now give me your answer."

"Señor!"

"You will wed me, of course. I shall intercede with the governor for your father and get a part of his estate restored. I shall take you to San Francisco de Asis, to the governor's house, where you will be admired by persons of rank."

"Señor! Let me go!"

"My answer, señorita! You have held me off enough."

She wrenched away from him, confronted him with blazing eyes, her tiny hands clenched at her sides.

"Wed with you?" she cried. "Rather would I remain a maid all my life, rather would I wed with a native, rather would I die than wed with you! I wed a caballero, a gentleman, or no man! And I cannot say that you are such!"

"Pretty words from the daughter of a man who is about ruined."

"Ruin would not change the blood of the Pulidos, Señor. I doubt whether you understand that, evidently having ill blood yourself. Don Diego shall hear of this. He is my father's friend—"

"And you would wed the rich Don Diego, eh, and straighten out your father's affairs? You would not wed an honorable soldier, but would sell yourself—"

"Señor!" she shrieked.

This was beyond endurance. She was alone, there was nobody near to resent the insult So her blood called upon her to avenge it herself.

Like a flash of lightning her hand went forward, and came against Captain Ramón's cheek with a crack. Then she sprang backward, but he grasped her by an arm and drew her toward him.

"I shall take a kiss to pay for that," he said. "Such a tiny bit of womanhood can be handled with one arm, thank the saints."

She fought him, striking and scratching at his breast, for

she could not reach his face. But he only laughed at her, and held her tighter until she was almost spent and breathless, and finally he threw back her head and looked down into her eyes.

"A kiss in payment, señorita," he said. "It will be a pleasure to tame such a wild one."

She tried to fight again, but could not. She called upon the saints to aid her. And Captain Ramón laughed more and bent his head, and his lips came close to hers.

But he never claimed the kiss. She started to wrench away from him again, and he was forced to strengthen his arm and pull her forward. And from a corner of the room there came a voice that was at once deep and stern.

"One moment, Señor!" it said.

Captain Ramón released the girl and whirled on one heel. He blinked his eyes to pierce the gloom of the corner; he heard Señorita Lolita give a glad cry.

Then Captain Ramón, disregarding the presence of the lady, cursed, once and loudly, for Señor Zorro stood before him.

He did not pretend to know how the highwayman had entered the house; he did not stop to think of it. He realized that he was without a blade at his side, and that he could not use it had he one, because of his wounded shoulder. And Señor Zorro was walking toward him from the corner.

"Outlaw I may be, but I respect women," the Curse of Capistrano said. "And you, an officer of the army, do not, it appears. What are you doing here, Captain Ramón?"

"And what do you here?"

"I heard a lady's scream, which is warrant enough for caballero to enter any place, señor. It appears to me that you have broken all the conventions."

"Perhaps the lady has broken them also."

"Señor!" roared the highwayman. "Another thought like that and I cut you down where you stand, though you are a wounded man! How shall I punish you?"

"Despensero! Natives!" the captain shouted suddenly. "Here is Señor Zorro! A reward if you take him!"

The masked man laughed. "'Twill do you small good to call for help," he said. "Spend your breath in saying your prayers, rather."

"You do well to threaten a wounded man."

"You deserve death, señor, but I suppose I must allow you to escape that. But you will go down upon your knees and apologize to this señorita. And then you will go from this house, slink from it like the cur you are, and keep your mouth closed regarding what has transpired here. If you do not, I promise to soil my blade with your life's blood."

"Ha!"

"On your knees, señor, and instantly!" Señor Zorro commanded. "I have no time to waste in waiting."

"I am an officer—"

"On your knees!" commanded Señor Zorro again, in a terrible voice. He sprang forward and grasped Captain Ramón by his well shoulder, and threw him to the floor.

"Quickly, poltroon! Tell the señorita that you humbly beg her pardon—which she will not grant, of course, since you are beneath speaking to—and that you will not annoy her again. Say it, or, by the saints, you have made your last speech!"

Captain Ramón said it. And then Señor Zorro grasped him by the neck and lifted him, and propelled him to the door and hurled him into the darkness. And had his boots not been soft, Captain Ramón would have been injured more deeply, both in feelings and anatomy.

Señor Zorro closed the door as the despensero came running into the room, to stare in fright at the masked man.

"Señorita, I trust that I have been of service," the highwayman said. "That scoundrel will not bother you further, else he feels the sting of my blade again."

"Oh, thank you, Señor—thank you!" she cried. "I shall tell my father this good deed you have done. Despensero, get him wine!"

There was nought for the butler to do except obey, since she had voiced the order, and he hurried from the room, pondering on the times and the manners.

Señorita Lolita stepped to the man's side.

"Señor," she breathed, "you saved me from insult. You saved me from the pollution of that man's lips. Señor, though you deem me unmaidenly, I offer you freely the kiss he would have taken."

She put up her face and closed her eyes.

"And I shall not look when you raise your mask," she said.

"It were too much, señorita," he said. "Your hand—but not your lips."

"You shame me, Señor. I was bold to offer it, and you have refused."

"You shall feel no shame," he said.

He bent swiftly, raised the bottom of his mask, and touched lightly her lips with his.

"Ah, señorita," he said. "I would I were an honest man and could claim you openly. My heart is filled with love of you."

"And mine with love of you."

"This is madness. None must know."

"I would not fear to tell the world, Señor."

"Your father and his fortunes! Don Diego!"

"I love you, Señor."

"Your chance to be a great lady! Do you think I did not know Don Diego was the man you meant when we spoke in your father's patio? This is a whim, señorita."

"It is love, señor, whether anything comes of it or not. And a Pulido does not love twice."

"What possibly could come of it but distress?"

"We shall see. God is good."

"It is madness—"

"Sweet madness, señor."

He clasped her to him and bent his head again, and again

she closed her eyes and took his kiss, only this time the kiss was longer. She made no effort to see his face.

"I may be ugly," he said.

"But I love you."

"Disfigured, señorita—"

"Still I love you."

"What hope can we have?"

"Go, señor, before my parents return. I shall say nothing except that you saved me from insult and then went your way again. They will think that you came to rob Don Diego. And turn honest, señor, for my sake. Turn honest, I say, and claim me.

"No man knows your face, and if you take off your mask forever, none ever will know your guilt. It is not as if you were an ordinary thief. I know why you have stolen—to avenge the helpless, to punish cruel politicians, to aid the oppressed. I know that you have given what you have stolen to the poor. Oh, señor!"

"But my task is not yet done, señorita, and I feel called upon to finish it."

"Then finish it, and may the saints guard you, as I feel sure they will. And when it is finished, come back to me. I shall know you in whatever garb you come."

"Nor shall I wait that long, señorita. I shall see you often. I could not exist else."

"Guard yourself."

"I shall in truth, now, since I have double reason. Life never was so sweet as now."

He backed away from her slowly. He turned and glanced toward a window near at hand.

"I must go," he said. "I cannot wait for the wine."

"That was but a subterfuge so that we could be alone," she confessed.

"Until the next time, señorita, and may it not be long."

"On guard, señor!"

"Always, loved one. Señorita, adios!"

Again their eyes met, and then he waved his hand at her, gathered his cloak close about his body, darted to the window, and went through it. The darkness outside swallowed him.

Chapter 14
Captain Ramoñe Writes a Letter

PICKING himself up out of the dust before Don Diego Vega's door, Captain Ramón darted through the darkness to the footpath that ran up the slope toward the presidio.

His blood was aflame with rage, his face was purple with wrath. There remained at the presidio no more than half a dozen soldiers, for the greater part of the garrison had gone with Sergeant Gonzales, and of these half-dozen four were on the sick list and two were necessary as guards.

So Captain Ramón could not send men down to the Vega house in an effort to effect a capture of the highwayman; moreover, he decided that Señor Zorro would not remain there more than a few minutes, but would mount his horse and ride away, for the highwayman had a name for not resting long in one place.

Besides, Captain Ramón had no wish to let it become known that this Señor Zorro had met him a second time, and had treated him much like a peon. Could he give out the information that he had insulted a señorita, and that Señor Zorro had punished him because of it, that Señor Zorro had caused him to get down upon his knees and apologize and then had kicked him through the front door like a dog?

The captain decided it were better to say nothing of the occurrence. He supposed that Señorita Lolita would tell her parents, and that the despensero would give testimony, but he doubted whether Don Carlos would do anything about it. Don Carlos would think twice before affronting an officer of the army, being the recipient already of the governor's frowns. Ramón only hoped that Don Diego would not learn much of the happening, for if a Vega raised hand against him, the captain would have difficulty maintaining his position.

Pacing the floor of his office, Captain Ramón allowed his wrath to grow, and thought on these things and many others. He had kept abreast of the times, and he knew that the governor and the men about him were sorely in need of more funds to waste in riotous living. They had plucked those men of wealth against whom there was the faintest breath of suspicion, and they would welcome a new victim.

Might not the captain suggest one, and at the same time strengthen his own position with the governor? Would the captain dare hint that perhaps the Vega family was wavering in its loyalty to the governor?

At least he could do one thing, he decided. He could have his revenge for the flouting the daughter of Don Carlos Pulido had given him.

Captain Ramón grinned despite his wrath as the thought came to him. He called for writing-materials, and informed one of his well men that he should prepare for a journey, being about to be named for a courier's job.

Ramón paced the floor for some minutes more, thinking on the matter and trying to decide just how to word the epistle he intended writing. And finally he sat down before the long table and addressed his message to his excellency the governor, at his mansion in San Francisco de Asis.

This is what he wrote:

Your intelligences regarding this highwayman, Señor Zorro,

as he is known, have come to hand. I regret that I am unable at this writing to report the rogue's capture, but I trust that you will be lenient with me in the matter, since circumstances are somewhat unusual.

I have the greater part of my force in pursuit of the fellow, with orders to get him in person or to fetch me his corpse. But this Señor Zorro does not fight alone. He is being given succor at certain places in the neighborhood, allowed to remain in hiding when necessary, given food and drink and, no doubt, fresh horses.

Within the past day he visited the hacienda of Don Carlos Pulido, a caballero known to be hostile to your excellency. I sent men there and went myself. While my soldiers took up his trail the man came from a closet in the living-room at Don Carlos's house and attacked me treacherously. He wounded me in the right shoulder, but I fought him off until he became frightened and dashed away, making his escape. I may mention that I was hindered somewhat by this Don Carlos in pursuing the man. Also, when I arrived at the hacienda, indications were that the man had been eating his evening meal there.

The Pulido hacienda is an excellent place for such a man to hide, being somewhat off the main highway. I fear that Señor Zorro makes it his headquarters when he is in this vicinity; and I await your instructions in the matter. I may add that Don Carlos scarcely treated me with respect while I was in his presence, and that his daughter, the Señorita Lolita, scarcely could keep from showing her admiration of this highwayman and from sneering at the efforts of the soldiery to capture him.

There are also indications of a famous and wealthy family of this neighborhood wavering in loyalty to your excellency, but you will appreciate the fact that I cannot write of such a thing in a missive sent you by courier.

      With deep respect,
      Roman, Comandante and Captain, Presidio,
      Reina de LosAngeles.

R AMÔN grinned again as he finished the letter. That last paragraph, he knew, would get the governor guessing. The Vega family was about the only famous and wealthy one that would fit the description. As for the Pulidos, Captain Ramón imagined what would happen to them. The governor would not hesitate to deal out punishment, and perhaps the Señorita Lolita would find herself without protection, and in no position to reject the advances of a captain of the army.

Now Ramón addressed himself to the task of making a second copy of the letter, intending to send one by his courier and preserve the other for his files, in case something came up and he wished to refer to it.

Having finished the copy, he folded the original and sealed it, carried it to the soldiers' lounging-room, and gave it to the man he had selected as courier. The soldier saluted, hurried out to his horse, and rode furiously toward the north, toward San Fernando and Santa Barbara, and on to San Francisco de Asis, with the orders ringing in his ears that he should make all haste and get a change of horses at every mission and pueblo in the name of his excellency.

Ramón returned to his office and poured out a measure of wine, and began reading over the copy of the letter. He half wished that he had made it stronger, yet he knew that it were better to make it mild, for then the governor would not think he was exaggerating.

He stopped reading now and then to curse the name of Señor Zorro, and frequently he reflected on the beauty and grace of the Señorita Lolita and told himself she should be punished for the manner in which she had treated him.

He supposed that Señor Zorro was miles away by this time, and putting more miles between himself and Reina de Los Angeles; but he was mistaken in that. For the Curse of Capistrano, as the soldiers called him, had not hurried away after leaving the house of Don Diego Vega.

Chapter 15
At the Presidio

SEÑOR ZORRO had gone a short distance through the darkness to where he had left his horse in the rear of a native's hut, and there he had stood, thinking of the love that had come to him.

Presently he chuckled as if well pleased, then mounted and rode slowly toward the path that led to the presidio. He heard a horseman galloping away from the place and thought Captain Ramón had sent a man to call back Sergeant Gonzales and the troopers and put them on the fresher trail.

Señor Zorro knew how affairs stood at the presidio, knew to a man how many of the soldiery were there, and that four were ill with a fever, and that there was but one well man now besides the captain since one had ridden away.

He laughed again and made his horse climb the slope slowly so as to make little noise. In the rear of the presidio building he dismounted and allowed the reins to drag on the ground, knowing that the animal would not move from the spot.

Now he crept through the darkness to the wall of the building and made his way around it carefully until he came to a window. He raised himself on a pile of adobe bricks and peered inside.

It was Captain Ramón's office into which he looked. He saw the comandante sitting before a table reading a letter which, it appeared, he had just finished writing. Captain Ramón was talking to himself, as does many an evil man.

"That will cause consternation for the pretty señorita," he was saying. "That will teach her not to flaunt an officer of his excellency's forces. When her father is in the cárcel charged with high treason, and his estates have been taken away, then perhaps she will listen to what I have to say."

Señor Zorro had no difficulty in distinguishing the words. He guessed instantly that Captain Ramón had planned a revenge, that he contemplated mischief toward the Pulidos. Beneath his mask the face of Señor Zorro grew black with rage.

He got down from the pile of adobe bricks and slipped on along the wall until he came to the corner of the building. In a socket at the side of the front door a torch was burning, and the only able-bodied man left in the garrison was pacing back and forth before the doorway, a pistol in his belt and a blade at his side.

Señor Zorro noted the length of the man's pacing. He judged the distance accurately, and just as the man turned his back to resume his march the highwayman sprang.

His hands closed around the soldier's throat as his knees struck the man in the back. Instantly they were upon the ground, the surprised trooper now doing his best to put up a fight. But Señor Zorro, knowing that a bit of noise might mean disaster for him, silenced the man by striking him on the temple with the heavy butt of his pistol.

He pulled the unconscious soldier back into the shadows, gagged him with a strip torn from the end of his serape, and bound his hands and feet with other strips. Then he drew his cloak about him, looked to his pistol, listened a moment to be sure the short fight with the soldier had not attracted the attention of any inside the building, and slipped once more toward the door.

He was inside in an instant. Before him was the big loungingroom with its hard dirt floor. Here were some long tables and bunks and wine mugs and harness and saddles and bridles. Señor Zorro gave it but a glance to assure himself that no man was there, and walked swiftly and almost silently across to the door that opened into the office of the comandante.

He made sure that his pistol was ready for instant use, and then threw the door open boldly. Captain Ramón was seated with his back toward it, and now he whirled around in his chair with a snarl on his lips, thinking one of his men had entered without the preliminary of knocking, and ready to rebuke the man.

"Not a sound, Señor," the highwayman warned. "You die if as much as a gasp escapes your lips."

He kept his eyes on those of the comandante, closed the door behind him, and advanced into the room. He walked forward slowly, without speaking, the pistol held ready in front of him. Captain Ramón had his hands on the table before him, and his face had gone white.

"This visit is necessary, Señor, I believe," Señor Zorro said. "I have not made it because I admire the beauty of your face."

"What do you here?" the captain asked, disregarding the order to make no sound, yet speaking in a tone scarcely above a whisper.

"I happened to look in at the window, Señor. I saw an epistle before you on the table, and I heard you speak. Tis a bad thing for a man to talk to himself. Had you remained silent I might have gone on about my business. As it is—"

"Well, Señor?" the captain asked, with a bit of his old arrogance returning to him.

"I have a mind to read that letter before you."

"Does my military business interest you that much?"

"As to that, we shall say nothing, señor. Kindly remove your hands from the table, but do not reach toward the pistol at your side unless you wish to die the death instantly. It would not grieve me to have to send your soul into the hereafter."

The comandante did as he had been directed, and Señor Zorro went forward cautiously and snatched up the letter. Then he retreated a few paces again, still watching the man before him.

"I am going to read this," he said, "but I warn you that I shall watch you closely, also. Do not make a move, señor, unless it is your wish to visit your ancestors."

He read swiftly, and when he had finished he looked the comandante straight in the eyes for some time without speaking, and his own eyes were glittering malevolently through his mask. Captain Ramón began to feel more uncomfortable.

Señor Zorro stepped across to the table, still watching the other, and held the letter to the flame of a candle. It caught fire, blazed, presently dropped to the floor, a bit of ash. Señor Zorro put one foot upon it

"The letter will not be delivered," he said. "So you fight women, do you, señor? A brave officer and an ornament to his excellency's forces! I doubt not he would grant you promotion if he knew of this. You insult a señorita because her father, for the time being, is not friendly with those in power, and because she repulses you as you deserve, you set about to cause trouble for the members of her family. Truly, it is a worthy deed."

He took a step closer and bent forward, still holding the pistol ready before him.

"Let me not hear of you sending any letter similar to the one I have just destroyed," he said. "I regret at the present time that you are unable to stand before me and cross blades. It would be an insult to my sword to run you through, yet would I do it to rid the world of such a fellow."

"You speak bold words to a wounded man."

"No doubt the wound will heal, señor. And I shall keep myself informed regarding it. And when it has healed and you have back your strength, I shall take the trouble to hunt you up, and call you to account for what you have attempted doing this night. Let that be understood between us."

Again their eyes blazed, each man's into those of the other, and Señor Zorro stepped backward and drew his cloak closer about him. To their ears there came suddenly a jangling of harness, the tramp of horses' feet, the raucous voice of Sergeant Pedro Gonzales.

"Do not dismount!" the sergeant was crying to his men at the door. "I but make report, and then we go on after the rogue! There shall be no rest until we take him!"

Señor Zorro glanced quickly around the room, for he knew escape by the entrance was cut off now. Captain Ramón's eyes flashed with keen anticipation.

"Ho, Gonzales!" he shrieked before Zorro could warn him against it. "To the rescue, Gonzales! Señor Zorro is here!"

And then he looked at the highwayman defiantly, as if telling him to do his worst.

But Señor Zorro had no desire to fire his pistol and let out the captain's lifeblood, it appeared, preferring to save him for the blade when his shoulder should have healed.

"Remain where you are!" he commanded, and darted toward the nearest window.

The big sergeant had heard, however. He called upon his men to follow, and rushed across the large room to the door of the office and threw it open. A bellow of rage escaped him as he saw the masked man standing beside the table, and saw the comandante sitting before it with his hands spread out before him.

"By the saints, we have him!" Gonzales cried. "In with you, troopers! Guard the doors! Some look to the windows!"

Señor Zorro had transferred his pistol to his left hand, and had whipped out his blade. Now he swept it forward and sidewise, and the candles were struck from the table. Zorro put his foot upon the only one that remained lighted and extinguished it in that manner—and the room was in darkness.

"Lights! Bring a torch!" Gonzales shrieked.

Señor Zorro sprang aside, against the wall, and made his way around it rapidly while Gonzales and two other men sprang into the room, and one remained guarding the door; while in the other room several ran to get a torch, and managed to get in one another's way.

The man with the torch came rushing through the door finally, and he shrieked and went down with a sword blade through his breast, and the torch fell to the floor and was extinguished. And then, before the sergeant could reach the spot, Señor Zorro was back in the darkness again and could not be found.

Gonzales was roaring his curses now and searching for the man he wished to slay, and the captain was crying to him to be careful and not put his blade through a trooper by mistake. The other men were storming around; in the other room one came with a second torch.

Zorro's pistol spoke, and the torch was shot from the man's hand. The highwayman sprang forward and stamped upon it, putting it out, and again retreated to the darkness, changing his position rapidly, listening for the deep breathing that would tell him the exact location of his various foes.

"Catch the rogue!" the comandante was shrieking. "Can one man thus make fools of the lot of you?"

Then he ceased to speak, for Señor Zorro had grasped him from behind and shut off his wind, and now the highwayman's voice rang out above the din.

"Soldiers, I have your captain! I am going to carry him before me and back out the door. I am going to cross the other room and so reach the outside of the building. I have discharged one pistol, but I am holding its mate at the base of the captain's brain. And when one of you attacks me, I fire, and you are without a captain."

The captain could feel cold steel at the back of his head, and he shrieked for the men to use caution. And Señor Zorro carried him to the doorway and backed out with the captain held in front of him, while Gonzales and the troopers followed as closely as they dared, watching every move, hoping for a chance to catch him unaware.

He crossed the big lounging-room of the presidio, and so came to the outside door. He was somewhat afraid of the men outside, for he knew that some of them had run around the building to guard the windows. The torch was still burning just outside the door, and Señor Zorro put up his hand and tore it down and extinguished it. But still there would be grave danger the moment he stepped out.

Gonzales and the troopers were before him, spread out fanfashion across the room, bending forward, waiting for a chance to get in a blow. Gonzales held a pistol in his hand—though he made out to despise the weapon—and was watching for an opportunity to shoot without endangering the life of his captain.

"Back, señores!" the highwayman commanded now. "I would have more room in which to make my start. That is it—I thank you. Sergeant Gonzales, were not the odds so heavy, I might be tempted to play at fence with you and disarm you again."

"By the saints—"

"Some other time, my sergeant. And now, señores, attention! It desolates me to say it, but I had only the one pistol. What the captain has been feeling all this time at the base of his brain is nought except a bridle buckle I picked up from the floor. Is it not a pretty jest? Señores, a Dios!"

Suddenly he whirled the captain forward, darted into the darkness, and started toward his horse with the whole pack at his heels and pistol flashes splitting the blackness of the night and bullets whistling by his head. His laughter came back to them on the stiffening breeze that blew in from the distant sea.

Chapter 16
The Chase that Failed

SEÑOR ZORRO charged his horse down the treacherous slope of the hill, where there was loose gravel and a misstep would spell disaster, and where the troopers were slow to follow. Sergeant Gonzales possessed courage enough, and some of the men followed him, while others galloped off to right and left, planning to intercept the fugitive when he reached the bottom and turned.

Señor Zorro, however, was before them, and took the trail toward San Gabriel at a furious gallop, while the troopers dashed along behind, calling to one another, and now and then discharging a pistol with a great waste of powder and ball and no result so far as capturing or wounding the highwayman was concerned.

Soon the moon came up. Señor Zorro had been anticipating that, and knew that it would make his escape more difficult. But his horse was fresh and strong, while those ridden by the troopers had covered many miles during the day, and so hope was not gone.

Now he could be seen plainly by those who pursued, and he could hear Sergeant Gonzales crying upon his men to urge their beasts to the utmost and effect a capture. He glanced behind him as he rode, and observed that the troopers were scattering out in a long line, the stronger and fresher horses gaining on the others.

So they rode for some five miles, the troopers holding the distance, but not making any gain, and Señor Zorro knew that soon their horses would weaken, and that the good steed he bestrode, which gave no signs of fatigue as yet, would outdistance them. Only one thing bothered him—he wanted to be traveling in the opposite direction.

Here the hills rose abruptly on either side of the highway, and it was not possible for him to turn aside and make a great circle, nor were there any trails he could follow; and if he attempted to have his horse climb, he would have to make slow progress, and the troopers would come near enough to fire their pistols, and mayhap wound him.

So he rode straight ahead, gaining a bit now, knowing that two miles farther up the valley there was a trail that swung off to the right, and that by following it he would come to higher ground and so could double back on his tracks.

He had covered one of the two miles before he remembered that it had been noised abroad that a landslide had been caused by the recent torrential rain and had blocked this higher trail. So he could not use that even when he reached it; and now a bold thought came to his mind.

As he topped a slight rise in the terrain, he glanced behind once more and saw that no two of the troopers were riding side by side. They were well scattered, and there was some distance between each two of them. It would help his plan.

He dashed around a bend in the highway and pulled up his horse. He turned the animal's head back toward whence he had come, and bent forward in the saddle to listen. When he could hear the hoofbeats of his nearest pursuer's horse, he drew his blade, took a turn of the reins around his left wrist, and suddenly struck his beast in the flanks cruelly with his sharp rowels.

The animal he rode was not used to such treatment, never having felt the spurs except when in a gallop and his master wished greater speed. Now he sprang forward like a thunderbolt, dashed around the curve like a wild stallion, and bore down upon the nearest of Señor Zorro's foes.

"Make way," Señor Zorro cried.

The first man gave ground readily, not sure that this was the highwayman coming back, and when he was sure of it he shrieked the intelligence to those behind, but they could not understand because of the clatter of hoofs on the hard road.

Señor Zorro bore down upon the second man, clashed swords with him, and rode on. He dashed around another curve, and his horse struck another fairly, and hurled him from the roadway. Zorro swung at the fourth man, and missed him, and was glad that the fellow's counter stroke missed as well.

And now there was naught but the straight ribbon of road before him, and his galloping foes dotting it. Like a maniac he rode them through, cutting and slashing at them as he passed. Sergeant Gonzales, far in the rear because of his jaded mount, realized what was taking place and screeched at his men, and even as he screeched a thunderbolt seemed to strike his horse, unseating him.

And then Señor Zorro was through them and gone, and they were following him again, a cursing sergeant at their head, but at a distance slightly greater than before.

He allowed his horse to go somewhat slower now, since he could keep his distance, and rode to the first cross trail, into which he turned. He took to higher ground and looked back to see the pursuit streaming out over the hill, losing itself in the distance, but still determined.

"It was an excellent trick," Señor Zorro said to his horse. "But we cannot try it often!"

He passed the hacienda of a man friendly to the governor, and a thought came to him—Gonzales might stop there and obtain fresh horses for himself and his men.

Nor was he mistaken in that. The troopers dashed up the driveway, and dogs howled a welcome. The master of the hacienda came to the door, holding a candelero high above his head.

"We chase Señor Zorro!" Gonzales cried. "We require fresh steeds, in the name of the governor!"

The servants were called, and Gonzales and his men hurried to the corral. Magnificent horses were there, horses almost as good as the one the highwayman rode, and all were fresh. The troopers quickly stripped saddles and bridles from their jaded mounts and put them on the fresh steeds, and then dashed for the trail again and took up the pursuit. Señor Zorro had gained quite a lead, but there was only one trail he could follow, and they might overtake him.

Three miles away, on the crest of a small hill, there was a hacienda that had been presented to the mission of San Gabriel by a caballero who had died without leaving heirs. The governor had threatened to take it for the state, but so far had not done so, the Franciscans of San Gabriel having a name for protecting their property with determination.

In charge of this hacienda was one Fray Felipe, a member of the order who was along in years, and under his direction the neophytes made the estate a profitable one, raising much livestock and sending to the storehouses great amounts of hides and tallow and honey and fruit, as well as wine.

Gonzales knew the trail they were following led to this hacienda, and that just beyond it there was another trail that split, one part going to San Gabriel and the other returning to Reina de Los Angeles by a longer route.

If Señor Zorro passed the hacienda, it stood to reason that he would take the trail that ran toward the pueblo, since, had he wished to go to San Gabriel, he would have continued along the highway in the first place, instead of turning and riding back through the troopers at some risk to himself.

But he doubted whether Zorro would pass. For it was well

known that the highwayman dealt harshly with those who prosecuted the frailes, and it was to be believed that every Franciscan held a friendly feeling for him and would give him aid.

The troopers came within sight of the hacienda, and could see no light. Gonzales stopped them where the driveway started, and listened in vain for sounds of the man they pursued. He dismounted and inspected the dusty road, but could not tell whether a horseman had ridden toward the house recently.

He issued quick orders, and the troop separated, half of the men remaining with their sergeant and the others scattering in such manner that they could surround the house, search the huts of the natives, and look at the great barns.

Then Sergeant Gonzales rode straight up the driveway with half his men at his back, forced his horse up the steps to the veranda as a sign that he held this place in little respect, and knocked on the door with the hilt of his sword.

Chapter 17
Sergeant Gonzales Meets a Friend

PRESENTLY light showed through the windows, and after a time the door was thrown open. Fray Felipe stood framed in it, shading a candle with his hand—a giant of a man now past sixty, but one who had been a power in his time.

"What is all this noise?" he demanded in his deep voice. "And why do you, son of evil, ride your horse on my veranda?"

"We are chasing this pretty Señor Zorro, fray—this man they call the Curse of Capistrano," Gonzales said.

"And you expect to find him in this poor house?"

"Stranger things have happened. Answer me, fray! Have you heard a horseman gallop past within a short time?"

"I have not."

"And has this Señor Zorro paid you a visit recently?"

"I do not know the man you mean."

"You have heard of him, doubtless?"

"I have heard that he seeks to aid the oppressed, that he has punished those who have committed sacrilege, and that he has whipped those brutes who have beaten Indians."

"You are bold in your words, fray."

"It is my nature to speak the truth, soldier."

"You will be getting yourself into difficulties with the powers, my robed Franciscan."

"I fear no politician, soldier."

"I do not like the tone of your words, fray. I have half a mind to dismount and give you a taste of my whip!"

"Señor!" Fray Felipe cried. "Take ten years off my shoulders and I can drag you in the dirt!"

"That is a question for dispute. However, let us get to the subject of this visit. You have not seen a masked fiend who goes by the name of Señor Zorro?"

"I have not, soldier."

"I shall have my men search your house."

"You accuse me of falsehood?" Fray Felipe cried.

"My men must do something to pass the time, and they may as well search the house. You have nothing you wish to hide?"

"Recognizing the identity of my guests, it might be well to hide the wine jugs," Fray Felipe said.

Sergeant Gonzales allowed an oath to escape him, and got down from his horse. The others dismounted, too, and the sergeant's mount was taken off the veranda and left with the horse holder.

Then Gonzales drew off his gloves, sheathed his sword, and stamped through the door with the others at his heels, as Fray Felipe fell back before him, protesting against the intrusion.

From a couch in a far corner of the room there arose a man, who stepped into the circle of light cast by the candelero.

"As I have eyes, it is my raucous friend!" he cried.

"Don Diego! You here?" Gonzales gasped.

"I have been at my hacienda looking over business affairs, and I rode over to spend the night with Fray Felipe, who has known me from babyhood. These turbulent times! I thought that here, at least, in this hacienda that is a bit out of the way and has a fray in charge of it, I could for a time rest in peace without hearing of violence and bloodshed. But it appears that

I cannot. Is there no place in this country where a man may meditate and consult musicians and the poets?"

"Meal mush and goat's milk!" Gonzales cried. "Don Diego, you are my good friend and a true caballero. Tell me—have you seen this Señor Zorro tonight?"

"I have not, my sergeant."

"You did not hear him ride past the hacienda?"

"I did not. But a man could ride past and not be heard here in the house. Fray Felipe and I have been talking together, and were just about to retire when you came."

"Then the rogue has ridden on and taken the trail toward the pueblo!" the sergeant declared.

"You had him in view?" Don Diego asked.

"Ha! We were upon his heels, caballero! But at a turn in the highroad he made connection with some twenty men of his band. They rode at us and attempted to scatter us, but we drove them aside and kept on after Señor Zorro. We managed to separate him from his fellows and give chase."

"You say he has a score of men?"

"Fully a score, as my men will testify. He is a thorn in the flesh of the soldiery, but I have sworn to get him! And when once we stand face to face—"

"You will tell me of it afterward?" Don Diego asked, rubbing his hands together. "You will relate how you mocked him as he fought, how you played with him, pressed him back, and ran him through—"

"By the saints! You make mock of me, caballero?"

"'Tis but a jest, my sergeant. Now that we understand each other, perhaps Fray Felipe will give wine to you and your men. After such a chase, you must be fatigued."

"Wine would taste good," the sergeant said.

His corporal came in then to report that the huts and barns had been searched, and the corral also, and that no trace had been found of Señor Zorro or his horse.

Fray Felipe served the wine, though he appeared to do it

with some reluctance, and it was plain that he was but answering Don Diego's request.

"And what shall you do now, my sergeant?" Don Diego asked, after the wine had been brought to the table. "Are you always to go chasing around the country and creating a tumult?"

"The rogue evidently has turned back toward Reina de Los Angeles, caballero," the sergeant replied. "He thinks he is clever, no doubt, but I can understand his plan."

"Ha! And what is it?"

"He will ride around Reina de Los Angeles and take the trail to San Luis Rey. He will rest for a time, no doubt, to throw off all pursuit, and then will continue to the vicinity of San Juan Capistrano. That is where he began this wild life of his, and for that reason the Curse of Capistrano he is called. Yes, he will go to Capistrano."

"And the soldiers?" Don Diego asked.

"We shall follow him leisurely. We shall work toward the place, and when the news of his next outrage is made known, we shall be within a short distance of him instead of in the presidio at the pueblo. We can find the fresh trail, and so take up the chase. There shall be no rest for us until the rogue is either slain or taken prisoner."

"And you have the reward," Don Diego added.

"You speak true words, caballero. The reward will come in handy. But I seek revenge, also. The rogue disarmed me once."

"Ah! That was the time he held a pistol in your face and forced you to fight not too well?"

"That was the time, my good friend. Oh, I have a score to settle with him."

"These turbulent times." Don Diego sighed. "I would they were at an end. A man has no chance for meditation. There are moments when I think I shall ride far out in the hills, where there can be found no life except rattlesnakes and coyotes, and there spend a number of days. Only in that manner may a man meditate."

"Why meditate?" Gonzales cried. "Why not cease thought and take to action? What a man you would make, caballero, if you let your eye flash now and then, and quarreled a bit, and showed your teeth once in a while. What you need is a few bitter enemies."

"May the saints preserve us!" Don Diego cried.

"It is the truth, caballero! Fight a bit—make love to some Señorita—get drunk! Wake up and be a man!"

"Upon my soul! You almost persuade me, my sergeant. But —no. I never could endure the exertion."

Gonzales growled something into his great mustache, and got up from the table.

"I have no special liking for you, fray, but I thank you for the wine, which was excellent," he said. "We must continue our journey. A soldier's duty never is at an end while he lives."

"Do not speak of journeys!" Don Diego cried. "I must take one myself on the morrow. My business at the hacienda is done, and I go back to the pueblo."

"Let me express the hope, my good friend, that you survive the hardship," Sergeant Gonzales said.

Chapter 18
Don Diego Returns

SEÑORITA LOLITA had to tell her parents, of course, what had happened during their absence, for the despensero knew and would tell Don Diego when he returned, and the Señorita was wise enough to realize that it would be better to make the first explanation.

The despensero, having been sent for wine, knew nothing of the love scene that had been enacted, and had been told merely that Señor Zorro had hurried away. That seemed reasonable, since the Señor was pursued by the soldiers.

So the girl told her father and mother that Captain Ramón had called while they were absent, and that he had forced his way into the big living-room to speak to her, despite the entreaties of the servant. Perhaps he had been drinking too much wine, else was not himself because of his wound, the girl explained, but he grew too bold, and pressed his suit with ardor that was repugnant, and finally insisted that he should have a kiss.

Whereupon, said the Señorita, this Señor Zorro had stepped from the corner of the room—and how he came to be there, she did not know—and had forced Captain Ramón to apologize, and then had thrown him out of the house. After which—and here she neglected to tell the entire truth—Señor Zorro made a courteous bow and hurried away.

Don Carlos was for getting a blade and going at once to the presidio and challenging Captain Ramón to mortal combat; but Doña Catalina was more calm, and showed him that to do that would be to let the world know that their daughter had been affronted, and also it would not aid their fortunes any if Don Carlos quarreled with an officer of the army; and yet again the don was of an age, and the captain probably would run him through in two passes and leave Doña Catalina a weeping widow, which she did not wish to be.

So the don paced the floor of the great living-room and fumed and fussed and wished he were ten years the younger, or that he had political power again, and he promised that when his daughter should have wedded Don Diego, and he was once more in good standing, he would see that Captain Ramón was disgraced and his uniform torn from his shoulders.

Sitting in the chamber that had been assigned to her, Señorita Lolita listened to her father's ravings, and found herself confronted with a situation. Of course, she could not wed Don Diego now. She had given her lips and her love to another, a man whose face she never had seen, a rogue pursued by soldiery—and she had spoken truly when she had said that a Pulido loved but once.

She tried to explain it all to herself, saying that it was a generous impulse that had forced her to give her lips to the man; and she told herself that it was not the truth, that her heart had been stirred when first he spoke to her at her father's hacienda during the siesta hour.

She was not prepared yet to tell her parents of the love that had come into her life, for it was sweet to keep it a secret; and, moreover, she dreaded the shock to them, and half feared that her father might cause her to be sent away to some place where she never would see Señor Zorro again.

She crossed to a window and gazed out at the plaza—

and she saw Don Diego approaching in the distance. He rode slowly, as if greatly fatigued, and his two native servants rode a short distance behind him.

Men called to him as he neared the house, and he waved his hand at them languidly in response to their greeting. He dismounted slowly, one of the natives holding the stirrup and assisting him, brushed the dust from his clothes, and started toward the door.

Don Carlos and his wife were upon their feet to greet him, their faces beaming, for they had been accepted anew into society the evening before, and knew it was because they were Don Diego's house guests.

"I regret that I was not here when you arrived," Don Diego said, "but I trust that you have been made comfortable in my poor house."

"More than comfortable in this gorgeous palace!" Don Carlos exclaimed.

"Then you have been fortunate, for the saints know I have been uncomfortable enough."

"How is that, Don Diego?" Doña Catalina asked.

"My work at the hacienda done, I rode as far as the place of Fray Felipe, there to spend the night in quiet. But as we were about to retire, there came a thundering noise at the door, and this Sergeant Gonzales and a troop of soldiers entered. It appears that they had been chasing the highwayman called Señor Zorro, and had lost him in the darkness!"

In the other room, a dainty señorita gave thanks for that.

"These are turbulent times," Don Diego continued, sighing and mopping the perspiration from his forehead. "The noisy fellows were with us an hour or more, and then continued the chase. And because of what they had said of violence, I endured a horrible nightmare, so got very little rest. And this morning I was forced to continue to Reina de Los Angeles."

"You have a difficult time," Don Carlos said. "Señor Zorro was here, caballero, in your house, before the soldiers chased him."

"What is this intelligence?" Don Diego cried, sitting up straight in his chair and betraying sudden interest.

"Undoubtedly he came to steal, else to abduct you and hold you for ransom," Doña Catalina observed. "But I scarcely think that he stole. Don Carlos and myself were visiting friends, and Señorita Lolita remained here alone. There—there is a distressing affair to report to you—"

"I beg of you to proceed," Don Diego said.

"While we were gone, Captain Ramón, of the presidio, called. He was informed we were absent, but he forced his way into the house and made himself obnoxious to the señorita. This Señor Zorro came in and forced the captain to apologize and then drove him away."

"Well, that is what I call a pretty bandit!" Don Diego exclaimed. "The señorita suffers from the experience?"

"Indeed, no," said Doña Catalina. "She was of the opinion that Captain Ramón had taken too much wine. I shall call her."

Doña Catalina went to the door of the chamber and called her daughter, and Lolita came into the room and greeted Don Diego as became a proper maiden.

"It makes me desolate to know that you received an insult in my house," Don Diego said. "I shall consider the affair."

Doña Catalina made a motion to her husband, and they went to a far corner to sit, that the young folk might be somewhat alone, which seemed to please Don Diego, but not the señorita.

CHAPTER 19
Captain Ramoñe Apologizes

"CAPTAIN RAMÔN is a beast!" the girl said in a voice not too loud.

"He is a worthless fellow," Don Diego agreed.

"He—that is—he wished to kiss me," she said.

"And you did not let him, of course."

"Señor!"

"I—confound it, I did not mean that. Certainly you did not let him. I trust that you slapped his face."

"I did," said the señorita. "And then he struggled with me, and he told me that I should not be so particular, since I was daughter of a man who stood in the bad graces of the governor."

"Why, the infernal brute!" Don Diego exclaimed.

"Is that all you have to say about it, caballero?"

"I cannot use oaths in your presence, of course."

"Do you not understand, señor? This man came into your house, and insulted the girl you have asked to be your wife!"

"Confound the rascal! When next I see his excellency, I shall ask him to remove the officer to some other post."

"Oh!" the girl cried. "Have you no spirit at all? Have him removed? Were you a proper man, Don Diego, you would go to the presidio, you would call this Captain Ramôn to account, you would pass your sword through his body and call upon all to witness that a man could not insult the señorita you admired and escape the consequences."

"It is such an exertion to fight," he said. "Let us not speak of violence. Perhaps I shall see the fellow and rebuke him."

"Rebuke him!" the girl cried.

"Let us talk of something else, señorita. Let us speak of the matter regarding which I talked the other day. My father will be after me again soon to know when I am going to take a wife. Cannot we get the matter settled in some manner? Have you decided upon the day?"

"I have not said that I would marry you," she replied.

"Why hold off?" he questioned. "Have you looked at my house? I shall make it satisfactory to you I am sure. You shall refurnish it to suit your taste, though I pray you do not disturb it too much, for I dislike to have things in a mess. You shall have a new carriage and anything you may desire."

"Is this your manner of wooing?" she asked, glancing at him from the corners of her eyes.

"What a nuisance to woo," he said. "Must I play a guitar, and make pretty speeches? Can you not give me your answer without all that foolishness?"

She was comparing this man beside her with Señor Zorro, and Don Diego did not compare to him favorably. She wanted to be done with this farce, to have Don Diego out of her vision, and none but Señor Zorro in it.

"I must speak frankly to you, caballero," she said. "I have searched my heart, and in it I find no love for you. I am sorry, for I know what our marriage would mean to my parents, and to myself in a financial way. But I cannot wed you, Don Diego, and it is useless for you to ask."

"Well, by the saints! I had thought it was about all settled," he said. "Do you hear that, Don Carlos? Your daughter says she cannot wed with me—that it is not in her heart to do so."

"Lolita, retire to your chamber!" Doña Catalina exclaimed.

The girl did so gladly. Don Carlos and his wife hurried across the room and sat down beside Don Diego.

"I fear you do not understand women, my friend," Don Carlos said. "Never must you take a woman's answer for the last. She always may change her mind. A woman likes to keep a man dangling, likes to make him blow cold with fear and hot with anticipation. Let her have her moods, my friend. In the end, I am sure, you shall have your way."

"It is beyond me!" Don Diego cried. "What shall I do now? I told her I would give her all her heart desired."

"Her heart desires love, I suppose," Doña Catalina said, out of the wealth of her woman's wisdom.

"But certainly I shall love and cherish her. Does not a man promise that in the ceremony? Would a Vega break his word regarding such a thing?"

"Just a little courtship," Don Carlos urged.

"But it is such a nuisance."

"A few soft words, a pressure of the hand now and then, a sigh or two, a languishing look from the eyes—"

"Nonsense!"

"It is what a maiden expects. Speak not of marriage for some time. Let the idea grow on her—"

"But my august father is liable to come to the pueblo any day and ask when I am to take a wife. He has rather ordered me to do it."

"No doubt your father will understand," said Don Carlos. "Tell him that her mother and myself are on your side and that you are enjoying the pleasure of winning the girl."

"I believe we should return to the hacienda tomorrow," Doña Catalina put in. "Lolita has seen this splendid house, and she will contrast it with ours. She will realize what it means to marry you. And there is an ancient saying that when a man and a maid are apart they grow fonder of each other."

"I do not wish to have you hurry away."

"I think it would be best under the circumstances. And do you ride out, say in three days caballero, and I doubt not you will find her more willing to listen to your suit."

"I presume you know best," Don Diego said. "But you must remain at least until tomorrow. And now I think I shall got to the presidio and see this Captain Ramón. Possibly that will please the señorita. She appears to think I should call him to account."

Don Carlos thought that such a course would prove disastrous for a man who did not practice with the blade and knew little of fighting, but he refrained from saying so. A gentleman never intruded his own thoughts at such a time. Even if a caballero went to his death, it was all right so long as he believed he was doing the proper thing, and died as a caballero should.

So Don Diego went from the house and walked slowly up thought of coming to combat with such a man.

But he was cold courtesy itself when Don Diego was ushered into the comandante's office.

"I am proud to know you have visited me here," he said, bowing low before the scion of the Vegas.

Don Diego bowed in answer, and the chair Ramón indicated. The captain marveled that Don Diego had no blade at his side.

"I was forced to climb your confounded hill to speak to you on a certain matter," Don Diego said. "I have been informed that you visited my house during my absence, and insulted a young lady who is my guest."

"Indeed?" the captain said.

"Were you deep in wine?"

"Señor?"

"That would excuse the offense in part, of course. And then you were wounded, and probably in a fever. Were you in a fever, captain?"

"Undoubtedly," Ramón said.

"A fever is an awful thing—I had a siege of it once. But you should not have intruded upon the señorita. Not only did you affront her, but you affronted me. I have asked the señorita to become my wife. The matter—er—is not settled as yet, but I have some rights in this case."

"I entered your house seeking news of this Señor Zorro," the captain lied.

"You—er—found him?" Don Diego asked.

The face of the comandante flushed red.

"The fellow was there and he attacked me," he replied. "I was wounded, of course, and wore no weapon, and so he could work his will with me."

"It is a most remarkable thing," observed Don Diego, "that none of you soldiers can meet this Curse of Capistrano when you can be on equal terms. Always he descends upon you when you are helpless, or threatens you with a pistol while he fights you with a blade, or has his score of men about him.

"I met Sergeant Gonzales and his men at the hacienda of Fray Felipe last night, and the big sergeant told some harrowing tale of the highwayman and his score of men scattering his troopers."

"We shall get him yet," the captain promised. "And I might call your attention to certain significant things, caballero. Don Carlos Pulido, as we know, does not stand high with those in authority. This Señor Zorro was at the Pulido hacienda, you will remember, and attacked me there, emerging from a closet to do it."

"Ha! What mean you?"

"Again, on last night, he was in your house while you were abroad and the Pulidos were your guests. It begins to look as if Don Carlos has a hand in the work of the Señor Zorro. I am almost convinced that Don Carlos is a traitor and is aiding the rogue. You had better think twice, or half a score of times, before seeking a matrimonial alliance with the daughter of such a man."

"By the saints, what a speech!" Don Diego exclaimed, as if in admiration. "You have made my poor head ring with it. You really believe all this?"

"I do, caballero."

"Well, the Pulidos are returning to their own place tomorrow, I believe. I but asked them to be my guests so they could be away from the scenes of this Señor Zorro's deeds."

"And Señor Zorro followed them to the pueblo. You see?"

"Can it be possible?" Don Diego gasped. "I must consider the matter. Oh, these turbulent times! But they are returning to their hacienda tomorrow. Of course I would not have his excellency think that I harbored a traitor."

He got to his feet, bowed-courteously, and then stepped slowly toward the door. And there he seemed to remember something suddenly and turned to face the captain again.

"Ha! I am at the point of forgetting all about the insult!" he exclaimed. "What have you to say, my captain, regarding the events of last night?"

"Of course, caballero, I apologize to you most humbly," Captain Ramón replied.

"I suppose that I must accept your apology. But please do not let such a thing happen again. You frightened my despensero badly, and he is an excellent servant."

Then Don Diego Vega bowed again and left the presidio, and Captain Ramón laughed long and loudly, until the sick men in the hospital room feared that their comandante must have lost his wits.

"What a man!" the captain exclaimed. "I have turned him away from that Pulido señorita, I think. And I was a fool to hint to the governor that he could be capable of treason. I must rectify that matter in some way. The man has not enough spirit to be a traitor!"

Chapter 20
Don Diego Shows Interest

THE threatened rain did not come that day nor that night, and the following morning found the sun shining brightly and the sky blue and the scent of blossoms in the air.

Soon after the morning meal, the Pulido carreta was driven to the front of the house by Don Diego's servants, and Don Carlos and his wife and daughter prepared to depart for their own hacienda.

"It desolates me," Don Diego said at the door, "that there can be no match between the señorita and myself. What shall I say to my father?"

"Do not give up hope, caballero," Don Carlos advised him. "Perhaps when we are home again, and Lolita contrasts our humble abode with your magnificence here, she will change her mind. A woman changes her mind, caballero, as often as she does the method of doing her hair."

"I had thought all would be arranged before now," Don Diego said. "You think there is still hope?"

"I trust so," Don Carlos said, but he doubted it, remembering the look that had been in the señorita's face. However, he intended having a serious talk with her once they were home, and possibly might decide to insist on obedience even in this matter of taking a mate.

So the usual courtesies were paid, and then the lumbering carreta was driven away, and Don Diego Vega turned back into his house with his head hanging upon his breast, as it always hung when he did himself the trouble to think.

Presently he decided that he needed companionship for the moment, and left the house to cross the plaza and enter the tavern. The fat landlord rushed to greet him, conducted him to a choice seat near a window, and fetched wine without being commanded to do so.

Don Diego spent the greater part of an hour looking through the window at the plaza, watching men and women come and go, observing the toiling natives, and now and then glancing up the trail that ran toward the San Gabriel road.

Down this trail, presently, he observed approaching two mounted men, and between their horses walked a third man, and Don Diego could see that ropes ran from this man's waist to the saddles of the horsemen.

"What, in the name of the saints, have we here?" he exclaimed, getting up from the bench and going closer to the window.

"Ha!" said the landlord at his shoulder. "That will be the prisoner coming now."

"Prisoner?" said Don Diego, looking at him with a question in his glance.

"A native brought the news a short tune ago, caballero. Once more a fray is in the toils."

"Explain, fat one!"

"The man is to go before the magistrado immediately for his trial. They say that he swindled a dealer in hides, and now must pay the penalty. He wished his trial at San Gabriel, but that was not allowed, since all there are in favor of the missions and the frailes."

"Who is the man?" Don Diego asked.

"He is called Fray Felipe, caballero."

"What is this? Fray Felipe is an old man, and my good friend. I spent night before the last with him at the hacienda he manages."

"No doubt he has imposed upon you, caballero, as upon others," the landlord said.

Don Diego showed some slight interest now. He walked briskly from the tavern and went to the office of the magistrado in a little adobe building on the opposite side of the plaza. The horsemen were just arriving with their prisoner. They were two soldiers who had been stationed at San Gabriel, the frailes having been forced to give them bed and board in the governor's name.

It was Fray Felipe. He had been forced to walk the entire distance fastened to the saddles of his guards, and there were indications that the horsemen had galloped now and then to test the fray's powers of endurance.

Fray Felipe's gown was almost in rags, and was covered with dust and perspiration. Those who crowded around him now gave him jeers and coarse jests, but the fray held his head proudly and pretended not to see or hear them.

The soldiers dismounted and forced him into the magistrado's office, and the loiterers and natives crowded forward and through the door. Don Diego hesitated a moment, and then stepped toward the door. "One side, scum!" he cried; and the natives gave way before him.

He entered and pressed through the throng. The magistrado saw him and beckoned him to a front seat. But Don Diego did not care to sit at that time.

"What is this we have here?" he demanded. "This is Fray Felipe, a godly man and my friend."

"He is a swindler," one of the soldiers retorted.

"If he is, then we can put our trust in no man," Don Diego observed.

"All this is quite irregular, caballero," the magistrado

insisted, stepping forward. "The charges have been preferred, and the man is here to be tried."

Then Don Diego sat down, and court was convened.

The man who made the complaint was an evil-looking fellow who explained that he was a dealer in tallow and hides, and had a warehouse in San Gabriel.

"I went to the hacienda this fray manages and purchased ten hides of him," he testified. "After giving him the coins in payment and taking them to my storehouse, I found that the hides had not been cured properly. In fact they were ruined. I returned to the hacienda and told the fray as much, demanding that he return the money, which he refused to do."

"The hides were good," Fray Felipe put in. "I told him I would return the money when he returned the hides."

"They were spoiled," the dealer declared. "My assistant here will testify as much. They caused a stench, and I had them burned immediately."

The assistant testified as much.

"Have you anything to say, fray?" the magistrado asked.

"It will avail me nothing," Fray Felipe said. "I already am found guilty and sentenced. Were I a follower of a licentious governor instead of a robed Franciscan, the hides would have been good."

"You speak treason?" the magistrado cried.

"I speak truth."

The magistrado puckered his lips and frowned.

"There has been entirely too much of this swindling," he said finally. "Because a man wears a robe he cannot rob with impunity. In this case, I deem it proper to make an example, that frailes will see they cannot take advantage of their calling.

"The fray must repay the man the price of the hides. And for the swindle he shall receive across his bare back ten lashes. And for the words of treason he has spoken, he shall receive five lashes additional. It is a sentence."

Chapter 21
The Whipping

THE natives jeered and applauded. Don Diego's face went white, and for an instant his eyes met those of Fray Felipe, and in the face of the latter he saw resignation.

The office was cleared, and the soldiers led the fray to the place of execution in the middle of the plaza. Don Diego observed that the magistrado was grinning, and he realized what a farce the trial had been.

"These turbulent times!" he said to a gentleman of his acquaintance who stood near.

They tore Felipe's robe from his back and started to lash him to the post. But the fray had been a man of great strength in his day, and some of it remained to him in his advanced years; and it came to him now what ignominy he was to suffer.

Suddenly he whirled the soldiers aside and stooped to grasp the whip from the ground.

"You have removed my robe!" he cried. "I am man now, not fray! One side, dogs!"

He lashed out with the whip. He cut a soldier across the face. He struck at two natives who sprang toward him. And then the throng was upon him, beating him down, kicking and striking at him, disregarding even the soldiers' orders.

Don Diego Vega felt moved to action. He could not see his friend treated in this manner despite his docile disposition. He rushed into the midst of the throng, calling upon the natives to clear the way. But he felt a hand grasp his arm, and turned to look into the eyes of the magistrado.

"These are no actions for a caballero," the judge said in a low tone. "The man has been sentenced properly.-When you raise hand to give him aid, you raise hand against his excellency. Have you stopped to think of that, Don Diego Vega?"

Apparently Don Diego had not. And he realized, too, that he could do no good to his friend by interfering now. He nodded his head to the magistrado and turned away.

But he did not go far. The soldiers had subdued Fray Felipe by now and had lashed him to the whipping-post. This was added insult, for the post was used for none except insubordinate natives. The lash was swung through the air, and Don Diego saw blood spurt from Fray Felipe's bare back.

He turned his face away then, for he could not bear to look. But he could count the lashes by the singing of the whip through the air, and he knew that proud old Fray Felipe was making not the slightest sound of pain and would die without doing so.

He heard the natives laughing and turned back again to find that the whipping was at an end.

"The money must be repaid within two days, or you shall have fifteen lashes more," the magistrado was saying.

Fray Felipe was untied and dropped to the ground at the foot of the post. The crowd began to melt away. Two frailes who had followed from San Gabriel aided their brother to his feet and led him aside while the natives hooted. Don Diego Vega returned to his house.

"Send me Bernardo," he ordered his despensero.

The butler bit his lip to keep from grinning as he went to do as he was bidden. Bernardo was a deaf-and-dumb native servant for whom Don Diego had a peculiar use. Within the minute he entered the great living-room and bowed before his master.

"Bernardo, you are a gem," Don Diego said: "You cannot speak or hear, cannot write or read, and have not sense enough to make your wants known by the sign language. You are the one man in the world to whom I can speak without having my ears talked off in reply. You do not 'Ha!' me at every turn."

Bernardo bobbed his head as if he understood. He always bobbed his head in that fashion when Don Diego's lips ceased to move.

"These are turbulent times, Bernardo," Don Diego continued. "A man can find no place where he can meditate. Even at Fray Felipe's night before last there came a big sergeant pounding at the door. A man with nerves is in a sorry state. And this whipping of old Fray Felipe—Bernardo, let us hope that this Señor Zorro, who punishes those who work injustice, hears of the affair and acts accordingly."

Bernardo bobbed his head again.

"As for myself, I am in a pretty pickle," Don Diego went on. "My father has ordered that I get me a wife, and the señorita I selected will have none of me. I shall have my father taking me by the ear in short order.

"Bernardo, it is time for me to leave this pueblo for a few days. I shall go to the hacienda of my father, to tell him I have got no woman to wed me yet, and ask his indulgence. And there, on the wide hills behind his house, may I hope to find some spot where I may rest and consult the poets for one entire day without highwaymen and sergeants and unjust magistrados bothering me. And you, Bernardo, shall accompany me, of course. I can talk to you without your taking the words out of my mouth."

Bernardo bobbed his head again. He guessed what was to come. It was a habit of Don Diego's to talk to him thus for a long time, and always there was a journey afterward. Bernardo liked that, because he worshiped Don Diego, and because he liked to visit the hacienda of Don Diego's father, where he always was treated with kindness.

The despensero had been listening in the other room and had heard what was said, and now he gave orders for Don Diego's horse to be made ready and prepared a bottle of wine and water for the master to take with him.

Within a short time Don Diego set out, Bernardo riding mule a short distance behind him. They hurried along the highroad and presently caught up with a small carreta, beside which walked two robed Franciscans, and in which was Fray Felipe, trying to keep back moans of pain.

Don Diego dismounted beside the carreta as it stopped. He went over to it and clasped Fray Felipe's hands in his own.

"My poor friend," he said.

"It is but another instance of injustice," Fray Felipe said. "For twenty years we of the missions have been subjected to it, and it grows. The sainted Junipero Serra invaded this land when other men feared, and at San Diego de Alcala he built the first mission of what became a chain, thus giving an empire to the world. Our mistake was that we prospered. We did the work, and others reap the advantages."

Don Diego nodded, and the other went on:

"They began taking our mission lands from us, lands we had cultivated, which had formed a wilderness and which my brothers had turned into gardens and orchards. They robbed us of worldly goods. And not content with that they now are persecuting us.

"The mission empire is doomed, caballero. The time is not far distant when mission roofs will fall in and the walls crumble away. Some day people will look at the ruins and wonder how such a thing could come to pass.

"But we can do naught except submit. It is one of our principles. I did forget myself for a moment in the plaza at Reina de Los Angeles, when I took the whip and struck a man. It is our lot to submit."

"Sometimes," mused Don Diego, "I wish I were a man of action."

"You give sympathy, my friend, which is worth its weight in precious stones. And action expressed in a wrong channel is worse than no action at all. Where do you ride?"

"To the hacienda of my father, good friend. I must crave his pardon and ask his indulgence. He has ordered that I get me a wife, and I find it a difficult task."

"That should be an easy task for a Vega. Any maiden would be proud to take that name."

"I had hoped to wed with the Señorita Lolita Pulido, she having taken my fancy."

"A worthy maiden! Her father, too, has been subjected to unjust oppression. Did you join your family to his, none would dare raise hand against him."

"All that is very well, fray, and the absolute truth, of course. But the señorita will have none of me," Don Diego complained. "It appears that I have not dash and spirit enough."

"She is hard to please, perhaps. Or possibly she is but playing at being a coquette with the hope of leading you on and increasing your ardor. A maid loves to tantalize a man, caballero. It is her privilege."

"I showed her my house in the pueblo and mentioned my great wealth and agreed to purchase a new carriage for her," Don Diego told him.

"Did you show her your heart, mention your love, and agree to be a perfect husband?"

Don Diego looked at him blankly, then batted his eyes rapidly, and scratched at his chin, as he did sometimes when he was puzzled over a matter.

"What a perfectly silly idea!" he exclaimed after a time.

"Try it, caballero. It may have an excellent effect."

CHAPTER 22
Swift Punishment

THE frailes drove the cart onward, Fray Felipe raised his hand in blessing, and Don Diego Vega turned aside into the other trail, the deaf-and-dumb Bernardo following at his heels on the mule.

Back in the pueblo, the dealer in hides and tallow was the center of attraction at the tavern. The fat landlord was kept busy supplying his guest with wine, for the dealer in hides and tallow was spending a part of the money of which he had swindled Fray Felipe. The magistrado was spending the rest.

There was boisterous laughter as one recounted how Fray Felipe lay about him with the whip, and how the blood spurted from his old back when the lash was applied.

"Not a whimper from him!" cried the dealer in hides and tallow. "He is a courageous old coyote! Now, last month we whipped one at San Fernando, and he howled for mercy, but some men said he had been ill and was weak, and possibly that was so. A tough lot, these frailes. But it is great sport when we can make one howl. More wine, landlord! Fray Felipe is paying for it!"

There was a deal of raucous laughter at that, and the dealer's assistant, who had given perjured testimony, was tossed a coin and told to play a man and do his own buying. Whereupon the apprentice purchased wine for all in the inn, and howled merrily when the fat landlord gave him no change from his piece of money.

"Are you a fray, that you pinch coins?" the landlord asked.

Those in the tavern howled with merriment again, and the landlord, who had cheated the assistant to the limit, grinned as he went about his business. It was a great day for the fat landlord.

"Who was the caballero who showed some mercy toward the fray?" the dealer asked.

"That was Don Diego Vega," the landlord replied.

"He will be getting himself into trouble—"

"Not Don Diego," said the landlord. "You know the great Vega family, do you not, señor? His excellency himself curries their favor. Did the Vegas hold up as much as a little finger, there would be a political upheaval in these parts."

"Then he is a dangerous man?" the dealer asked.

A torrent of laughter answered him.

"Dangerous? Don Diego Vega?" the landlord cried, while tears ran down his fat cheeks. "You will be the death of me! Don Diego does nought but sit in the sun and dream. He scarcely ever wears a blade, except as a matter of show. He groans if he has to ride a few miles on a horse. Don Diego is about as dangerous as a lizard basking in the sun.

"But he is an excellent gentleman, for all that!" the landlord added hastily, afraid that his words would reach Don Diego's ears, and Don Diego would take his custom elsewhere.

It was almost dusk when the dealer in hides and tallow left the tavern with his assistant, and both reeled as they walked, for they had partaken of too much wine.

They made their way to the carreta in which they traveled, waved their farewells to the group about the door of the tavern, and started slowly up the trail toward San Gabriel.

They made their journey in a leisurely manner, continuing

to drink from a jug of wine they had purchased. They went over the crest of the first hill, and the pueblo of Reina de Los Angeles was lost to view, and all they could see was the highway twisting before them like a great dusty serpent, and the brown hills, and a few buildings in the distance, where some man had his hacienda.

They made a turning and found a horseman confronting them, sitting easily in the saddle, with his horse standing across the road in such manner that they could not pass.

"Turn your horse—turn your beast!" the dealer in hides and tallow cried. "Would you have me drive over you?"

The assistant gave an exclamation that was part of fear, and the dealer looked more closely at the horseman. His jaw dropped; his eyes bulged.

"'Tis Señor Zorro!" he exclaimed. "By the saints! Tis the Curse of Capistrano, away down here near San Gabriel. You would not bother me, Señor Zorro? I am a poor man, and have no money. Only yesterday, a fray swindled me, and I have been to the Rein a de Los Angeles seeking justice."

"Did you get it?" Señor Zorro asked.

"The magistrado was kind, señor. He ordered the fray to repay me, but I do not know when I shall get the money."

"Get out of the carreta, and your assistant also!" Señor Zorro commanded.

"But I have no money—" the dealer protested.

"Out of the carreta with you! Do I have to request it twice? Move, or lead finds a lodging-place in your carcass!"

Now the dealer saw that the highwayman held a pistol in his hand, and he squealed with sudden fright and got out of the cart as speedily as possible, his assistant tumbling out at his heels. They stood in the dusty highway before Señor Zorro, trembling with fear, the dealer begging for mercy.

"I have no money with me, kind highwayman, but I shall get it for you!" the dealer cried. "I shall carry it to where you say, whenever you wish—"

"Silence, beast!" Señor Zorro cried. "I do not want your money, perjurer. I know all about the farce of a trial at Reina de Los Angeles; I have ways of finding out about such things speedily.

"So the aged fray swindled you, eh? Liar and thief! 'Tis you who are the swindler. And they gave that old and godly man fifteen lashes across his bare back because of the lies you told. And you and the magistrado will divide the money of which you swindled him."

"I swear by the saints—"

"Do not. You have done enough false swearing already. Step forward."

The dealer complied, trembling as if with a disease; and Señor Zorro dismounted swiftly and walked around in front of his horse. The dealer's assistant was standing beside the carreta, and his face was white.

"Forward!" Señor Zorro commanded again.

Again the dealer complied; but suddenly he began to beg for mercy, for Señor Zorro had taken a mule whip from beneath his long cloak, and held it ready in his right hand, while he held the pistol in his left.

"Turn your back!" he commanded now.

"Mercy, good highwayman! Am I to be beaten as well as robbed? You would whip an honest merchant because of a thieving fray?"

The first blow fell, and the dealer shrieked with pain. His last remark appeared to have given strength to the highwayman's arm. The second blow fell, and the dealer in hides and tallow went to his knees in the dusty highroad.

Then Señor Zorro returned his pistol to his belt and stepped forward and grasped the dealer's mop of hair with his left hand, so as to hold him up, and with the right he rained heavy blows with the mule whip upon the man's back, until his tough coat and shirt were cut to ribbons, and the blood soaked through.

"That for a man who perjures himself and has an honest

fray punished!" Señor Zorro cried.

And then he gave his attention to the assistant.

"No doubt, young man, you but carried out your master's orders when you lied before the magistrado," he said. "but you must be taught to be honest and fair, no matter what the circumstances."

"Mercy, señor!" the assistant howled.

"Did you not laugh when the fray was being whipped? Are you not filled with wine now because you have been celebrating the punishment that godly man received for something he did not do?"

Señor Zorro grasped the youth by the nape of his neck, whirled him around, and sent a stiff blow at his shoulders.; The boy shrieked and then began whimpering. Five lashes in all he received, for Señor Zorro apparently did not wish to render him unconscious. And finally he hurled the boy from him, and looped his whip.

"Let us hope both of you have learned your lesson," he said. "Get into the carreta and drive on. And when you speak of this occurrence, tell the truth, else I hear of it and punish you again! Let me not learn that you have said some fifteen or twenty men surrounded and held you while I worked with the whip."

The apprentice sprang into the cart, and his master followed, and they whipped up and disappeared in a cloud of dust toward San Gabriel. Señor Zorro looked after them for a time, then lifted his mask and wiped the perspiration from his face, and then mounted his horse again, fastening the mule whip to the pommel of his saddle.

CHAPTER 23
More Punishment

SEÑOR ZORRO rode quickly to the crest of the hill beneath which was the pueblo, and there he stopped his horse and looked down at the village:

It was almost dark, but he could see quite well enough for his purpose. Candles had been lighted in the tavern; and from the building came the sounds of raucous song and loud jest. Candles were burning at the presidio, and from some of the houses came the odor of cooking food.

Señor Zorro rode on down the hill. When he reached the edge of the plaza he put spurs to his horse and dashed up to the tavern door, before which half a dozen men were congregated, the most of them under the influence of wine.

"Landlord!" he cried.

None of the men about the door gave him particular attention at first, thinking he was but some caballero on a journey wishing refreshment. The landlord hurried out, rubbing his fat hands together, and stepped close to the horse. And then he saw that the rider was masked, and that the muzzle of a pistol was threatening him.

"Is the magistrado within?" Señor Zorro asked.

"Si, Señor!"

"Stand where you are and pass the word for him. Say there is a caballero here who wishes speech with him regarding a certain matter."

The terrified landlord shrieked for the magistrado, and the word was passed inside. Presently the judge came staggering out, crying in a loud voice to know who had summoned him from his pleasant entertainment.

He staggered up to the horse, and put one hand against it, and looked up to find two glittering eyes regarding him through a mask. He opened his mouth to shriek, but Señor Zorro warned him in time.

"Not a sound or you die," he said. "I have come to punish you. Today you passed judgment on a godly man who was innocent. Moreover, you knew of his innocence, and his trial was but a farce. By your order he received a certain number of lashes. You shall have the same payment."

"You dare—"

"Silence!" the highwayman commanded. "You about the door there—come to my side!" he called.

They crowded forward, the most of them peons who thought that here was a caballero who wished something done and had gold to pay for it. In the dusk they did not see the mask and pistol until they stood beside the horse, and it was too late to retreat then.

"We are going to punish this unjust magistrado" Señor Zorro told them. "The five of you will seize him now and conduct him to the post in the middle of the plaza, and there you will tie him. The first man to falter receives a slug of lead from my pistol, and my blade will deal with the others. And I wish speed, also."

The frightened magistrado began to screech now.

"Laugh loudly, that his cries may not be heard," the highwayman ordered; and the men laughed as loudly as they could, albeit there was a peculiar quality to their laughter.

They seized the magistrado by the arms and conducted him

to the post and bound him there with thongs.

"You will line up," Señor Zorro told them. "You will take this whip, and each of you will lash this man five times. I shall be watching, and if I see the whip fall lightly once I shall deal out punishment. Begin."

He tossed the whip to the first man, and the punishment began. Señor Zorro had no fault to find with the manner in which it was given, for there was great fear in the hearts of the peons, and they whipped with strength, and willingly.

"You, also, landlord," Señor Zorro said.

"He will put me in for it afterward," the landlord wailed.

"Do you prefer cárcel or a coffin, Señor?" the highwayman asked.

It became evident that the landlord preferred the cárcel. He picked up the whip, and he surpassed the peons in the strength of his blows.

The magistrado was hanging heavily from the thongs now. Unconsciousness had come to him with about the fifteenth blow, more through fear than through pain and punishment.

"Unfasten the man," the highwayman ordered.

Two men sprang forward to do his bidding.

"Carry him to his house," Señor Zorro went on. "And tell the people of the pueblo that this is the manner in which Señor Zorro punishes those who oppress the poor and helpless, who give unjust verdicts, and who steal in the name of the law. Go your ways."

The magistrado was carried away, groaning, consciousness returning to him now. Señor Zorro turned once more to the landlord.

"We shall return to the tavern," he said. "You will go inside and fetch me a mug of wine, and stand beside my horse while I drink it. It would be only a waste of breath for me to say what will happen to you if you attempt treachery on the way."

But there was fear of the magistrado in the landlord's heart as great as his fear of Señor Zorro. He went back to the tavern

beside the highwayman's horse, and he hurried inside as if to get the wine. But he sounded the alarm.

"Señor Zorro is without," he hissed at those nearest the table. "He has just caused the magistrado to be whipped cruelly. He has sent me to get him a mug of wine."

Then he went on to the wine cask and began drawing the drink slowly as possible.

There was sudden activity inside the tavern. Some half-dozen caballeros were there, men who followed in the footsteps of the governor. Now they drew their blades and began creeping toward the door, and one of them who possessed a pistol and had it in his sash, drew it out, saw that it was prepared for work, and followed in their wake.

Señor Zorro, sitting his horse some twenty feet from the door of the tavern, suddenly beheld a throng rush out at him, saw the light flash from half a dozen blades, heard the report of a pistol, and heard a ball whistle past his head.

The landlord was standing in the doorway, praying that the highwayman would be captured, for then he would be given some credit, and perhaps the magistrado would not punish him for having used the lash.

Señor Zorro caused his horse to rear high in the air, and then raked the beast with the spurs. The animal sprang forward, into the midst of the caballeros, scattering them.

That was what Señor Zorro wanted. His blade already was out of its scabbard, and it passed through a man's sword arm, swung over and drew blood on another.

He fenced like a maniac, maneuvering his horse to keep his antagonists separated, so that only one could get at him at a time. Now the air was filled with shrieks and cries, and men came tumbling from the houses to ascertain the cause of the commotion. Señor Zorro knew that some of them would have pistols, and while he feared no blade, he realized that a man could stand some distance away and cut him down with a pistol ball.

So he caused his horse to plunge forward again, and before the fat landlord realized it, Señor Zorro was beside him and had reached down and grasped him by the arm. The horse darted away, the fat landlord dragging, shrieking for rescue and begging for mercy in the same breath. Señor Zorro rode with him to the whipping-post.

"Hand me that whip," he commanded.

The shrieking landlord obeyed, and called upon the saints to protect him. And then Señor Zorro turned him loose, and curled the whip around his fat middle, and as the landlord tried to run he cut at him again and again. He left him once to charge down upon those who had blades and so scatter them, and then he was back with the landlord again, applying the whip.

"You tried treachery!" he cried. "Dog of a thief! You would send men about my ears, eh? I'll strip your tough hide—"

"Mercy!" the landlord shrieked, and fell to the ground.

Señor Zorro cut at him again, bringing forth a yell more than blood. He wheeled his horse and darted at the nearest of his foes. Another pistol ball whistled past his head, another man sprang at him with blade ready. Señor Zorro ran the man neatly through the shoulder and put spurs to his horse again. He galloped as far as the whipping-post, and there he stopped his horse and faced them for an instant.

"There are not enough of you to make a fight interesting, Señores!" he cried.

He swept off his sombrero and bowed to them in nice mockery, and then he wheeled his horse again and dashed away.

CHAPTER 24
At the Hacienda of Don Alejando

BEHIND him he left a tumult in the town. The shrieks of the fat landlord had aroused the pueblo. Men came running, servants hurrying at their sides and carrying torches. Women peered from the windows of the houses. Natives stood still wherever they happened to be and shivered, for it had been their dear experience that whenever there was a tumult natives paid the price.

Many young caballeros of hot blood were there, and for some time there had been no excitement in the pueblo of Reina de Los Angeles. These young men crowded into the tavern and listened to the wails of the landlord, and some hurried to the house of the magistrado and saw his wounds, and heard him declaim on the indignity that had been offered the law, and therefore his excellency the governor.

Captain Ramôn came down from the presidio, and when he heard the cause of the tumult he swore great oaths, and sent his only well man to ride along the Pala Road, overtake Sergeant Gonzales and his troopers, and bid them return and take the trail, since at the time being they were following a false scent.

But the young caballeros saw in this circumstance a chance

for excitement that was to their liking, and they asked permission of the comandante to form a posse and take after the highwayman, a permission they received immediately.

Some thirty of them mounted horses, looked to weapons, and set out, with the intention of dividing into three bands of ten each when they came to forks in the trail.

The townsmen cheered them as they started, and they galloped rapidly up the hill and toward the San Gabriel road, making a deal of noise, glad that now there was a moon to let them see the foe when they approached him.

In time they separated, ten going toward San Gabriel proper, ten taking the trail that led to the hacienda of Fray Felipe, and the last ten following a road that curved down the valley to the neighborhood of a series of landed estates owned by wealthy dons of the day.

Along this road, Don Diego Vega had ridden some time before, the deaf-and-dumb Bernardo behind him on the mule. Don Diego rode with leisure, and it was long after nightfall when he turned from the main road and followed a narrower one toward his father's house.

Don Alejandro Vega, the head of the family, sat alone at his table, the remains of the evening meal before him, when he heard a horseman before the door. A servant ran to open it, and Don Diego entered, Bernardo following close behind him.

"Ah, Diego, my son!" the old don cried, extending his arms.

Don Diego was clasped for an instant to his father's breast, and then he sat down beside the table and grasped a mug of wine. Having refreshed himself, he faced Don Alejandro once more.

"It has been a fatiguing journey," he remarked.

"And the cause for it, my son?"

"I felt that I should come to the hacienda," Don Diego said. "It is no time to be in the pueblo. Wherever a man turns, he finds nought but violence and bloodshed. This confounded

Señor Zorro—"

"Ha! What of him?"

"Please do not 'Ha!' me, sir and father. I have been 'Ha'd!' at from morning until night these several days. These be turbulent times.

"This Señor Zorro has made a visit to the Pulido hacienda and frightened everyone there. I went to my hacienda on business, and from there I went over to see old Fray Felipe, thinking I might get a chance to meditate in his presence. And who makes an appearance but a big sergeant and his troopers seeking this Señor Zorro."

"They caught him?"

"I believe not, sir and father. I returned to the pueblo; and what think you happened there this day? They brought in Fray Felipe, accused of having swindled a dealer, and after a mockery of a trial they lashed him to a post and gave him the whip fifteen times across his back."

"The scoundrels!" Don Alejandro cried.

"I could stand it no longer, and so I decided to pay you a visit. Wherever I turn there is turmoil. It is enough to make a man insane. You may ask Bernardo if it is not."

Don Alejandro glanced at the deaf-and-dumb native and grinned. Bernardo grinned back as a matter of course, not knowing it was no manner in which to act in the presence of a don.

"You have something else to tell me?" Don Alejandro asked his son, looking at him searchingly.

"By the saints! Now it comes. I had hoped to avoid it, father and sir."

"Let me hear about it."

"I paid a visit to the Pulido hacienda and spoke with Don Carlos and his wife, also the Señorita Lolita."

"You were pleased with the señorita?"

"She is as lovely as any girl of my acquaintance," Don Diego said. "I spoke to Don Carlos of the matter of marriage, and he appeared to be delighted."

"Ah! He would be," said Don Alejandro.

"But the marriage cannot take place, I fear."

"How is this? There is some shadow concerning the señorita?"

"Not to my knowledge. She appears to be a sweet and innocent maiden, father and sir. I had them come to Reina de Los Angeles and spend a couple of days at my house. I had it arranged so that she could see the furnishings, and learn of my wealth."

"That was a wise arrangement, my son."

"But she will have none of me."

"How is this? Refuses to wed with a Vega? Refuses to become allied to the most powerful family in the country, with the best blood in the land?"

"She intimated, father and sir, that I am not the sort of man for her. She is prone to foolishness, I believe. She would have me play a guitar under her window, perhaps, and make eyes, and hold hands when her duenna is not looking, and all that silliness."

"By the saints! Are you a Vega?" Don Alejandro cried. "Would not any worthy man want a chance like that? Would not any caballero delight to serenade his love on a moonlight night? The little things you term silly are the very essence of love. I doubt not the señorita was displeased with you."

"But I did not see that such things were necessary," Don Diego said.

"Did you go to the señorita in a cold-blooded manner and suggest that you wed and have it done with? Had you the idea, young sir, that you were purchasing a horse or a bull? By the saints! And so there is no chance for you to wed the girl? She has the best blood by far, next to our own."

"Don Carlos bade me have hope," Diego replied. "He took her back to the hacienda, and suggested that perhaps when she had been there a time and had reflected she might change her mind."

"She is yours, if you play the game," Don Alejandro said. "You are a Vega, and therefore the best catch in the country. Be but half a lover, and the señorita is yours. What sort of blood is in your veins? I have half a mind to slit one of them and see."

"Cannot we allow this marriage business to drop for the time being?" Don Diego asked.

"You are twenty-five. I was quite old when you were born. Soon I shall go the way of my fathers. You are the only son, the heir, and you must have a wife and offspring. Is the Vega family to die out because your blood is water? Win you a wife within the quarter-year, young sir, and a wife I can accept into the family, or I leave my wealth to the Franciscans when I pass away."

"My father!"

"I mean it. Get life into you! I would you had half the courage and spirit this Señor Zorro, this highwayman, has! He has principles and he fights for them. He aids the helpless and avenges the oppressed.

"I salute him! I would rather have you, my son, in his place, running the risk of death or imprisonment, than to have you a lifeless dreamer of dreams that amount to nought!"

"My father! I have been a dutiful son."

"I would you had been a little wild—it would have been more natural." Don Alejandro sighed. "I could overlook a few escapades more easily than I can lifelessness. Arouse yourself, young sir! Remember that you are a Vega.

"When I was your age, I was not a laughingstock. I was ready to fight at a wink, to make love to every pair of flashing eyes, to stand up to any caballero in sports rough or refined. Ha!"

"I pray you, do not 'Ha!' me, sir and father. My nerves are on edge."

"You must be more of a man."

"I shall attempt it immediately," Don Diego said, straightening himself somewhat in his chair. "I had hoped to avoid it, but it appears that I cannot. I shall woo the Señorita Lolita as other men woo maidens. You meant what you said about your fortune?"

"I did," said Don Alejandro.

"Then I must bestir myself. It would never do, of course, to let that fortune go out of the family. I shall think these matters over in peace and quiet tonight. Perhaps I can meditate here, far from the pueblo. By the saints!"

The last exclamation was caused by a sudden tumult outside the house. Don Alejandro and his son heard a number of horsemen stop, heard their calls to one another, heard bridles jingling and blades rattling.

"There is no peace in all the world," Don Diego said with deepened gloom.

"It sounds like half a score of men," Don Alejandro said.

"It was—exactly. A servant opened the door, and into the great room there strode ten caballeros, with blades at their sides and pistols in their belts.

"Ha, Don Alejandro! We crave hospitality!" the foremost cried.

"You have it without asking, caballeros. What manner of journey is this you take?"

"We pursue Señor Zorro, the highwayman."

"By the saints!" Don Diego cried. "One cannot escape it even here. Violence and bloodshed!"

"He invaded the plaza at Reina de Los Angeles," the spokesman went on. "He had the magistrado whipped because he sentenced Fray Felipe to receive the lash, and he whipped the fat landlord, and he fought half a score of men while he was about it. Then he rode away, and we made up a band to pursue him. He has not been in this neighborhood?"

"Not to my knowledge," Don Alejandro said. "My son arrived off the highway but a short time ago."

"You did not see the fellow, Don Diego?"

"I did not," Don Diego said. "That is one stroke of good fortune that came my way."

Don Alejandro had sent for servants, and now wine mugs were on the long table, and heaps of small cakes, and the caballeros began to eat and drink. Don Diego knew well what that meant. Their pursuit of the highwayman was at an end, their enthusiasm had waned. They would sit at his father's table and drink throughout the night, gradually getting intoxicated, shout and sing and tell stories, and in the morning ride back to Reina de Los Angeles like so many heroes.

It was the custom. The chase of Señor Zorro was but a pretext for a merry time.

The servants brought great stone jugs filled with rare wine and put them on the table, and Don Alejandro ordered that meat be fetched also. The young caballeros had a weakness for these parties at Don Alejandro's, for the don's good wife had been dead for several years, and there were no womenfolk except servants, and so they could make what noise they pleased throughout the night.

In time they put aside pistols and blades, and began to boast and brag, and Don Alejandro had his servants put the weapons in a far corner out of the way, for he did not wish a drunken quarrel, with a dead caballero or two in his house.

Don Diego drank and talked with them for a time, and then sat to one side and listened, as if such foolishness bored him,

"It were well for this Señor Zorro that we did not catch up with him," one cried. "Any one of us is a match for the fellow. Were the soldiers men of merit he would have been taken long before this."

"Ha, for a chance at him!" another screeched. "How the landlord did howl when he was whipped!"

"He rode in this direction?" Don Alejandro asked.

"We are not sure as to that. He took the San Gabriel trail, and thirty of us followed. We separated into three bands, each going a different direction. It is the good fortune of one of the other bands to have him now, I suppose. But it is our excellent good fortune to be here."

Don Diego stood before the company.

"Señores, you will pardon me, I know, if I retire," he said. "I am fatigued with the journey."

"Retire, by all means," one of his friends cried. "And when you are rested, come out to us again and make merry."

They laughed at that; and Don Diego bowed ceremoniously, and observed that several scarcely could get to their feet to bow in return; and then the scion of the house of Vega hurried from the room with the deaf-and-dumb man at his heels.

He entered a room that always was ready for him, and in which a candle already was burning, and closed the door behind him, and Bernardo stretched his big form on the floor just outside it, to guard his master during the night.

In the great living-room, Don Diego scarcely was missed. His father was frowning and twisting his mustache, for he would have had his son like other young men. In his youth, he was remembering, he never left such a company early in the evening. And once again he sighed and wished that the saints had given him a son with red blood in his veins.

The caballeros were singing now, joining in the chorus of a popular love song, and their discordant voices filled the big room. Don Alejandro smiled as he listened, for it brought his own youth back to him.

They sprawled on chairs and benches on both sides of the long table, pounding it with their mugs as they sang, laughing boisterously now and then.

"Were this Señor Zorro only here now!" one of them cried.

A voice from the doorway answered him. "Señores, he is here!"

Chapter 25
A League is Formed

THE SONG ceased; the laughter was stilled. They bunked their eyes and looked across the room. Señor Zorro stood just inside the door, having entered from the veranda without them knowing it. He wore his long cloak and his mask, and in one hand he held his accursed pistol, and its muzzle was pointed at the table.

"So these are the manner of men who pursue Señor Zorro and hope to take him," he said. "Make not a move, else lead flies. Your weapons, I perceive, are in the corner. I could kill some of you and be gone before you could reach them."

"'Tis he! 'Tis he!" a tipsy caballero was crying.

"Your noise may be heard a mile away, señores. What a posse to go pursuing a man! Is this the way you attend to duty? Why have you stopped to make merry while Señor Zorro rides the highway?"

"Give me my blade and let me stand before him!" one cried.

"If I allowed you to have blade, you would be unable to stand," the highwayman answered. "Think you there is one in this company who could fence with me now?"

"There is one!" cried Don Alejandro, in a loud voice, springing to his feet. "I openly say that I have admired some of the things you have done, señor; but now you have entered my house and are abusing my guests, and I must call you to account!"

"I have no quarrel with you, Don Alejandro, and you have none with me," Señor Zorro said. "I refuse to cross blades with you. And I am but telling these men some truths."

"By the saints, I shall make you!"

"A moment, Don Alejandro! Señores, this aged don would fight me, and that would mean a wound or death for him. Will you allow it?"

"Don Alejandro must not fight our battles!" one of them cried.

"Then see that he sits in his place, and all honor to him."

Don Alejandro started forward, but two of the caballeros sprang before him and urged him to go back, saying that his honor was safe, since he offered combat. Raging, Don Alejandro complied.

"A worthy bunch of young blades," Señor Zorro sneered. "You drink wine and make merry while injustice is all about you. Take your swords in hand and attack oppression! Live up to your noble names and your blue blood, señores! Drive the thieving politicians from the land! Protect the frailes whose work gave us these broad acres! Be men, not drunken fashion plates!"

"By the saints!" one cried and sprang to his feet.

"Back, or I fire! I have not come here to fight you in Don Alejandro's house. I respect him too much for that. I have come to tell you these truths concerning yourselves.

"Your families can make or break a governor! Band yourselves together in a good cause, caballeros, and make some use of your lives. You would do it, were you not afraid. You seek adventure? Here is adventure a plenty, fighting injustice."

"By the saints, it would be a lark!" cried one in answer.

"Look upon it as a lark if it pleases you, yet you would be doing some good. Would the politicians dare stand against you, scions of the most powerful families? Band yourselves together and give yourselves a name. Make yourselves feared the length and breadth of the land."

"It would be treason—"

"It is not treason to down a tyrant, caballeros! Is it that you are afraid?"

"By the saints—no!" they cried in chorus.

"Then make your stand!"

"You would lead us?"

"Si, Señores!"

"But stay! Are you of good blood?"

"I am a caballero, of blood as good as any here," Señor Zorro told them.

"Your name? Where resides your family?"

"Those things must remain secrets for the present. I have given you my word."

"Your face—"

"Must remain masked for the time being, señores."

They had lurched to their feet now, and were acclaiming him wildly.

"Stay!" one cried. "This is an imposition upon Don Alejandro. He may not be in sympathy, and we are planning and plotting in his house—"

"I am in sympathy, caballeros, and give you my support," Don Alejandro said.

Their cheers filled the great room. None could stand against them if Don Alejandro Vega was with them. Not even the governor himself would dare oppose them.

"It is a bargain!" they cried. "We shall call ourselves the Avengers! We shall ride El Camino Real and prove terrors to those who rob honest men and mistreat natives! We shall drive the thieving politicians out!"

"And then you shall be caballeros in truth, knights protecting the weak," Señor Zorro said. "Never shall you repent this decision, señores! I lead, and I give you loyalty and expect as much. Also, I expect obedience to orders."

"What shall we do?" they cried.

"Let this remain a secret. In the morning return to Reina de Los Angeles and say you did not find Señor Zorro—say rather that you did not catch him, which will be the truth. Be ready to band yourselves together and ride. I shall send word when the time arrives."

"In what manner?"

"I know you all. I shall get word to one, and he can inform the others. It is agreed?"

"Agreed!" they shouted.

"Then I will leave you here and now. You are to remain in this room, and none is to try to follow me. It is a command. Buenos noches, caballeros!"

He bowed before them, swung the door open, and darted through it and slammed it shut behind him.

They could hear the clatter of a horse's hoofs on the driveway.

And then they raised their wine mugs and drank to their new league for the suppression of swindlers and thieves and to Señor Zorro, the Curse of Capistrano, and to Don Alejandro Vega, somewhat sobered by the agreement they had made and what it meant. They sat down again and began speaking of wrongs that should be righted, each of them knowing half a dozen.

And Don Alejandro Vega sat in one corner, by himself, a grief-stricken man because his only son was asleep in the house and had not red blood enough to take a part in such an undertaking, when by all rights he should be one of the leaders.

As if to add to his misery, Don Diego at that moment came slowly into the room, rubbing his eyes and yawning and looking as if he had been disturbed.

"It is impossible for a man to sleep in this house tonight," he said. "Give me a mug of wine, and I shall take my place with you. Why was the cheering?"

"Señor Zorro has been here—" his father began.

"The highwayman? Been here? By the saints! It is as much as a man can endure."

"Sit down, my son," Don Alejandro urged. "Certain things have come to pass. There will be a chance now for you to show what sort of blood flows in your veins."

Don Alejandro's manner was very determined.

Chapter 26
An Understanding

THE remainder of the night was spent by the caballeros in loud boasts of what they, intended doing, and in making plans to be submitted to Señor Zorro for his approval; and, though they appeared to look upon this thing as a lark and a means to adventure, yet there was an undercurrent of seriousness in their manner. For they knew well the state of the times and realized that things were not as they should be, and in reality they were exponents of fairness to all; they had thought of these things often, but had made no move because they had not been banded together and had no leader, and each young caballero waited for another to start the thing. But now this Señor Zorro had struck at the psychological moment, and things could be done.

Don Diego was informed of the state of affairs, and his father informed him, likewise, that he was to play a part and prove himself a man. Don Diego fumed considerably and declared that such a thing would cause his death, yet he would do it for his father's sake.

Early in the morning the caballeros ate a meal that Don Alejandro caused to be prepared, and then they started back to Reina de Los Angeles, Don Diego riding with them at his father's order. Nothing was to be said about their plans. They were to get recruits from the remainder of the thirty who had set out in pursuit of Señor Zorro. Some would join them readily, they knew, while others were the governor's men pure and simple, and would have to be kept in the dark concerning the thing contemplated.

They rode leisurely, for which Don Diego remarked that he was grateful. Bernardo was still following him on the mule, and was a little chagrined because Don Diego had not remained longer at his father's house. Bernardo knew something momentous was being planned, but could not guess what, of course, and wished that he was like other men, and could hear and speak.

When they reached the plaza, they found that the other two parties already were there, saying that they had not come up with the highwayman. Some declared that they had seen him in the distance, and one that he had fired a pistol at him, at which the caballeros who had been at Don Alejandro's put their tongues in their cheeks and looked at one another in a peculiar manner.

Don Diego left his companions and hurried to his house, where he donned fresh clothing and refreshed himself generally. He sent Bernardo about his business, which was to sit in the kitchen and await his master's call. And then he ordered his carriage around.

That carriage was one of the most gorgeous along El Camino Real, and why Don Diego had purchased it had always been a mystery. There were some who said he did it to show his wealth, while others declared a manufacturer's agent had worried him so much that Don Diego had given him the order to be rid of him.

Don Diego came from his house dressed in his best; but he did not get into the carriage. Again there was a tumult in the plaza, and into it rode Sergeant Pedro Gonzales and his troopers. The man Captain Ramón had sent after them had overtaken them easily, for they had been riding slowly and had not covered many miles.

"Ha, Don Diego, my friend!" Gonzales cried. "Still living in this turbulent world?"

"From necessity," Don Diego replied. "Did you capture this Señor Zorro?"

"The pretty bird escaped us, caballero. It appears that he turned toward San Gabriel that night, while we went chasing him toward Pala. Ah, well, 'tis nothing to make a small mistake. Our revenge shall be the greater when we find him."

"What do you now, my sergeant?"

"My men refresh themselves, and then we ride toward San Gabriel. It is said the highwayman is in that vicinity, though some thirty young men of blood failed to find him last night after he had caused the magistrado to be whipped. No doubt he hid himself in the brush and chuckled when the caballeros rode by."

"May your horse have speed and your sword arm strength," Don Diego said and got into his carriage.

Two magnificent horses were hitched to the carriage, and a native coachman in rich livery drove them. Don Diego stretched back on the cushions and half closed his eyes as the carriage started. The driver went across the plaza and turned into the highway and started toward the hacienda of Don Carlos Pulido.

Sitting on his veranda, Don Carlos saw the gorgeous carriage approaching, and growled low down in his throat, and then got up and hurried into the house, to face his wife and daughter.

"Señorita, Don Diego comes," he said. "I have spoken words regarding the young man, and I trust that you have given heed to them as a dutiful daughter should."

Then he turned and went out to the veranda again, and the señorita rushed into her room and threw herself upon a couch to weep. The saints knew she wished that she could feel some love for Don Diego and take him for a husband, for it would help her father's fortunes, yet she felt that she could not.

Why did not the man act the caballero? Why did he not exhibit a certain measure of common sense? Why did he not show that he was a young man bursting with health, instead of acting like an aged don with one foot in the grave?

Don Diego got from the carriage and waved to the driver to continue to the stable yard. He greeted Don Carlos languidly, and Don Carlos was surprised to note that Don Diego had a guitar beneath one arm. He put the guitar down on the floor, removed his sombrero, and sighed.

"I have been out to see my father," he said.

"Ha! Don Alejandro is well, I hope?"

"He is in excellent health, as usual. He has instructed me to persist in my suit for the Señorita Lolita's hand. If I do not win me a wife within a certain time, he says, he will give his fortune to the Franciscans when he passes away."

"Indeed?"

"He said it, and my father is not a man to waste his words. Don Carlos, I must win the señorita. I know of no other young woman who would be as acceptable to my father as a daughter-in-law."

"A little wooing, Don Diego, I beg of you. Be not so matter-of-fact, I pray."

"I have decided to woo as other men, though it no doubt will be much of a bore. How would you suggest that I start?"

"It is difficult to give advice in such a case," Don Carlos replied, trying desperately to remember how he had done it when he had courted Doña Catalina. "A man really should be experienced, else be a man to whom such things come naturally."

"I fear I am neither," Don Diego said, sighing again and raising tired eyes to Don Carlos's face.

"It might be an excellent thing to regard the señorita as if you adored her. Say nothing about marriage at first, but speak rather of love. Try to talk in low, rich tones, and say those meaningless nothings in which a young woman can find a world of meaning. 'Tis a gentle art—saying one thing and meaning another."

"I fear that it is beyond me," Don Diego said. "Yet I must try, of course. I may see the Señorita now?"

Don Carlos went to the doorway and called his wife and daughter, and the former smiled upon Don Diego in encouragement, and the latter smiled also, yet with fear and trembling. For she had given her heart to the unknown Señor Zorro, and could love no other man, and could not wed where she did not love, not even to save her father from poverty.

Don Diego conducted the Señorita to a bench at one end of the veranda, and started to talk of things in general, plucking at the strings of his guitar as he did so, while Don Carlos and his wife removed themselves to the other end of the veranda and hoped that things would go well.

Señorita Lolita was glad that Don Diego did not speak of marriage as he had done before. Instead, he told of what had happened in the pueblo, of Fray Felipe's whipping, and of how Señor Zorro had punished the magistrado, and fought a dozen men, and made his escape. Despite his air of languor, Don Diego spoke in an interesting manner, and the Señorita found herself liking him more than before.

He told, too, of how he had gone to his father's hacienda, and of how the caballeros had spent the night there, drinking and making merry; but he said nothing of Señor Zorro's visit and the league that had been formed, having taken his oath not to do so.

"My father threatens to disinherit me if I do not get my wife within a specified time," Don Diego said then. "Would you like to see me lose my father's estate, Señorita?"

"Certainly not," she replied. "There are many girls who would be proud to wed you, Don Diego."

"But not you?"

"Certainly, I would be proud. But can a girl help it if her heart does not speak? Would you wish a wife who did not I love you? Think of the long years you would have to spend beside her, and no love to make them endurable."

"You do not think, then, that you ever could learn to love me, señorita?"

Suddenly the girl faced him and spoke in lower tones, and earnestly.

"You are a caballero of the blood, señor. I may trust you?"

"To death, señorita."

"Then I have something to tell you. And I ask that you let it remain your secret. It is an explanation in a way."

"Proceed, señorita."

"If my heart bade me do so, nothing would please me more than to become your wife, señor, for I know that it would mend my father's fortunes. But perhaps I am too honest to wed where I do not love. There is one great reason why I cannot love you."

"There is some other man in your heart?"

"You have guessed it, señor. My heart is filled with his - image. You would not want me for wife in such case. My parents do not know. You must keep my secret. I swear by the saints that I have spoken the truth."

"The man is worthy?"

"I feel sure that he is, caballero. Did he prove to be otherwise, I should grieve my life away, yet I never could love another man. You understand now?"

"I understand fully, señorita. May I express the hope that you will find him worthy and in time the man of your choice?"

"I knew you would be the true caballero."

"And if things should go amiss, and you need a, friend, command me, señorita."

"My father must not suspect at the present time. We must let him think that you still seek me, and I will pretend to be thinking more of you than before. And gradually you can cease your visits—"

"I understand, Señorita. Yet that leaves me in bad case. I have asked your father for permission to woo you, and if I go to wooing another girl now, I will have him about my ears in just anger. And if I do not woo another girl, I shall have my own father upbraiding me. It is a sorry state."

"Perhaps it will not be for long, señor."

"Ha! I have it! What does a man do when he is disappointed in love? He mopes, he pulls a long face, he refuses to partake of the actions and excitements of the times.

"Señorita, you have saved me in a way. I shall languish because you do not return my love. Then men will think they know the reason when I dream in the sun and meditate instead of riding and fighting like a fool. I shall be allowed to go my way in peace, and there shall be a romantic glamour cast about me. An excellent thought!"

"Señor, you are incorrigible!" the Señorita Lolita exclaimed, laughing.

Don Carlos and Doña Catalina heard that laugh, looked around, and then exchanged quick glances. Don Diego Vega was getting along famously with the señorita, they thought.

Then Don Diego continued the deception by playing his guitar and singing a verse of a song that had to do with bright eyes and love. Don Carlos and his wife glanced at each other again, this time in apprehension, and wished that he would stop, for the scion of the Vegas had many superiors as musician and vocalist, and they feared that he might lose what ground he had gained in the señorita's estimation.

But if Lolita thought little of the caballero's singing, she said nothing to that effect, and she did not act displeased. There was some more conversation, and just before the siesta hour Don Diego bade them buenos dias and rode away in his gorgeous carriage. From the turn in the driveway, he waved back at them.

Chapter 27
Orders for Arrest

CAPTAIN RAMÔN'S courier, sent north with the letter for the governor, had dreams of gay times in San Francisco de Asis before returning to his presidio at Reina de Los Angeles. He knew a certain señorita there whose beauty caused his heart to burn.

So he rode like a fiend after leaving his comandante's office, changed mounts at San Fernando and at a hacienda along the way, and galloped into Santa Barbara a certain evening just at dusk, with the intention of changing horses again, getting meat and bread and wine at the presidio, and rushing on his way.

And at Santa Barbara his hopes of basking in the señorita's smiles at San Francisco de Asis were cruelly shattered. For before the door of the presidio there was a gorgeous carriage that made Don Diego's appear like a carreta, and a score of horses were tethered there, and more troopers than were stationed at Santa Barbara regularly moved about the highway, laughing and jesting with one another.

The governor was in Santa Barbara.

His excellency had left San Francisco de Asis some days before on a trip of inspection, and intended to go as far south as San Diego de Alcala, strengthening his political fences, rewarding his friends, and awarding punishment to his enemies.

He had reached Santa Barbara an hour before, and was listening to the report of the comandante there, after which he intended remaining during the night with a friend. His troopers were to be given quarters at the presidio, of course, and the journey was to continue on the morrow. Captain Ramón's courier had been told that the letter he carried was of the utmost importance, and so he hurried to the office of the comandante and entered it like a man of rank.

"I come from Captain Ramón, comandante at Reina de Los Angeles, with a letter of importance for his excellency," he reported, standing stiffly at salute.

The governor grunted and took the letter, and the comandante motioned for the courier to withdraw. His excellency read the letter with speed, and when he had finished there was an unholy gleam in his eyes, and he twirled his mustache with every evidence of keen satisfaction. And then he read the letter again and frowned.

He liked the thought that he could crush Don Carlos Pulido more, but he disliked to think that Señor Zorro, the man who had affronted him, was still at liberty. He got up and paced the floor for a time, and then whirled upon the comandante.

"I shall leave for the south at sunrise," he said. "My presence is urgently needed at Reina de Los Angeles. You will attend to things. Tell that courier he shall ride back with my escort. I go now to the house of my friend."

And so, in the morning, the governor started south, his escort of twenty picked troopers surrounding him, the courier in their midst. He traveled swiftly, and on a certain day at midmorning entered the plaza of Reina de Los Angeles unheralded. It was the same morning that Don Diego rode to the Pulido hacienda in his carriage, taking his guitar with him.

The cavalcade stopped before the tavern, and the fat landlord almost suffered an apoplexy because he had not been warned of the governor's coming and was afraid he would enter the inn and find it in a dirty state.

But the governor made no effort to leave his carriage and enter the tavern. He was glancing around the square, observing many things. He never felt secure concerning the men of rank in this pueblo; he felt that he did not have the proper grip on them.

Now he watched carefully as news of his arrival was spread and certain caballeros hurried to the plaza to greet him and make him welcome. He noted those who appeared to be sincere, observed those who were in no particular haste to salute him, and noticed that several were absent.

Business must receive his first attention, he told them, and he must hasten up to the presidio. After that he would gladly be the guest of any of them. He accepted an invitation and ordered his driver to proceed. He was remembering Captain Ramón's letter, and he had not seen Don Diego Vega in the plaza.

Sergeant Gonzales and his men were away pursuing Señor Zorro, of course, and so Captain Ramón himself was awaiting his excellency at the presidio entrance, and saluted him gravely, and bowed low before him and ordered the commander of the escort to take charge of the place and police it, stationing guards in honor of the governor.

He led his excellency to the private office, and the governor sat down.

"What is the latest news?" he asked.

"My men are on the trail, excellency. But, as I wrote, this pest of a Señor Zorro has friends—a legion of them, I take it. My sergeant has reported that twice he found him with a band of followers."

"They must be broken up, killed off!" the governor cried. "A man of that sort always can get followers, and yet more followers, until he will be so strong that he can cause us serious trouble. Has he committed any further atrocities?"

"He has, excellency. Yesterday a fray from San Gabriel was whipped for swindling. Señor Zorro caught the witnesses against him on the highroad, and whipped them almost to death. And then he rode into the pueblo just at dusk and had the magistrado whipped.

"My soldiers were away looking for him at the time. It appears that this Señor Zorro knows the movements of my force and always strikes where the troopers are not."

"Then spies are giving him warnings?"

"It appears so, excellency. Last night some thirty young caballeros rode after him but did not find track of the scoundrel. They returned this morning."

"Was Don Diego Vega with them?"

"He did not ride out with them, but he returned with them. It seems that they picked him up at his father's hacienda. You perhaps guessed that I meant the Vegas in my letter. I am convinced now, your excellency, that my suspicions in that quarter were unjust. This Señor Zorro even invaded Don Diego's house one night while Don Diego was away."

"How is this?"

"But Don Carlos Pulido and his family were there."

"Ha! In Don Diego's house? What is the meaning of that?"

"It is amusing," said Captain Ramón, laughing lightly. "I have heard that Don Alejandro ordered Don Diego to get him a wife. The young man is not the sort to woo women. He is lifeless."

"I know the man. Proceed."

"So he rides straightway to the hacienda of Don Carlos and asks permission to pay his addresses to Don Carlos's only daughter. Señor Zorro was abroad, and Don Diego, going to his own hacienda on business, asked Don Carlos to come to the pueblo with his family, where it would be safer, and occupy his house until he returned. The Pulidos could not refuse, of course. And Señor Zorro, it appears, followed them."

"Ha! Go on."

"It is laughable that Don Diego fetched them here to escape Señor Zorro's wrath, when, in reality, they are hand in glove with the highwayman. Remember, this Señor Zorro had been at the Pulido hacienda. We got word from a native, and almost caught him there. He had been eating a meal. He was hiding in a closet, and while I was alone there and my men searching the trails, he came from the closet, ran me through the shoulder from behind, and escaped."

"The low scoundrel!" the governor exclaimed. "But do you think there will be a marriage between Don Diego and the Señorita Pulido?"

"I imagine there need be no worry in that regard, excellency. I am of the opinion that Don Diego's father put a flea in his ear. He probably called Don Diego's attention to the fact that Don Carlos does not stand very high with your excellency, and that there are daughters of other men who do.

"At any rate, the Pulidos returned to their hacienda after Don Diego's return. Don Diego called upon me here at the presidio and appeared to be anxious that I would not think him a man of treason."

"I am glad to hear it! The Vegas are powerful. They never have been my warm friends, yet never have they raised hands against me, so I cannot complain. It is good sense to keep them friendly, if that be possible. But these Pulidos—"

"Even the señorita appears to be giving aid to this highwayman," Captain Ramón said. "She boasted to me of what she called his courage. She sneered at the soldiers.

"Don Carlos Pulido and some of the frailes are protecting the man, giving him food and drink, hiding him, sending him news of the troopers' whereabouts. The Pulidos are hindering our efforts to capture the rogue. I would have taken steps, but I thought it best to inform you and await your decision."

"There can be but one decision in such a case," said the; governor loftily. "No matter how good a man's blood may be, or what his rank, he cannot be allowed to commit treason without suffering the consequences. I had thought that Don Carlos had learned his lesson, but it appears that he has not. Are any of your men in the presidio?"

"Some who are ill, excellency."

"That courier of yours returned with my escort. Does he know the country well hereabouts?"

"Certainly, excellency. He has been stationed here for some little time."

"Then he can act as guide. Send half my escort at once to the hacienda of Don Carlos Pulido. Have them arrest the don and fetch him to cárcel and incarcerate him there. That will be a blow to his high blood. I have had quite enough of these Pulidos."

"And the haughty Doña, who sneered at me, and the proud señorita who scorned the troopers?"

"Ha! It is a good thought. It will teach a lesson to all in this locality. Have them fetched to cárcel and incarcerated also," the governor said.

Chapter 28
The Outrage

DON DIEGO'S carriage had just pulled up before his house when a squad of troopers went by it in a cloud of dust. He did not recognize any of them for men he had seen about the tavern.

"Ha! There are new soldiers on the trail of Señor Zorro?" he asked a man standing near

"They are a part of the escort of the governor, caballero."

"The governor is here?"

"He arrived but a short time ago, caballero, and has gone to the presidio."

"I suppose they must have fresh news of this highwayman to send them riding furiously through dust and sun like that. He appears to be an elusive rascal. By the saints! Had I been here when the governor arrived, no doubt he would have put up at my house. Now some other caballero will have the honor of entertaining him. It is much to be regretted."

And then Don Diego went into the house, and the man who had heard him speak did not know whether to doubt the sincerity of that last remark.

Led by the courier, who knew the way, the squad of troopers galloped swiftly along the highroad, and presently turned up the trail toward Don Carlos's house. They went at this business as they would have gone about capturing a desperado. As they struck the driveway, they scattered to left and right, tearing up Doña Catalina's flower beds and sending chickens squawking out of the way, and so surrounded the house in almost an instant of time.

Don Carlos had been sitting on the veranda in his accustomed place, half in a doze, and he did not notice the advance of the troopers until he heard the beating of their horses' hoofs. He got to his feet in alarm, wondering whether Señor Zorro was in the vicinity again and the soldiers after him.

Three dismounted in a cloud of dust before the steps, and the sergeant who commanded them made his way forward, slapping the dust from his uniform.

"You are Don Carlos Pulido?" he asked in a loud voice.

"I have that honor, señor."

"I have orders to place you under military arrest."

"Arrest!" Don Carlos cried. "Who gave you such orders?"

"His excellency, the governor. He now is in Reina de Los Angeles, señor."

"And the charge?"

"Treason and aiding-the enemies of the state."

"Preposterous!" Don Carlos cried. "I am accused of treason when, though the victim of oppression, I have withheld my hand against those in power? What are the particulars of the charges?"

"You will have to ask the magistrado that, señor. I know nothing of the matter except that I am to arrest you."

"You wish me to accompany you?"

"I demand it, señor."

"I am a man of blood, a caballero—"

"I have my orders."

"So I cannot be trusted to appear at my place of trial? But perhaps the hearing is to be held immediately. So much the better, for all the quicker can I clear myself. We go to the presidio?"

"I go to the presidio when this work is done. You go to cárcel," the sergeant said.

"To cárcel?" Don Carlos screeched. "You would dare? You would throw a caballero into the filthy jail? You would place him where they keep insubordinate natives and common felons?"

"I have my orders, Señor. You will prepare to accompany us at once."

"I must give my superintendent instructions regarding the management of the hacienda."

"I'll go along with you, señor."

Don Carlos's face flamed purple. His hands clenched as he regarded the sergeant.

"Am I to be insulted with every word?" he cried. "Do you think I would run away like a criminal?"

"I have my orders, Señor," the sergeant said.

"At least I may break this news to my wife and daughter without an outsider being at my shoulder?"

"Your wife is Doña Catalina Pulido?"

"Certainly."

"I am ordered to arrest her also, Señor."

"Scum!" Don Carlos cried. "You would put hands on a lady? You would remove her from her house?"

"It is my orders. She, too, is charged with treason and with aiding the enemies of the state."

"By the saints! It is too much! I shall fight against you and your men as long as there is breath in my body!"

"And that will not be for long, Don Carlos, if you attempt to give battle. I am but carrying out my orders."

"My beloved wife placed under arrest like a native wench! And on such a charge! What are you to do with her, sergeant?"

"She goes to cárcel."

"My wife in that foul place? Is there no justice in the land?

She is a tender lady of noble blood—"

"Enough of this, Señor. My orders are my orders, and I carry them out as instructed. I am a soldier and I obey."

Now Doña Catalina came running to the veranda, for she had been listening to the conversation just inside the door. Her face was white, but there was a look of pride in it. She feared Don Carlos might make an attack on the soldier, and she feared he would be wounded or slain if he did, and knew that at least it could only double the charge held against him.

"You have heard?" Don Carlos asked.

"I have heard, my husband. It is but more persecution. I am too proud to argue the point with these common soldiers, who are but doing as they have been commanded. A Pulido can be a Pulido, my husband, even in a foul cárcel."

"But the shame of it!" Don Carlos cried. "What does it all mean? Where will it end? And our daughter will be here alone with the servants. We have no relatives, no friends—"

"Your daughter is Señorita Lolita Pulido?" the sergeant asked. "Then do not grieve, señor, for you will not be separated. I have an order for the arrest of your daughter, also."

"The charge?"

"The same, señor."

"And you would take her—"

"To cárcel."

"An innocent, high-born, gentle girl?"

"My orders, señor," said the sergeant.

"May the saints blast the man who issued them!" Don Carlos cried. "They have taken my wealth and lands. They have heaped shame upon me and mine. But, thank the saints, they cannot break our pride!"

And then Don Carlos's head went erect, and his eyes flashed, and he took his wife by the arm and turned about to enter the house, with the sergeant at his heels. He broke the news to the Señorita Lolita, who stood as if stricken dumb for an instant, and then burst into a torrent of tears. And then the pride of the Pulidos came to her, and she dried her eyes, and curled her pretty lips with scorn at the big sergeant, and pulled aside her skirts when he stepped near.

Servants brought the carreta before the door, and Don Carlos and his wife and daughter got into it, and the journey of shame to the pueblo began.

Their hearts might be bursting with grief, but not one of the Pulidos showed it. Their heads were held high, they looked straight ahead, they pretended not to hear the low taunts of the soldiers.

They passed others, who were crowded off the road by the troopers, and who looked with wonder at those in the carreta, but they did not speak. Some watched in sorrow, and some grinned at their plight, according to whether those who passed were of the governor's party or of the honest folk who abhorred injustice.

And so, finally, they came to the edge of Reina de Los Angeles, and there they met fresh insult. For his excellency had determined that the Pulidos should be humbled to the dust; and he had sent some of his troopers to spread news of what was being done, and to give coins to natives and peons if they would jeer the prisoners when they arrived. For the governor wished to teach a lesson that would prevent other noble families from turning against him, and wished it to appear that the Pulidos were hated by all classes alike.

At the edge of the plaza they were met by the mob. There were cruel jeers and jests, some of which no innocent señorita should have heard. Don Carlos's face was red with wrath, and there were tears in Doña Catalina's eyes, and Señorita Lolita's lips were trembling, but they gave no other sign that they heard.

The drive around the plaza to the cárcel was made slow purposely. At the door of the inn there was a throng of rascals who had been drinking wine at the expense of the governor, and these added to the din.

One man threw mud, and it splashed on Don Carlos's breast, but he refused to notice it. He had one arm around his wife, the other around his daughter, as if to give them what protection he could, and he was looking straight ahead

There were some men of blood who witnessed the scene, yet took no part in the tumult. Some of them were as old as Don Carlos, and this thing brought to their hearts fresh, yet passive, hatred of the governor.

And some were young, with the blood running hot in their veins, and they looked upon the suffering face of Doña Catalina and imagined her their own mother, and upon the lovely face of the señorita and imagined her their sister or betrothed.

And some of these men glanced at one another furtively, and though they did not speak they were wondering the same thing—whether Señor Zorro would hear of this, and whether he would send word around for the members of the new league to gather.

The carreta stopped before the cárcel finally, the mob of jeering natives and peons surrounding it. The soldiers made some pretense of holding them back, and the sergeant dismounted and forced Don Carlos and his wife and daughter to step to the ground.

Uncouth and intoxicated men jostled them as they walked up the steps to the door. More mud was thrown, and some of it spattered upon Doña Catalina's gown. But if the mob expected an outburst on the part of the aged caballero, it was disappointed. Don Carlos held his head high, ignoring those who were striving to torment him, and so led his ladies to the door.

The sergeant beat against it with the heavy hilt of his sword. An aperture was opened, and in it appeared the evil, grinning face of the jailer.

"What have we here?" he demanded.

"Three prisoners charged with treason," the sergeant replied.

The door was thrown open. There came a last burst of jeers from the mob, and then the prisoners were inside, and the door had been closed and bolted again.

The jailer led the way along an evil-smelling hall and threw open another door.

"In with you," he directed.

The three prisoners were thrust inside, and this door was closed and barred. They blinked their eyes in the semi-gloom. Gradually they made out two windows, some benches, some human derelicts sprawled against the walls.

They had not even been given the courtesy of a clean, private room. Don Carlos and his wife and daughter had been thrust in with the scum of the pueblo, with drunkards and thieves and dishonored women and insulting natives.

They sat down on a bench in one corner of the room, as far from the others as possible. And then Doña Catalina and her daughter gave way to tears, and tears streamed down the face of the aged don as he tried to comfort them.

"I would to the saints that Don Diego Vega were only my son-in-law now," the don breathed.

His daughter pressed his arm.

"Perhaps—my father—a friend will come," she whispered. "Perhaps the evil man who caused this suffering will be punished."

For it seemed to the Señorita that a vision of Señor Zorro had appeared before her; and she had great faith in the man to whom she had given her love.

Chapter 29
Don Pulido Feels Ill

ONE HOUR after Don Carlos Pulido and his ladies had been incarcerated in the cárcel, Don Diego Vega, dressed most fastidiously, made his way slowly on foot up the slope to the presidio to make his call on his excellency, the governor.

He walked with swinging stride, gazing both to right and left as if at the hills in the distance, and once he stopped to observe a blossom that bloomed beside the path. His rapier was at his side, his most fashionable one with its jeweled hilt, and in his right hand he carried a handkerchief of flimsy lace, which he wafted this way and that like a dandy, and now and then touched it to the tip of his nose.

He bowed ceremoniously to two or three caballeros who passed him, but spoke to none beyond the necessary words of greeting, and they did not seek conversation with him. For, remembering that they had thought Don Diego Vega was courting the daughter of Don Carlos, they wondered how he would take the matter of her imprisonment along with her father and mother. They did not care to discuss the matter, for their own feelings were high, and they feared they might be betrayed into utterances that might be termed treasonable.

Don Diego came to the front door of the presidio, and the sergeant in charge called the soldiers to attention, giving Vega the salute due his station in life. Don Diego answered it with a wave of his hand and a smile, and went on to the comandante's office, where the governor was receiving such caballeros as cared to call and express their loyalty.

He greeted his excellency with carefully chosen words, bowed over his hand, and then took the chair the governor was kind enough to indicate.

"Don Diego Vega," the governor said, "I am doubly glad that you have called upon me today, for in these times a man who holds high office would know his friends."

"I should have called sooner, but I was away from my house at the time you arrived," Don Diego said. "You contemplate remaining long in Reina de Los Angeles, excellency?"

"Until this highwayman, known as Señor Zorro, is either slain or taken," the governor said.

"By the saints! Am I never to hear the last of that rogue?" Don Diego cried. "I have heard of nothing else for these many days. I go to spend an evening with a fray, and in comes a crowd of soldiers chasing this Señor Zorro. I repair to the hacienda of my father to get me peace and quiet, and along comes a crowd of caballeros seeking news of Señor Zorro.

"These be turbulent Times! A man whose nature inclines him to music and the poets has no right to exist in the present age."

"It desolates me that you have been annoyed," the governor said, laughing. "But I hope to have the fellow soon, and so put an end to that particular annoyance. Captain Ramón has sent for his big sergeant and his troopers to return. I brought an escort of twenty. And so we have ample men to run down this Curse of Capistrano when next he makes his appearance."

"Let us hope it will end as it should," said Don Diego.

"A man in high office has many things with which to contend," the governor went on. "Look at what I was forced to do this day. I am called upon to put in prison a man of good blood and his lady wife and tender daughter. But the state must be protected."

"I suppose you mean Don Carlos Pulido and his family?"

"I do, caballero."

"Now that it is called to my mind again, I must say a few words regarding that," Don Diego said. "I am not sure that my honor is not involved."

"Why, caballero, how can that be?"

"My father has ordered that I get me a wife and set up my establishment properly. Some days ago I requested of Don Carlos Pulido permission to pay my addresses to his daughter."

"Ha! I understand. But you are not the betrothed of the young lady?"

"Not yet, excellency."

"Then your honor is not involved, Don Diego, that I can see."

"But I have been paying court to her."

"You may thank the saints that it has gone no further, Don Diego. Think how it would look if you were allied with this family now. As for getting you a wife—come north with me to San Francisco de Asis, caballero, where the señoritas are far more lovely than here in your south land.

"Look over those of good blood, and let me know your preference, and I'll guarantee that the lady will listen to your suit and accept your hand and name. And I can guarantee, also, that she will be of a loyal family with which it will be no shame to make a contract. We shall get you a wife of the proper sort, caballero."

"If you will pardon me, is it not taking stern measures to have Don Carlos and his ladies thrown into the cárcel? Don Diego asked, flicking dust from his sleeve.

"I find it necessary, señor."

"Do you think it will add to your popularity, excellency?"

"Whether it does or not, the state must be served."

"Men of good blood hate to see such a thing, and there may be murmurings," Don Diego warned. "I should hate to see your excellency make a wrong step at this juncture."

"What would you have me do?" the governor asked.

"Place Don Carlos and the ladies under arrest, if you will, but do not incarcerate them. It is unnecessary; they will not run away. Bring them to trial as gentle folk should be brought to trial."

"You are bold, caballero."

"By the saints, am I talking too much?"

"It were better to leave these matters to the few of us who are trusted with attention to them," the governor said. "I can understand, of course, how it irks a man of good blood to see a don thrown into a cárcel, and to see his ladies treated likewise, but in such a case as this—"

"I have not heard the nature of the case," Don Diego said.

"Ha! Perhaps you may change your mind when you learn it. You have been speaking of this Señor Zorro. What if I tell you that the highwayman is being shielded and protected and fed by Don Carlos Pulido?"

"That is astonishing!"

"And that the Doña Catalina is a party to the treason? And that the lovely señorita has seen fit to talk treasonably and dip her pretty hands into a conspiracy against the state?"

"This is past belief!" Don Diego cried.

"Some nights ago Señor Zorro was at the Pulido hacienda. Warning was fetched the comandante by a native who is loyal. Don Carlos aided the bandit in tricking the soldiers, hid him in a closet, and when Captain Ramón was there alone, this highwayman stepped from the closet and attacked him treacherously and wounded him."

"By the saints!"

"And while you were gone and the Pulidos were your house guests, señor, Señor Zorro was in your house, speaking to the señorita, when the comandante walked in upon them. And the señorita grasped Captain Ramón by the arm and annoyed him until this Señor Zorro had made good his escape."

"It is past comprehension!" Don Diego exclaimed.

"Captain Ramón has placed before me a hundred such items of suspicion. Can you wonder now that I had them placed in cárcel? Did I merely have them put under arrest, this Señor Zorro would combine forces with them and aid them to escape."

"And your intentions, excellency?"

"I shall keep them in cárcel while my troopers run down this highwayman. I shall force him to confess and implicate them—and then they shall have a trial."

"These turbulent times!" Don Diego complained.

"As a loyal man—and I hope an admirer of mine—you should hope to see foes of the state confounded."

"I do. Most sincerely do I. All real foes of the state should receive punishment."

"I am joyed to hear you say that, caballero!" the governor cried, and he reached across the table and grasped Don Diego fervently by the hand.

There was some more talk that amounted to nothing, and then Don Diego took his leave, for there were other men waiting to see the governor. After he had left the office the governor looked across at Captain Ramón and smiled.

"You are right, comandante," he said. "Such a man could not be a traitor. It would tire him too much to think treasonable thoughts. What a man! He must be enough to drive that old fire-eater of a father of his insane."

Don Diego made his way slowly down the hill, greeting those he passed, and stopping again to regard the little flowers that blossomed by the wayside. At the corner of the plaza he met a young caballero who was glad to call him friend, one of the small band of men who had spent the night at Don Alejandro's hacienda.

"Ha! Don Diego, a fair day to you!" he cried. And then he lowered his voice and stepped nearer. "Has, by any chance, the man we call leader of our league of avengers, sent you a message this day.'

"By the bright blue sky-no!" Don Diego said. "Why should the man?"

"This Pulido business. It seems an outrage. Some of us have been wondering whether our leader does not intend to take a hand in it. We have been anticipating a message."

"By the saints! Oh, I trust not," Don Diego said. "I could not endure an adventure of any sort tonight. I—er—my head aches, and I fear I am going to have a fever. I shall have to see an apothecary about it. There are shiverings up and down my spine, also. Is not that a symptom? During the siesta hour I was bothered with a pain in my left leg just above the knee. It must be the weather."

"Let us hope that it will not result seriously." His friend laughed and hurried on across the plaza.

Chapter 30
The Sign of the Fox

AN HOUR after dusk that night a native sought out one of the caballeros with the intelligence that a gentleman wished to speak to him immediately, and that this gentleman was evidently wealthy since he had given the native a coin for carrying the message, when he might just as well have given nothing more than a cuff alongside the head, also that the mysterious gentleman would be waiting along the path that ran toward the San Gabriel trail, and to be sure that the caballero would come he had bade the native say that there was a fox in the neighborhood.

A fox! Zorro—fox! the caballero thought, and then he ruined the native forever by giving him another coin.

He went to the rendezvous immediately, and there he found Señor Zorro sitting his big horse, his face masked, the cloak wrapped around his body.

"You will pass the word, caballero," Señor Zorro said. I would have all men who are loyal and wish to do so, meet at midnight in the little valley beyond the hill. You know the place? So? I shall be waiting."

Then Señor Zorro wheeled his horse and dashed away in the darkness, and the caballero went back to the pueblo and passed the word to those men he knew could be depended upon, and urged upon them that they pass it to others of the league. One went to Don Diego's house, but was told by the despensero that Don Diego had complained of a fever and had retired to his chamber and had left word that he would flay alive any servant who dared enter the room unless he called.

Near the hour of midnight the caballeros began slipping from the pueblo one at a time, each upon the back of his best horse, and each armed with sword and pistol. Each man had a mask that could be put over his features instantly, for that had been decided upon at Don Alexandra's hacienda, among other things.

The pueblo was in darkness, save that there were lights in the tavern, where some of his excellency's escort made merry with the local troopers. For Sergeant Pedro Gonzales had returned with his men just before nightfall, glad to be back from a fruitless chase and hoping that the next scent would be warmer.

Those in the tavern had gone down the hill from the presidio, some leaving their horses there without paddles or bridles on, and they had no thought of an encounter with Señor Zorro this night. The fat landlord was kept busy, for the soldiers from the north had coins in their purses and were willing to spend them. Sergeant Gonzales, holding the attention of the company as usual, was detailing at length what he would do to this Señor Zorro if the saints were kind enough to let them meet and grant him his blade in his hand.

There were lights in the big lounging-room of the presidio, too, for few of the soldiers had retired. And there were lights in the house where his excellency was a guest, but the remainder of the pueblo was in darkness, and the people slept.

In the cárcel there was no light at all except one candle burning in the office, where a sleepy man was on guard. The jailer was in his bed. Prisoners moaned on the hard benches in the prison room. Don Carlos Pulido stood before a window, looking up at the stars; and his wife and daughter huddled on a bench beside him, unable to sleep in such surroundings.

The caballeros found Señor Zorro waiting for them as he had said he would be, but he remained aloof, speaking scarcely a word, until all were present.

"Are all here?" he asked then.

"All except Don Diego Vega," one replied. "He is ill with a fever, señor."

And all the caballeros chuckled, for they had an idea the fever was caused by cowardice.

"I take it that you know something of what is in my mind," Señor Zorro said. "We know what has happened to Don Carlos Pulido and the ladies of his family. We know they are innocent of any treason, and were they not, they should not have been taken to cárcel and incarcerated with common felons and drunkards.

"Think of those gentle ladies in such surroundings! Think of it—because Don Carlos has the ill will of the governor! Is it the sense of the league that something be done in this matter? If it is not, then will I do something by myself!"

"Rescue them!" a caballero said; and the others growled their approval. Here was a chance for risk and adventure and an opportunity to do a good deed.

"We must enter the pueblo quietly," Señor Zorro said. "There is no moon, and we will not be observed if we use caution. We shall approach the cárcel from the south. Each man will have his task to do.

"Some will surround the building to give notice if any approach it. Others must be ready to beat off the soldiers, if they respond to an alarm. Others will effect an entrance to the cárcel with me and rescue the prisoners."

"It is an excellent plan," one said.

"That is but a small part of it. Don Carlos is a proud man and, if given time for reflection, may refuse to be rescued. We cannot allow that. Certain ones will seize him and take him from the place. Others will attend to the Doña Catalina. I will undertake to care for the Señorita. Now—we have them free. And then what?"

He heard murmurs, but no distinct reply, and so he continued to outline the plan.

"All will ride to the highway just below this place," he said. "At that point we shall scatter. Those who have the Doña Catalina in charge will hasten with her to the hacienda of Don Alejandro Vega, where she can be hidden if necessary, and where the governor's soldiers will hesitate before entering and seizing her.

"Those who have Don Carlos in charge will take the road to Pala, and at a certain point some ten miles from this pueblo they will be met by two natives of understanding, who will give the sign of the fox. The natives will take Don Carlos in charge and care for him.

"When these things are done, each caballero will ride to his home quietly and alone, telling what story pleases him and using great caution. I shall have conducted the señorita to a safe place by that time. She shall be given into the keeping of old Fray Felipe, a man we can trust, and he will hide her if he must. Then we will watch to see what the governor does."

"What can he do?" a caballero asked. "Have them searched for, of course."

"We must await developments," Señor Zorro said. "Are all now ready?"

They assured him that they were, and so he named the men for each task, and then they left the little valley and rode slowly and cautiously around the little town and approached it from the south.

They heard the soldiers shouting and singing in the tavern, saw the lights in the presidio, and crept toward the cárcel quietly, riding two by two.

In a short time it had been surrounded by quiet, determined men, and then Señor Zorro and four others dismounted and went to the door of the building.

Chapter 31
The Rescue

SEÑOR ZORRO knocked upon the door with the hilt of his sword. They heard a man gasp inside, presently heard his steps on the stone flooring, and after a little time light showed through the cracks, and the aperture was opened, and the sleepy face of the guard appeared.

"What is wanted?" he asked.

Señor Zorro thrust the muzzle of his pistol through the aperture and into the man's face, and in such fashion that the little door could not be closed.

"Open, if you value your life! Open—and make not the slightest sound!" Señor Zorro commanded.

"What—what is this?"

"Señor Zorro is talking to you!"

"By the saints—"

"Open, fool, or you die instantly!"

"I—I'll open the door. Do not shoot, good Señor Zorro! I am only a poor guard and not a fighting man! I pray you do not shoot!"

"Open quickly!"

"As soon as I can fit key to lock, good Señor Zorro!"

They heard him rattling the keys; presently one was turned

in the lock, and the heavy door was thrown open.

Señor Zorro and his four companions rushed inside and slammed and fastened the door again. The guard found the muzzle of a pistol pressed against the side of his head, and would have knelt before these five masked and terrible men, only one of them caught him by the hair and held him up.

"Where sleeps the keeper of this infernal hole?" Señor Zorro demanded.

"In yonder room, señor."

"And where have you put Don Carlos Pulido and his ladies?"

"In the common prison room, señor."

Señor Zorro motioned to the others, strode across the room, and threw open the door to the jailer's chamber. The man already was sitting up in bed, having heard the sounds in the other room, and he blinked in fright when he beheld the highwayman by the light of the candle.

"Do not make a move, señor," Zorro warned. "One screech, and you are a dead man. Señor Zorro confronts you."

"May the saints preserve me—"

"Where are the keys to the prison rooms?"

"On—on that table, señor."

Señor Zorro picked them up and then whirled upon the jailer again and rushed toward him.

"Lie down!" he commanded. "On your face, scoundrel!"

Señor Zorro tore strips from a blanket and bound the jailer's hands and feet, and made a gag which he affixed.

"To escape death," he said then, "it is necessary for you to remain exactly as you are now, without making a sound, for some time after we have left the cárcel. I shall leave it to your own judgment to decide the length of time."

Then he hurried back into the main office, beckoned the others, and led the way down the evil-smelling hall.

"Which door?" he asked of the guard.

"The second one, señor."

They hurried to it, and Señor Zorro unlocked it and threw it open. He forced the guard to hold a candle high above his head.

A gasp of pity came from beneath the highwayman's mask He saw the aged don standing by the window, saw the two women crouched on the bench, saw the vile companions they had in this miserable place.

"Now may Heaven forgive the governor!" he cried.

Señorita Lolita looked up in alarm, and then gave a glad cry. Don Carlos whirled at the highwayman's words.

"Señor Zorro!" he gasped.

"The same, Don Carlos. I have come with some friends to rescue you."

"I cannot allow it, señor. I shall not run away from what is in store for me. And it would avail me little to have you do the rescuing. I am accused now of harboring you, I understand. How will it look, then, if you effect my escape?"

"There is no time for argument," Señor Zorro said. "I am not alone in this, but have twenty-six men with me. And a man of your blood, and gentle ladies such as those of your family, shall not spend an entire night in this miserable hole if we can prevent it. Caballeros!"

The last word was one of command. Two of the caballeros threw themselves upon Don Carlos, subdued him quickly, and half carried him into the hall and along it toward the office. Two others grasped the Doña Catalina by the arms, as gently as they could, and so carried her along.

Señor Zorro bowed before the Señorita and extended a hand, which she clasped gladly.

"You must trust me, Señorita," he said.

"To love is to trust, señor."

"All things have been arranged. Ask no questions, but do as I bid. Come."

He threw an arm around her, and so led her from the prison room, leaving the door open behind him. If some of the miserable wretches there could win through and out of the building, Señor Zorro had no wish to prevent them. More than half of them, he judged, were there because of prejudice or injustice.

Don Carlos was causing an unearthly clamor, shouting that he refused to be rescued, and that he would stay and face the governor at the trial, and show the blood that was in him. Doña Catalina was whimpering a bit because of fright, but made no resistance.

They reached the office, and Señor Zorro ordered the guard to a corner of it, with instructions to remain there quietly for some time after they had gone. And then one of the caballeros threw open the outside door.

There was a tumult outside at that moment. Two soldiers had approached with a fellow caught stealing at the tavern, and the caballeros had stopped them. One glance at the masked faces had been enough to tell the troopers that here was something wrong.

A soldier fired a pistol, and a caballero answered the fire, neither hitting the mark. But the shooting was enough to attract the attention of those in the tavern, and also of the guards at the presidio.

Troopers at the presidio were awakened immediately and took the places of the guards, while the latter mounted and spurred down the hill to ascertain the cause of the sudden tumult at that hour of the night. Sergeant Pedro Gonzales and others hurried from the tavern. Señor Zorro and his companions found themselves facing a resistance when they least expected it.

The jailer had gathered courage enough to work himself free of gag and bonds, and he shrieked through a window of his chamber that prisoners were being rescued by Señor Zorro. His shriek was understood by Sergeant Gonzales, who screeched for his men to follow him and earn a part of his excellency's reward.

But the caballeros had their three rescued prisoners on

horseback, and they spurred through the gathering throng and so dashed across the plaza and toward the highway.

Shots flew about them, but no man was hit. Don Carlos Pulido was still screaming that he refused to be rescued. Doña Catalina had fainted, for which the caballero who had her in charge was grateful, since he could give more attention to his horse and weapons.

Señor Zorro rode wildly with the Señorita Lolita in the saddle before him. He spurred his magnificent horse ahead of all the others, and so led the way to the highroad. And when he had reached it, he pulled up his mount and watched the others come galloping to the spot, to ascertain whether there had been casualties.

"Carry out your orders, caballeros!" he commanded, when he saw that all had won through safely.

And so the band was broken into three detachments. One rushed along the Pala Road with Don Carlos. Another took the highway that would lead them to the hacienda of Don Alejandro. Señor Zorro, riding without any of his comrades at his side, galloped toward Fray Felipe's place, the señorita's arms clasped tightly about his neck, and the señorita's voice in his ear.

"I knew that you would come for me, señor," she said. "I knew you were a true man, and would not see me and my parents remain in that miserable place."

Señor Zorro did not answer her with words, for it was not a time for speech with his enemies so close at his heels, but his arm pressed the señorita closer to him.

He had reached the crest of the first hill, and now he stopped the horse to listen for sounds of pursuit, and to watch the flickering lights far behind.

For there was a multitude of lights in the plaza now, and in all the houses, for the pueblo had been aroused. The presidio building was ablaze with light, and he could hear a trumpet being blown, and knew that every available trooper would be sent on the chase.

The sound of galloping horses came to his ears. The troopers knew in what direction the rescuers had traveled; and the pursuit would be swift and relentless, with his excellency on the scene to offer fabulous rewards and urge on his men with promises of good posts and promotion.

But one thing pleased Señor Zorro as his horse galloped down the dusty highway and the señorita clung to him and the keen wind cut into his' face—he knew that the pursuit would have to be divided into three parties.

He pressed the señorita to him again, put spurs to his horse, and rode furiously through the night.

Chapter 32
Close Quarters

OVER the hills peeped the moon.

Señor Zorro would have had the sky heavy with clouds this night and the moon obscured, could he have had things his own way, for now he was riding along the upper trail, and his pursuers were close behind and could see him against the brightening sky.

The horses ridden, by the troopers were fresh, too, and the most of those belonging to the men of his excellency's escort were magnificent beasts, as swift as any in the country and able to endure many miles of travel at a terrific pace.

But now the highwayman thought only of getting all the speed possible out of his own mount and of making as great as he could the distance between himself and those who followed; for at the end of his journey he would need quite a little time, if he was to accomplish what he had set out to do.

He bent low over the señorita and felt his horse with the reins, making himself almost a part of the animal he rode, as any good horseman can. He reached the crest of another hill and glanced back before he began the descent into the valley. He could see the foremost of his pursuers.

Had Señor Zorro been alone, no doubt the situation would

have caused him no uneasiness, for many times he had been in a position more difficult and had escaped. But the señorita was on the saddle before him now, and he wanted to get her to a place of safety, not only because she was the señorita and the woman he loved, but also because he was not the sort of man to let a prisoner he had rescued be recaptured. Such an event, he felt, would be a reflection on his skill and daring.

Mile after mile he rode, the señorita clinging to him, and neither speaking a word. Señor Zorro knew that he had gained some on those who followed, but not enough to suit his purpose.

Now he urged his horse to greater effort, and they flew along the dusty highway, past haciendas where the hounds barked in sudden alarm, past the huts of natives where the clamor of beating hoofs on the hard road caused bronze men and women to tumble from their bunks and rush to their doors.

Once he charged through a flock of sheep that were being driven to Reina de Los Angeles and the market there, and scattered them to either side of the road, leaving cursing herders behind him. The herders gathered the flock again, just in time to have the pursuing soldiers scatter it once more.

On and on he rode, until he could see, far ahead, the mission buildings at San Gabriel glistening in the moonlight. He came to a fork in the road and took the trail that ran to the right, toward the hacienda of Fray Felipe.

Señor Zorro was a reader of men, and he was trusting to his judgment tonight. He had known that the Señorita Lolita would have to be left either where there were women or else where there was a robed Franciscan to stand guard over her, for Señor Zorro was determined to protect his lady's good name. And so he was pinning his faith to old Fray Felipe.

Now the horse was galloping over softer ground, and was not making such good speed. Señor Zorro had little hope that the troopers would turn into the San Gabriel Road when they arrived at the fork, as they might have done had it not been moonlight and they had been unable to catch sight now and then of the man they pursued. He was within a mile of Fray Felipe's hacienda now, and once more he gave his horse the spurs in an effort to obtain greater speed.

"I shall have scant time, Señorita," he said, bending over her and speaking into her ear. "Everything may depend upon whether I have been able to judge a man correctly. I ask only that you trust me."

"You know that I do that, Señor."

"And you must trust the man to whom I am carrying you, señorita, and listen well to his advice upon all matters concerned with this adventure. The man is a fray."

"Then everything will be well, Señor," she replied, clinging to him closely.

"If the saints are kind, we shall meet again soon, señorita. I shall count the hours and deem each one of them an age. I believe there are happier days ahead for us."

"May Heaven grant it," the girl breathed.

"Where there is love, there may be hope, señorita."

"Then my hope is great, Señor."

"And mine," he said.

He turned his horse into Fray Felipe's driveway now and dashed toward the house. His intention was to stop only long enough to leave the girl, hoping that Fray Felipe would afford her protection, and then ride on, making considerable noise and drawing the troopers after him. He wanted them to think that he was merely taking a short cut across Fray Felipe's land to the other road, and that he had not stopped at the house.

He reined in his horse before the veranda steps, sprang to the ground, and lifted the señorita from the saddle, hurrying with her to the door. He beat against it with his fist, praying that Fray Felipe was a light sleeper and easily aroused. From the far distance there came a low drumming sound that he knew was made by the hoofs of his pursuers' horses.

It seemed to Señor Zorro that it was an age before the old

fray threw open the door and stood framed in it, holding a candle in one hand. The highwayman stepped in swiftly and closed the door behind him, so no light would show outside. Fray Felipe had taken a step backward in astonishment when he had beheld the masked man and the señorita he escorted.

"I am Señor Zorro, fray" the highwayman said, speaking swiftly and in low tones. "Perhaps you may feel that you owe me a small debt for certain things?"

"For punishing those who oppressed and mistreated me, I owe you a large debt, caballero, though it is against my principles to countenance violence of any sort," Fray Felipe replied.

"I was sure that I had made no mistake in reading your character," Señor Zorro went on. "This señorita is Lolita, the only daughter of Don Carlos Pulido."

"Ha!"

"Don Carlos is a friend of the frailes, as you well know, and has known oppression and persecution the same as they. Today the governor came to Reina de Los Angeles and had Don Carlos arrested and thrown into the cárcel on a charge that has no true worth, as I happen to know. He also had the Doña Catalina and this young lady put in cárcel, in the same prison room with drunkards and dissolute women. With the aid of some good friends, I rescued them."

"May the saints bless you, señor, for that kind action!" Fray Felipe cried.

"Troopers are pursuing us, fray. It is not seemly, of course, that the señorita ride farther with me alone. Do you take her and hide her, fray—unless you fear that such a course may cause you grave trouble."

"Señor!" Fray Felipe thundered.

"If the soldiers take her, they will put her in cárcel again, and probably she will be mistreated. Care for her, then, protect her, and you will more than discharge any obligation you may feel that you owe me."

"And you, señor?"

"I shall ride on, that the troopers may pursue me and not stop here at your house. I shall communicate with you later, fray. It is agreed between us?"

"It is agreed," Fray Felipe replied solemnly. "And I would clasp you by the hand, señor."

That handclasp was short, yet full of expression for all that. Señor Zorro then whirled toward the door.

"Blow out your candle," he directed. "They must see no light when I open the door."

In an instant Fray Felipe had complied, and they were in darkness. Señorita Lolita felt Señor Zorro's lips press against her own for an instant, and knew that he had raised the bottom of his mask to give her this caress. And then she felt one of Fray Felipe's strong arms around her.

"Be of good courage, daughter," the fray said. "Señor Zorro, it appears, has as many lives as a cat, and something tells me he was not born to be slain by troopers of his excellency."

The highwayman laughed lightly at that, opened the door, and darted through, closed it softly behind him, and so was gone.

Great eucalyptus trees shrouded the front of the house in shadows, and in the midst of these shadows was Señor Zorro's horse. He noticed, as he ran toward the beast, that the soldiers were galloping down the driveway, that they were much nearer than he had expected to find them when he emerged from the house.

He ran quickly toward his mount, tripped on a stone, and fell, and frightened the animal so that it reared and darted half a dozen paces away, and into the full moonlight.

The foremost of his pursuers shouted when he saw the horse, and dashed toward it. Señor Zorro picked himself up, gave a quick spring, caught the reins from the ground, and vaulted into the saddle.

But they were upon him now, surrounding him, their blades flashing in the moonlight. He heard the raucous voice of Sergeant Gonzales ordering the men.

"Alive, if you can, soldiers! His excellency would see the rogue suffer for his crimes. At him, troopers! By the saints!"

Señor Zorro parried a stroke with difficulty and found himself unhorsed. On foot he fought his way back into the shadows, and the troopers charged after him. With his back to the bole of a tree, Señor Zorro fought them off.

Three sprang from their saddles to rush in at him. He darted from the tree to another, but could not reach his horse. But one belonging to a dismounted trooper was near him, and he vaulted into the saddle and dashed down the slope toward the barns and corral.

"After the rogue!" he heard Sergeant Gonzales shouting. "His excellency will have us flayed alive if this pretty highwayman escapes us now!"

They charged after him, eager to win promotion and the reward. But Señor Zorro had some sort of a start of them, enough to enable him to play a trick. As he came into the shadow cast by a big barn, he slipped from the saddle, at the same time giving the horse he rode a cut with his rowels. The animal plunged ahead, snorting with pain and fright, running swiftly through the darkness toward the corral below. The soldiers dashed by in pursuit.

Señor Zorro waited until they were past and then he ran rapidly up the hill again. But he saw that some of the troopers had remained behind to guard the house, evidently with the intention of searching it later, and so he found he could not reach his horse.

And once more there rang out that peculiar cry, half shriek and half moan, with which Señor Zorro had startled those at the hacienda of Don Carlos Pulido. His horse raised its head, whinnied once in answer to his call, and galloped toward him.

Señor Zorro was in the saddle in an instant, spurring across a field directly in front of him. His horse went over a stone fence as if it had not been in the way. And after him speedily came a part of the troopers.

They had discovered the trick he had used. They charged at him from both sides, met behind him, followed, and strained to cut down his lead. He could hear Sergeant Pedro Gonzales shouting lustily for them to make a capture in the name of the governor.

He hoped that he had drawn them all away from Fray Felipe's house but he was not sure, and the thing that demanded his attention the most now was the matter of his own escape.

He urged his horse cruelly, knowing that this journey across plowed ground was taking the animal's strength. He longed for a hard trail, the broad highway.

And finally he reached the latter. Now he turned his horse's head toward Reina de Los Angeles, for he had work to do there. There was no señorita before him on the saddle now, and the horse felt the difference.

Señor Zorro glanced behind and exulted to find that he was running away from the soldiers. Over the next hill and he would be able to elude them!

But he had to be on guard, of course, for there might be troopers in front of him, too. His excellency might have sent reinforcements to Sergeant Gonzales, or might have men watching from the tops of the hills.

He glanced at the sky and saw that the moon was about to disappear behind a bank of clouds. He would have to make use of the short period of darkness, he knew.

Down into the little valley he rode, and looked back to find that his pursuers were only at the crest of the hill. Then came the darkness, and at the proper time. Señor Zorro had a lead of half a mile on the pursuing soldiers now, but it was not his intention to allow them to chase him into the pueblo.

He had friends in this locality. Beside the highway was an adobe hut, where there lived a native Señor Zorro had saved from a beating. Now he dismounted before the hut and kicked against the door. The frightened native opened it.

"I am pursued," Señor Zorro said.

That appeared to be all that was necessary, for the native immediately threw the door of the hut open wider. Señor Zorro led his horse inside, almost filling the crude building, and the door was hastily shut again.

Behind it, the highwayman and the native stood listening, the former with pistol in one hand and his naked blade in the other.

CHAPTER 33
Flight and Pursuit

THAT the determined pursuit of Señor Zorro and his band of caballeros from the cárcel had been taken up so quickly was due to Sergeant Pedro Gonzales.

Sergeant Gonzales had heard the shots and had rushed from the tavern with the other troopers at his heels, glad of an excuse to escape without paying for the wine he had ordered. He had heard the shout of the jailer and had understood it, and immediately had grasped the situation.

"Señor Zorro is rescuing the prisoners!" he screeched. "The highwayman is in our midst again! To horse, troopers, and after him! There is a reward—"

They knew all about the reward, especially the members of the governor's bodyguard, who had heard his excellency rave at mention of the highwayman's name and declare he would make a captain of the trooper who captured him or brought in his carcass.

They rushed for their horses, swung themselves into their saddles, and dashed across the plaza toward the cárcel with Sergeant Gonzales at their head.

They saw the masked caballeros galloping across the plaza, and Sergeant Gonzales rubbed his eyes with the back of one hand and swore softly that he had been taking too much wine. He had lied so often about Señor Zorro having a band of men at his back, that here was the band materialized out of his falsehoods.

When the caballeros split into three detachments, Sergeant Gonzales and his troopers were so near them that they observed the maneuver. Gonzales quickly made three troops of the men who followed him, and sent a troop after each band.

He saw the leader of the caballeros turn toward San Gabriel, he recognized the leap of the great horse the highwayman rode, and he took after Señor Zorro with an exultant heart, being of a mind to capture or slay the highwayman rather than to retake any of the rescued prisoners. For Sergeant Pedro Gonzales had not forgotten the time Señor Zorro had played with him in the tavern at Reina de Los Angeles, nor had he given up the idea of taking his vengeance for it.

He had seen Señor Zorro's horse run before, and he wondered a bit now because the highwayman was not putting greater distance between himself and his pursuers. And Sergeant Gonzales guessed the reason—that Señor Zorro had Señorita Lolita Pulido on the saddle before him and was carrying her away.

Gonzales was in the lead, and now and then he turned his head and shouted orders and encouragement to his troopers. The miles flew beneath them, and Gonzales was glad because he was keeping Señor Zorro in sight.

"To Fray Felipe's—that is where he is riding!" Gonzales told himself. "I knew that old fray was in league with the bandit! In some manner he tricked me when I sought this Señor Zorro at his hacienda before. Perhaps this highwayman has a clever hiding-place there. Ha! By the saints, I shall not be tricked again!"

On they rode, now and then catching glimpses of the man they pursued, and always in the minds of Gonzales and his troopers were thoughts of the reward and promotion a capture would mean. Their horses were beginning to show some fatigue already, but they did not spare the animals.

They saw Señor Zorro turn into the driveway that led to Fray Felipe's house; and Sergeant Gonzales chuckled low down in his throat because he felt that he had guessed correctly.

He had the highwayman now! If Señor Zorro continued to ride, he could be seen and followed because of the bright moonlight; if he stopped, Señor Zorro could not hope to cope successfully with half a score of troopers with Gonzales at their head.

They dashed up to the front of the house and started to surround it. They saw Señor Zorro's horse. And then they saw the highwayman himself, and Gonzales cursed because half a dozen troopers were between him and his prey, and were at him with their swords, threatening to end the business before Gonzales could reach the scene.

He tried to force his horse into the fight He saw Señor Zorro spring into a saddle and dash away, and the troopers after him. Gonzales, not being close, gave his attention to the other half of his duty—he bade some of his soldiers surround the house so that none could leave it.

Then he saw Señor Zorro take the stone fence, and started in pursuit, all except the guards around the house joining him. But Sergeant Gonzales went only as far as the crest of the first hill. He noticed how the highwayman's horse was running, and realized that he could not be overtaken. Perhaps the sergeant could gain some glory if he returned to Fray Felipe's house and recaptured the señorita.

The house was still being guarded when he dismounted before it, and his men reported that none had attempted to leave the building. He called two of his men to his side and knocked on the door. Almost instantly it was opened by Fray Felipe.

"Are you just from bed, fray?" Gonzales asked.

"Is it not a time of night for honest men to be abed?" Fray

Felipe asked in turn.

"It is, fray—yet we find you out of it. How does it happen that you have not come from the house before? Did we not make enough noise to awaken you?"

"I heard sounds of combat—"

"And you may hear more, fray, else feel the sting of a whip again, unless you answer questions swiftly and to the point. Do you deny that Señor Zorro has been here?"

"I do not."

"Ha! Now we have it. You admit, then, that you are in league with this pretty highwayman, that you shield him upon occasion? You admit that, fray?"

"I admit nothing of the sort," Fray Felipe replied. "I never set my eyes on this Señor Zorro, to my knowledge, until a very few minutes ago."

"That is a likely story. Tell it to the stupid natives, but do not try to tell it to a wise trooper, fray. What did this Señor Zorro wish?"

"You were so close upon the man's heels, señor, that he scarce had time to wish for anything," Fray Felipe said.

"Yet you had some speech with him?"

"I opened the door at his knock, señor, the same as I opened it at yours."

"What said he?"

"That soldiers were pursuing him."

"And he asked that you hide him, so he could escape capture at our hands?"

"He did not."

"Wanted a fresh horse, did he?"

"He did not say as much, señor. If he is such a thief as he is painted, undoubtedly he would merely have taken a horse without asking, had he wanted it."

"Ha! What business had he with you, then? It would be well for you to answer openly, fray."

"Did I say that he had business with me?"

"Ha! By the saints—"

"The saints are better off your lips, señor—boaster and drunkard!"

"Do you wish to receive another beating, fray? I am riding on his excellency's business. Do not you delay me further! What said this pretty highwayman?"

"Nothing that I am at liberty to repeat to you, señor," Fray Felipe said.

Sergeant Gonzales pushed him aside roughly and entered the living-room, and his two troopers followed at his heels.

"Light the candelero," Gonzales commanded his men. "Take candles, if you can find any. We search the house."

"You search my poor house?" Fray Felipe cried. "And what do you expect to find?" Fray Felipe asked.

"I expect to find the piece of merchandise this pretty Señor Zorro left here, fray."

"What do you imagine he left?"

"Ha! A package of clothing, I suppose! A bundle of loot! A bottle of wine! A saddle to be mended! What would the fellow leave, fray? One thing impresses me—Señor Zorro's horse carried double when he arrived at your house, and was carrying none but Señor Zorro when he departed."

"And you expect to find—"

"The other half of the horse's load," replied Gonzales. "Failing to find it, we may try a twist or two of your arm to see whether you can be made to speak."

"You would dare? You would so affront a fray? You would descend to torture?"

"Meal mush and goat's milk!" quoth Sergeant Gonzales. "You fooled me once in some manner, but you will not so fool me again. Search the house, troopers, and be sure that you search it well. I shall remain in this room and keep this entertaining fray company. I shall endeavor to discover what his sensations were while he was being whipped for swindling."

"Coward and brute!" Fray Felipe thundered. "There may

come a day when persecution shall cease."

"Meal mush and goat's milk!"

"When this disorder ends and honest men be given their just dues!" Fray Felipe cried. "When those who have founded a rich empire here shall receive the true fruits of their labor and daring instead of having them stolen by dishonest politicians and men who stand in their favor!"

"Goat's milk and meal mush, fray!"

"When there shall be a thousand Señor Zorros, and more if necessary, to ride up and down El Camino Real and punish those who do wrong! Sometimes I would that I were not a fray, that I might play such a game myself!"

"We'd run you down in short order and stretch a rope with your weight," Sergeant Gonzales told him. "Did you help his excellency's soldiers more, perhaps his excellency would treat you with more consideration."

"I give aid to no spawn of the devil," Fray Felipe said.

"Ha! Now you grow angry, and that is against your principles. Is it not the part of a robed fray to receive what comes his way and give thanks for it, no matter how much it chokes him? Answer me that, angry one."

"You have about as much knowledge of a Franciscan's principles and duties as has the horse you ride."

"I ride a wise horse, a noble animal. He comes when I call and gallops when I command. Do not deride him until you ride him. Ha! An excellent jest."

"Imbecile!"

"Meal mush and goat's milk!" said Sergeant Gonzales.

Chapter 34
The Blood of the Pulidos

THE TWO troopers came back into the room. They had searched the house well, they reported, invading every corner of it, and no trace had been found of any person other than Fray Felipe's native servants, all of whom were too terrified to utter a falsehood, and had said they had seen nobody around the place who did not belong there.

"Ha! Hidden away well, no doubt!" Gonzales said. "Fray, what is that in the corner of the room?"

"Bales of hides," Fray Felipe replied. "I have been noticing it from time to time. The dealer from San Gabriel must have been right when he said the hides he purchased of you were not properly cured. Are those?"

"I think you will find them so."

"Then why did they move?" Sergeant Gonzales asked. "Three times I saw the corner of a bale move. Soldiers, search there."

Fray Felipe sprang to his feet.

"Enough of this nonsense," he cried. "You have searched and found nothing. Search the barns next and then go! At least let me be master in my own house. You have disturbed my rest enough as it is."

"You will take a solemn oath, fray, that there is nothing alive behind those bales of hides?"

Fray Felipe hesitated, and Sergeant Gonzales grinned.

"Not ready to forswear yourself, eh?" the sergeant asked. "I had a thought you would hesitate at that, my robed Franciscan. Soldiers, search the bales."

The two men started toward the corner. But they had not covered one half the distance when Señorita Lolita Pulido stood up behind the bales of hides and faced them.

"Ha! Unearthed at last!" Gonzales cried. "Here is the package Señor Zorro left in the fray's keeping! And a pretty package it is! Back to cárcel she goes, and this escape will but make her final sentence the greater!"

But there was Pulido blood in the señorita's veins, and Gonzales had not taken that into account. Now the señorita stepped to the end of the pile of hides, so that light from the candelero struck full upon her.

"One moment, señores," she said.

One hand came from behind her back, and in it she held a long, keen knife such as sheep skinners used. She put the point of the knife against her breast, and regarded them bravely.

"Señorita Lolita Pulido does not return to the foul cárcel now or at any time, señores," she said. "Rather would she plunge this knife into her heart, and so die as a woman of good blood should. If his excellency wishes for a dead prisoner, he may have one."

Sergeant Gonzales uttered an exclamation of annoyance. He did not doubt that the señorita would do as she had threatened, if the men made an attempt to seize her. And while he might have ordered the attempt in the case of an ordinary prisoner, he did not feel sure that the governor would say he had done right if he ordered it now. After all, Señorita Pulido was the daughter of a don, and her self-inflicted death might cause trouble for his excellency. It might prove the spark to the powder magazine.

"Señorita, the person who takes his or her own life risks eternal damnation," the sergeant said. "Ask this fray if it is not so. You are only under arrest, not convicted and sentenced. If you are innocent, no doubt you soon will be set at liberty."

"It is no time for lying speeches, Señor," the girl replied. "I realize the circumstances only too well, I have said that I will not return to cárcel, and I meant it—and mean it now. One step toward me, and I take my own life."

"Señorita—" Fray Felipe began.

"It is useless for you to attempt to prevent me, good fray," she interrupted. "I have pride left me, thank the saints. His excellency gets only my dead body, if he gets me at all."

"Here is a pretty mess," Sergeant Gonzales exclaimed. "I suppose there is nothing for us to do except retire and leave the señorita to her freedom."

"Ah, no, señor!" she cried quickly. "You are clever, but not clever enough by far. You would retire and continue to have your men surround the house? You would watch for an opportunity, and then seize me?"

Gonzales growled low in his throat, for that had been his intention, and the girl had read it.

"I shall be the one to leave," she said. "Walk backward, and stand against the wall, señores. Do it immediately, or I plunge this knife into my bosom."

They could do nothing except obey. The soldiers looked to the sergeant for instructions, and the sergeant was afraid to risk the señorita's death, knowing it would call down upon his head the wrath of the governor, who would say that he had bungled.

Perhaps, after all, it would be better to let the girl leave the house. She might be captured afterward, for surely a girl could not escape the troopers.

She watched them closely as she darted across the room to the door. The knife was still held at her breast.

"Fray Felipe, you wish to go with me?" she asked. "You may

be punished if you remain."

"Yet I must remain, señorita. I could not run away. May the saints protect you!"

She faced Gonzales and the soldiers once more.

"I am going through this door," she said. "You will remain in this room. There are troopers outside, of course, and they will try to stop me. I shall tell them that I have your permission to leave. If they call and ask you, you are to say that it is so."

"And if I do not?"

"Then I use the knife, señor."

She opened the door, turned her head for an instant and glanced out.

"I trust that your horse is an excellent one, señor, for I intend to use it," she told the sergeant.

She darted suddenly through the door, and slammed it shut behind her.

"After her!" Gonzales cried. "I looked into her eyes! She will not use the knife—she fears it!"

He hurled himself across the room, the two soldiers with him. But Fray Felipe had been passive long enough. He went into action now. He did not stop to consider the consequences. He threw out one leg, and tripped Sergeant Gonzales. The two troopers crashed into him, and all went to the floor in a tangle.

Fray Felipe had gained some time for her, and it had been enough. For the señorita had rushed to the horse and had jumped into the saddle. She could ride like a native. Her tiny feet did not reach halfway to the sergeant's stirrups, but she thought nothing of that.

She wheeled the horse's head, kicked at his sides as a trooper rushed around the corner of the house. A pistol ball whistled past her head. She bent lower over the horse's neck and rode.

Now a cursing Sergeant Gonzales was on the veranda,

shouting for his men to get to horse and follow her. The moon was behind a bank of clouds again. They could not tell the direction the señorita was taking except by listening for the sounds of the horse's hoofs. And they had to stop to do that —and if they stopped they lost time and distance.

Chapter 35
The Clash of Blades Again

SEÑOR ZORRO stood like a statue in the native's hut, one hand grasping his horse's muzzle. The native crouched at his side.

Down the highway came the drumming of horses' hoofs. Then the pursuit swept by, the men calling to one another and cursing the darkness, and rushed down the valley.

Señor Zorro opened the door and glanced out, listened for a moment, and then led out his horse. He tendered the native a coin.

"Not from you, señor," the native said.

"Take it. You have need of it, and I have not," the highwayman said.

He vaulted into the saddle and turned his horse up the steep slope of the hill behind the hut. The animal made little noise as it climbed to the summit. Señor Zorro descended into the depression on the other side, and came to a narrow trail, and along this he rode at a slow gallop, stopping his mount now and then to listen for sounds of other horsemen who might be abroad.

He rode toward Reina de Los Angeles, but he appeared to be in no hurry about arriving at the pueblo. Señor Zorro had another adventure planned for this night, and it had to be accomplished at a certain time and under certain conditions.

It was two hours later when he came to the crest of the hill above the town: He sat quietly in the saddle for some time, regarding the scene. The moonlight was fitful now, but now and then he could make out the plaza.

He saw no troopers, heard nothing of them, decided that they had ridden back in pursuit of him, and that those who had been sent in pursuit of Don Carlos and the Doña Catalina had not yet returned. In the tavern there were lights, and in the presidio, and in the house where his excellency was a guest.

Señor Zorro waited until it was dark and then urged his horse forward slowly, but off the main highway. He circled the pueblo, and in time approached the presidio from the rear.

He dismounted now and led his horse, going forward slowly, often stopping to listen, for this was a very ticklish business and might end in disaster if a mistake were made.

He stopped the horse behind the presidio where the wall of the building would cast a shadow if the moon came from behind the clouds again, and went forward cautiously, following the wall as he had done on that other night.

When he came to the office window, he peered inside. Captain Ramón was there alone, looking over some reports spread on the table before him, evidently awaiting the return of his men.

Señor Zorro crept to the corner of the building and found there was no guard. He had guessed and hoped that the comandante had sent every available man to the chase, but he knew that he would have to act quickly, for some of the troopers might return.

He slipped through the door and crossed the big lounging-room, and so came to the door of the office. His pistol was in his hand, and could a man have seen behind the mask, he would have observed that Señor Zorro's lips were crushed in a thin, straight line of determination.

As upon that other night, Captain Ramón whirled around in his chair when he heard the door open behind him, and once more he saw the eyes of Señor Zorro glittering through his mask, saw the muzzle of the pistol menacing him.

"Not a move. Not a sound. It would give me pleasure to fill your body with hot lead," Señor Zorro said. "You are alone—your silly troopers are chasing me where I am not."

"By the saints—" Captain Ramón breathed.

"Not so much as a whisper, señor, if you hope to live. Turn your back to me."

"You would murder me?"

"I am not that sort, comandante. And I said for you to make not a sound. Put your hands behind your back, for I am going to bind your wrists."

Captain Ramón complied. Señor Zorro stepped forward swiftly, and bound the wrists with his own sash, which he tore from his waist. Then he whirled Captain Ramón around so that he faced him.

"Where is his excellency?" he asked.

"At Don Juan Estados's house."

"I knew as much, but wanted to see whether you prefer to speak the truth tonight. It is well if you do so. We are going to call upon the governor."

"To call—"

"Upon his excellency, I said. And do not speak again. Come with me."

He grasped Captain Ramón by the arm and hurried him from the office, across the lounging-room, out of the door. He piloted him around the building to where the horse was waiting.

"Mount!" he commanded. "I shall sit behind you, with the muzzle of this pistol at the base of your brain. Make no mistake, comandante, unless you are tired of life. I am a determined man this night."

Captain Ramón had observed it. He mounted as he was

directed, and the highwayman mounted behind him, and held the reins with one hand and the pistol with the other. Captain Ramón could feel the touch of cold steel at the back of his head.

Señor Zorro guided his horse with his knees instead of with the reins. He urged the beast down the slope and circled the town once more, keeping away from the beaten trails, and so approached the rear of the house where his excellency was a guest.

Here was the difficult part of the adventure. He wanted to get Captain Ramón before the governor, to talk to both of them, and to do it without having anybody else interfere. He forced the captain to dismount, and led him to the rear wall of the house. There was a patio there, and they entered it.

It appeared that Señor Zorro knew the interior of the house well. He entered it through a servant's room, taking Captain Ramón with him, and passed through into a hall without awakening the sleeping native. They went along the hall slowly. From one room came the sound of snoring. From beneath the door of another light streamed.

Señor Zorro stopped before that door and applied an eye to a crack at the side of it. If Captain Ramón harbored thoughts of voicing an alarm, or of offering battle, the touch of the pistol at the back of his head caused him to forget them.

And he had scant time to think of a way out of this predicament, for suddenly Señor Zorro threw open the door, hurled Captain Ramón through it, followed himself, and shut the door quickly behind him. In the room there were his excellency and his host.

"Silence, and do not move," Señor Zorro said. "The slightest alarm, and I put a pistol ball through the governor's head. That is understood? Very well, señores."

"Señor Zorro!" the governor gasped.

"The same, your excellency. I ask your host to be not frightened, for I mean him no harm if he sits quietly until I am done.

Captain Ramón, kindly sit across the table from the governor. I am delighted to find the head of the state awake and awaiting news from those who are chasing me. His brain will be clear, and he can understand better what is said."

"What means this outrage?" the governor exclaimed. "Captain Ramón, how comes this? Seize this man! You are an officer—"

"Do not blame the comandante," Señor Zorro said. "He knows it is death to make a move. There is a little matter that needs explanation, and since I cannot come to you in broad day as a man should, I am forced to adopt this method. Make yourselves comfortable, Señores. This may take some little time."

His excellency fidgeted in his chair.

"You have this day insulted a family of good blood, your excellency," Señor Zorro went on. "You have forgotten the proprieties to such an extent that you have ordered thrown into your miserable cárcel a hidalgo and his gentle wife and innocent daughter. You have taken such means to gratify a spite—"

"They are traitors," his excellency said.

"What have they done of treason?"

"You are an outlaw with a price put upon your head. They have been guilty of harboring you, giving you aid."

"Where got you this information?"

"Captain Ramón has an abundance of evidence."

"Ha! The comandante, eh? We shall see about that! Captain Ramón is present, and we can get at the truth. May I ask the nature of your evidence?"

"You were at the Pulido hacienda," the governor said.

"I admit it."

"A native saw you and carried word to the presidio. The soldiers hurried out to effect your capture."

"A moment. Who said a native sounded the alarm?"

"Captain Ramón assured me so."

"Here is the first chance for the captain to speak the truth.

As a matter of fact, comandante, was it not Don Carlos Pulido himself who sent the native? The truth!"

"It was a native brought word."

"And he did not tell your sergeant that Don Carlos had sent him? Did he not say that Don Carlos had slipped him the information in whispers while he was carrying his fainting wife to her room? Is it not true that Don Carlos did his best to hold me at his hacienda until the soldiers arrived, that I might be captured? Did not Don Carlos thus try to show his loyalty to the governor?"

"By the saints, Ramón, you never told me as much!" his excellency cried.

"They are traitors," the captain declared stubbornly.

"What other evidence?" Señor Zorro asked.

"Why, when the soldiers arrived, you concealed yourself by some trick," the governor said. "And presently Captain Ramón himself reached the scene, and while he was there you crept from a closet, ran him through treacherously from behind, and made your escape. It is an evident fact that Don Carlos had hidden you in the closet"

"By the saints!" Señor Zorro swore. "I had thought, Captain Ramón, that you were man enough to admit defeat, though I knew you for a scoundrel in other things. Tell the truth!"

"That is—the truth."

"Tell the truth!" Señor Zorro commanded, stepping closer to him and bringing up the pistol. "I came from that closet and spoke to you. I gave you time to draw blade and get on guard. We fenced for fully ten minutes, did we not?

"I admit freely that for a moment you puzzled me, and then I solved your method of giving battle and knew you were at my mercy. And then, when I could have slain you easily, I but scratched your shoulder. Is not that the truth? Answer, as you hope to live!"

Captain Ramón licked his dry lips, and could not meet the governor's eyes.

"Answer!" Señor Zorro thundered.

"It is—the truth," the captain acknowledged.

"Ha! So I ran you through from behind, eh? It is an insult to my blade to have it enter your body. You see, your excellency, what manner of man you have for comandante here. Is there more evidence?"

"There is," the governor said. "When the Pulidos were guests at the house of Don Diego Vega, and Don Diego was away, Captain Ramón went to pay his respects and found you there alone with the señorita."

"And that shows what?"

"That you are in league with the Pulidos. That they harbored you even in the house of Don Diego, a loyal man. And when the captain discovered you there, the señorita flung herself upon him and held him—delayed him, rather—until you made your escape through a window. Is not that enough?"

Señor Zorro bent forward, and his eyes seemed to burn through the mask and into those of Captain Ramón.

"So that is the tale he told, eh?" the highwayman said. "As a matter of fact, Captain Ramón is enamored of the señorita. He went to the house, found her alone, forced his attentions upon her, even told her that she should not object, since her father was in the bad graces of the governor. He attempted to caress her, and she called for help. I responded."

"How did you happen to be there?"

"I do not care to answer that, but I take my oath the señorita did not know of my presence. She called for aid, and I responded.

"I made this thing you call a comandante kneel before her and apologize. And then I took him to the door and kicked him out into the dust! And afterward I visited him at the presidio and told him that he had given insult to a noble señorita—"

"It appears that you hold some love for her yourself," the governor said.

"I do, your excellency, and am proud to admit it."

"Ha! You condemn her and her parents by that statement! You deny now they are in league with you?"

"I do. Her parents do not know of our love."

"This señorita is scarcely conventional."

"Señor! Governor or no, another thought like that and I spill your blood," Señor Zorro cried. "I have told you what happened that night at the house of Don Diego Vega. Captain Ramón will testify that what I have said is the exact truth. Is it not, comandante? Answer!"

"It—it is the truth." The captain gulped, looking at the muzzle of the highwayman's pistol.

"Then you have told me falsehood, and can no longer be an officer of mine!" the governor cried. "It appears that this highwayman can do as he pleases with you. Ha! But I still believe that Don Carlos Pulido is a traitor, and the members of his family, and it has availed you nothing, Señor Zorro, to play this little scene.

"My soldiers shall continue to pursue them—and you! And before they are done, I'll have the Pulidos dragged in the dirt, and I'll have you stretching a rope with your carcass!"

"Quite a bold speech," observed Señor Zorro. "You set your soldiers a pretty task, your excellency. I rescued your three prisoners tonight, and they have escaped."

"They shall be retaken."

"Time alone will tell that. And now I have another duty to perform here. Your excellency, you will take your chair to that far corner and sit there, and your host will sit beside you. And there you shall remain until I have finished."

"What do you mean to do?"

"Obey me," Señor Zorro cried. "I have scant time for argument, even with a governor."

He watched while the two chairs were placed and the governor and his host had seated themselves. And then he stepped nearer Captain Ramón.

"You insulted a pure and innocent girl, comandante," he

said. "For that, you shall fight. Your scratched shoulder is healed now, and you wear your blade by your side. Such a man as you is not fit to breathe God's pure air. The country is better for your absence. On your feet, señor, and on guard!"

Captain Ramón was white with rage. He knew that he was ruined. He had been forced to confess that he had lied. He had heard the governor remove his rank. And this man before him had been the cause of all of it.

Perhaps in his anger he could kill this Señor Zorro, stretch this Curse of Capistrano on the floor with his life blood flowing away. Perhaps, if he did that, his excellency would relent.

He sprang from his chair and backward to the side of the governor.

"Unfasten my wrists!" he cried. "Let me at this dog!"

"You were as good as dead before—you certainly are dead after using that word," Señor Zorro said calmly.

The comandante's wrists were untied. He whipped out his blade, sprang forward with a cry, and launched himself in a furious attack upon the highwayman.

Señor Zorro gave ground before this onslaught, and so obtained a position where the light from the candelero did not bother his eyes. He was skilled with a blade, and had fenced for life many times, and he knew the danger in the attack of an angered man who did not fence according to the code.

And he knew, too, that such anger is spent quickly unless a fortunate thrust makes the possessor of it victor almost at once. And so he retreated step by step, guarding well, parrying vicious strokes, alert for an unexpected move.

The governor and his host were sitting in their corner, but bending forward and watching the combat.

"Run him through, Ramón, and I reinstate and promote you!" his excellency cried.

The comandante thus was urged to do it. Señor Zorro found his opponent fighting much better than he had before in Don Carlos Pulido's house at the hacienda. He found himself forced

to fight out of a dangerous corner, and the pistol he held in his left hand to intimidate the governor and his host bothered him.

And suddenly he tossed it to the table, and then swung around so that neither of the two men could dart from a corner and get it without running the chance of receiving a blade between the ribs. And there he stood his ground and fought.

Captain Ramón could not force him to give way now. His blade seemed to be a score. It darted in and out, trying to find a resting place in the captain's body; for Señor Zorro was eager to have an end of this and be gone. He knew that the dawn was not far away, and he feared that some trooper might come to the house with a report for the governor.

"Fight, insulter of girls!" he cried. "Fight, man who tells a falsehood to injure a noble family! Fight, coward and poltroon! Now death stares you in the face, and soon you'll be claimed! Ha! I almost had you then! Fight, cur!"

Captain Ramón cursed and charged, but Señor Zorro received him and drove him back, and so held his position. The perspiration was standing out on the captain's forehead in great globules. His breath was coming heavily from between his parted lips. His eyes were bright and bulging.

"Fight, weakling!" The highwayman taunted him. "This time I am not attacking from behind. If you have prayers to say, say them—for your time grows short."

The ringing blades, the shifting feet on the floor, the heavy breathing of the combatants and of the two spectators of this life-and-death struggle were the only sounds in the room. His excellency sat far forward on his chair, his hands gripping the edges of it so that his knuckles were white,

"Kill me this highwayman!" he shrieked. "Use your good skill, Ramón! At him!"

Captain Ramón rushed again, calling into play his last bit of strength, fencing with what skill he could command. His arms were as lead; his breath was fast. He thrust, he lunged—

and made a mistake of a fraction of an inch.

Like the tongue of a serpent, Señor Zorro's blade shot in. Thrice it darted forward, and upon the fair brow of Ramón, just between the eyes, there flamed suddenly a red, bloody letter Z.

"The Mark of Zorro!" the highwayman cried. "You wear it forever now, comandante!"

Señor Zorro's face became more stern. His blade shot in again and came out dripping red. The comandante gasped and slipped to the floor.

"You have slain him!" the governor cried. "You have taken his life, wretch!"

"Ha! I trust so. The thrust was through the heart, excellency. He never will insult a señorita again."

Señor Zorro looked down at his fallen foe, regarded the governor a moment, then wiped his blade on the sash that had bound the comandante's wrists. He returned the blade to its scabbard and picked up his pistol from the table.

"My night's work is done," he said.

"And you shall hang for it!" his excellency cried.

"Perhaps—when you catch me," replied the Curse of Capistrano, bowing ceremoniously.

Then, without glancing again at the twitching body of him who had been Captain Ramône, he whirled through the door and was in the hall, and rushed through it to the patio and to his horse.

CHAPTER 36
All Against Them

AND HE rushed into danger.

The dawn had come; the first pink streaks had appeared in the eastern sky, and then the sun had risen quickly above the heights to the east, and now the plaza was bathed in brilliance. There was no mist, no high fog even, and objects on the hillsides far away stood out in relief. It was no morning in which to ride for life and freedom.

Señor Zorro had delayed too long with the governor and comandante, else had misjudged the hour. He swung into his saddle and urged his beast out of the patio—and then a full realization of his imminent peril came to him.

Down the trail from San Gabriel came Sergeant Pedro Gonzales and his troopers. Down the Pala road came another detachment of soldiers that had been trailing the caballeros and Don Carlos and had given up in disgust. Over the hill toward the presidio came the third body of men, who had been in chase of those who had rescued the Doña Catalina. Señor Zorro found himself hemmed in by his foes.

The Curse of Capistrano deliberately stopped his horse and for a moment contemplated the outlook. He glanced at the three bodies of troopers, estimated the distance. And in that instant one with Sergeant Gonzales's detachment saw him and raised the alarm.

They knew that magnificent horse, that long purple cloak, that black mask and wide sombrero. They saw before them the man they had been pursuing throughout the night, the man who had made fools of them and played with them, about the hills and valleys. They feared the rage of his excellency and their superior officers, and in their hearts and minds was determination to capture or slay this Curse of Capistrano now as this last chance was offered them.

Señor Zorro put spurs to his horse and dashed across the plaza, in full view of some score of citizens. Just as he did that, the governor and his host rushed from the house, shrieking that Señor Zorro was a murderer and should be taken. Natives scurried like so many rats for shelter; men of rank stood still and gaped in astonishment.

Señor Zorro, having crossed the plaza, drove his horse at highest speed straight toward the highway. Sergeant Gonzales and his troopers rushed to cut him off and turn him back, shrieking at one another, pistols in their hands, blades loosened in their scabbards. Reward and promotion and satisfaction were to be their lot if they made an end of the highwayman here and now.

Señor Zorro was forced to swerve from his first course, for he saw that he could not win through. He had not taken his pistol from his belt, but he had drawn his blade, and it dangled from his right wrist in such fashion that he could grip the hilt of it instantly and put it into play.

He cut across the plaza again, almost running down several men of rank who were in the way. He passed within a few paces of the infuriated governor and his host, darted between two houses, and rushed toward the hills in that direction.

It appeared that he had some small chance of escaping the cordon of his foes now. He scorned paths and trails, and cut across the open ground. From both sides the troopers galloped to meet him, flying toward the angle of the wedge, hoping to reach it in time and turn him back once more.

Gonzales was shouting orders in his great voice, and he was sending a part of his men down into the pueblo, so they would be in proper position in case the highwayman turned back again, and could keep him from escaping to the west.

He reached the highway and started down it toward the south. It was not the direction he would have preferred, but he had no choice now. He dashed around a curve in the road, where some natives' huts cut off the view—and suddenly he pulled up his horse, almost unseating himself.

For here a new menace presented itself. Straight at him along the highway flew a horse and rider, and close behind came half a dozen troopers in pursuit.

Señor Zorro whirled his horse. He could not turn to the right because of a stone fence. His horse could have jumped it, but on the other side was soft plowed ground, and he knew he could make no progress across it, and that the troopers might cut him down with a pistol bullet.

Nor could he turn to the left, for there was a sheer precipice down which he could not hope to ride with safety. He had to turn back toward Sergeant Gonzales and the men who rode with him, hoping to get a distance of a couple of hundred yards, where he could make a descent, before Gonzales and his men arrived at the spot

He gripped his sword now, and was prepared for fight, for he knew it was going to be close work. He glanced back over his shoulder—and gasped his surprise.

For it was Señorita Lolita Pulido who rode that horse and was pursued by the half-dozen troopers, and he had thought her safe at the hacienda of Fray Felipe. Her long black hair was down and streaming out behind her. Her tiny heels were glued to the horse's flanks. She bent forward as she rode, holding the reins low down, and Señor Zorro, even in that instant, marveled at her skill with a mount.

"Señor!" he heard her shout.

And then she had reached his side, and they rode together, dashing down upon Gonzales and his troopers.

"They have been chasing me—for hours!" she gasped. "I escaped them—at Fray Felipe's!"

"Ride close! Do not waste breath!" he screeched.

"My horse is almost done, señor!"

Señor Zorro glanced aside at the beast, and saw that he I was suffering from fatigue. But there was scant time to consider that now. The soldiers behind had gained some; those in front presented a menace that required consideration.

Down the trail they flew, side by side, straight at Gonzales and his men. Señor Zorro could see that pistols were out, and he doubted not that the governor had given orders to get him dead or alive, but to see that he did not escape again.

Now he spurred a few paces in advance of the señorita, and called upon her to ride his horse's tracks. He dropped the reins on his mount's neck, and held his blade ready. He had two weapons—his blade and his horse.

Then came the crash. Señor Zorro swerved his horse at the proper instant, and the señorita followed him. He cut at the trooper on his left, swung over and cut at the one on his right. His horse crashed into that of a third trooper, and hurled it against the animal the sergeant rode.

He heard shrill cries about him. He knew that the men who had been pursuing Señorita Lolita had run into the others, and that there was a certain amount of confusion, that they could not use blades for fear of cutting down one another.

And then he was through them, with the señorita riding at his side again. Once more he was at the edge of the plaza. His horse was showing signs of weariness, and he had gained nothing.

For the way to San Gabriel was not open, the way to Pala was closed, he could not hope to escape by cutting across soft ground, and on the opposite side of the plaza were more troopers, in saddle and waiting to cut him off, no matter in which direction he started.

"We are caught!" he shouted. "But we are not done, señorita!"

"My horse is stumbling!" she cried.

Señor Zorro saw that it was so. He knew that the beast could not make another hundred yards.

"To the tavern!" he cried.

They galloped straight across the plaza. At the door of the tavern the Señorita's horse staggered and fell. Señor Zorro caught the girl in his arms in time to save her from a hard fall and, still carrying her, darted through the tavern door.

"Out!" he cried to the landlord and the native servant. "Out!" he shrieked to half a dozen loiterers, exhibiting his pistol. They rushed through the door and into the plaza.

The highwayman threw the door shut and bolted it. He saw that every window was closed except the one that fronted on the plaza, and that the board and skin coverings were in place. He stepped to the table and then whirled to face the señorita.

"It may be the end," he said.

"Señor! Surely the saints will be kind to us."

"We are beset by foes, Señorita. I care not, so that I die fighting as a caballero should. But you, señorita—"

"They shall never put me in the foul cárcel again, Señor! I swear it! Rather would I die with you."

She took the sheep skinner's knife from her bosom, and he caught a glance of it.

"Not that, señorita!" he cried.

"I have given you my heart, Señor. Either we live together or we die together."

Chapter 37
The Fox at Bay

He darted to the window and glanced out. The troopers were surrounding the building. He could see the governor stalking across the plaza, crying his orders. Down the San Gabriel trail came the proud Don Alejandro Vega, to pay his visit to the governor, and he stopped at the plaza's edge and began questioning men regarding the cause for the tumult.

"All are in at the death," Señor Zorro said, laughing. "I wonder where my brave caballeros are, those who rode with me?"

"You expect their aid?" she asked.

"Not so, señorita. They would have to stand together and face the governor, tell him their intentions. It was a lark with them, and I doubt whether they take it seriously enough to stand by me now. It is not to be expected. I fight it out alone."

"Not alone, Señor, when I am by your side." He clasped her in his arms, pressed her to him.

"I would we might have our chance," he said. "But it would be folly for you to let my disaster influence your life. You never have seen my face even, señorita. You could forget me. You could walk from this place and surrender, send word to Don Diego Vega that you will become his bride, and the governor then would be forced to release you and clear your parents of all blame."

"Ah, Señor—"

"Think, Señorita. Think what it would mean. His excellency would not dare stand an instant against a Vega. Your parents would have their lands restored. You would be the bride of the richest young man in the country. You would have everything to make you happy—"

"Everything except love, señor, and without, love the rest is as naught."

"Think, señorita, and decide for once and all. You have but a moment now!"

"I made my decision long ago, señor. A Pulido loves but once, and does not wed where she cannot love."

"Cara!" he cried, and pressed her close again. Now there came a battering at the door.

"Señor Zorro!" Sergeant Gonzales cried.

"Well, señor?" Zorro asked.

"I have an offer for you from his excellency the governor."

"I am listening, loud one."

"His excellency has no wish to cause your death or injury to the señorita you have inside with you. He asks that you open the door and come out with the lady."

"To what end?" Señor Zorro asked.

"You shall be given a fair trial, and the señorita also. Thus you may escape death and receive imprisonment instead."

"Ha! I have seen samples of his excellency's fair trials," Señor Zorro responded. "Think you I am an imbecile?"

"His excellency bids me say that this is the last chance, that the offer will not be renewed."

"His excellency is wise not to waste breath renewing it. He grows fat, and his breath is short"

"What can you expect to gain by resistance, save death?" Gonzales asked. "How can you hope to offstand a score and a half of us?"

"It has been done before, loud one."

"We can batter in the door and take you."

"After a few of you have been stretched lifeless on the floor," Señor Zorro observed. "Who will be the first through the door, my sergeant?"

"For the last time—"

"Come in and drink a mug of wine with me," said the highwayman, laughing.

"Meal mush and goat's milk!" swore Sergeant Gonzales.

There was quiet then for a time, and Señor Zorro, glancing through the window cautiously, so as not to attract a pistol shot, observed that the governor was in consultation with the sergeant and certain of the troopers.

The consultation ended, and Señor Zorro darted back from the window. Almost immediately, the attack upon the door began. They were pounding at it with heavy timbers, trying to smash it down. Señor Zorro, standing in the middle of the room, pointed his pistol at the door and fired, and as the ball tore through the wood and somebody outside gave a shriek of pain, he darted to the table and started loading the pistol again.

Then he hurried across to the door, and observed the hole where the bullet had gone through. The plank had been split, and there was quite a crack in it. Señor Zorro put the point of his blade at this crack, and waited.

Again the heavy timber crashed against the door, and some trooper threw his weight against it, also. Señor Zorro's blade darted through the crack like a streak of lightning, and came back red, and again there was a shriek outside. And now a volley of pistol balls came through the door, but Señor Zorro, laughing, had sprung back out of harm's way.

"Well done, señor!" Señorita Lolita cried.

"We shall stamp our mark on several of these hounds before we are done," he replied.

"I would that I could aid you, señor."

"You are doing it, señorita. It is your love that gives me my strength."

"If I could use a blade—"

"Ah, señorita, that is for a man to do. Do you pray that all may be well."

"And at the last, señor, if it is seen that there is no hope—may I then see your dear face?"

"I swear it, señorita, and feel my arms about you, and my lips on yours. Death will not be so bitter then."

The attack on the door was renewed. Now pistol shots were coming through it regularly, and through the one open window also, and there was nothing for Señor Zorro to do except stand in the middle of the room and wait, his blade held ready. There would be a lively few minutes, he promised, when the door was down and they rushed in at him.

It seemed to be giving way now. The señorita crept close to him, tears streaming down her cheeks, and grasped him by the arm.

"You will not forget?" she asked.

"I'll not forget, señorita."

"Just before they break down the door, señor. Take me in your arms and let me see your dear face and kiss me. Then I can die with good grace, too."

"You must live—"

"Not to be sent to a foul cárcel, señor. And what would life be without you?"

"There is Don Diego—"

"I think of nobody but you, señor. A Pulido will know how to die. And perhaps my death will bring home to men the perfidy of the governor. Perhaps it may be of service."

Again the heavy timber struck against the door. They could hear his excellency shouting encouragement to the troopers, could hear the natives shrieking and Sergeant Gonzales crying his orders in his loud voice.

Señor Zorro hurried to the window again, chancing a bullet, and glanced out. He saw that half a dozen troopers had their blades ready, were prepared to rush over the door the moment it was down. They would get him—but he would get some of them first! Again the ram against the door.

"It is almost the end, Señor," the girl whispered.

"I know it, señorita."

"I would we had had better fortune, yet I can die gladly since this love has been in my life. Now—señor—your face and lips. The door—is crashing in!"

She ceased to sob, and lifted her face bravely. Señor Zorro sighed, and one hand fumbled with the bottom of his mask.

But suddenly there was a tumult outside in the plaza, and the battering at the door ceased, and they could hear loud voices that they had not heard before.

Señor Zorro let go of his mask, and darted to the window.

Chapter 38
The Man Unmasked

TWENTY-THREE horsemen were galloping into the plaza. The beasts they rode were magnificent, their saddles and bridles were heavily chased with silver, their cloaks were of the finest materials, and they wore hats with plumes, as if this was somewhat of a dress affair and they wished the world to know it. Each man sat straight and proud in his saddle, his blade at his side, and every blade had a jeweled hilt, being at once serviceable and a rich ornament.

They galloped along the face of the tavern, between the door and the soldiers who had been battering it, between the building and the governor and assembled citizens, and there they turned and stood their horses side by side, facing his excellency.

"Wait! There is a better way!" their leader cried.

"Ha!" screeched the governor. "I understand. Here we have the young men of all the noble families in the southland. They have come to show their loyalty by taking this Curse of Capistrano. I thank you, caballeros. Yet it is not my wish to have any of you slain by this fellow. He is not worthy your blades, señores. Do you ride to one side and lend the strength of your presence, and let my troopers deal with the rogue.

Again I thank you for this show of loyalty, for this demonstration that you stand for law and order and all it means, for constituted authority—"

"Peace!" their leader cried. "Your excellency, we represent power in this section, do we not?"

"You do, caballeros," the governor said.

"Our families say who shall rule, what laws shall be just, do they not?"

"They have great influence," the governor said.

"You would not care to stand alone against us?"

"Most assuredly not!" his excellency cried. "But I pray you, let the troopers get this fellow. It is not seemly that a caballero should suffer wound or death from his blade."

"It is to be regretted that you do not understand."

"Understand?" queried the governor, in a questioning tone, glancing up and down the line of mounted men.

"We have taken counsel with ourselves, excellency. We know our strength and power, and we have decided upon certain things. There have been things done that we cannot countenance.

"The frailes of the missions have been despoiled by officials. Natives have been treated worse than dogs. Even men of noble blood have been robbed because they have not been friendly to the ruling powers."

"Caballero—"

"Peace, excellency, until I have done. This thing came to a crisis when a hidalgo and his wife and daughter were thrown into a cárcel by your orders. Such a thing cannot be countenanced, excellency, and so we have banded ourselves together, and here we take a hand. Be it known that we ourselves rode with this Señor Zorro when he invaded the cárcel and rescued the prisoners, that we carried Don Carlos and the Doña Catalina to places of safety, and that we have pledged our words and honors and blades that they shall not be persecuted more."

"I would say—"

"Silence, until I have done! We stand together, and the strength of our united families is behind us. Call upon your soldiers to attack us, if you dare! Every man of noble blood up and down the length of El Camino Real would flock to our defense, would unseat you from your office, would see you humbled. We await your answer, excellency."

"What—what would you?" his excellency gasped.

"First, proper consideration for Don Carlos Pulido and his family. No cárcel for them. If you have the courage to try them for treason, be sure that we will be on hand at the trial, and deal with any man who gives perjured testimony, and with any magistrado who does not conduct himself properly. We are determined, excellency."

"Perhaps I was hasty in the matter, but I was led to believe certain things," the governor said. "I grant you your wish. One side now, caballeros, while my men get at this rogue in the tavern."

"We are not done," their leader said. "We have things to say regarding this Señor Zorro. What has he done—actually—excellency? Is he guilty of any treason? He has robbed no man except those who robbed the defenseless first. He has whipped a few unjust persons. He has taken sides with the persecuted, for which we honor him. To do such a thing, he took his life in his own hands. He successfully evaded your soldiers. He resented insults, as any man has the right to do."

"What would you?"

"A complete pardon, here and now, for this man known as Señor Zorro!"

"Never!" the governor cried. "He has affronted me personally. He shall die the death!" He turned around and saw Don Alejandro Vega standing near him. "Don Alejandro, you are the most influential man in this south country," he said. "You are the one man against whom even the governor dare not stand. You are a man of justice. Tell these young caballeros that what they wish cannot be granted. Bid them retire to their homes, and this show of treason will be forgotten."

"I stand behind them!" Don Alejandro thundered.

"You—you stand behind them?"

"I do, your excellency! I echo every word they have spoken in your presence. Persecution must cease. Grant their requests, see that your officials do right hereafter, return to San Francisco de Asis, and I take my oath that there shall be no treason in this southland.

"I shall see to it myself. But oppose them, excellency, and I shall take sides against you, see you driven from office and ruined, and your foul parasites with you."

"This terrible, willful southland!" the governor cried.

"Your answer?" Don Alejandro demanded.

"I can do nothing but agree," the governor said. "But there is one thing—"

"Well!"

"I spare the man's life if he surrenders, but he must stand trial for the murder of Captain Ramón."

"Murder?" queried the leader of the caballeros, "It was a duel between gentlemen, excellency. Señor Zorro resented an insult on the part of the comandante to the señorita."

"Ha! But Ramón was a caballero—"

"And so is this Señor Zorro. He told us as much, and we believe him, for there was no falsehood in his voice. So it was a duel, excellency, and between gentlemen, according to the code, and Captain Ramón was unfortunate that he was not a better man with a blade. That is understood? Your answer."

"I agree," the governor said weakly. "I pardon him, and I go home to San Francisco de Asis, and persecution ceases in this locality. But I hold Don Alejandro to his promise—that there be no treason against me here if I do these things."

"I have given my word," Don Alejandro said.

The caballeros shrieked their happiness and dismounted. They drove the soldiers away from the door, Sergeant Gonzales growling into his mustache because here was a reward gone glimmering again.

"Within there, Señor Zorro!" one cried. "Have you heard?"

"I have heard, caballero!"

"Open the door and come out amongst us—a free man!"

There was a moment's hesitation, and then the battered door was unbarred and opened, and Señor Zorro stepped out with the señorita on his arm. He stopped just in front of the door, removed his sombrero and bowed low before them.

"A good day to you, caballeros!" he cried. "Sergeant, I regret that you have missed the reward, but I shall see that the amount is placed to the credit of you and your men with the landlord of the tavern."

"By the saints, he is a caballero!" Gonzales cried.

"Unmask, man!" cried the governor. "I would see the features of the person who has fooled my troopers, has gained caballeros to his banner, and has forced me to make a compromise."

"I fear that you will be disappointed when you see my poor features," Señor Zorro replied. "Do you expect me to look like Satan? Or can it be possible, on the other hand, that you believe I have an angelic countenance?"

He chuckled, glanced down at the Señorita Lolita, and then put up a hand and tore off his mask.

A chorus of gasps answered the motion, an explosive oath or two from the soldiers, cries of delight from the caballeros, and a screech of mingled pride and joy from one old hidalgo.

"Don Diego, my son—*my son!*"

And the man before them seemed to droop suddenly in the shoulders, and sighed, and spoke in a languid voice.

"These be turbulent times. Can a man never meditate on music and the poets?"

And Don Diego Vega, the Curse of Capistrano, was clasped for a moment in his father's arms.

Chapter 39
"Meal Mush and Goat's Milk!"

THEY crowded forward—troopers, natives, caballeros, surrounding Don Diego Vega and the Señorita who clutched at his arm and looked up at him from proud and glistening eyes.

"Explain! Explain!" they cried.

"It began ten years ago, when I was but a lad of fifteen," he said. "I heard tales of persecution. I saw my friends, the frailes, annoyed and robbed. I saw soldiers beat an old native who was my friend. And then I determined to play this game.

"It would be a difficult game to play, I knew. So I pretended to have small interest in life, so that men never would connect my name with that of the highwayman I expected to become. In secret, I practiced horsemanship and learned how to handle a blade—"

"By the saints, he did," Sergeant Gonzales growled.

"One half of me was the languid Don Diego you all knew, and the other half was the Curse of Capistrano I hoped one day to be. And then the time came, and my work began.

"It is a peculiar thing to explain, señores. The moment I donned cloak and mask, the Don Diego part of me fell away. My body straightened, new blood seemed to course through my veins, my voice grew strong and firm, fire came to me! And the moment I removed cloak and mask I was the languid Don Diego again. Is it not a peculiar thing?

"I had made friends with this great Sergeant Gonzales, and for a purpose."

"Ha! I guess the purpose, caballeros!" Gonzales cried. "You tired whenever this Señor Zorro was mentioned, and did not wish to hear of violence and bloodshed, but always you asked me in what direction I was going with my troopers—and you went in the other direction and did your confounded work."

"You are an excellent guesser," said Don Diego, laughing, as did the others about him. "I even crossed blades with you, so you would not guess I was Señor Zorro. You remember the rainy night at the tavern? I listened to your boasts, went out and donned mask and cloak, came in and fought you, escaped, took off mask and cloak, and returned to jest with you."

"Ha!"

"I visited the Pulido hacienda as Don Diego and a short time later returned as Señor Zorro and held speech with the señorita here. You almost had me, sergeant, that night at Fray Felipe's—the first night, I mean."

"Ha! You told me there that you had not seen Señor Zorro."

"Nor had I. The fray does not keep a mirror, thinking that it makes for vanity. The other things were not difficult, of course. You can easily understand how, as Señor Zorro, I happened to be at my own house in town when the comandante insulted the señorita.

"And the señorita must forgive me the deception. I courted her as Don Diego, and she would have none of me. Then I tried it as Señor Zorro, and the saints were kind, and she gave me her love.

"Perhaps there was some method in that, also. For she turned from the wealth of Don Diego Vega to the man she loved, though she deemed him, then, an outcast and outlaw.

"She has showed me her true heart, and I am rejoiced at it. Your excellency, this señorita is to become my wife, and I take it you will think twice before you will annoy her family further."

His excellency threw out his hands in a gesture of resignation.

"It was difficult to fool you all, but it has been done," Don Diego continued. "Only years of practice allowed me to accomplish it. And now Señor Zorro shall ride no more, for there will be no need, and moreover a married man should take some care of his life."

"And what man do I wed?" the Señorita Lolita asked, blushing because she spoke the words where all could hear.

"What man do you love?"

"I had fancied that I loved Señor Zorro, but it comes to me now that I love the both of them," she said. "Is it not shameless? But I would rather have you Señor Zorro than the old Don Diego I knew."

"We shall endeavor to establish a golden mean," he replied, laughing again. "I shall drop the old languid ways and change gradually into the man you would have me. People will say that marriage made a man of me."

He stooped and kissed her there before them all.

"Meal mush and goat's milk!" swore Sergeant Gonzales.

Zorro Saves a Friend

*The keen rapier and quick wit of the masked outlaw
Zorro were legend in Spanish California—
and there was need for them now!*

CHAPTER I
A Pirate Drops A Hint

EMERGING from his father's pretentious town house, Don Diego Vega stood for a moment on the stoop, dainty scented handkerchief brushing his nostrils, his left hand resting on the jeweled hilt of his rapier.

The siesta hour was at an end, the cool breeze was starting to drift in from the distant sea, and the shadows were lengthening and pointing toward the east in the little plaza of the pueblo of Reina de Los Angeles.

Persons of quality were coming forth, dressed in their best finery, to promenade and greet one another, to visit from house to house, purchase wares from the merchants, gossip and chat, frolic and flirt and mayhap quarrel a bit.

Young caballeros wandered toward the inn for a mug of spiced wine and a fling at cards or dice. Dainty señoritas tripped along, each with a grim duenna at heel. Proud hidalgos strutted. Robed Franciscans went leisurely about their serious business of mending bodies and souls. Natives, both neophyte and gentile, ran errands, or stretched in the dust and sand on the shady sides of adobe huts, to drowse and dream, perhaps to tell tall tales of that new and astonishing young outlaw who called himself Señor Zorro, and robbed the rich and tyrannical to befriend such as themselves.

Don Diego Vega sighed and began his stroll. Something of a dandy was this Don Diego Vega, too quiet by far to please his impetuous father, too lacking in fire and spirit. He disliked the usual pursuits of the other young bloods. He did not indulge much in strong drink, did not play much at dice or cards, seldom indulged in a quarrel, never strummed a guitar beneath a window, and refused to mount the fiery stallion his father had purchased for him and race with others out to some hacienda for a day and night of frolic; then back through the misty dawn. He even perused the works of poets!

Yet all made obeisance to Don Diego Vega as he passed, for his father was a powerful man who could not be affronted with impunity, and Don Diego himself had personal qualities which endeared him to many, despite his disinclination to be a man of intense action.

Don Diego appeared to be almost half asleep this day as he sauntered along, seeking the shady spots, his scented handkerchief at his nostrils, saluting those he passed but not loitering for conversation. Natives bowed before him and backed out of his path, and for some strange reason looked after him with expressions of adoration in their usually dull faces.

Don Diego seemed to have no particular objective this day, but to be taking the air aimlessly. He kept to the west side of the plaza, as though making his way leisurely around it and toward the inn. But his course brought him past the adobe hut wherein lived a certain Bardoso, a reformed and retired pirate.

This Bardoso, a man with only one good eye—he having lost the other in some brawl on the high seas years before—sat on a bench on the shady side of his hut, a jug of wine at his side, and a cutlass strapped to his thigh.

He was a thing to terrify children, this Bardoso, regarding whom many bloody tales had been told, some of them fact and a great many fiction. He had unusual visitors at times—men who traveled, mostly by night, up and down El Camino Real, as they called the highway which connected the Franciscan missions in a long chain.

With his one good eye this Bardoso beheld the approach of Don Diego Vega, straightened himself somewhat on the bench, and seemed to be collecting his courage. Don Diego often stopped for a word with him, which was queer for a man loving peaceful pursuits. It was the attraction of opposites, said the Franciscans and other educated folk.

Bardoso got to his feet and bowed from the waist, an act which caused him to expel his breath in a peculiar, choking grunt, for he was somewhat inclined to fat around his middle, as a result of much food and little exercise.

"A good day to you, Bardoso!" Don Diego greeted, waving his hand languidly. Then he would have passed on, but Bardoso's words halted him.

"It is truly an excellent day, Don Diego Vega," Bardoso replied. "The high fog has tempered the burning rays of the sun, and there is a fresh breeze. A beautiful day, indeed, upon which there should be no evil. Yet evil we have, Don Diego, to mar the splendor of this perfect weather."

"How is this?" Don Diego asked, arching his brows in question. "You perhaps have received news of some atrocity? There is new trouble in the land or on the sea?"

"The thing at which I have hinted is here at home, Don Diego—here in Reina de Los Angeles, under our very noses," Bardoso replied.

"These are, indeed, turbulent times." Don Diego sighed, and brushed his scented handkerchief across his nostrils again, at which motion Bardoso winced, knowing that perhaps he did not smell any too sweet.

"It is a thing, Don Diego, in which you may be interested personally," Bardoso went on to say. "It has to do with one of your friends."

"What is this?" Don Diego turned toward the erstwhile pirate and betrayed a sudden interest.

"If the señor will be gracious enough to allow me to explain—"

"Do so, good Bardoso. But shorten your words as much as possible."

BARDOSO bowed low, and grunted again. "Lately come to the pueblo," he said, "is a certain Marcos Lopez, a man of fine raiment and furtive eyes. He apes the caballero, but his soul is that of scum."

"I have noted him."

"He is a professional gambler, that one, and each afternoon and evening holds his game at the inn or in the big barracks room at the presidio. He is adept alike with cards and dice."

"It does not interest me," Don Diego said. "There are many such traveling up and down El Camino Real, from San Francisco de Asis to San Diego de Alcala. They are pests indeed, but serve to aid some men to while away dull hours."

"At the expense of their purses."

"Quite true! But a man is expected to pay for his pleasure, is he not?"

"Any man of real spirit, Don Diego, is inclined to take a fling at the gods of chance on occasion, to try his fortune. But, if there is no chance?"

"What is this you say?"

"The man is a cheat, señor—a professional cheat. I know of him, Don Diego. He can make the cards and dice do as he wills. And, behind his presence here in Reina de Los Regales there also is a plot."

"Get to the meat of it!" Don Diego begged.

"The air is warm, and I am overdue now for a cup of chilled

wine. Moreover, there is dust in the air."

"It is well known—is it not?—that his excellency, the Governor, is jealous of this Southland and the foremost men in it. The hidalgos do not bow to him enough to please his excellency. They are of better blood, which irks him."

"Quite true," Don Diego admitted. "His excellency is but a scurvy politician."

"And he can fight his betters only through underhand methods, Don Diego. Let us suppose, then, that he sends a clever gambling cheat this way. This cheat, this Marcos Lopez, ruined a dozen good men in the vicinity of Santa Barbara. He is trying to ruin some here, being under orders to do so. Do you not comprehend, señor? He gets a young caballero in his cups, gets him to play. The caballero loses heavily–and a debt of honor always must be satisfied."

"Again, true," said Don Diego.

"He is in league with Capitán Torello, the comandante of the presidio, who is, quite naturally, the Governor's man."

"This is a serious accusation you make, Bardoso."

"But I know the truth of these things, señor, else I'd not bother your ears with them. I have friends who bring me reliable information."

"And why bother my ears with it at all?" Don Diego wished to know. "I have not diced with the fellow, nor flipped a card with him."

"You perhaps are too wise to do so, Don Diego—but some others are not. Others are not so well controlled as you when it comes to games of chance. With some men, it is like a fever in the veins. I speak to you thus because of your friend."

"I have many friends."

"But this is a very special friend of yours, Don Diego; one unto you almost as a blood brother. I am speaking of Don Carlos Cassara. Have you not noticed that lately he wears a worried look?"

"I have," Don Diego replied, sudden concern in his face. "I

had thought it a bit of stomach trouble, because of too much rich food and wine."

"Purse trouble, Don Diego. Remorse. The pain that afflicts a man when he realizes that he has made a fool of himself. The agony of a man trapped and unable to escape."

"Speak more clearly."

"This Marcos Lopez has cheated him, mulcted him, kept him playing on in a hopeless endeavor to regain his losses," Bardoso explained.

"The old folly of tossing good gold after bad," Don Diego observed.

"Your friend, Don Carlos Cassara, who lately inherited his father's estate, is on the verge of ruin. It is being talked about. He will be taking his own life, as a matter of honor—"

"Dios!" Don Diego breathed.

"Your pardon for speaking to you of such things, Don Diego, but I thought you should know."

"I thank you, Bardoso. You did right to so inform me. But what can be done in the matter? Can I, Don Diego Vega, soil my hands or my blade by use on such scum as this Marcos Lopez?"

"Possibly Don Diego Vega cannot," Bardoso admitted, almost closing his good eye. "But Señor Zorro can!"

CHAPTER II
Certain Plans Are Made

DON DIEGO Vega was about to brush his handkerchief across his nostrils again as Bardoso spoke, but his hand stopped abruptly half way to his face. Into that face came a queer expression, and the eyes opened wider, and Don Diego drew in his breath sharply. But immediately he was master of himself again.

"Señor Zorro?" he questioned. "Ah, yes! He is the rogue lately come to these parts, whom men call the Curse of Capistrano; who puts a mask over his face and rides abroad on a big black horse."

"And rights the wrongs of the oppressed," Bardoso added. "Defends the natives against cruel masters. Whips those who abuse the robed Franciscans. Takes his blade and carves the letter Z on the faces of rogues he encounters, that all men may know he has met and punished them. Señor Zorro–The Fox– may he live long and prosper!"

"You appear to admire the fellow," Don Diego said, smiling slightly.

"He is a man." Bardoso replied, "though there be some who seem to doubt it. A man after my own heart!" The reformed and retired pirate stepped a bit closer, but not on the windward side, and lowered his voice as he continued: "Some things are known to me, Don Diego. Jose, the chief of the Cocopahs, is my friend and brother. What secrets I hold in my breast, hot irons could not tear out of me."

"I thank you, good Bardoso."

"Regarding this Marcos Lopez, this card cheat, things are as I have told you. He was sent here by the Governor, to ruin young caballeros and so shame their families. And Capitán Torello, of the presidio, aids and abets him. Was it not Capitán Torello who introduced him around?"

"I believe so," Don Diego said.

"And does not the rogue conduct his crooked game in the barracks room at times?"

"So you say. But I am more interested in the affairs of my friend, Don Carlos Cassara. He has told me nothing of this."

"Perhaps he is too proud to do so," Bardoso replied. "Some men do not like to speak of their follies. This Marcos Lopez has bills of honor against Don Carlos for large sums, all won through cheating. The rogue cannot play an honest game. It has been in my mind to carve him with my cutlass, but I have no chance at him. Such as I cannot dice with him, accuse him of cheating, grow angry and pick a quarrel that would end in his undoing. He will have none of me. I offend his nostrils."

"No doubt," Don Diego agreed.

"As to this Señor Zorro—he should be warned also. It is my understanding that Capitán Torello believes he knows the identity of the man. He and his soldiers watch, to trap him. The capitán thinks that Señor Zorro is a young man of quality seeking adventure. And were he to be caught and hanged, another proud family of the Southland would be humbled, and the Governor have cause for rejoicing."

Don Diego smiled a bit. "Perhaps Señor Zorro knows that he is being watched," he said. "Have done, Bardoso! Your many words tire me. I must be on my way. Señor a' Dios!"

Bardoso bowed, and returned to his bench in the shade beside the adobe hut, and reached for his wine jug. His one good eye was sparkling as he lifted the jug and took a deep drink. Bardoso could read men after a fashion.

THE idle Don Diego Vega continued his tour of the plaza, bowing to the dainty señoritas and their mothers, waving a hand languidly at men he knew. He neared the inn, into which he seldom ventured. But upon this particular afternoon he decided to honor the establishment with his presence.

From the blazing sun of the plaza, he stepped into the cool, semi-dark interior of the inn, into a big, low-ceilinged room redolent with odors of food and drink. The fat landlord hurried forward, smirking and bowing, gesturing toward a bench beside a table.

But Don Diego waved the landlord aside, and went on down the room, past benches where merchants and soldiers, caballeros and rogues, strangers and townsmen ate and drank, saluting some and ignoring others.

Marcos Lopez had a gaming table beneath a window at the far end of the room. Men were dicing there now, and Don Carlos Cassara was one. That Don Carlos was losing, there could be little doubt. His pale face, and eyes too bright, told the story of strain and intense excitement.

The eyes of Marcos Lopez glowed when he saw Don Diego Vega approach. Here was a proper young blood to get into the game! He had wealth, and position unquestioned. And Capitán Torello had whispered to the gambler some suspicions regarding him. Here was a big fish for the net!

"Make way, there, for Don Diego Vega!" Lopez commanded. He bowed and smiled. "Welcome to my poor game, Don Diego. You'll try your fortune with the dice?"

Don Diego looked at him, through him, without speaking, and the face of Marcos Lopez grew red with wrath. Don Diego, it appeared, did not intend to play, but had come into the inn to find his friend. He slapped Don Carlos familiarly on the shoulder, and drew him aside, and the game was continued with the others playing.

Beside the wall in the corner they stood side by side, the two young caballeros, garbed in the finery of the hour. About twenty-five they were, scions of noble families, proud and haughty, secure in the positions they held in the world.

"How goes it with you, my friend?" Don Diego asked.

"As usual."

"That remark may have one of several meanings. We have not seen much of you lately," Don Diego rebuked. "You are looking tired and ill. Suppose we take horse tomorrow, and ride out to my father's hacienda. The country air will benefit you."

"Though it would please me, I cannot," Don Carlos replied. "There are things I must do."

"It is a delicate subject, and I hesitate to speak of it even to you, my friend," Don Diego said. "But—is it possible that you have been losing heavily to this fellow?"

"It is true that the dice and cards both have been running against me."

"A man may take his chances with dice and cards," Don Diego observed, "when they are handled fairly. I have it, on good authority, he is a cheat."

"A cheat? Capitán Torello himself introduced him, vouched for him."

"Quite true!" Don Diego admitted. "There is also a meaning behind that, I understand. They are cousins in intrigue. The man would ruin you and shame your family–as he ruined and shamed men in Santa Barbara, much to the delight of the Governor."

"There is a plot to do so? Then, indeed, I am ruined," Don Carlos declared. "The man holds my promises to pay. I have been trying to win them back, and have been only losing more. There is but one way out–the caballero's way."

"The coward's way," Don Diego corrected. "Let us have no thought of that! Give me your promise!"

"I cannot!"

"At least, promise me this—that you'll dice no more, play at cards no more, and do nothing to hurt yourself until this time tomorrow."

"And what will that avail, my friend? The fever is upon me. If you are thinking of paying my debts–"

"Would that not be an act of friendship?"

"I could not allow it, Don Diego, could not endure it. To take such a sum from you–"

"Easy!" Don Diego cautioned. "You need not humble your pride. Did I speak of money? There are several ways of paying debts, my friend. Your promise?"

"You have it!" Don Carlos Cassara bowed.

"I thank you," Don Diego said. "Now you are to leave the inn, as though in answer to some message I brought. And keep away from Marcos Lopez's table tonight."

"You are leaving with me?"

"I watch the game for a time," Don Diego said. "Perhaps I shall play for a moment."

"He will get you in his clutches."

"Have no fear of that," Don Diego said. "Get you gone!"

DON Carlos hurried from the inn, as though to keep an appointment, and Don Diego drifted back to the gaming table and watched the play. And presently he took a money pouch from his girdle, and extracted a handful of coins from it, at which the eyes of Marcos Lopez sparkled. Only get him started, Lopez thought! The fever soon would claim him.

Don Diego played for the space of half an hour, first with the dice and then with the cards, winning at times and losing at other times, Marcos Lopez allowing him to keep about even in an effort to whet his interest.

Don Diego watched carefully, and saw what he had expected to see. Marcos Lopez could do with cards or dice as he willed. There was no doubt that the fellow was a cheat.

"Perhaps a larger stake some time?" Don Diego suggested.

"At your pleasure, Don Diego." Marcos Lopez bowed courteously. "I hold my game this evening at the presidio. Come you there, if it please you."

"At the presidio?" Don Diego lifted his brows. "You are expecting me to play with common soldiers?"

"Not so, Señor. Capitán Torello is my good friend. He loves to play. And there undoubtedly will be some others, gentlemen of blood and station."

"Perhaps," Don Diego said.

He brushed his handkerchief across nostrils and went forth into the plaza again, languidly, and once outside he used the handkerchief to rub his hands briskly, as though rubbing away some sort of stain. For he had handled the same dice and cards that this Marcos Lopez had handled.

At the presidio! In the midst of Capitán Torello's troopers! There would be a rare place for Señor Zorro to strike!

Don Diego strolled around the border of the plaza and toward his home. He walked slowly, with head proudly erect, looking into the face of the setting sun, every inch a caballero.

Near one of the stores loitered a group of natives, one of them much taller and larger than the rest. This was José, the chief of the Cocopahs. All backed away and bowed as Don Diego passed. And Don Diego—careless of him—dropped his handkerchief.

José of the Cocopahs glided forward like a shadow, picked up the dainty handkerchief, ran after Don Diego, half knelt before him, and proffered it.

"Have it for yourself," Don Diego said, waving the man aside. Then, in lower tones: *"Zorro rides tonight!"*

CHAPTER III
Zorro Plays A Trick

THAT night a myriad of stars studded a clear sky, but there was no moon. It was spring, and the natives were courting and mating, and some not natives were doing the same and old men were out walking and looking at the stars and dreaming of the time when they had been young. So one wishing to pass unseen would have to be cautious, since almost every dark corner held a witness.

Don Diego, having dined with his father, retired to his own quarters on the second floor of the casa, and his father went to spend the evening with a friend. Don Diego perused a tome of poetry for a time, and then clapped his hands, and his personal servant entered.

This native was named Bernardo, and he was a jewel of a body servant, for he could hear orders but could not speak, being dumb.

"Zorro rides," Don Diego said.

Bernardo bowed and smiled, and backed out of the room. A moment later Don Diego followed. He went through a passage and up a flight of steps which led to the roof. But he did not go on to the roof, but passed through a panel in the wall, descended another flight of steps, and finally came to a small room beneath the ground.

Bernardo was there. Don Diego divested himself of his

embroidered dressing gown and his other apparel, and dressed as Señor Zorro always dressed, putting on thin black gloves and his black mask as a finishing touch. From a peg in the wall he took down the sword of Zorro, an excellent blade, but a bit heavier than a rapier, and buckled it on.

Then Bernardo went ahead through a narrow passage and opened a door, and Señor Zorro—Don Diego Vega no longer—passed forth into the night, emerging near the well in the patio.

He wrapped his cloak around him, up to his ears, after the manner of some man wishing to avoid recognition as he went to keep tryst. Keeping in the deeper shadows as much as possible, he crept away from the house, got behind the huts of the servants, and fared forth.

At the edge of the pueblo there was a depression in the earth, made years ago by a torrential rain, around which brush grew—a spot avoided by all as worthless. Señor Zorro crept to the edge and gave a peculiar whistle, so low that it could not be heard more than a score of feet away.

It was answered, and José of the Cocopahs crept out of the darkness and to his side.

"The horse is ready?" Zorro asked.

"Ready, master."

"Attend me, while I give you orders," Zorro instructed.

He spoke rapidly and at length. Then he crawled from the depression, wrapped his cloak around him again, and walked back toward the buildings of the pueblo. Jose, on a horse which was not that of Señor Zorro, followed cautiously at a distance.

BY A circuitous route, Zorro approached the inn. On the dark side of the building he went forward until he was against the wall, and could creep along it to the nearest open window. Beneath the window he crouched and listened, ascertaining the number and quality of those inside.

Then he went to the rear of the building, where the door

of the kitchen stood open, with odors of roasting meat wafting forth into the night air to agonize the stomachs of such natives as had not eaten recently.

Two natives were there, working among the pots and pans, but Zorro wished nothing with them. He waited until the fat landlord came into the kitchen, until he was busy berating one of the servants for some fault, and then slipped inside, and got between the landlord and the door of the big room, there to stand with his arms folded across his chest, and a pistol held in his right hand.

The fat landlord turned, in time, and saw him, and turned gray and gasped. One of the natives gave a screech of fear, and the other seemed stricken dumb.

"Let there be no noise!" Zorro commanded, using a deep monotone when he spoke. "Landlord, come you here to me! The men will remain as they are."

The servants cringed against the wall, yet they did not seem to be much afraid, knowing that Señor Zorro always had befriended them. The quaking landlord, wringing his hands, hobbled forward as though his legs scarcely would carry him.

"You know me?" Zorro asked.

"If you are a highwayman—"

"I am Zorro!"

"Ah!" The fat landlord dropped to his knees and lifted his hands in earnest supplication. "I have done nothing, good Señor Zorro. Do not mark me with your blade. Do not put bullet through my body."

"Silence your tongue!" Zorro ordered. "Obey me, and you have nothing to fear."

"Command me, Señor Zorro!"

"This Marcos Lopez, the gambler, lives in a room off your patio, does he not?"

"It is so, Señor."

"Conduct me to his room. Be cautious about it. If you try to play me false, one thrust of my blade, one shot from this pistol—"

"It shall be as you wish, Señor Zorro."

"And quickly!" Zorro added, turning toward the door.

The landlord opened the door, and they went into the patio, where the shadows were deep and there was no light save one tallow pot which only served to cast uncertain streaks of illumination. Past the bubbling fountain they went, and toward the end of the patio, and there the landlord stopped in front of a door.

"Open it, and enter," Zorro said.

They went inside, and at Zorro's order the landlord lighted a candle. The room was small, and contained little beyond a cot and night coverings. There was a small traveling box of wood, which was unfastened.

Zorro lifted the lid of the box and examined the contents, clothing for the greater part. He examined the cot and the coverings, tapped around the walls, while the landlord stood in the doorway and shivered, and wondered whether Zorro would blame him if somebody happened into the patio and discovered his presence.

Zorro had not found what he sought. He extinguished the candle and stood beside the landlord outside the door of the room.

"Where does this Marcos Lopez keep his papers?" Zorro asked.

"He has a pouch, señor, which he carries attached to his belt. It is a pouch of fine leather–"

"Enough! I care not of what it is made. Its contents are my chief concern. Lead the way back into the inn."

"Would you crave a portion of roast mutton, beef, or a cup of my choicest wine, Señor Zorro?"

"I crave your silence only—and do not mention my name aloud again," Zorro told him.

"Some day, I shall punish you, when I get around to it. To men in their cups, you sell wine mixed with water, and charge them for the real article. Your nimble fingers often make mistakes when you are changing coins. You purchase mutton stolen by native thieves from haciendas—"

"Have mercy, señor! I shall mend my ways."

"See that you do so. That were easier than mending a slit in your fat belly," Zorro said. "Into the inn!"

THEY went into the kitchen, where the affrighted servants were still cringing against the walls.

"On with your work!" Zorro commanded them. And then, to the landlord: "We go into the big room, and you will serve me wine."

"Señor! A dozen men are there, including Sergeant Pedro Gonzales of the soldiery."

"I know it. I listened at a window," Zorro admitted. "Do as I tell you. Open the door!"

The landlord opened the door, and Zorro strode into the dimly lighted room and sat on a bench beside one of the tables. The frantic landlord put a cup of wine before him, and he drank.

Sergeant Pedro Gonzales was sprawled on a bench, boasting as usual. He did not notice the presence of Zorro, nor did any of the others. Some were listening to the wild tales of the sergeant, and others were playing cards at a table on the far side of the room, and still others were half stupefied with the wine they had taken.

Zorro quaffed his wine, while the landlord stood by ready to fill the cup again. But Zorro waved him aside, got to his feet, hurled the wine cup across the room to strike beside the bench whereon Sergeant Gonzales sat, and laughed.

Every man in the room turned his way. Every man lurched to his feet and started forward.

"It is a masked highwayman!" somebody shouted.

"It is Zorro!" another cried.

"At him!" Gonzales bellowed, whipping out his blade. "Let

us take him! There is a reward—"

One of the troopers nearest the door bolted through it and into the plaza, shouting that Zorro was at the inn, and rushing on toward the presidio with this intelligence. Others took up the cry, until it rang around the plaza and startled half the town.

Señor Zorro darted forward, still laughing, his eyes gleaming through the holes in the mask he wore. His blade crashed against that of the big sergeant, there was a quick exchange, and Gonzales found himself disarmed and his sword flying through the air to clatter to the floor.

"Back!" Zorro cried. And then he darted through the kitchen door, and was gone.

"After him! Catch me this rogue!" Gonzales bellowed. "I have said it—there is a rich reward!"

Out into the night they poured. Down the hill from the presidio came some of the troopers on their horses. Gonzales got into his own saddle, and began bellowing commands.

Away from the inn, a big black horse rushed through the night, and the eager troopers pursued.

But they pursued José of the Cocopahs, while Señor Zorro, having thus drawn the troopers away, hurried through the shadows to the depression in the earth where his own horse was waiting.

CHAPTER IV
Zorro Marks His Man

NOT far from the back wall of the presidio was a clump of stunted trees, and Señor Zorro reached this without discovery, dismounted, and tethered his horse.

From the far distance came sounds which told where the troopers rode in vain pursuit, and he could hear the hoarse bellowing of Sergeant Gonzales as he led them.

Leaving the trees, Zorro crept toward the building. In front of it a light burned, and several soldiers were there, looking down toward the plaza and wishing that they had been in the chase instead of here on guard.

Zorro had no intention of going to the front. He went along a wall, keeping in the deep shadows, and came to an open window through which light streamed. Through that window also came men's voices.

Crouching against the wall just outside the streak of light, Señor Zorro listened intently. Capitán Torello was there, and also Marcos Lopez, and two young caballeros Zorro knew well, were talking with them.

"This Zorro is a pest, but one day we shall have him," the capitán was saying. "I have a clue as to his identity. When he is caught he shall swing from the end of a rope for the world to see, and no doubt some persons will be surprised. For there will be no mask on his face then."

"What did he do at the inn?" one asked.

"According to the report just brought me, the fellow showed himself there, but took flight when he found my big sergeant, Gonzales, ready to do battle with him. They pursue him now, and may bring him in."

"He has interrupted our game," Marcos Lopez remarked.

"Let us play on," Capitán Torello suggested. "A highway man should not be allowed to interfere with the pleasure of gentlemen."

Señor Zorro almost chuckled at what he heard. He went back along the wall and came to a door which was without bar on the inside, due to somebody's carelessness. Through this door he entered the building, finding himself in a sort of storeroom filled with casks and tubs of supplies for the soldiery.

For a short time he listened at the wall, and then he opened another door and slipped into a corridor and along it to the entrance of the room wherein they played at cards. He could see the four around the table, in the center of which a candelabrum furnished light.

Marcos Lopez was dealing, and between him and the capitán flashed a look of understanding that Señor Zorro did not miss. The two caballeros were being victimized. They were far gone in their cups, which the capitán kept well filled. Too befuddled were they to pay close attention to the dealing.

"Never have I seen this Señor Zorro," Capitán Torello was saying. "He avoids me and my troopers. He always strikes where we are not."

"And what gains he by his work, if he does not steal?" Marcos Lopez asked.

" 'Tis the adventure he seeks," the capitán declared. "To befriend the oppressed, he gives out. But he upsets order, hence his excellency has offered a reward. When first I set my eyes on this Señor Zorro, I claim it!"

"You have your opportunity, señor!" rang out a voice at the door.

ZORRO had slipped inside the room, closed the door behind him, put the heavy bar up in place. And now he stood before it, menacing them with his pistol. Torello and Marcos Lopez sprang to their feet, and the two caballeros gasped and stared at him, but remained seated.

"Steady, señores!" Zorro warned. "Make no violent move, else somebody dies."

"Zorro!" Torello gasped.

"The same. Are you about to claim the reward, my capitán?"

"For this insolence—" Torello began.

"Spare me your threats," Zorro snapped in interruption. "You are but a monkey in uniform, a worthy satellite for a licentious Governor."

"Treason!" Torello cried.

"Make the most of it," Zorro told him.

"What do you do here? Have you come to assassinate us?" the capitán asked.

"I am no assassin," Zorro said. "You recently remarked that I crave adventure. What better thrill than to come here, with mask on my face and your troopers near, and have a game of cards and a fling of dice? Seldom do I get into a game. I would try my luck with Señor Lopez."

"You would play with me?" Lopez cried, nervously, licking at his lips as though they suddenly were parched.

"Why not? I am not particular, señor. I have funds with me. It will, perhaps, be a thrill for us both."

One of the caballeros seemed to realize what was happening. "Have at him!" he cried, trying to lurch to his feet, and trying to draw his sword.

"Steady!" Zorro snapped at him. "Sit back against the wall, you two, with your arms folded."

"No thief can tell me—" the other began.

"Silence!" Zorro cried. "You are taking orders from me now. Put your stools against the wall, and sit there and be quiet. You may enjoy the show Capitán Torello, you'll sit beside them. My game is with this Señor Lopez."

"You order around your betters as though they were scum," the capitán complained. "Or, perhaps they are not your betters, eh?"

"No man is!"

"Perhaps your own blood is blue—" the capitán hinted.

"No man yet has been able to let out enough that such may be ascertained."

Capitán Torello retired to the wall, placing a stool beside it and sitting down, urging the caballeros to do the same. The capitán was noticing things, even in the flickering and uncertain light that came from the candelabrum. Behind the left ear of the masked man, and a little down, he saw a sizable wart. He would remember that!

Señor Zorro advanced to the gaming, while the capitán watched every move he made, striving to identify. Lopez had sat down again.

"Why not seize this rogue?" one of the caballeros was asking Torello. "You are a soldier, are you not, señor?"

"Let us wait—and watch," the capitán begged. "Perhaps there is a plan in my mind."

LOPEZ looked across the table. "What sort of game do you wish, señor?" he asked.

Upon the table, Zorro tossed a pouch which clinked as it struck. He waved his left hand toward it, retaining the pistol in his right.

"Count it, and match it," he said.

Lopez opened the pouch, and his eye bulged at what he saw. He counted the gold rapidly.

"I have not this much with me, señor," he said. "I am but a poor man."

"How much can you cover?"

"Perhaps the half of it."

"Cover the half, then," Zorro directed. "And for the other half throw upon the table the leather pouch you wear on your belt."

"This pouch? No gold is in it, señor—only papers."

"I am aware of that," Zorro told him.

"They are promises to pay, señor, and, if you won, you probably would have difficulty collecting."

"Do you expect to have difficulty?" Zorro asked. "I can collect as readily as you. Perhaps I know the contents of the pouch, señor! Perhaps it would give me pleasure to collect the promises to pay, knowing who wrote them for you."

"Ha! An enemy of his, are you?"

"Enough of this prattle!" Zorro said. "Cover my bet, with your gold and the pouch. I am in a fever to play."

Watching him carefully, Marcos Lopez put out gold, and counted it, and made a little pile of it beside Zorro's. Then he tossed the pouch upon the table.

"I wish to be sure of its contents, since I am matching them with gold," Zorro told him. "Expose them."

Lopez opened the pouch and revealed a sheaf of documents, upon some of which Zorro saw the signature of Don Carlos Cassara.

"It is well," he said. "Return them to the pouch, and the gold also, and let us play."

"And what sort of game does the señor desire?" Lopez asked. "The dice, or cards?"

"Cards," Zorro told him. "But—a moment! Attend me, caballeros, as I speak. This man, this Marcos Lopez, is a cheat."

"How is this?" Lopez cried.

"Be quiet!" Zorro warned, lifting the muzzle of the pistol a bit. "And keep your hands flat on the table in front of you. Yes, señor, you are a cheat! You were sent here by the Governor to ruin men. You ruined several near Santa Barbara. You get young caballeros filled with wine, and rob them. You do not know how to play an honest game."

"Prove that, Zorro, and I run him through!" one of the victims cried.

"Stay as you are, señor! This is my affair. When I am done with this fellow, you may have what is left of him. Not only is he a common cheat, but Capitán Torello knows it, and aids him. Like flies to the web of the spider you have drifted—"

"For this—" Torello began, starting to his feet.

But Zorro threatened him with the pistol, and he subsided. Marcos Lopez was pale, nervous, trembling. His eyes bulged, and his lips were quivering.

"Shuffle the pack," Zorro ordered him. "And use caution, señor, as you do so. I know every trick that may be done with cards."

Lopez shuffled, cut, and shuffled again, and put the pack in the middle of the table.

"You will deal me the fifth card, face down," Zorro directed, "and take the tenth for yourself. It will be a quick game of high cards, and a simple one. At it, señor!"

WITH trembling fingers, Lopez slowly counted off the cards, tossed one in front of Zorro, and retained the tenth for himself. Zorro's eyes were glittering at him through the holes in the mask. They seemed to be threatening torture and death. Lopez wondered at the identity of this man, as did Capitán Torello—and the latter was not forgetting the wart behind the ear. He had suspected Don Diego Vega of being Señor Zorro, and never had he noticed whether Don Diego had such a wart. He would make sure when next he saw him.

"Well, señor?" Lopez was saying.

"We have not yet seen our cards. You have dealt, señor, no doubt anticipating that I would say the high card is to win. Such would be the usual game, eh, señor? One moment."

Zorro suddenly whipped out his dagger, it flashed through the light, and the card Lopez had dealt himself was transfixed and so fastened to the table.

"What is this?" Lopez cried.

"We now announce the game, señor," Zorro said. "The high card loses, Señor Gambler." Watching them all, he picked up his own card, made swift glance at it, then flipped it over upon the table, face up.

"We have here an eight," he said. "And what did you deal yourself, señor, under the anticipation that the high card would have merit?"

"Why, I–I do not know, señor, not having looked at it."

"Did I have the time to spend, and the inclination to spend it, I would make another wager that, whatever it is, the card is in excess of an eight. Withdraw my dagger and toss it across the table to me, and then expose the card."

Zorro held his wrist on the edge of the table, so that the muzzle of the pistol covered Lopez's heart.

"You are being unfair—" Torello began.

"Unfair?" Zorro laughed. "And what is this man, I ask you?

Is he not a common cheat? Does he give men a chance for their money? Señor Lopez, expose the card."

Lopez licked at his dry lips again, and again his hand trembled. He withdrew the dagger and tossed it to Zorro, picked up the card slowly and turned it over.

"A knave!" Zorro cried. "As I thought, Señor Cheat. You dealt yourself an excellent card—had the game been the reverse." He got to his feet, gathered up the pouches and stowed them away, and stepped back. "It has been a great game," he added. "It desolates me that I cannot remain and play for a longer time with you. But I fear the capitán's troopers will be returning from their senseless chase, and I have no wish to do battle with them all."

"Then do battle with one—with me," Torello cried.

"This is not my night to deal with you," Zorro said. "That may come later. This is my night to deal with Señor Lopez, the swindler who ruins men. Draw your blade, Lopez!"

NOW it happened that Marcos Lopez fancied himself as a swordsman. His rapier had been removed when the gambling began that evening, and was on the end of the long table. Now he sprang up and back, a bellow of rage rumbling from his throat, and whipped out the blade.

Zorro transferred his pistol to his left hand, and drew with his right, and placed himself on guard.

"You others will remain against the wall," he ordered. "If not, my weapon shall speak. This is to be a fair combat, though Marcos Lopez is not used to fairness."

Then they were at it, with Zorro compelled to glance now and then toward Capitán Torello, to make certain that he did not try a foul attack and rush to the aid of his confederate. And Marcos Lopez found, in the first few seconds of swordplay, that he knew nothing at all of handling a blade as compared to Señor Zorro. There came an instant when he felt a sting on his cheek, felt a trickle of blood run warmly down toward his throat.

"There is the top bar of my mark—the letter Z—señor," Zorro said. "Three times I shall strike, and the letter then will be completed. And all men shall know that you have met me and been punished for some fault."

"Demon!" Lopez cried, and made a furious attack.

Zorro retreated and guarded well while the other's fury expended itself without effect, and then Lopez felt another burning sting on his cheek.

"The slant of the Z," Zorro told him. "But one stroke remains, señor." He continued to talk as he fought. "Then, get you gone from Reina de Los Angeles! Turn your nose north, señor, and follow it back to the Governor!"

Capitán Torello had edged along the wall to the open window, looked out, and saw some of his men returning from the fruitless chase. He bellowed out into the night.

"Gonzales! Troopers! To me! Zorro is here!"

A chorus of cries answered him, and hoofs pounded the hard earth.

Zorro retreated swiftly to the barred door. Torello started toward him.

"Back!" Zorro thundered, lifting the pistol again.

"Throw the gun aside, and try it," Torello begged.

"The odds are too great, señor. I must retire. I cannot fight an army. And I have not finished the Z on your face, Señor Lopez. But that perhaps shall be done before dawn. Get you to the inn, get your belongings, and leave Reina de Los Angeles!"

Zorro unbarred the door, pulled it open, and dashed out into the corridor. Toward the rear of the building he ran, with Torello bellowing orders, and Lopez crying for help, and the two befuddled caballeros joining in.

Led by Sergeant Gonzales, the troopers rushed into the presidio, through it, some returning to mount again.

Zorro sped through the night to the grove of trees, and they saw him and gave chase over the uneven ground. Out of the trees a big horse dashed, a figure stretched along its neck. Once more, the troopers gave chase.

And once more they chased José of the Cocopahs, as he rode wildly and led them away from Señor Zorro, who stood beside his own horse in the grove of stunted trees and watched.

CHAPTER V
Concerning A Wart

ZORRO waited for a time, until the noise of the chase had died away, then got into his saddle and rode by a circuitous route through the darkness and back to the vicinity of the inn. He put his horse once more in the depression, where José later would find him and take him away. Then, afoot, he went toward the inn once more, cautious and alert.

And once more he crouched beneath a window to listen to what was being said inside. Men were talking of Zorro and the chase, some hoping that he would be captured and others that he would get free of the soldiery. Some trooper from the presidio was there already, sure of free wine since he brought news.

"Marcos Lopez, the gambler, has two-thirds of the mark of Zorro on his face," the man related. "This Zorro came into the presidio, and gambled with Lopez, and beat him. Then they fought. He proved Lopez a cheat, 'tis said, and ordered him to leave Reina de Los Angeles."

"It occurs to me that the man had rare good luck with cards and the dice," some caballero put in. "A cheat, is he? Unless he obeys this Zorro's order, we shall deal with him ourselves, scum though he be."

"He is coming to the inn," the trooper continued. "He was washing the blood from his face when I left. And Capitán Torello will be coming with him, to learn if there is any news here. The capitán is hot to catch him, this Zorro."

"He has been hot for it for some time," another remarked, "but there have been no results."

There was a tumult in front of the inn, and Zorro risked standing back and lifting his head and peering through the low window. He saw Marcos Lopez enter through the front door, with Torello at his side.

And he saw his friend, Don Carlos Cassara, sitting at one of the tables with wine cup before him, drinking to excess as he brooded on his folly. He glared at the gambler, but made no move.

"Wine!" Torello was shouting at the fat landlord. "Sit you down here, Lopez. My troopers shall catch this rogue, and you'll see him hanged. A rare spectacle that, eh? And perhaps some will be surprised when they see the face behind the mask."

"If he had not held a pistol—" Lopez said.

"He is a ready man with a blade, that one, and there can be no denying it," the capitán put in. "It is no disgrace to be beaten at swordplay by Zorro. As for the mark on your face–it will heal."

"And leave a scar."

"He did not finish the mark. The scar will be a thing of distinction. You can tell the señoritas that you got it in a duel while defending some fair lady's honor. It will attract attention to you, and mayhap win you preference over others. There is something romantic about a scar on the face."

"This hurts like the devil," Lopez said, as he sat down on a bench and reached for the mug of wine the landlord placed at his elbow. "How comes it that this Zorro has not been captured before?"

"He is aided by the natives, and sometimes, I believe, by the frailes of the missions. They hide him, no doubt, when he is hard pressed. But we'll have him yet!"

CERTAIN natives at that moment were gathering near the public corral on the side of the plaza, slipping like shadows through the starlit night, acting under José's orders.

José himself had eluded the troopers again, and had

circled to return to the pueblo, where he rode his horse to the neighborhood of the inn. There, another man met him, and carried his commands to those near the corral.

And suddenly there was a tumult, shouts and screeches and groans. Men rushed from the inn to learn the cause of the commotion. But Lopez and Torello remained, as did also Don Carlos Cassara.

Zorro slipped to the kitchen door and through it, waited until the landlord entered for more wine, thrust the man aside, and strode into the big room.

"I have come to finish my letter!" he said.

Marcos Lopez and the capitán sprang to their feet, whipping out their blades. Don Carlos Cassara stirred and looked up with sudden interest.

"The both of you—and no pistol this time," Zorro said. "Let us have an end of it."

Together they advanced upon him, while Zorro took station in a corner of the room near the end of the big fireplace. Then began swift swordplay. Advancing, retreating, lunging, cutting, panting with heavy breath, they fought, while the others rushed across the plaza to where the natives were conducting their disconcerting demonstration.

Capitán Torello thought he saw an opportunity, and went in, and went out again with blood gushing from a wound in his right shoulder. His sword clattered to the floor, and the capitán sank upon one of the benches, groaning with the pain of his wound.

Marcos Lopez, fear suddenly heavy upon him, now that he fought alone, retreated, with Zorro following. The gambler's face was gray save where it was inflamed by the wound Zorro had made at the presidio.

"I finish the letter!" Zorro cried, and his blade darted in like the tongue of a serpent, brought a streak of fire to the gambler's cheek. "'Tis finished! You bear my brand, Señor Cheat!"

Now Lopez became as a madman. He retreated to the wall,

still fighting, almost stumbling over the feet of Don Carlos Cassara, whom he seemed to see for the first time.

"At the rogue, Don Carlos!" he cried. "Get him for me! There is a reward for this highwayman! Get him—and I hand you back all your promises to pay!"

Don Carlos lurched to his feet, his blade coming from its scabbard. What was in his mind, he scarcely knew, save that he yearned to fight. He engaged furiously, as Lopez fell back and gave him room.

Don Carlos was good with the blade, as Señor Zorro knew well, having fenced with him on a thousand occasions. And Zorro knew also that Don Carlos was not himself now, did not realize what he was doing, and certainly did not recognize him.

Zorro retreated in front of the fireplace, backing toward the kitchen door. Torello remained on his bench, Lopez kept in the background, and the fat landlord cringed against a wall, shivering with fright.

And so Zorro, pretending to retreat before the furious onslaught of Don Carlos, got some distance from them, where he could speak without being overheard.

He advanced as though to an attack, and for an instant the swords were locked to the hilt.

"Carlos, my friend! Easy! Do you not know me? It is Diego!" he hissed.

The light of understanding came into the face of Don Carlos Cassara and an appreciation of the situation.

"Lopez lied! I have your papers. I got them from him in the presidio. Fight on—pretend!"

"Disarm me," Carlos whispered, as they clashed again.

AN INSTANT later, Don Carlos's sword went spinning through the air and crashed to the floor in a far corner of the room, and Don Carlos reeled back against the wall. And Señor Zorro laughed loudly and waved his blade at them, and darted into the kitchen.

Capitán Torello was on his feet instantly, shouting. The landlord rushed to the front door and out into the night, screeching for men to come. Marcos Lopez, holding hand to bloody cheek, added his cries to the din. Don Carlos Cassara lurched in front of the kitchen door, to deter any who would pursue.

Sergeant Gonzales and the troopers returned at that instant. Once more, for the third time that night they chased a big horse that was ridden furiously away from the place–chased José of the Cocopahs, who bestrode a piece of horseflesh no trooper's mount could catch. Guns spoke, and bullets whistled, and hoofs pounded, and back through the din came a mocking laugh.

"Gonzales—Sergeant!" Torello roared.

"My capitán!"

"Recall your men. Have the trumpeter sound! Surround the town house of Don Alejandro Vega, Don Diego's father! Quickly, my man!"

"I fail to understand—"

"Obey, do it! I shall be there presently."

In the darkness at the end of the inn, Señor Zorro heard the words. Now a fear came to him, not for himself, but for his father's and family's good name. It was one thing to ride as Zorro and right wrongs. It could be quite another to be captured and tried by court-martial as a highwayman, and possibly hanged. And he knew that he could expect no mercy from the Governor's man.

Torello suspected him, as Zorro had known for some time. He had been watched. And now the capitán was ordering the house surrounded, thinking that Zorro had ridden away, and would be coming back quietly to enter his father's casa.

Through the night Zorro fled afoot, while some of the soldiers already rode furiously toward the house, with big Sergeant Gonzales barking his orders at them.

"Come with me, Lopez ," Torello said, in a low voice. "This may be our great night. If things are as I think, we shall receive rare thanks from his excellency. The son of Don Alejandro Vega, haughty don! Ha! To see him dance at the end of a rope—!"

"A sight that would gladden my eyes. I am marked for life," Lopez said.

" 'Tis the fortunes of war. You are not the only one who bears a wound."

"But yours is in the shoulder, and the scar will be covered by your uniform," Lopez complained.

They went across the plaza toward the Vega house. Half the doors in town were open, and servants ran about, seeking to learn news and take it back to their masters. Señor Zorro was compelled to exercise great caution as he made his way toward his home. The mask remained on his face. His pistol had been tucked into his sash, but his blade was ready in his hand.

DON Carlos Cassara had heard Torello's words, and a great fear for his friend came upon him. Don Diego had done this for him, he knew. And if the house was surrounded, with Diego out of it, and being forced to return wearing the garb of Zorro, there could be but one end.

Don Carlos hurried after the capitán.

"Señor, you go too far," he said. "If you thus affront Don Alejandro Vega, you had best send in your resignation—if you live to write it."

"I do not need you to tell me my duty, señor."

"Somebody should," Don Carlos observed. "A capitán who aids and abets a gambling cheat—"

"What is this?" Torello raged. Then a crafty expression came into his face. "I understand, and it verifies my suspicions," he added. "You are perhaps trying to entice me into a fight, that matters may be delayed. I shall attend to you later, señor! Just now, I have work to do."

The capitán hurried on, shouting to the sergeant, and the troopers rushed toward the Vega house to surround it, dismounting and taking up positions of advantage in the front and rear, and to either side.

Señor Zorro had gone on through the night, avoiding those in the plaza and careful not to be seen. He went to the rear of his father's house, and so to the well in the patio. A moment later, Bernardo had let him in.

"Make haste!" Zorro snapped.

They ascended the steps and came to the hidden room, and there Señor Zorro stripped himself of mask and gloves, blade and costume, while Bernardo helped him. Swiftly, he dressed as he had been earlier in the evening, even to the flowered dressing gown. He wiped the perspiration from his face, straightened his hair, fought to compose his breathing, that it might seem normal.

Up through the house he went, and to his own quarters on the second floor. As he picked up the tome of poetry and sank into an upholstered chair, there was a furious pounding below at the front door.

The pounding was repeated, and there were shouted demands for recognition. Don Alejandro Vega, his white hair bristling with anger, stalked down the wide tiled stairs and to the immense living room, bellowing for servants.

Natives scurried to his side and got orders. Candelabra were lighted. Don Alejandro stalked on to the front door, with a servant at his side.

"Open!" Don Alejandro commanded.

The man took down a metal bar, affixed a chain which would allow the heavy door to come open for the space of a foot, and pulled it back. In the candlelight, Don Alejandro Vega stood there as angry as he was proud.

"What is all this tumult around a gentleman's house?" he demanded, in stentorian tones. "Shall I have my servants whip you, scum?" Then he saw Capitán Torello. "Ha! So you are with them," he added. "Perhaps you can explain, Señor Capitán."

"I would see you alone, Don Alejandro."

"Enter!"

DON Alejandro motioned to the servant, who took down the chain and pulled the door open wider. Torello stepped through, with Marcos Lopez at his heels.

"And who is this?" Don Alejandro asked.

"A friend of mine."

"You have queer friends, capitán. If I mistake not, he is the common gambler who has been playing in the pueblo recently. My house is not for such."

"This is an investigation, Don Alejandro, and he is a witness."

"That entirely alters the situation. Enter!"

The door was closed.

"Now, capitán, I demand an explanation," Don Alejandro said. "And it had best be an excellent one."

"Señor Zorro has been abroad again," Torello said.

"That is none of my affair."

"Perhaps it is, señor. Just now, I wish to see Don Diego, your son. He is home?"

"As far as I know, he is in his room," Don Alejandro said.

"Will you make sure, señor?"

Don Alejandro glared at him, clapped his hands, and another servant entered.

"My compliments to my son, and ask him to be kind enough to visit me here immediately," Don Alejandro said. "Be seated, señores, and I'll have wine served you."

"We have no time for wine, and this is not a visit of courtesy," Capitán Torello said. "Frankly, Don Alejandro, I suspect your son of being this Señor Zorro."

Consternation flooded Don Alejandro's face for an instant, and then he threw back his head and laughed heartily.

"Some men have no brains at all," he observed. "My son?

Playing at being Zorro? I wish to Heaven that were true. My son, it happens, does not care for such things as furious riding, fighting with a blade, indulging in violent sports. The whole world knows how it irks me that this is so. I wish he were this Zorro! My old heart would rejoice, for Zorro has done some wonderful things."

"Nevertheless, I am waiting to see your son," Torello said.

"Here he is, señor!"

Don Diego Vega came slowly down the stairs, trailing his flowered dressing gown, the tome of poetry beneath his left arm, his right hand politely stifling a yawn. He reached the bottom and moved languidly across the big room.

"You wished to see me, my father?" he asked. He glanced at the two others as though he never had seen them before.

"It is I who wished to see you, Don Diego Vega," Capitán Torello said. "May I ask what you have been doing this evening?"

Don Diego's face broke into a soft smile. "For a time, I was on the roof, looking at the stars, and wondering," he replied. "Then I returned to my room, and read the works of the poets. I have here a verse—"

"This soldier thinks that you are Señor Zorro, who rides abroad and slashes with his blade," his father interrupted, laughing again. "Were it not so amusing, I'd have him tossed out of the house like a scurvy knave. Zorro—you? Hah!"

"One moment!" Torello said. "Allow me, Don Diego, to have a look at your neck, just behind the left ear. If there is a large wart there—"

"A wart?" Don Diego said, yawning again.

"That is almost an insult, Señor Capitán. We Vegas do not run to such blemishes as warts."

Nevertheless, Torello looked–and found no wart.

"It is an error, and I apologize," he said, retreating toward the door.

"Another such error, another bit of annoyance, and I shall

take measures against you, señor!" Don Alejandro thundered. "Take yourself out of my house—and take your foul gambler friend with you!"

And so they went forth, crestfallen, and Don Carlos Cassara came in from the plaza, as though to see his friend and offer him help in case there should be trouble.

And, some minutes later, they were in Don Diego's room, the two friends, laughing and chatting, and speaking in whispers.

"There is a taint to the affair," Don Carlos declared. "I lost money to the man—"

"He cheated," Don Diego interrupted. "Hence, it is not an unworthy thing to refuse to pay. And, if I mistake not, he will leave at dawn—and how can you pay him if you never see him again? Gamble no more with strangers, my friend!"

And, just before he fell asleep that night, Don Diego Vega chuckled softly. He was thinking of the matter of the wart. Certainly there was no wart on his neck. For Don Diego had removed it with the costume of Zorro—had removed the bit of wax fashioned as a wart, and placed on his neck for the special purpose of being seen.

Zorro Hunts a Jackal

The human jackals of Spanish California needed taming, said the night-riding Zorro, so ...

CHAPTER I
"Zorro Rides Tonight!"

NOW the siesta hour was at an end in the little pueblo of Reina de Los Angeles. The cool breeze was starting to drift in from the distant sea, and again life came to the plaza. House doors were opened, and men and women came forth to go about their pursuits. Native servants scurried on errands, dealers prepared to extol the merits of their wares, and lethargy gave place to activity.

In the tavern at the corner of the plaza, there were some who still dozed as they sprawled on benches their backs against the adobe wall, mostly because of the wine they had guzzled. And some others were not dozing, notably a certain Don Diego Vega, scion of a proud and wealthy family, who had everything that a young man might desire—save spirit.

For, according to common report, this Don Diego was perfumed youth with a languid air, who seemed to find life a bore. It was whispered that he read the works of poets, shuddered at thought of blade-wielding and blood-letting, disdained to play a guitar beneath a window or flirt with a dainty señorita when her dueña was looking the other way, cared little for gaming or racing, and was about as lifeless as a man may be and still breathe and move.

Don Diego had gone to the inn in search of a friend. He had not found the friend, however, and the fat landlord was aflutter because of his visit, and servile to the point of abasement.

"A cup of rare wine, Don Diego, with my compliments?" the landlord asked.

"'Twould be of rare vintage, no doubt, if found in this place. I have a cellar of my own, dolt!" said Don Diego. "Would I shrivel my throat with the poor stuff you sell?"

"My private stock—"

"Keep it private, and save the stomachs of men!" Don Diego interrupted. "If my good friend, Don Carlos Cassara, comes to this your vile establishment, tell him to call upon me forthwith at my father's house."

"It shall be done, Don Diego."

"And in payment for the wine which you offered me gratis, and for the insults it has pleased me to heap upon you, take this."

Don Diego tossed down a gold piece as though it had been a bit of filth, wiped his fingers with his scented lace handkerchief, yawned, and turned toward the door.

BUT there was a sudden tumult outside, at the corner of the plaza. Men began running, both whites and natives. Wild shrieks rang out, and a raucous bellowing was heard. There was the ominous whack-whack! of a whip striking against bare human flesh.

Don Diego Vega made a grimace of disgust, and the fat landlord hurried past him to the door, to peer out into the blazing sunshine that drenched the dusty plaza.

"It is somebody administering a beating to one of the natives, Don Diego," the tavern keeper made report.

"And is it necessary for the wretch to howl and scream as

though attacked by wild beasts?"

"He is being given a sound beating with a whip, Don Diego. —Ah! The man with the whip is the strange horse dealer who came to the pueblo a few days ago. He does nothing, that man, except eat, drink, sleep, talk about horses, and beat the natives."

"A full life," Don Diego observed languidly.

"If this Señor Zorro who has been winning such fame of late would but ride the highways once more, this man might meet with proper punishment. They say that Señor Zorro is hard on ruffians who mistreat natives."

"Señor Zorro?—Ah, yes, I remember! The fellow who took it upon himself to defend the weak and oppressed. That," Don Diego said, "is quite a task!"

"It is some time since this Señor Zorro was active," the landlord recalled. "Were he here now—well, this man not only beats natives, but also is a thief."

"How is this?"

"He is a dealer in horses, and all such are swindlers, Don Diego—as doubtless you know. But this man purchases stolen animals from the natives, gives them a small part of what he promised, then compels them to dice or play at cards with him, and so wins back the little he paid—undoubtably through some trick."

"Undoubtedly," Don Diego agreed, smiling slightly.

Holding his scented handkerchief to his nostrils, Don Diego Vega stepped through the door and made bold to risk the open air. The native was still squealing, and the whip was striking home. The man who wielded it continued his raucous denunciation:

"Native dog!—Scum!—The next time I'll take off your hide in strips!—Begone!"

The whip cracked a last time, and the native gave a final screech and fled. Don Diego glanced at toward the horse trader and appraised him swiftly. The crowd melted away, and Don

Diego strolled forward.

"What is all this tumult?" asked the young man.

The man with the whip whirled to face him. "Who questions—and by what right?" he demanded.

"This is Don Diego Vega, señor, a man to be treated with the utmost consideration," the landlord warned, quickly.

"Ah! Your pardon, Don Diego. I regret it if you were disturbed. I was but whipping a native cur."

"And what was his offense?"

"Such as he are a stench in my nostrils—and he was walking to windward of me."

"There are stenches and stenches," Don Diego observed. "And you, señor, are standing to windward of me." Don Diego touched his nostrils with the scented handkerchief again, and shifted his position slightly.

"What is this?" the other cried. His face turned almost purple.

"What is your name and your business?" Don Diego asked.

"I am Felipe Garzo, and I deal in horses."

"And do you also break and train the beasts, señor? That is rough work."

"It is, as you say, rough work—labor for a man of strength, Don Diego."

"You are buying horses here?"

"I am hoping to sell some to Capitán Torello, of the presidio, for the use of his troopers. My herdsmen even now are driving some animals north from San Juan Capistrano."

"You appear to be quite handy with the whip, señor. It is an accomplishment which may lead you into trouble," Don Diego warned. "You must have enemies scattered up and down the length of El Camino Real."

"I attend to such enemies as dare face me, señor!"

"Violence," Don Diego told him, "is something that I cannot understand. It seems such a waste of energy and time."

THEN he turned his back without another word, and started around the plaza, strolling toward a row of poor huts past which he was compelled to go to get to his father's house.

He looked ahead, and saw a man sitting on a rough bench in the shade beside a hut—a massive man with a huge paunch, with one good eye and a green patch over the empty socket of the other. He was a retired pirate—and he also pretended to be a reformed one—Bardoso by name.

This Bardoso blinked his good eye rapidly when he beheld Don Diego's approach, for Don Diego was not beyond stopping for a friendly chat. "The attraction of opposites," said the wise Franciscans.

Don Diego did slacken pace as he came near, and finally he stopped in the shade beside the hut.

"Retain your present seat on the bench, good Bardoso," Don Diego ordered. "If that jug beside you is empty, mayhap you could not rise anyhow. —I have just witnessed a disgraceful brawl on the other side of the plaza."

"I heard the disturbance, Don Diego."

"It seems that a horse dealer, Felipe Garzo by name, loves to swindle natives and beat them."

"He appears to make a business of it." Bardoso replied. "It is in my mind, Don Diego, that you have no love for gossip or rumor, being a true caballero in all things. Yet you may find some amusement in it."

"Say on."

"This Felipe Garzo gives out publicly that he is a rough man, a buyer and breaker of horses. Yet he does not appear to be rough. He walks with a certain amount of grace, using the balls of his feet, I have noted. His hands are well kept, the fingers long and tapered, his wrist that of a man skilled in the use of blade. A pirate notices such things."

"I noticed such myself, good Bardoso."

"And I have done some speculation regarding him, Don Diego, putting together fragments of information and kneading them into a surmise. My conclusion is that the fellow is a jackal."

"Ah! And the lion for whom he finds prey—?"

"Is Capitán Torello, commanding officer at our presidio, and the governor's representative here in Reina de Los Angeles—if you care to call him a lion."

"Interesting!" Don Diego commented.

"As is well known, Capitán Torello is eager to capture Señor Zorro, friend of the oppressed, or to see him slain. There is a rich reward offered by the governor. But how can Capitán Torello capture or slay Señor Zorro if the latter remains in his fox's den, wherever it is?"

"I am quite sure that it would be impossible," Don Diego said.

"So, this Señor Zorro must be drawn out of his den. There must be a decoy. Something must happen to make Zorro want to ride again, and use his whip and blade. So the jackal comes to town, pretending to be what he is not; and he beats and swindles natives—a thing likely to bring Señor Zorro out into the open. Pitfalls have been prepared for him, no doubt."

"No doubt," Don Diego agreed.

"LET us assume that Señor Zorro wishes to punish this Felipe Garzo. He discovers that he is dealing with an expert swordsman instead of a lout. If he dies on the point of a blade, there is an end of Zorro! If he wins, perhaps others will be near to have at him and make a capture. For the jackal is watched always, as he walks abroad, by those who are prepared to rush to his assistance."

"A pretty plot," Don Diego said, yawning.

"Capitán Torello believes that the capture or slaying of Señor Zorro will mean reward and promotion for him. He thinks this Zorro is a man of quality, a caballero who plays at highwayman, and that his defeat would humble a proud family already in the ill grace of the governor, but too powerful for the governor to affront openly."

Don Diego met Bardoso's good eye with two good ones of his own. "Conversation is such tiresome stuff," he commented. "Bardoso, I recall that I asked you to procure for me a certain drug, you being a clandestine dealer in chemicals and nostrums."

"I have what you require, Don Diego."

Bring it to my house after nightfall. Bernardo, my servant, will be in the patio."

"I shall obey, Don Diego."

Then Don Diego walked on, past the row of humble huts and toward his father's splendid house.

A native shuffled from the patch of shade beside one of the huts—a giant of a native, who towered above the others in the town. He was a Cocopah, who had been named José by the Franciscans, and was a man of influence among his kind.

José of the Cocopahs backed away slightly, and stood with bowed head as Don Diego approached. Don Diego was looking straight forward, and his nose seemed to be tilted a trifle, as though the presence of the native offended him. He brushed his nostrils with his perfumed handkerchief again.

But, as he passed José of the Cocopahs, the corner of Don Diego's mouth twisted slightly, and whispered words came forth:

"Zorro rides tonight! The hacienda trail!"

CHAPTER II
A Change Of Identity

DUSK came to Reina de Los Angeles, and lights glowed in the buildings, smoke issued from chimneys, and odors of burning wood and cooking food filled the air.

At the presidio, the troopers were eating and attending to their duties; and in the private quarters of Capitán Torello, the latter held speech with Felipe Garzo, who had been the guest of the capitán for the evening meal. They were conversing in low tones, so that not even the guard in the corridor could hear.

"He took the bait," Felipe Garzo was saying. "His manner was mild enough, but he could not keep the flame out of his eyes. I grabbed the native wretch in front of the door of the inn, and beat him soundly so this Don Diego could not but hear and see."

"I feel certain that he is this Señor Zorro," the capitán said. "If we win in this, Felipe, our fortunes are made. The man's proud father is a thorn in the side of the governor. If this Don Diego Vega is unmasked as Zorro, either dead or alive, the family is shamed—and His Excellency will be well pleased."

"And what to do now?" Felipe Garzo asked.

"You will sleep in the guest house, as usual. Perhaps this Zorro will come to punish you during the night. Three troopers will be on guard and within call. If he comes, he walks into a trap."

"I itch to hold blade and face him!" Felipe Garzo said fiercely. "He treated me as dirt beneath his boots."

"He has treated me in a similar fashion—and his proud father also. But Zorro is clever with a blade. If he bests you—"

"Give me a chance at him!"

"Help will be near at hand," Capitán Torello said, smiling slightly. "If Señor Zorro visits you, there must be no slip. He dies, or is captured—and I care not which."

There came a discreet tap on the door, and the capitán called permission to enter. One of his troopers opened the door and made salute.

"Don Diego Vega to see the capitán," he said.

"Don Diego Vega—here?" Capitán Torello betrayed a measure of astonishment. "Usher him within, and at once."

"Now, what do you suppose—?" Garzo began softly.

"Hush! Let us talk of horses," the capitán whispered. He

raised his voice. "I have told you the price that I am allowed to pay, señor. And the horses must pass strict inspection. My troopers are entitled to the best in horseflesh."

"Mine are prime animals," Felipe Garzo replied. "I can assure you—"

"Ah! Don Diego Vega!" Capitán Torello was on his feet, bowing as Don Diego stepped through the door.

"Your pardon, Capitán Torello, for this intrusion," Don Diego said.

"It is an honor!"

"I have a favor to ask. If it is against your policy to grant it, do not hesitate to say so."

"It is granted already, Don Diego, if within my power. Is it something secret and personal? I am discussing business with this horse dealer, but he can retire—"

DON Diego lifted a hand to stop him. "It is nothing that cannot be spoken openly. Scarcely an affair of state. I ride out to the Pulido place to make a social call. It is a dark night, and the servant who usually attends me is ill. My father is out at his hacienda—"

"Ah! And you desire an escort?" the capitán put in. "You may have one, surely. There are highwaymen and cutthroats abroad these nights."

"If I may have that big sergeant of yours, Pedro Gonzales, it will please me. He has an amusing chatter."

"I'll issue the order immediately, Don Diego, and Sergeant Gonzales will be ready as soon as he can saddle his horse. If you will partake of wine—?"

"Your pardon if I do not at this time," Don Diego said. "You are an officer, and you have business to transact. In your line of duty, you must consort with many queer folk. —But there is nothing, capitán, which compels me to breathe the same air as a man who plays at dice and cards with natives."

"How now—!" Felipe Garzo cried, and sprang from the stool

upon which he was sitting.

"Be silent, señor!" Capitán Torello snapped at him. He bowed to Don Diego again. "Some other time, the wine," he said. "I can well understand your situation."

"I wait in front for the sergeant."

As Capitán Torello struck the gong to summon his orderly, Don Diego retreated through the corridor. They could hear his boot-heels tapping the hard floor.

"The fiend!" Felipe Garzo gurgled angrily. "He gets under my skin! To run him through would be a pleasure!"

"Quiet!" the capitán begged. "If he is Zorro, you may have the chance. Otherwise—a caballero such as Don Diego Vega need not fight such a man as you are posing to be."

Garzo sank upon the stool again. "Now what?" he asked. "If he is going visiting, and taking along one of your troopers for escort—"

"If he is Zorro, that would be like him. He will return, pretend to be fatigued and go home and to bed. Then he will put on his costume and mask, and as Zorro he will come back to the presidio. It is but an elegant gesture—asking for an escort. Or, perhaps he wished to learn whether you are at the presidio"

"I'll have his blood!" Felipe Garzo fumed.

"Keep your own cool, and your head also. The angry man is always at a disadvantage," Torello warned...

OUT along the dusty highway, through the deep dust and the soft black night, rode Don Diego Vega with Sergeant Pedro Gonzales just on his left, and half a horse's length behind, as was proper.

"Highwaymen are active again, so the capitán says," Don Diego remarked over his shoulder.

"It is not for me to question the statement of my superior," Gonzales replied.

"This Señor Zorro, who created some excitement along the

highway—nothing more is heard of him."

"Attune your ears, Don Diego, and you may hear of him soon. I know certain things which lead me to believe—"

"Tell me not your official secrets!" Don Diego begged. "I am grateful to you for riding with me tonight. I am compelled to go to the Pulido hacienda for a time. It will be a dreary assignment for you, no doubt, for of course you could be drinking wine at the presidio."

"There is a certain bronze native wench at the Pulido place whom it is a rare pleasure to chuck under the chin," the sergeant said.

"Then you will not find time hanging heavy on your hands while I am the house."

Don Diego laughed a bit, and then turned through a huge stone archway and went along a winding road on either side of which great trees grew. At the end of this lane was the Pulido house, and the scattered outbuildings around it. From the servants' huts in the rear came soft laughter and the tinkling of a guitar. Those who worked at the Pulido hacienda were fortunate in having a kind employer who liked to see his people happy.

They dismounted before the front door, and Don Diego handed his reins to the sergeant.

"Take my mount along with your own," he said. "When I am ready to return to Reina de Los Angeles, I'll send a servant for you. Enjoy yourself."

Sergeant Pedro Gonzales hurried around the corner of the big house with the horses, eager to tether them near the servants' huts and to hunt up his wench. Don Diego approached the great front door, but he did not use the knocker.

None knew better than Don Diego that the Señorita Pulido, to whom he was betrothed, was off with her mother paying a visit, and that Don Carlos Pulido was alone in his big house. Don Carlos undoubtedly would be dozing after a heavy meal, and it would be impolite to disturb him.

Through the darkness Don Diego slipped swiftly, dodging the lighter spots, and glad that there was no moon and that a heavy mist partially obscured the light of the stars. Safe away from the house and the buildings, he skipped lightly down a slope, dodging the scattered trees, and finally stopped beside a narrow trail. He gave a low whistle.

"Señor?" The answer came almost immediately, in a whisper, from a clump of brush a few feet away.

"Is it you, José?"

"Sí, señor!"

"Is everything prepared?"

"Here, señor, behind the brush."

WHILE José of the Cocopahs kept close watch a few feet away, piercing the darkness with his keen eyes and straining his ears to catch the slightest sound, Don Diego Vega divested himself of certain of his garments and quickly donned others instead. Across his face he fastened a black mask with slits for the eyes. A blade was strapped at his side.

The garments he had discarded were piled neatly at the base of a tree. From a pouch he took a small bottle, which he handled carefully.

"José!"

"Señor?"

"The torch!"

"Behind this rock, señor, it may not be seen."

Don Diego dropped down behind a big rock, and there was a sudden flare as José kindled a small torch into flame. Don Diego took something from the bottle, propped a mirror against the rock, and worked diligently for a time. He was chuckling as he returned the bottle to the pouch.

"The horse?"

"Ten paces straight ahead, señor."

"You will remember everything?"

"Everything, señor."

"I go. Put out the torch. Zorro rides!"

As he spoke, he draped his form with a long black cloak of thin material. Then he darted forward, to where a black horse was waiting. Don Diego Vega was gone—and in his stead was Señor Zorro, the Fox. And it was Señor Zorro, quite another person, who got into the saddle to ride.

Down the narrow trail he went through the soft night, the horse picking the path; and presently he turned into the highway and rode swiftly toward the town. He was keenly alert, quick to catch sight and sound, his eyes gleaming through the slit's in the mask he wore.

What a game he played, this Don Diego Vega, supposed to be too languid to be a spirited young caballero. Yet it was a dangerous game, he knew well. One fatal slip—and shame would descend upon the Vegas and the jealous governor have his moment of gloating. In truth, Zorro struck only to aid the oppressed and to right wrongs; yet, nevertheless, he acted outside the law.

He topped a hill and saw in the distance the few twinkling lights of Reina de Los Angeles. Now he rode from the trail and over rough ground, and approached the hillside in which stood the presidio, with a deep gulch running behind it.

Zorro rode into the gulch, sent his black horse forward at a walk, and finally emerged behind the low, sprawling presidio buildings, tethering his horse to a tree.

He kept the black cloak wrapped closely around his body as he crept through the fringe of brush on the gulch's rim. His black mask covered his entire face. He was but an unseen part of the night, as he went cautiously toward the presidio buildings. These were on three sides of a large patio, the main barracks on one side, storehouses on another, and a guest house on the third. A commodious structure, this guest house, partitioned into two apartments for the use of both men and women.

It was toward the guest house that Zorro went now, half

crawling at times, careful to keep the black cloak wrapped tightly around his body, to refrain from striking a boot against a rock. Careful also that the blade he wore hit against nothing to give forth a warning metallic sound.

Behind a clump of brush he crouched, silent and motionless. It was quiet in the barracks, and he knew that the troopers slept, since all of them save the guard always retired early. No light gleamed through the windows of the guest house. Zorro knew that only one guest reposed there, the man who called himself Felipe Garzo.

Nor was he sure that Garzo was there now. The fellow might be at the inn, or prowling around the pueblo under the protection of a couple of troopers. If so, things were but delayed a bit. And there were others to be considered, too.

Zorro watched and listened, and finally he located them—the lurking guards. There were three, resting on the ground near a clump of brush, not far from the door of the guest house. They were waiting for Zorro to make an attack on Felipe Garzo and so walk into a trap.

Silently, Señor Zorro crept toward them.

CHAPTER III
"On Guard, Señor!"

WHEN he was but a short distance away, and they were yet unaware of his presence, Zorro stopped behind another clump of brush. He stood up, rested a moment, and prepared to remove the cloak that shrouded his form.

He could hear the guards whispering to one another as a wine jug was passed from hand to hand.

"He is a decoy, this Señor Horse Trader," one said. "He beats natives so that Zorro will come to get him. Then we shall get Zorro."

"And a handful of gold pieces into the bargain!" another added, chuckling.

"And mayhap divers cuts and slashes from Zorro's blade," the third reminded them.

"We allow this Señor Garzo to do the fighting, merely seeing that Zorro does not escape if he wins," the first said. "If he bests the horse dealer, the three of us must account for him."

"He is a demon! He slips around like a ghost. It may be he is not human man at all."

It was at this moment that Señor Zorro whipped off the light cloak and stepped from behind the clump of brush. An eerie wail rumbled from his throat, grew in volume, and seemed to shatter the silence of the night. It beat back from the walls of the presidio buildings, rushed away on the hill breeze.

The three troopers sprang to their feet, alarm striking at them. They glanced around quickly, as Zorro wailed again.

And then they saw! A short distance from them, in the midst of the Stygian blackness of the night and seemingly drifting toward them, was the skull and chest of a skeleton.

Again there came that eerie wail. The apparition bore toward them. They could see the gleaming outline of the skull, the great gleaming eye sockets. The throat and shoulder bones and the upper ribs were also visible.

Brave men they might have been in physical combat. None of them would have retreated even from a superior foe. Soldiers they were, and skilled in the use of weapons; but they also were superstitious.

They could have understood a charging enemy and prepared to clash and fight it out; but when the third eerie wail came rumbling through the night at them, the gleaming skeleton apparently starting to advance toward them again, it was more than their nerves could endure.

"Dios!" one cried.

Their shrieks of superstitious fear rang out. As one man they turned and charged away toward the barracks, howling for their comrades to come to their aid, to bring blazing torches. Together the three made a tumult equal to the noise of a frenzied score.

Voices answered them from the barracks, and in front of the building the sentinel on regular post shouted for the capitán. From the guest house came the raucous bellowing of Señor Felipe Garzo. He demanded to know what was happening.

Zorro quickly wrapped the dark cloak around him again, and put the hood of it up over his head. The gleaming skeleton disappeared. Through the black night he rushed noiselessly to the corner of the guest house, and there watched the door.

Light gleamed within, and the door was hurled open. Señor Felipe Garzo stood framed in it, partly clothed, holding a flaming torch above his head with his left hand, a naked blade in his right.

"What is it?" he shouted.

THE guards had rushed across the patio to the corner of the barracks, where a door had been opened for them. Out of the barracks, the other troopers were tumbling in their night clothing, shouting and clashing weapons. Capitán Torello appeared, crying for order and silence, and for somebody to tell him what had happened. Felipe Garzo left the guest house and rushed across the patio, carrying his sword and his torch.

Quickly, Zorro slipped through the guest house door and got inside the big room. In a corner was a huge clothes press, and into this he went, but for the time being kept its door half open. Thus he was able to see across the room and into the patio.

There were a dozen torches in the patio now, and troopers were commencing a search, the capitán's angry shouts urging them on. Felipe Garzo came back toward the guest house with Capitán Torello beside him.

"It was a fiery skeleton," one of the guards kept repeating. "A skeleton with flaming bones. All of us saw it, capitán. It screeched threats at us."

"And where did you see it first?"

"Over there, by the clump of brush. It seemed to be floating through the air at us. And the screech it gave—!"

"It probably came out of this empty wine jug I find here on the ground," the capitán suggested. "Strange sights and sounds may be found in a jug!"

"But we all saw it at the same time, capitán, and heard it. It was a terrible thing!"

"What think you, Garzo?" the capitán asked.

"That you have some strange troopers, capitán," Garzo replied. "A flaming skeleton that screeched—um! There's nobody here."

Capitán Torello whirled upon his men. "Idiots and cowardly fools!" he stormed. "Whoever saw a flaming skeleton? And can any skeleton shriek? Wine has robbed you of what wits you possessed. And perhaps it also has ruined our plans for the night. Return to your post—and you others get to your beds!"

"We are to continue the watch?" a guard asked. "And in the darkness?"

"You are, though probably it will avail nothing now. You were put on a secret post, to keep quiet and perhaps trap a fox. And you have howled enough to frighten away every fox in the land."

"A terrible thing!" a guard moaned.

"Remain on post, imbeciles, though you shiver and shake! Do not desert, for I may come out at any time to see if you are attending to duty. And do not make a light."

The three returned to the clump of brush where they had been watching, and the others retired to the barracks. Torello remained with Felipe Garzo at the door of the guest room. By the light of the torches they carried, they could view the interior. They saw nothing unusual, for Zorro had by this time closed the door of the huge press, and was snug inside.

"What do you make of it, capitán?" Garzo asked.

"I scarce know, señor!"

"The guards were badly frightened—no pretense there."

"They are a superstitious lot. Something undoubtedly happened to frighten them. But, a skeleton that shrieks—!"

"It is yet early in the night. Perhaps the man we expect will come to us yet."

"I doubt it," the capitán said. "Zorro strikes when men expect it not. Perhaps he has been near, had something planned, and the howling of the guards ruined his calculations."

"I'll to bed again," Felipe Garzo decided.

" 'Noches!"

THE capitán stalked away toward the barracks building with rage in his stride, and Felipe Garzo closed the door of the guest house and walked across to his bed. He surveyed the room an instant, then plunged the head of the torch into the bowl of sand to extinguish it. That made the interior of the big room black dark, for the heavy draperies had been drawn across the windows.

Garzo stretched out upon the couch half dressed, as he had appeared at the door a while before, and reached down to pull the protecting quilt of skins up to his chin, for he had grown cold running about the patio. He turned on one side, so facing the opposite wall of the room. And suddenly he gave a gasp of surprise and struggled to sit up. For there, on the adobe wall of the room, in quivering shining letters, was the one word: *Muerte*. And below it was a big jagged letter Z.—"Death!" And the sign of Zorro.

Felipe Garzo sprang out of bed and grasped the torch again. Feverishly, he kindled it, meanwhile straining his ears for sounds inside the room, but hearing nothing. The light flared up and Garzo gave a sigh of relief to find that Señor Zorro was not standing before him, his eyes gleaming through the slits in his mask.

Across the room he went, and to the wall. But it seemed innocent of anything except a damp smear. He could not understand it.

"Am I, too, growing into an imbecile?" Felipe Garzo growled aloud to himself. "A pest, this Zorro! He grows on the imagination of a man. If ever I stand face to face with him, blade in hand—!"

He left the threat unfinished and retired to the couch again. Once more he extinguished the torch. And as he did so, there flamed out on the wall again the letter and the sign!

"I shall go mad!" Garzo breathed. "It is some trick, such as was played on the guards.—A boy's trick!—It will take something more substantial than writing on a wall to harm me."

He closed his eyes and turned his head away, but his ears were open. He could hear the faint rustling of the wind through the brush outside, and the howling of a dog down near the plaza. But nothing else. Inside the guest house, all was as still as death.

After a time he looked at the wall again. The word and the sign were still there, though seemingly they did not shine with such great radiance. Felipe Garzo fought with himself to remain calm, to keep from lighting the torch and making a fresh investigation.

INSIDE the big clothes press, Señor Zorro was growing cramped and uncomfortable. It was hot and stuffy, and the perspiration was trickling down his neck, causing a delicious kind of agony. He opened the door of the press for the space of a couple of inches, looked out into the darkness of the room, listened.

Felipe Garzo was tossing on his bed. His breathing became heavier, and once it approached a snore. Then Zorro opened the door wider, and finally stepped gingerly down to the floor, closing the door of the press behind him slowly and noiselessly.

His long dark cloak was wrapped closely around him, covering him from head to feet. As he stood against the wall, he could not be seen. All at once he dropped the cloak to the floor and drew himself up. He began to speak in a weak monotone:

"You who call yourself Felipe Garzo!—You are an impostor and a wretch!—Jackal!—Cheap decoy!"

"Dios!" Felipe Garzo threw the skin quilt aside and sat erect on the couch. His first glance was at the opposite wall, where the word and the ragged letter Z still gleamed faintly at him. "I am going mad!" he breathed. "The wine at dinner was too strong. A pest on this accursed place!"

The perspiration was standing out on his forehead in great globules. That word on the wall seemed to dance before his eyes. He had not yet observed the presence of the stranger.

"Jackal!" the hissed whisper came to his ears again. "So you would trap and trick Señor Zorro, eh?"

Felipe Garzo jerked his head around. Then he sprang from the couch and crashed back against the wall, making a wild grab for the sword and dagger which he had left handy on a stool. The stool went over with a crash, sword and dagger flew aside. For across the room, Felipe Garzo beheld what the guards had seen—the upper half of a skeleton in gleaming, quivering light. And from that direction came also a soft, mocking laugh, and a sound such as that made by blade being drawn from scabbard, deliberately, with evident morbid purpose.

Garzo did not cry out; he did not screech to attract the attention of the guards supposed to be outside. He did not care to make a fool of himself, as the others had made laughing stocks of themselves. First of all, this thing called for investigation. Though his heart hammered at his ribs and his ears were strained to catch sounds of footsteps, his eyes never left that quivering, flaming skeleton.

Felipe Garzo reached for the torch and made shift to kindle it into flame. As the light flared up, there was a quick step on the other side of the room. He whirled. And there he saw a man in dark clothing, with a black mask across his face, and on the forehead of the mask a ragged letter Z.

"Zorro!" Felipe Garzo gasped.

"At your service, beater of natives! Swindler and cheat and thief!"

Garzo backed to the wall, stooped swiftly, and retrieved sword and dagger. This was the moment for which he had waited. And now that the queer apparition had gone with the coming of the light, courage returned to him. He was not without skill with a blade.

"This shall be the end of you, Zorro!" he hissed.

"A thing to be proved!"

"In a moment, señor, I shall strip off your mask and have a look at your dead face!"

"You'll find it much more pleasant than your own. Are you going to call to the guards for help? Are you about to summon the soldiery? How many men do you need for aid, Felipe Garzo, when you cross blades with another man?"

"None!" Garzo said.

"I warn you, out of the kindness of my heart, that it will be safer for you to call."

But here was a business which Felipe Garzo wished to finish himself, that he might gain greater notoriety. To take the notorious Zorro alone and unaided—there was a feat!

He thrust the torch into its holder on the wall, and it cast a flickering and uncertain light across the big room.

"Now, highwayman—!"

"On guard, señor!" Zorro said.

CHAPTER IV
Combat

THEY met, clashed, felt each other's strength, and then were at it. At the first encounter, Zorro knew that here was a swordsman, and no poor novice to be disarmed and marked or done to death. The first clash of steel seemed to turn Felipe Garzo into a cold fighting machine. The man had shaken off his disguise, in a manner of speaking; no longer was he Felipe

Garzo, uncouth horse trader and breaker.

"Beater of natives!" Zorro taunted. "Jackal for the capitán and the governor!"

"Highwayman!" the other gasped.

But they did not waste breath in epithets, for breath was a thing which both needed in this combat. Around and around the room they fought, each trying to get the advantage of light, avoiding the heavy articles of furniture, using what skill they possessed.

The perspiration was glistening on the forehead of the man who called himself Felipe Garzo, and the expression in his face was that of a man who knows he has met his match.

Zorro's features were hidden by the mask he wore, wherein he had an advantage, for the other could not read the workings of his mind. The eyes gleamed through the slits malevolently. Now and then teeth glistened in a provoking smile. Feet slipped over the rough flooring of the guest house, and steel hissed and sang.

Neither cried out, but they gasped and panted as they fought, and their ringing blades could be heard. Outside, the guards heard them, and approached the building, listening at the door and beneath one of the windows. They knew that these were sounds of fight which came from inside. But nobody cried to them for help. There was no shout that Zorro was at hand. Merely the clash of good steel and the panting breaths of the swordsmen. And the troopers were loath to enter and distub, and gain a rebuke if they made error.

"Get to the capitán and tell him," one ordered, and a comrade rushed away.

"If Gonzales were only here!" another suggested.

"He has gone with Don Diego Vega to the Pulido place, as an escort. Perhaps the capitán will come. If there was but a cry for help—"

Inside the big room, the torch flickered and cast shadows. Footing was uncertain. Felipe Garzo felt himself being bested by this masked man who taunted now in low tones. His strength was leaving him rapidly. He had met his match in fence, and a man who was in better condition physically.

Fear of death came to him, and also the fear that this man might escape after having slain him. He retreated toward the wall and prepared to shout an alarm. For an instant, he grew careless. The blade of Zorro darted in like the tongue of a snake, and Felipe Garzo felt a streak of fire across his check.

"The first stroke, señor," Zorro said. "I write my mark on your face in three strokes, señor—for all the world to see—always. You will not have to tell them with whom you have fought."

GARZO attacked furiously then, and blindly, for rage consumed him and wrecked caution.

Again Zorro's blade darted in, and Felipe Garzo felt another streak of flame. Blood trickled down his cheek from the wound.

"The last stroke is a delicate matter," Zorro said. "I like to join the scratches, so that the letter Z will be perfect. And, after having marked you—!"

The sentence was left unfinished, but Garzo's imagination ran on. In fancy, he felt the blade slip through his body, to protrude at the back, felt it whipped out again and himself falling to crash to the floor, and then the dark oblivion of an unknown future—

"Help!—Guards!—Zorro is here!" he shouted.

"Craven!" Zorro hissed. As he spoke, his blade darted forward again, and the letter Z was now completed. Felipe Garzo darted back against the wall to make his last desperate stand.

Now the guards were pounding at the door, howling to know whether they should enter.

"Help!—Zorro is here!" Felipe Garzo's last cry strangled in his throat.

But Señor Zorro had not slain him. He had merely disarmed him neatly, then run his blade through a shoulder. Garzo dropped to the floor, moaning more with fright than with pain, disarmed and helpless, expecting a death blow at any moment.

"Quiet, or you die!" Zorro hissed at him.

Then Felipe Garzo did a foul thing. He still clutched his dagger in his left hand; and now he transferred it swiftly to his right, hurling it straight at the masked man before him, in open defiance of all rules of fair combat. Instantly, Zorro darted aside, and the flying weapon glanced from the steel of his blade.

"*Scum!*" Zorro cried, and his blade flashed again, and came back red.

Nor had he struck to kill this time—but only to give a wound that would bring unconsciousness. For if, as Zorro believed, this "horse trader" was a proud swordsman of the governor's retinue, to go through life shamed with Zorro's brand would be a sterner lesson to him, and to other bravos like him, than a swift and painless death.

Zorro whirled away from his fallen adversary, even as he heard the voice of Capitán Torello shouting for his men to get through the door. From his pouch, he took the little bottle, and for a time worked swiftly at the wall, and on the face of the fallen man.

An instant later he had darted across the room and had extinguished the torch, and grasping his long black cloak he enveloped himself in it. Then he darted to the big door and stood so it would cover him when it was hurled open.

The next moment it crashed inward. The guest room was in total blackness, for those who carried torches had not yet reached the building. Immediately the guards who had opened the door recoiled, cries of awe rumbling from their throats. For gleaming on the opposite wall was a huge skull, and below it a jagged letter Z. And on the floor in a corner was something that moaned and tossed and might have been a man. On it was another Z, that gleamed and quivered in the midst of the darkness.

The guards howled, terrified, and then the capitán was there with the others and the place was lit by torches. Blades out and ready, they stormed into the room. Their first swift glances revealed nothing except Felipe Garzo, wounded and bleeding, and the indications of combat—overturned furniture, blotches of blood upon the floor. For Señor Zorro was behind the very door which they had hurled open and back against the wall. He was only a few feet from them in reality, though not in their thoughts.

AND now, since they had all rushed past him, Señor Zorro darted from behind the door and prepared to rush forth into the black night. —But his work was not yet done. He had punished Felipe Garzo, but he must also disabuse the capitán of the idea that Señor Zorro was in reality Don Diego Vega.

"Ha! Señores! You look for me, perhaps?" he cried.

They whirled, and in that instant he had darted through the door and was gone, his mocking laugh ringing back at them.

"After him!" Torello cried. "Get horses for a chase, some of you! Saddle my own mount!"

Some were in night clothing, and some in boots and breeches only, notably the capitán. Some chased out into the black night and in the direction Zorro had taken, guided by his mocking laugh. But he reached his horse safely enough and got himself into the saddle, and then he was quiet, listening to the troopers as they charged toward the stables.

Horses were always ready for the trail, at the presidio, and men mounted these. Others were soon made ready rapidly. Capitán Torello mounted his own horse, not stopping to finish his dressing, and making neither a brave nor an attractive picture in his present half attire.

But out of the night and past them there suddenly rode a demon on a black horse, who howled at them as he passed. The flaming upper half of a skeleton again—for Zorro had not put on his cloak.

Troopers gave cries of alarm, but their capitán silenced them.

"It is but Zorro! It is a trick!" Torello howled. "After him! A reward to the man who catches or slays him!"

And back to them, as they began their hard ride, came the mocking laugh of Zorro.

CHAPTER V
The Last Taunt

OUT of the pueblo they flew, along the hard highway which ran toward San Fernando. There was no moon, but the mist had now been dispelled by the sea breeze. Ahead, now and then, they caught sight of horse and rider against the starlit sky. They gained some, and that heartened them. Capitán Torello, leading, urged them on. Half-naked they rode, the troopers from Reina de Los Angeles, rage burning within them. In some strange manner he had made babies and fools of them, this Zorro, and they sought revenge—as well as the reward that had been offered. Over hills they went, around great curves in the highway, up slopes and down through gulches. And because of the mocking laugh that came back to them, and the hoofs pounding on ahead, they knew they still followed Zorro.

"Flaming skeleton!" Zorro chuckled as he rode. "A man may have a certain amusement by the use of phosphorus—A glow in the night!"

He laughed yet again, so that his pursuers heard as they slackened pace to negotiate a steep hill. Then Zorro increased speed a little, gradually increasing the distance between himself and the enemy—yet not so much that the pounding of his mount's hoofs could not be heard.

They swept after him, around another long curve in the road and up another slope. Zorro increased his speed again, and presently skidded his big black to a stop near the edge of a sea of brush.

"José!" Zorro called softly.

"Here, señor!"

"All is well, José! Ride!"

Zorro sprang out of the saddle, and José of the Cocopahs sprang into it. The black started again, and again the ringing hoofs gave signal to those behind. Crouching in the brush, Zorro watched them ride furiously past, chasing José, who had a way of losing them when he willed, and of caring for the black in a secret hiding place.

Zorro rushed along a little trail and came to the spot where he had left his clothes. Swiftly he stripped the Zorro costume from him, put aside mask and blade, and donned the clothing of Don Diego Vega. The Zorro costume, streaked with phosphorus, was hidden beneath a rock, where José would get it later.

Through the brush Don Diego Vega hurried, then, and up the side of the hill, approaching the great house of the Pulidos cautiously. From the servants' huts there came a gale of laughter, and he heard the raucous voice of Sergeant Pedro Gonzales, evidently happy.

Zorro went up to the big front door, and used the knocker. A servant opened to him, and he strode across a wide room to find Don Carlos Pulido rising to greet him.

"**D**ON Diego! At this hour! There is something amiss?"

"Why, no, señor," Don Diego said, and yawned. "Two or three hours ago I came to your fine house to make you a visit of courtesy and to have speech with the father of my betrothed. Do you not remember?"

"How is this?"

"We have been talking of politics, all this while, and I have been greatly bored. I am just now taking leave of you, señor. I came with the big sergeant, Gonzales, for escort. Will you have the kindness to send a servant and tell the sergeant to bring my horse to the front?"

"Certainly, Don Diego!"

The servant was called by a clapping of hands, and the order given.

"This man realizes that I have been here for hours, does he not? He admitted me again just now, it is true, but I had only stepped out to ascertain the meaning of some sound we heard."

"Have no fear." Don Carlos Pulido smiled.

"There is but one soiled wine glass on the table," Don Diego observed.

"And there should be two when two men have been talking for hours? Do me the honor, Don Diego, of soiling another."

Don Diego did so, and as their eyes met over the tops of their glasses, Don Carlos Pulido's brows arched questioningly.

"Zorro has been riding?" he asked.

"So I understand."

"Good fortune attend him always!" Don Carlos said earnestly.

"I thank you."

"And wipe the red dust from your boots before you leave. Can you imagine even a dolt of a trooper thinking you got that dust on your boots in my house?"

Don Diego turned scarlet, took out his scented handkerchief and wiped his boots with it, then tucked it away where no other could find it.

"The best of us grow careless at times," he muttered.

Then they went to the door together, a servant holding a torch; and there was Sergeant Pedro Gonzales with the horses.

Don Diego Vega mounted, waved to his host, and rode

away, down the lane and toward the main road that ran to Reina de Los Angeles.

"Did you find your wench, Gonzales?" he asked haughtily.

"She was away on a visit to an aunt—but I found another."

"And the wine was good?"

"Excellent—and plenty of it. I ask a favor, Don Diego. Whenever you need an escort to come to the Pulido hacienda, ask for my services."

"You had sport, and I but talked politics," Don Diego said. "But what is this we have ahead?" he demanded all at once.

"Ha!" Gonzales gasped, and whipped out his blade.

Ahead of them was a body of horsemen, riding slowly into the highway from a cross trail. Three of them carried torches.

"Troopers!" Gonzales said, and sighed in relief.

He had expected to fight a band of highwaymen in defense of Don Diego Vegas's proud and wealthy person.

"And what can they be doing here?" Don Diego asked.

THEY were heard, and the troop rushed toward them, the torches being held high, Capitán Torello in the van. Arms gleamed in the light. Strained faces looked at Gonzales and the man who rode beside him.

"What is all this?" Don Diego asked. "Capitán! You ride abroad half-naked, like a native? And your men—some in their night clothing! Is it a lark of some sort?"

Capitán Torello did not like the bantering tone, but he was on guard. He was suspicious of Don Diego Vega, but a man had to have more than mere suspicion when he affronted one of the mighty Vega family.

"We have been chasing Zorro," the capitán said. "He came to the presidio and attacked the horse trader."

"The fellow who beats natives?"

"The same," Torello replied. "You have been to the Pulido hacienda?"

"For a lifetime, it seems," Don Diego said. "And now I am

eager to get me home and to bed."

The troopers made way for him, and he rode forward.

Capitán Torello urged his mount beside that of the sergeant.

"What has this Don Diego been doing?" the capitán asked.

"He visited in the big house."

"His horse?"

"I cared for it the entire time."

"Take charge of the troop!"

Capitán Torello spurred forward to a place beside Don Diego Vega again.

"This Zorro marked the—er—horse trader," he said. "Carved his accursed letter on the fellow's cheek."

"Spare me!" Don Diego begged. "Am I always to hear of blood-letting? Capitán, you are commanding officer under the governor for this district. It is your duty to catch or slay this Zorro and put an end to the turmoil, the constant fighting and pursuits. Why do you not do so?"

Capitán Torello had no adequate answer.

From Pulp Page to Silver Screen

From Pulp Page to Silver Screen

by Ed Hulse

JOHNSTON McCULLEY'S fiction had been appearing in pulp magazines for more than a decade when he sold the story for which he is best remembered to legendary Munsey editor Bob Davis. A 68,000-word novel serialized in five installments, "The Curse of Capistrano" began in *All-Story Weekly's* August 9, 1919 issue, which prominently featured the swashbuckling yarn's masked and cloaked protagonist in a lackluster cover painting by P. J. Monahan.

McCulley seemed comfortable working in all genres, but he demonstrated particular facility with crook melodramas and thrillers. He was a mainstay of Street & Smith's *Detective Story Magazine,* having created for that pulp a handful of series characters—among them Black Star, Thubway Tham, The Spider, and Terry Trimble—before placing "Curse of Capistrano" with *All-Story Weekly.* The new serial was by way of a follow-up to "Captain Fly-by-Night" (May 27, 1916), which also took place in Old California and described frequent displays of derring-do.

"The Curse of Capistrano" remains one of McCulley's most

pleasing stories. Obviously inspired by Baroness Emmuska Orczy's 1903 play, *The Scarlet Pimpernel*, and the novelization of it published two years later, "Curse" offers a more full-bodied and richly melodramatic treatment of Orczy's premise. The prose is crisp and uncluttered, with period detail and description kept to a minimum. A plenitude of dialogue keeps the story moving rapidly, although references to events that have occurred off stage, so to speak, occasionally prove disappointing, as the reader wants to see even more of Zorro in action than McCulley gives us. The novel contains romance, humor, and adventure in exactly the right proportions; unlike many pulp yarns of the period, it can be easily digested and enjoyed by today's readers.

Certainly it appealed to one Douglas Fairbanks, who saw significant cinematic potential in "The Curse of Capistrano." At that time, *All-Story Weekly* was second only to the mighty *Saturday Evening Post* in supplying stories for screen adaptation. Fairbanks, having recently formed his own production company and now distributing his films through the newly organized United Artists, had been making light-hearted Westerns and comedies for years, and was looking to new genres for successful vehicles in which to exploit his increasingly larger-than-life persona.

Like his United Artists partners Charlie Chaplin and Mary Pickford (the latter also being his wife at the time), Doug sought complete creative control over the properties he brought to the screen. The motion-picture version of McCulley's novel, which was eventually titled *The Mark of Zorro*, was a phenomenal success that guaranteed such autonomy and literally changed the direction of his career. The modest Westerns and breezy romantic comedies were out; swashbuckling period adventures were in. The patented Fairbanks flamboyance was ideally suited to such film fare.

It's unclear exactly how or when Fairbanks discovered "The Curse of Capistrano." His niece later claimed that her father,

Douglas Fairbanks (left) and Robert McKim clash swords in *The Mark of Zorro*. Marguerite De La Motte played Lolita, the love interest and damsel-in-distress.

Robert Fairbanks, brought the story to Doug's attention. The famous stuntman Richard Talmadge reported that Native American actor Charles Stevens—who frequently worked with Fairbanks—showed Doug the yarn. Mary Pickford wrote that she gave McCulley's novel to her new husband during their European honeymoon trip in the spring of 1920. In any case, Fairbanks purchased the screen rights from Munsey and began work straightaway on his most elaborate producing venture to date. The planned film was announced to the trade as *The Curse of Capistrano*.

Doug adapted the story himself, retaining all of McCulley's principal characters and most of the novel's incidents. His additions consisted mainly of stunt sequences designed to show off the exuberant athleticism that was an integral part of his persona. He passed the adaptation to Eugene Miller, who crafted the scenario that would be followed closely by director Fred

Don Diego Vega (Fairbanks, left) banters with Sergeant Gonzales (Noah Beery).

Niblo and his assistant, Theodore Reed. Miller incorporated much of McCulley's dialogue into the spoken intertitles.

The San Fernando Valley, just north of Hollywood and Los Angeles proper, was rapidly becoming a favorite location of filmmakers. At that time still largely rural, it seemed the perfect place to replicate 18th-century California, images of which were still reflected in the Spanish architecture of hacienda-style homes with adobe walls and red tile roofs. Fairbanks had a construction crew build an entire Spanish plaza in the Valley, the largest such collection of building facades outside the Universal back lot, located further east near the Cahuenga Pass. The purchase and construction of additional props, added to the cost of costuming, swelled the project's budget. Doug had a small fortune tied up in *Capistrano* before a single foot of film was exposed. A screen star since 1915, he was quite wealthy, but with no way of knowing if audiences would accept him in a new type of movie, Doug and his manager Dennis O'Brien had good reason to be nervous about the expenditures.

Fairbanks was extremely canny about casting Capistrano. Eighteen-year-old Marguerite De La Motte, a chestnut-haired beauty with nearly a dozen motion-picture appearances to her credit, made a perfect Lolita. Robert McKim, a veteran of William S. Hart Westerns already well established as a heavy, was suitably suave and sinister as Captain Ramon. Big, bluff Noah Beery proved the ideal embodiment of Sergeant Gonzales, slightly recast as a serio-comic menace. Charles Hill Mailes and Claire McDowall played Lolita's parents with appropriate dignity, which Sidney De Grey also brought to his characterization of Diego's father. As the governor, George Periolat engaged in some of the hammy, eyeball-rolling overacting often (but not always appropriately) associated with silent movies— although, in all fairness, the role didn't call for subtlety.

Released nationwide in December 1920, now retitled *The Mark of Zorro*, Doug's rousing adaptation of McCulley's pulp story elicited reasonably favorable if not wildly congratulatory reviews. The *New York Times* appraised it this way:

"Certainly there are moments in the motion picture which must delight anyone, no matter how preposterous they are. There is a duel scene, for example, which is something distinctly original in the history of mortal combat on the stage or screen, and there are spirited races and pursuits, sudden appearances, quick changes and flashes of tempestuous lovemaking that are typically and entertainingly Fairbanksian.

"But *The Mark of Zorro* is also different in some respects from the usual Fairbanks picture. It is somewhat tamer, for one thing, the scenery especially having more of the quality of inertia. There are no mountain slides or floods in it, and the hero himself actually appears sometimes as a constitutionally languid individual wearied by the exertions of a carriage ride.... There may be those who will find [it] a little tedious in places because Fairbanks is not frolicking through every scene of it, and, as he never creates a character and will not confine himself to any possible plot or plan, his pictures must depend almost entirely upon his own athletics and absurdities, supplemented by those of scenery and cast. So, whenever *The Mark of Zorro* calms down, something seems to be missing."

Variety, the preeminent show-business trade paper, had this to say:

"Here is romance and into the bargain a commercial film started on a clean-up.... Fred Niblo directed, and while he often lost the thread of his story, much of this fault may have been due to the cutting. Things were clipped when obviously there must have been more taken, but on the whole despite a slow start the picture moves right along and carries the interest with it.... The yarn itself is based on 'The Curse of Capistrano,' a novel by Johnston McCulley. What the screen version needed most was a competent scenario writer, for all the basic elements for excellent Fairbanks stuff were there."

Fortunately for Doug, the movie-going public took to Zorro with more alacrity and enthusiasm than the critics. The film's November 29 premiere at New York's Capitol Theatre broke the existing record for single-day grosses. Some 19,547 people paid $11,708 to see *The Mark of Zorro* on its first day. Think of it: nearly 20,000 people at *one* theater on one day. And that was just the beginning. Doug's gamble paid off handsomely; Zorro became the fifth highest-grossing movie of 1921, and Fairbanks was anointed the year's top screen star. United Artists kept the film in release for longer than the usual play-off period and it did substantial business overseas.

Most people today find silent movies tough to watch. *The Mark of Zorro* fares better than most in holding the attention of present-day audiences. For the most part, Fred Niblo's direction is pedestrian, keeping the camera too far from the actors and relying on long takes when shorter ones would have benefited the pace. The action scenes are reasonably well handled, but their staging and photography were dictated more by

Douglas Fairbanks refused doubles for all but the most dangerous stunts.

Doug's acrobatics than Niblo's narrative sense.

The film's most exhilarating sequence unfolds in the penultimate reel. After freeing the Pulidos from jail, Zorro buys them time to escape by discarding his sword and daring the soldiers to follow him back to the pueblo. Bounding over fences and wagons, swinging from balcony to balcony, leaping from rooftop to rooftop, clambering up and down adobe walls, the highwayman leads his feckless pursuers on a merry chase around the plaza, at one point slipping into a chapel and donning a monk's robes—a disguise that only momentarily fools the troopers. He finally manages to elude them, stopping momentarily for a quick breakfast prepared by a grateful peon.

Daredevil stunting had been part of Doug's repertoire almost from the beginning of his screen career, and he refused doubles for all but the most dangerous stunts (such as the famous slide down the galleon sail in *The Black Pirate*, which was undertaken by Richard Talmadge). Fairbanks developed a method all his own to make his amazing physical feats always seem effortless. If he could only vault a six-foot-high fence by straining, he replaced it with one five foot high, so as to sail over it gracefully. Sets were designed and constructed based on his capabilities; if the script called for him to scale the side of a three-story building, meticulously measured and artfully concealed handholds were built into the wall. The illusions were invariably enhanced by showing clumsy pursuers or combatants fumbling and stumbling around him.

The Mark of Zorro made lasting and valuable contributions to the character's lore and iconography. The all-black costume, for example, was Doug's idea, as was the strip mask that barely covered his eyes. McCulley's Zorro wore a full-face mask with thin eye-slits; when he kisses Lolita, the author specifically mentions that he lifts his mask to do so.

Fairbanks gave a comic-relief edge to Don Diego by making him a dabbler in silly sleight-of-hand tricks, an affectation adopted by Tyrone Power's Diego in the 1940 remake, also titled *The Mark of Zorro*. Additionally, Doug somewhat enlarged the role of deaf-mute servant Bernardo, who does very little in the novel but provides considerable aid to Diego in the movie. And his adaptation of the story adds a secret room to Diego's town house, a neat touch McCulley should have thought of. These elements were incorporated into subsequent cinematic and TV incarnations of Zorro.

The success of Doug's movie inspired McCulley to write a sequel, "The Further Adventures of Zorro," which was serialized in *Argosy All-Story Weekly* (May 6–June 10, 1922). Grosset & Dunlap reprinted "Curse of Capistrano" in a 1924 hardcover edition, retitling it *The Mark of Zorro* for obvious reasons. (And putting a color photo of Fairbanks as Diego on the dust wrapper.)

After producing and starring in *The Three Musketeers* (1921), *Robin Hood* (1922), and *The Thief of Bagdad* (1924),

Fairbanks responded to the pleas of exhibitors and moviegoers alike by returning to his career-altering role in a 1925 sequel. But *Don Q, Son of Zorro* wasn't based on a McCulley story. Instead, Jack Cunningham's scenario grafted Zorro onto the plot of Hesketh and Kate Prichard's "Don Q's Love Story," a novel cobbled together from adventure yarns published in *Pearson's Magazine* and *Short Stories*. Opulent, overlong, and lethargic, Don Q lumbered through ten reels of tedious intrigue before bringing father and son together (using superb double-exposure camerawork) for an exciting finale.

Johnston McCulley, one of the most prolific pulp fictioneers ever to pound a typewriter, churned out dozens, perhaps hundreds, of stories before returning to his most famous creation in 1931. A few years later Hollywood would once again come knocking at McCulley's door for the screen rights to Zorro.

Ed Hulse is the editor and publisher of *Blood 'N' Thunder*, a quarterly journal for fans, scholars and collectors of adventure, mystery and melodrama in American popular culture of the late 19th and early 20th centuries. He is also the author of the award-winning *Blood 'N' Thunder Guide to Pulp Fiction* and various books on motion-picture history, including *The Films of Betty Grable, Filming The West of Zane Grey*, and his two-volume history of silent-era movie serials, *Distressed Damsels and Masked Marauders* and *Handsome Heroes and Vicious Villains*. Ed's books and back issues of *Blood 'N' Thunder* are available at muraniapress.com.

About the author
Johnston McCulley

Johnston McCulley (1883-1958) was born in Ottowa, Illinois, and began his writing career as a police reporter. He became a prolific fiction author, filling thousands of pages of popular pulp magazines. Southern California became a frequent backdrop for his fiction. His most notable use of the locale was in his ongoing adventures of Zorro, the masked highwayman who defended a pueblo's citizens from an oppressive government.

McCulley contributed to popular magazines of the day like *Argosy, Western Story Magazine, Blue Book, Detective Story Magazine,* and *Rodeo Romances.* Many of his novels were published in hardcover and paperback. Eventually he branched out into film and television screenplays.

McCulley developed several continuing characters including The Crimson Clown, Thubway Tham, The Green Ghost, and The Thunderbolt. But Zorro proved to be his most popular and enduring character, becoming the subject of numerous television programs, motion pictures, comic books, and cartoon programs.

In the 1950s, he assigned all Zorro rights agent to Mitchell Gertz. Having retired to Los Angeles, McCulley died in 1958.

ZORRO

The Complete Pulp Adventures by Johnston McCulley

The Curse of Capistrano's original adventures — collected for the first time in paperback and hardcover.

www.boldventuepress.com

Zorro ® & © 2019 Zorro Productions, Inc. All rights reserved.

Watch for the Curse of Capistrano's wildest adventure!

ZORRO®

and the LITTLE DEVIL

A thrilling new novel by New York Times best-selling author

Peter David

BOLD VENTURE
www.boldventurepress.com

Zorro ® & © Zorro Productions, Inc. All rights reserved.

Made in the USA
Middletown, DE
16 June 2021